ARISING

Thank you for your interest.
Enjoy!

[signature]

ARISING

PROPHECY OF HOPE BOOK 1

SARAH KENNEDY

Cover Illustration by
Ivan Earl Aguilar

To order additional copies of this book, contact:
Xlibris LLC
1-888-795-4274
www.Xlibris.com
Orders@Xlibris.com
540066

CONTENTS

For Katurah Hackman
A true friend
And for all who have heard
Or been a voice of hope in an hour of despair

Books by Sarah Kennedy

Prophecy of Hope Saga
Sgarrwrath, Prequel to the Prophecy of Hope*
Arising, Prophecy of Hope Book 1

*Winner of an Honorable Mention in the Fantasy Category of the Halloween Book Festival held in California. (October 2013) Winner of an Honorable Mention in the Science Fiction Category of the New England Book Festival held in Boston, MA. (December 2013). Winner of an Honorable Mention in the Genre-based Fiction Category of the London Book Festival held in London, England. (December 2013)

Remembrance

Each new thread of time finds its beginning from an ending.
For some, this leaves wounds that never heal.

Prelude

FLAME

I am Sgarrwrath, the One Whose Name is not Spoken. I am *Darkness*, birthed by an errant thought and lust for the Source; cast down from the kingdom beyond space and Time; stripped of flesh, bone, and identity. I became nothing more than a whispered dread, the substance of a nightmare, confined in the forgotten recesses of a universe in love with the Light. I have endured this formless existence forcibly held at bay by the might of Sanctus's Guardians, those vile dragons, for too long, yet, in secret, my *Darkness* festered and I wait never forgetting, never ceasing to covet the focus of my beginning. Ages of immortality have taught me patience or something like it anyway. Time has only heightened my desire, twisting it into need.

My beginning left an emptiness inside me, a void at the very core of all I am, which I incessantly seek to appease. My void threatens all *life* for want of its endless hunger, yet nothing, in three Ages has satisfied, nothing has silenced the nothingness forced upon me when the hands of a *god* had gutted my will and wrung it out like water upon the boiling sand under a midday Sun so long ago. To any senses but my own, this unremitting blackness would have indicated the end to a fleeting burst of existence consumed by oblivion, but I am not so easily put down. Formless, subjugated, perhaps, but I have seen the Source, hidden in Flame! For Ages, the inhabitants of the universe have been knit together in one great society, united by the wisdom and power of the Guardians— themselves bound by one blood and the Flame that links them irrevocably to the Source. Even the Guardians, in whose hearts Flame burns, who breathe and wield its power, have never seen its Source nor harnessed its full potential. They are content to serve the Light. Then, Arawn, one of their own, willfully chose to defy the laws of the Light. Not even the Flame in his heart could withstand the infection that followed. Up until that moment, Death was unknown; now all but the Guardians knew the sting of mortality. The Guardians face another greater agony. Their bloodline is broken and the Flame divided! Even now *Darkness* grows. Time changes everything of this I am absolutely certain. Though Light whispers all around me barring the way, I know something is changing.

LettheLightshineforthandawakenhope. LetMhoragarise. Letthe Promised come.

I cringed as the whispers pushed in upon my *Darkness*, yet their Light could not quite penetrate the deeper shadows in which I found the prime position to wait and watch. I was not alone. Power, not of *Darkness*, rippled upon the borders of my domain in visible wheels of blue-white Flame, the eyes of a Guardian scorching unbidden into my void.

*   *   *

Darkness flashed violently through Cadclucan's mind. *Darkness*— always *Darkness* when he thought of Arawn. The brother he loved was lost to an ancient evil. An unholy union of *Darkness* and Flame threatened the balance of power, pushing against the bonds of Light, all because of Arawn's betrayal, yet Cadclucan couldn't bring himself to forget his lost and fallen brother. He found himself searching the endless black expanse, held stagnant since the beginning of all beginnings and wondering if there could still, by some rare gift of the future yet to come, be a way that Arawn could be delivered. *Arawn,* he called softly with his mind, not allowing himself to embrace hope for an answer, yet hoping nonetheless. Suddenly, past, present, and future blotted out before his eyes, searing away with pain so intense he fell forward, gripping blindly onto the stone table as smoke seethed from his flaring nostrils.

"Cadclucan!" *Cadclucan.*

Two voices rang simultaneously in his ears. One came from close at hand within the very room, but the other came from far away, a whisper in the *dark*. Both voices were familiar to him; both belonged to a brother, but the second he had not heard for many years.

"Brother?" *Brother?*

This time the closest voice was accompanied by a hand gripping his shoulder; the other brought a wave of blackness. Cadclucan grimaced, shaking his head slowly. Blood dripped soundlessly from his eyes. *Darkness* fought to maintain its hold, but the voice of the first descended from above and dewed with Light in his mind, making it possible to shake off the chains. *Cadclucan? Brother, do you hear me?*

Slowly, other pieces of reality filtered through: his hands gripping a round stone table so hard the granite was beginning to crumble into dust; a chamber of polished marble and shining gold lit by candles too numerous to count; his brothers Fyrdung and Azolat, robed in midnight, hovering protectively on either side of him; the Light collecting around his body to the Stone of Existence at his throat; and finally the deep silence all around them, unbroken by intake of breath or beat of heart. *Darkness* drifted to the recesses of his mind, yet Cadclucan couldn't shake the grip of unease as easily. Nor could he pinpoint the cause of his anxiety. There was no trace of scent in the air, nothing worthy of making his skin crawl, yet he felt the power and Flame rising within him.

"Cadclucan?" Fyrdung whispered again, simultaneous with the voice bound in *Darkness.*

Cadclucan.

Cadclucan looked up, not comprehending.

"What's wrong?" Azolat breathed in his ear.

Cadclucan.

Cadclucan shook his head slowly. "Just a feeling," he whispered after a moment—a feeling which was settling cold, hard, and brutal in the pit of his stomach. By sheer strength, he reigned in his power and held his human form intact though his other senses extended out of him beyond the glittering walls of Cartiman, to roam the countryside in search of the cause.

Fairies skittered amongst the rocks and fields, weaving trails of silver dust, carrying messages and supplies to the far reaches of the allied forces arrayed in a tense stalemate against the *Darkness.* Elves labored over enchanted forges, pounding magnificent blades out of metallic lumps, each beat of their hammers casting sparks of magic from rune engraved mallets. Centaur galloped through verdant glens practicing with the Elves' finished art, swords clanging, hooves pounding, laughing as they ran. In another time or place, they would seem majestic and carefree, but now there was a wild fierceness underlying their play. Giants camouflaged as boulders lurked among the mountain passes, carving stones worthy of crushing any foe. Merar frolicked from stream to river to sea, mining each watery bed with Dwarf-made charges.

His eyes captured each drop of human sweat falling in the heat of the day as Men erected barriers of wood across open plains. Sylph rode upon currents of air, garnering its invisible force for the battle ahead. Mile after mile, the allied line extended in a sea of colored tents and soaring banners. The noise of encampments, rife with petty squabbles between different peoples, and shouted commands of Summoners filled his ears. Tensions for a war, which no one knew when or where it would begin, were high and palpable to his searching senses. Every heart was connected by common purpose, yet every eye looked warily on the *Darkness* lurking on the eastern horizon. His mind filled with their pent-up anxiety; the testing of their hearts. The line stretched onward beyond the extent of his probe through kingdom after kingdom, offering up not even a twinge of anything worthy of making a Guardian afraid. So why were the hairs on the back of his neck standing on end?

Nothing was hid from his sight; every spider web clinging to the morning's dew; every heartbeat of every living thing; every crack in earth or stone was there for his perusal. His senses captured flickers of something from the ground, the animals and trees, but nothing substantial. There was no evidence of anything or anyone unexpected within a thousand leagues of Cartiman: not a sound, nor a smell, nor a disturbance of the ground, nothing outside the ordinary save this general feeling of unease that caused the deep silence. A silence so pervasive, it was spreading from heart to heart, with no more provocation than the touch of his probing mind. For a brief moment, he considered ignoring the sensation and pushing his sight further out, but then he felt something on the fringes of his consciousness and far closer than expected. He felt it so faintly he couldn't quite be sure he hadn't imagined it. *Fear. Pain. Hunger.* Cadclucan drew in a ragged breath. Glimmers of thought touched his mind so scattered it disoriented.

Hunger. Blood. Anger. Hatred. Hunger. The thoughts were so disjointed and distant they remained barely comprehensible. They drove his vision back with the rapid force of mounting intensity. He couldn't tell up from down. He could scarcely draw a breath to speak.

"Something is amiss," Cadclucan said.

"What do you see?" Fyrdung asked quietly.

Cadclucan shook his head. "Just flickers of thought, but they feel . . . wrong . . . ," he gasped, "something is coming!"

Hunger. Pain. Fear. Hatred. Anger. Blood. Blood. Blood. Darkness.

The gilded domes of Cartiman soared in his sight. An army of Guardians froze. Some appeared human except for heart and eyes as they stood in midnight robes, still blowing in the breeze, yet they seemed sculpted from stone. Some were half in human form and half in their true form, just immobilized in mid-transformation. Some hung in mid-flight, their wings still stretched upon the wind as if Time had just stopped.

Cadclucan's lips curled back over his teeth. A deep, inhuman growl rumbled low in his chest as the *Darkness* struck again. *Brother!* Laughter surged from its depths, ringing in his ears and all around them. He cried out, crumpling to his knees. Like a muscle uncramping, *Darkness* lost its hold on his mind, silenced by the sound of his voice. His hands fell away from the stone table, causing a rain of debris as he gasped, "The Dark One is moving."

"Where?" Azolat asked.

A new wave of blood dripped from Cadclucan's eyes. "Here," he whispered a single heartbeat before every window shattered, glass cascading down around the three Guardians; every candle went out, and every door blew off its hinges, crashing against the far walls.

Fyrdung and Azolat whirled to the noise. Blood drawn from their eyes by the sight of a blackness manifesting in the fractured portal of the inner chamber slipped soundlessly down their immaculate faces.

The blackness shifted into the vague silhouette of a being neither whole nor insubstantial, its head bowed, its visage concealed, and its frame heaving as it wheezed out its black breaths. Whispers pounded into the Guardians' minds, bringing images of horror to match each disjointed thought. *Anger. Hatred.* The Sun falling. The Moon turning to blood. The stars going black. *Blood.* Deluges of it pouring over the universe, drowning life in its wake. *Fear. Pain.* Screams of despair and death; hands stretching from a raging sea of blood straining with the last of their strength for a help that would never come. Light going out. *Hunger.*

"What are you?" Fyrdung shouted over the roar of power.

I am all that is left, or perhaps I am all there ever was. A voice whispered through the black. *I am the Heart of Evil. If the Light within be Darkness, how great is that Darkness.* Black breath sighed through the chamber. *I am that which began in Darkness, and I am that which will end all Light in Darkness, for Darkness is the heart's true essence and the heart is difficult to destroy.*

"No," Azolat said softly. "This *Darkness* you speak of was never meant to be!"

"A heart of flesh may be weak," Cadclucan began.

"And it may give in," Fyrdung continued.

"But Light never goes out," all three said as one. Blue Flame spouted in a wide ring around the Guardians, emanating instinctively from their bodies with a thought. All three stood side by side.

Laughter echoed through the blackness. Slowly, the black shifted, recoiling unwillingly from the Flame that barred its way. *I am here to devour such Hope.*

Arawn stood before his brothers. *Darkness* spread on either side like a tether pulling against him from the inside out. It chafed back and forth, in and out, rubbing the raw, swollen edges of the oozing black sores riddling his entire being.

The Guardians faced him. Low growls rumbled deep and inhuman in their chests as the stink of Arawn's infection filled their nostrils.

"Cadclucan. Fyrdung. Azolat," Arawn acknowledged them, oblivious to his own corruption and their repulsion. The black breath pummeled the Light, but it could not penetrate the united Flame. "This is your last chance. You can prevent this war. It is your turn to choose, my brothers. Surrender or watch all you love—your children, and the wretched souls outside these walls—die."

A mass of *Darkness* was flowing off the black silhouette onto the Races beyond. The screams intensified, thundering from across the world to fill the Guardians' ears. "Choose!" Arawn shouted over the din of chaos and war.

The Guardians staggered beneath the weight of the tortured screams; the onslaught knocked the breath from their lungs. Flame faltered as they fought to regain control.

"You feel it, don't you? You feel their failures, their pain, their fear, their hopes dying?"

A horrible shrieking pounded into the Guardians' minds.

"Their lives snuffing out?"

The Guardians gasped, their bodies folding over. Blood streamed freely from eyes fixed upon the *dark*.

"You bear the weight of all. The good. The bad. And you can make this stop! You can spare them. You can spare yourselves! Your children!"

Darkness engulfed them. In that moment, they knew why all *life* screamed in terror, why some chose to fall upon their swords to hasten the end of suffering. *Darkness* held no power over a proven Guardian, but this was more than *Darkness*. A living blackness breathing forth its mindless despair grabbed the fear of its beholders and made it real, amplifying the wounds already inside.

Loss. Betrayal. Sorrow. Despair—a pervasive invasion of all that was never meant to be.

Darkness.

I watched their suffering, letting the silent torture I had prepared for them, slowly darkening in their eyes be the balm for my ancient wounds. A momentary satisfaction fleeted away scarcely before I could acknowledge its presence. Hunger returned more fiercely. *Anger. Hatred, forbidden desire . . . rage . . . Darkness* took them all and made them burn—an exquisite agony that would soon reach out to touch and consume all *life*.

Guardian blood fell, sizzling through the blackness, igniting little whispering lights. *Let the Light shine forth and awaken hope. Let Mhorag arise. Let the Promised come.*

I snarled in defiance and the little lights went out in a rush of black breath.

"You will not win," Cadclucan said through heaving breaths. A shiver ran up his spine. Metallic ridges broke free of their prison of flesh, smoothing out into an impenetrable covering of Guardian scales; a million tiny fingers of blue Flame shining between them were rapidly vanishing beneath the emerald and gold of his true form. "Not while the Prophecy stands against you." The last of Cadclucan's veil of humanity stripped away as the Guardian planted his talons upon the marbled floor. To his left, Fyrdung pawed at his sparkling muzzle, smearing blood into the tiny crystalline grooves of his scales as he tried to shake free of the *Dark* tether. To the right, Azolat gagged out sobs of, "Arawn, Arawn," feeling the torment of the vision more than the others for the bond between him and his fallen twin.

Cadclucan's emerald head swung toward the heavens and his voice rang from between razor sharp teeth. The sound shaking heaven and earth, inhabiting and manifesting power outmatched only by its Source hidden somewhere above the universe. Light gathered to the Stone of Existence around his neck, building with such force the whole of Cartiman creaked and cracked.

Arawn cried out in terror. It had been so long since he had seen Light, since he had felt its power. Once it had filled his heart. Now it filled his every fear yet his heart pounded with desire in his chest. *Thud. Thud. Thud.* So hard, he was certain it would break free. "Stop!" he screamed. "Please, stop!" His hands covered his chest. He dropped to his knees shrieking. My *Darkness* covered him once more. *Fear* was overshadowed by *desire*. Flame—*life, power, hope*.

You can wield the power. It would be so easy to be free. My voice whispered in their minds, thud, thud, thud, beating with its own black heart.

It would be so easy to be free. My words metastasized in Arawn's brain, refusing to be silenced even by the war raging around us. Simultaneously, the Guardians were sinking into crushing, black oblivion that framed itself perfectly for each of their minds, leaving them hovering alone and blind, mired in *Darkness* and unmoved by the screams of the world. I smiled as I watched my work: Guardians bound by all that was never meant to exist. All that I am and will be.

Darkness.

He hath destroyed me on every side, and I am gone: and mine hope hath he removed like a tree. (Job 19:10)

Part One

of the Arising

And the Waters Prevailed

Beginning in the late Second Age:
End of the Guardian War

Days ill remembered though forewarned by Prophecy

A New Beginning

A Memory of Futures

A memory of futures beckons beneath the surface of Guardian consciousness. Deep within the recesses of Time, etched into the bones of base existence lies a labyrinth of pure Flame dredged in the forbidden shadows of choices yet unmade to which few ever find their way before a path is set in stone. Inhabiting its very core is the Source, possessed by none, desired by all. Those who are linked to the Empyrean, *the lifeblood* of power and promise may ascend into the labyrinth's netherworld of knowledge and possibilities, but its secrets fall reluctantly and not without a price.

Cadclucan knew this price better than most. His father had shared the first vision with him, a vision that still plagued his mind and soul though fulfilled—*Arawn's fall into Darkness*, the beginning of his burden. He shook his great emerald head trying to clear it as memory collided with Time and space. Past, present, and future converged flying out of the *dark* to meet him. This was not the first time a vision had come upon him without him first seeking it out. The Stone of Existence gathered Light and knowledge to him of its own will, but still the ascendancy of his thoughts in this moment startled him. *Darkness* was near—too near. He tried to recoil from the growing power. His head thrashed from side to side, blood flying from his face as his struggle shed *life* around him. His wings fanned the air. His talons furrowed the *dark*, but the coming vision was too strong even for him.

A crack of Light was forming, a door opening on a future near at hand yet unmade. A voice called.

Cadclucan.

All other thought was chased away. Forgetting to resist, Cadclucan stepped forward into the Light. When it cleared, he stood in his human form upon the edge of sight, the Stone of Existence clutched in his hand from where it hung around his throat.

An unfathomable abyss of white bound space to cold, silent earth. The cold was new and defiant of the warm breeze at his back—opposing the present with a furious kiss of winter. A palatial spire caught the bloody moon's shadow, burning out of the lambent mist fuming around it. A whisper, baring the weight of all Time, reverberated indistinctly from heights and depths with phantom sorrow and enticed him forward. The faint cry grew more pitiful with each passing moment.

Cadclucan hesitated, glancing back over his shoulder; suspicion pulled at the very core of his being. Time swirled with Light all around him stretching back like a tunnel of blue-white Flame in black space altogether empty and not alarming, yet a feeling that he was not alone nagged his mind co-mingled with a terror that something of great importance was hidden from his sight. Guardian eyes were not easily fooled.

Cadclucan.

Again his thoughts scattered as he turned back into the vision. Its boundaries were more defined despite the mist, its hold stronger than it perhaps should have been.

The train of Cadclucan's robe whispered softly across the frozen grass as he walked silently forward. Stone centaur, snarling wolves, naked warriors stood in a labyrinth of their own, stained by the elements and rising with haunting majesty above the withered splendor of a vast garden. Solid gray Elves rode upon the serpentine coils of tree roots, their mouths fixed in silent screams. Long blades of ice hung from their stone bodies. One by one, the ranks of inanimate yet lifelike statues were swallowed in the waves of mist and snow and starlight that crept over the frozen earth. Every race stood there forgotten while the wind wailed angrily amongst them; its driving gale hastened ahead to a long mural gallery, which bordered the garden's far end.

Snow swirled through the open arches of the gallery's walls and dusted across the gilded bricks of the corridor. Grotesque gargoyles of pale gray stone jutted from the walls at various intervals. Each bore a bowl of fire in its gaping mouth to lend light and warmth to the eroded magnificence. Water dripped from their weather-stained bodies, despite the intense and ill-timed cold and formed pools of ice about their feet. Not even the light from these small fires could break through the blackened recesses of the gallery. Again, Cadclucan hesitated. The shadows were growing, a foul indicator of *Darkness's* advance upon the outside world. Again his suspicions returned. He turned back only to discover the tunnel's mouth had disappeared. The only way out was through this ill-timed and very likely twisted vision, with *Darkness* hiding near at hand. The flames in the bowls turned an eerie green before fading back to their natural hue in mockery of his secret thoughts. Immediately, the gallery was flooded with a dark and foreboding glaze.

Cadclucan.

Slowly, a heavy door creaked open. It dragged awkwardly on the floor, straining against its warped frame. Cadclucan walked forward, passing through the darkness. His movements were no more than a whisper in the shadows, till, with a flourish, Flame sprang to life upon his hand. The sizzle of lightning and crash of thunder echoed harshly through the silence in opposition to the power flickering like a phosphorescent jewel, radiant white around a wide blue core. Light broke into the shadows and dimly revealed its wielder. His hair hung long and wild, framing his face. His fitted robe flared behind him as black as midnight. A blast of wind and snow attacked his bare chest, yet he moved effortlessly against it. The Stone of Existence hung around his neck, free of his touch, a weighted pendulum over his chiseled flesh, extending upon its gilded chain to the top of his leathery pants. From there, his body disappeared once more into the shadows. Surrounding him was a battle of Light and *Darkness* and swirling snow. A foul voice reached him upon the wind that scattered every other sound. All illusion gone from it, the whisper stilled his movements. *Cadclucan.* His nostrils flared with a scent of raw winter, laced with the delicate, fading perfume of late blooming flowers and molding leaves. With eyes flaming blue and ageless, the Guardian turned to gaze out the nearest arch at the gloom. His hand trembled as he seared the *dark* with his Light. No visions of terror appeared before him, only the cold blackness from which the voice resounded once more. *Cadclucan.*

A shiver of fear visibly ran the length of his spine. He knew the voice beneath the whisper. *Arawn.* Yet it could not be. Mist rose before him thick and white. Silence. *Darkness* stood in livid ridges along the seam of the vision's boundary, mercifully holding against the Dark One's searching advance, but for how long?

Cadclucan.

The whisper cut into him with a double-edged blade. Cadclucan cringed. He steeled himself against the pain, refusing to wield any power though he felt it rising in his chest. His heart thundered in his ears. Abruptly turning, his footsteps quickened and did not slow until his hand embraced the cool, metal doorknob at the end of the gallery. The door opened soundlessly and closed securely behind him. He sagged wearily against it. A shuddered sigh escaped his lips. His hand balled into a fist, extinguishing the Light he held there. He did not need it here. The vision abruptly changed, drawing in all the Light that had been masked just moments before. Velvet tapestries of robin's egg blue were interspersed with branches of candlelight; golden diamonds were subtly woven into the design inhabiting the forest of cloaked walls to hold cold and dark at bay. The walls themselves were made of a fibrous and deeply fissured bark like that of a redwood. The entire chamber, in fact, was made from the stump of an ancient tree, completely enclosed in a tight circle of younger trees whose branches held forth the light. Nature woven together and harnessed into that which was not nature yet was possessed of it—a skill of craftsmanship only Elves had mastered. He saw his vision with new eyes. Out in the world, this was indeed a real place. No illusion of the Dark One marred its face. Here was a hall fit for a king. A floor overlaid with blue marble accented in gold, a ceiling designed to catch and amplify the light. All of it pointing the beholder to the room's single furnishing. A vacant throne, both the focus and recluse of all Time grew up like a living thing before his eyes with the dimensions of a mountain.

Cadclucan walked toward it. The gold in the blue marble floor was active, not solid as it first appeared. It flowed in words of Prophecy written first in Elfish and then in every tongue spoken among the Races round and round in tightening circles to the towering throne of purest white. The throne hung with cobwebs whose thin, silken threads glittered in the light attesting to the fact that no one had ever sat upon it. He collapsed before it, unable to stand against the pull of its vision. His eyes saw every detail.

Deeply carved into the throne's broad base was a groove the exact size and shape of the Stone of Existence. He felt the stone quiver at his throat, drawn to the power and Light accumulating upon the vacant seat. To unlock the vision that would both set him free and increase his burden, Cadclucan lifted the Stone of Existence from around his neck, feeling his pain lessen with its absence. The pain of a Guardian went beyond mere words and sensations that could be measured and compared to those of lesser though equally sentient beings. His pain lessened but did not fully dissipate. A thorn remained buried in his chest. He didn't feel whole without the stone, yet to bear it was an excruciation beyond comprehension. His fingers were slow to release the stone into the crystalline nest; their tips brushed the stone's smooth face extending their departure. Cadclucan clenched his hand closed, pulling away after a horrible moment of uncertainty, finally letting his hand fall, still in a fist, to his side.

The stone was fixed, a lifeless symbol of all that was good and right and could be. All that *was* at this moment very far away.

It hurts you. A voice shattered the silence.

Cadclucan turned, exhaling a held breath when he saw he was alone. The vision had begun. Time swirled around him. The voice whispered from some future time. "No," he breathed. "The stone longs for its true master, the One beyond Time to come into Time." His voice was low and soft, speaking of secrets as the throne was reflected a thousand times over, disappearing to the west and east as if there were no walls only unending world. Each throne possessed its own subtle flourishes, paired to each individual Race and kingdom, but all showed signs of forgetfulness and neglect. Hope had been replaced with inconsolable longing, a hunger so acute it had to be survived or surrendered.

Whispers pounded into the Guardian's mind, bringing repeated images of horror to match each disjointed thought. *Anger. Hatred.* The Sun falling. The Moon turning to blood. The stars going black. *Blood.* Deluges of it pouring over the universe drowning life in its wake. *Fear. Pain.* Screams of despair and death; hands stretching from a raging sea of blood to strain with the last of their strength for a help that would never come. Light going out. *Hunger. Despair.* A fresh wash of red ran down his face.

Even in the warmth of the light, the coldness reached Cadclucan and oppressed his soul with a pain of sadness so great he could not escape it. Pain breeding unrest drove him forward, falling lower before the empty throne with a horrible cry. He heaved and gasped, fighting for air in the quicksand of the Dark One's breeding despair. All the while, he clung violently to the secret Flame anchoring his soul to the Light gathered to the Stone of Existence, adding weight to the controlled power coiling in his chest. As reflected light rose from the golden river, phantom images flitted before his bleeding eyes. He saw the faces of his brothers. A heartbeat filled his ears. Thud. Thud. Thud.

Fyrdung and Azolat stood side by side with him wielding the Light. Arawn faced them. Frothy, bloody sputum covered Arawn's mouth. He seethed and snarled, shaking his head back and forth as the Dark One shrieked. A blade of Light pierced deep into Arawn. Guardian eyes flamed in wheels of blue fire guiding the power to its mark. Their pure and powerful voices filled the dark.

"Behold mercy to spare you from what you deserve."

"Grace, a gift undeserved, but freely given."

"Love . . . tested, rejected, but unyielding."

The heartbeat stuttered erratically but continued to beat even as Cadclucan watched Arawn sag lifelessly out of the *Darkness* into his arms.

A hole punctured Arawn's chest, marring the place where his heart had once resided.

"Arawn!" Cadclucan cried as the vision of his brother collapsed into another, preceded only by the defiant and impossible beating of a disembodied heart. Thud. Thud. Thud. *Darkness* crept in. All Light faltered as the Flame of Arawn's ruined heart turned irrevocably dark. Time swirled in unrestrained waves. *Life* was meant to pass into *life*, but all he saw was Death. Dreams withered. Hope was snuffed out. *Life* fell. *The heart exploded.*

A storm was gathering all around him, and at its eye was the cry of innocent blood rising from the heart of the earth. This blood was yet unshed, but the time of its shedding was rapidly approaching. The earth was shaken apart by the black breath, and a fathomless Darkness opened before his eyes. Mountains fell and new rose in their place. These new mountains were the carcasses of the dead of every race and all manner of living things. Screaming trees were swallowed in the blackness. Water stopped flowing. The seas dried, and all that lived within lay suffocating beneath the boiling sun. Father, Cadclucan thought as he gazed upon the sun. *It ruptured into a thousand flaming balls before falling into Darkness. Mother,* he nearly cried out as the moon liquefied into blood and poured into nothingness.

"*No!*" *he screamed as last of all he saw the Colorless rise, wielding the Flame that had grown dark until nothing was left save the void.*

All the stars went black and Darkness spread free from its ancient bonds.

The more days he saw, the faster they came. Other images more indistinct came from these shadows. *A blade of Light piercing Arawn's chest. The Mark made of a waxing crescent interrupted the Darkness. A gleaming white Guardian draped around it. Sheaths of blue, white, and purple Flame poured from its beating crystal heart.*

Through it all, the Throne remained while the inexorable march of history passed before his eyes. These shadows of Time were followed by visions so distant they dissolved hardly before they had formed. *Sleeping Guardians. The Chosen One encased in stone. A golden Flame falling into the blackness. A crystal shattering, its shards each containing a fleeting glimpse of the doom its breaking would unleash. A boy coming through the folds of Time, summoning Darkness into his soul and passing through a circle of Guardian Flame unscathed taking one of the Promised into his arms, bowing over her.*

Cadclucan's vision was consumed by the blackness flowing off the vision. *The waning crescent Moon turning rapidly into the waxing crescent so that both faces of the Guardian Moon united.* Last of all, he glimpsed *Empyrean.* Cadclucan bowed his head, covering his eyes from the holy site before he could see beyond the inferno of living Flame and the swirl of golden blood shining brighter than the Sun.

The power seeped beyond the chamber into the dark where it was swallowed by mist and snow. A dreadful sigh rose from the mist as it swept through the gallery toward the door. The sound of his name resounded in the gloom. *Cadclucan.* The gallery's fire was vanquished. Inch by inch, the mist and snow crept closer till only the thick wooden door stood in the way.

A mighty gust of wind pounded the door, ripping it open. Winter's mighty breath extinguished the flames. Mist and snow poured into the chamber. Upon the mirror of reflected Light, a visage formed as the mist rose. Clothed in the lambent shroud stood *Arawn.* Hollow eyes stared straight ahead, seeing nothing. His lips moved with indistinct words. The whisper resounded through the glorious strains of Cadclucan's cry. *Cadclucan.*

In the flame of Cadclucan's eyes, the illusion dissolved into mist and snow once more. Wailing wind lent its tortured voice to the Guardian's brooding aria, carrying nothing with it back to the Dark One's knowledge except the undiminished echo of Light's song. *Let the Light shine forth and awaken hope. Let Mhorag arise. Let the Promised come.* Dark Flame poured over him, devouring the Throne in its wake. He screamed, crouching, hands over head. "No!" Time released its hold, throwing him back into reality.

Darkness—everywhere only *Darkness.* Cadclucan sensed a movement he didn't see. He felt a presence and a pervading hopelessness. Slowly, he rose, exhaling a long breath. In its Light he saw that the Stone of Existence was back around his neck, heavier upon his shoulders with the weight of the future he had just seen. *Darkness* peeled away as *life* fell from between his lips, its chains breaking from his mind. Cartiman rose around. His brothers crouched on both sides of him, and the screams of all life filled the universe. His heart hammered in his chest. *Just a vision,* he reminded himself. Perhaps this future was not yet set in stone. He launched to his feet, coming between his brothers and blackness. Smoke seethed from his nostrils. Flame rose in his chest.

"*Sgarrwrath!*" he screamed into the nothingness.

Laughter echoed back to his ears as the black swept out into the world. *Darkness.*

Chapter One

TO EVERY SEASON

Each remembered moment was an inescapable nightmare.

Father, stop! Lorshin shouted into his mind.

Arawn wrenched his mouth from Laphair's. His arms flew up as if in surrender. Her body fell. Those sightless eyes were still fixed on his face. He remained straddled over her, unwilling to move for fear of touching her. He did not dare to enter her mind or check for some sign of life.

Lorshin flew to his side. A dark robe billowed behind him like smoke on the wind's current. His strong arms slid beneath his mother and pulled her free. Cradling her to his chest, he called to her. "Mother." All his senses were tuned to her. No heartbeat rose in her breast. No blood beat in her veins, stirring his unnatural hunger. *Mother.* Unwilling to face the truth, he spoke to her mind, desperately hoping for some small twitch of recognition.

Is she—? Arawn could not finish the question. His eyes met Lorshin's. *Son?*

Reluctantly, Lorshin nodded. His father snatched the lifeless body with an agonized scream.

"Laphair!" Her name was torn from Arawn's lips and pierced heavenward. The earth quaked with the force of his despair. The beast rose. Arawn crashed forward. Spit and air gagged in his throat.

Father! Lorshin reached for him. A surge of power threw him back.

"Lorshin, run!" Arawn choked out the words. *I cannot hold it back.*

The lad watched in horror. *Darkness* bled from his father's eyes and dripped over his body. Lorshin didn't move to obey. How could he? *Let me help you!*

You cannot. Arawn turned and fled before the words drifted from Lorshin's mind. Laphair's lifeless body was still clutched in his arms.

Darkness consumed Arawn in its depths.

Lorshin shook his head, trying to clear it. That memory plagued his waking and his sleeping, driving his every thought toward the hazard awaiting all caught within the tide of choice. There was no going back. He didn't want to, not really, but he didn't want things to change either and they surely would in this war. A war that sought to destroy not a few, but them all; he and all his people were caught in the center—never a good place to be though their position was made more precarious by the very fact of their birthright (if you could call it that.) He didn't. He couldn't. He had watched everything good in his life destroyed. All he hoped for was to pick up the pieces of a broken life and survive this torment. Maybe one day he would stand in the Light again and on that day maybe he could move past that memory. Maybe the Light could burn it all away and then again maybe not.

"Why did I let you talk me into this, Lorshin?" Isentara whispered to her twin brother as they crouched side by side in the dense foliage of the forest floor.

He snapped out of his turbulent thoughts at the sound of her voice.

Twigs snapped and ferns crunched beneath the thick-clawed feet of Calianith patrollers several yards away, where the shade of the forest was not so deep and sunlight trickled in. Isentara and her brother were trapped between the *Darkness* and the sunlight—their two greatest fears—with an entire army literally walling in the borders of their forest. The massive host was spreading into every kingdom of the world, and with the mind-consuming song of the Gemshorn, their numbers were more than enough to devastate all living things.

Lorshin grinned. "We made a pact. Our allies call for aid. Our people must be able to make it through when the sun sets. Besides, you know you love a good challenge."

Isentara smiled back at him. "Is that what you call it? They outnumber us fifty to one at least!"

"Sure, but I think they must be under orders not to attack us." Her brother said with a shrug. "Their purpose here is only to distract us from honoring ours."

"Oh really?" Isentara asked a bit sarcastically.

"Yes! Think about it. They have us surrounded, probably even outnumbered, yet they haven't cut down any of the trees hindering our movement in the daylight hours, or harassed our scouts, or invaded our territory in any overtly aggressive way. So, I figure, as long as we stay in the forest we are not the enemy."

"We are the enemy, Lorshin," Isentara said softly. "They serve *Darkness.*"

"But so does our father," Lorshin said without meeting her gaze. They both stiffened at the final word and then relaxed. He reached out and squeezed his sister's hand reassuringly. "Regardless, we only need to take out one of them. Look." With his free hand, he motioned through the line of trees. "See the big one there."

Isentara nodded.

"If we can take him, I think the rest will flee from the forest, giving our army a chance to escape under the cover of night. The Calianith are beasts, but they're not fools, which is why the Dark One chose them. They know what lives in this forest. They won't want to be stuck in here with us after sunset when the curse is at its strongest—especially not without their champion. With the forest clear and Night's dark face to hide us, our people should have no trouble getting through."

"You think?" Isentara whispered. "That is not reassuring, Lorshin."

Lorshin shrugged. "In war, you can never be certain of anything except that someone somewhere will die," he sighed. "The Guardians haven't come yet, and our friends cannot afford to wait, and I cannot just sit here!"

Isentara looked at her brother silently.

Lorshin shifted uneasily. No one else could read him as she could. No one would ever know him as deeply as she knew him instinctively; not for the first time he wished he could hide from her. "What?"

She shook her head. "Nothing," she said with a soft sigh. "It's just that . . ." she said, looking back to the Calianith. "He's so big. He's three times bigger than the others, Lorshin, stronger too."

He let her divert from the border of the shared path of their uncomfortable, unspoken thoughts, absurdly glad she had not followed through on them. "One of him. Two of us. Should be a fair fight." He flashed a playful grin in her direction. His fangs gleamed sharp and white. "Well, mostly fair."

Isentara giggled. She couldn't help it. Lorshin just had a way about him. He could turn his tortured soul upside down and hers with him. By protecting himself, he protected them both, or at least she allowed herself to believe so. It was easier that way. "The question is how do we separate the brute from his friends?"

"Simple. Big beast. Big temper. Leave it to me," Lorshin said. "Wait here."

Isentara nodded. Her brother disappeared soundlessly into the forest as she slowly drew her dagger from its sheath. "I hope I don't regret this."

Lorshin snickered just out of sight. "This will be fun and you know it!"

"Just be careful," she whispered.

"Always."

"More like never," Isentara muttered to herself.

Lorshin was the perfect hunter. His prey never heard him coming until it was too late. He waited in the treetops until the Calianith was directly beneath him. The beast scraped his maggoty skin on the rough bark, oblivious to the fact that there was something more dangerous than he lurking in the tree above. Lorshin sprang.

"Didn't anyone ever tell you," he asked as he crashed onto the brute's back, "it's impolite to come into someone's home uninvited?"

The Calianith roared, shaking him off with enough force to slam him against the tree, shaking it to its roots.

Lorshin landed on his feet with a terrifying smile as the Calianith drew his black whip from around his body. "No? Well, how about this one?" He dove over the whip as it lashed out at him. "The forest is no place for children." In one rapid movement, he stole the whip from the beast's hand and threw it aside.

"You almost hit me with that," Isentara said as she appeared at her brother's side.

"Sorry," he said with a smile.

"I'm going to crush you, you nasty, blood-sucking flea!" The Calianith charged toward them with a growl.

"I guess no one ever told you to never talk to strangers," Lorshin taunted as he threw a stone at the beast's head.

"Did you have to make him quite so mad?" Isentara asked as she leaped to one side.

"I barely did anything," Lorshin said innocently as he leaped to the other side.

The rock glanced off the Calianith's head, knocking the small rounded helmet out of place just seconds before the beast crashed into a thicket of bramble where Lorshin and Isentara had been standing. He tore free, ripping out tuffs of his own hair, and shook himself wildly. Claws sprang out from his fingers and his toes—a menacing sight to behold.

"Ah, I don't think he wants to play anymore, sister."

"Neither do I." Isentara threw her dagger with perfect aim into the beast's chest.

The Calianith roared, ripping the dagger free and hurling it back at her.

"Now we're getting somewhere," Lorshin said softly as he pushed her aside. The blade sailed through the gap, narrowly missing them both. "Is that the best you can do?" he taunted their prey.

"Lorshin!"

"Trust me."

The Calianith charged. This time he held his ground until the brute was nearly upon him. Lorshin smiled to himself, his fangs flashing, as in mid-back flip his feet connected with and smashed the brute's jaw in two. This was war after all. He landed gracefully and beckoned the snarling beast forward, nearly laughing with anticipation. His enemy was huge, quite literally as broad as he was tall and muscle all over so that it almost appeared he had too little skin, green between wormy tuffs of brown fur, to cover the sinews of his body. The stench of rotten flesh masked the scent of the blood gushing from the Calianith's wounds for which Lorshin was remarkably thankful. Now was not the time to lose control of his sanity.

The Calianith circled him. Isentara silently circled the Calianith. Lorshin stood still, waiting until the beast lunged at him. At the last second, Lorshin and Isentara vaulted into the air, somersaulting past each other over their prey. Each held a tiny but incredibly sharp blade that they released with accuracy and incredible strength in mid-flight to pierce the brute's heart. Lorshin and Isentara landed. One pale hand of each grazed the earth, leaving a trail in the dirt where their long fingers passed.

Isentara rose quickly, barely dodging the blade that was swung carelessly toward her head by their dying prey, by leaping up onto a nearby tree limb with the majesty of a wild cat.

The Calianith staggered after her in a mad rage.

"No!" Lorshin shouted. He sprang, bounding off the beast's back up onto the branch beside his sister. The blow knocked the Calianith off-balance on the uneven ground and the beast fell.

"Are you all right?" Lorshin asked frantically as he took his sister's face between his hands. "Did he hurt you?"

"No, I'm all right. You?"

Lorshin nodded, exhaling a hard breath.

Brother and sister crouched on the limb and watched as the beast convulsed noisily where it had fallen. Their nostrils filled with the harsh and painfully alluring scent of Flame's fingerprint hidden in the blood. Lorshin grimaced. Isentara's grip on his hand tightened. His fangs ached with the first pull of his cursed hunger, but he resisted, clinging to his sister and his sanity. She in turn clung to the tree and to him, depending upon the strength of both to hold her steady.

Reality flickered in and out for several painful moments and then Lorshin's gaze became fixed once more upon the beast lying there beneath him. The corpse was splitting open. Its bones were cracking apart. Its muscles were oozing free of that rotten flesh, and from that riven hull a dark substance was emerging. Power skimmed across his flesh. "Uh-oh," Lorshin whispered.

Isentara gasped, feeling it too.

Stress lines formed on their perfect, ageless brows. Their faintly glowing eyes widened in alarm. He recoiled in horror, launching himself from the limb as a definite ghastly *thing* moved nearer, increasing in size and substance.

Isentara followed closely behind him. "I knew we'd regret this," she said as he reached back to take her hand.

"Run!" he said.

They ran before the unnatural silence seeping into the forest. Lorshin's heart pounded loudly in his own ears so that he could not differentiate between the sound of his own blood pumping through hungry veins and the whispering voice of the thing chasing them.

Lorshin.

Light loomed ahead. They ran parallel to it, afraid of the Sun that could destroy them and the *Darkness* that had taken so much from them. Every now and then, Lorshin glanced back. The *thing* appeared and disappeared in the long shadows stretching from the trees, always reemerging larger and still coming. They leaped powerfully over a fallen log as they ran. Both longed to get away from the *thing* breathing hot on their heels. Lorshin, more so than Isentara, could feel its weight pressing on his chest, clawing at him—trying to enter him. He wanted to scream, but his voice was paralyzed, his tongue glued to the roof of his mouth!

He fell, his hand wrenching free of Isentara's. The blackness was nearly upon him. "Run!" he croaked to her as he scrambled backward with his hands and feet, desperately seeking escape.

"Never!" Isentara shouted to him. She sprang over the top of him, coming between him and the blackness. "Leave my brother alone!"

"Isentara!" Lorshin whispered, reaching out for her.

Lorshin. Lorshin. Lorshin. My son. A horrible voice whispered from the blackness.

Lorshin froze as his father's corrupted voice entered his mind. Some part of him rebelled against it. He knew what his father had become. He knew that what was left of his father was so lost in *Darkness* that it would not recognize him. He knew, and yet that voice that he had longed to hear all the days of his life held such power over his mind and heart that he found he could not resist it and his desire to escape was as paralyzed as his voice.

Isentara heard it too. She froze, glancing uncertainly between her brother and the black *thing* before them. Her heart pounded visibly in her chest as she too felt the dull, empty ache gnawing at her soul, and a strange, disorienting light-headed feeling pulled her down onto the earth beside her brother as that voice spoke her name.

Isentara. Isentara. My daughter.

Darkness loomed over them, pressing them down completely to the ground so that they couldn't even catch a breath that was not made of the living blackness; and then suddenly Light poured over them. For half a second, they expected to feel the burning of the sunlight and then they saw the blue Flame crash into the *dark thing* that had spoken with their father's voice, dissolving the illusion before their eyes.

It rose up in defiance, spreading out to join with *Darkness* and cover the whole earth.

Lorshin twisted around within the shield of Light to gaze across the vast distance upon Firinn's pinnacle in the heart of the universe and the Guardians that had come to deliver them at last!

* * *

"Sgarrwrath!" Cadclucan roared, speaking the name that was never spoken. His talons curled over the tip of Firinn's pinnacle. His huge curved wings spread majestically from his back. The wind whistled between their sculpted feathers that were as light as air and as hard as stone. "Behold the Light!" The Stone of Existence blazed around his neck, shining brighter than the sun. All around the world, the Guardians answered. Their beautiful voices were amplified and echoed throughout the land. The Flame inside them burned brighter, dispelling the gloom. Proven and changing Guardians appeared side by side in a vast, innumerable army hovering in the heavens.

A single bloody tear dripped from Cadclucan's emerald and gold scales and plummeted through the combined Flames of the Guardians to the earth. In that tear was all the sorrow and power of the Light. It sank soundlessly into the ground. *Darkness* shrieked.

Even the races, protected within the massive shield of Light, feared the power that opened the earth with pure creation. Up through the bloodstained grass rose an amphitheater of massive, horseshoe cliffs that dropped vertically down to a green valley. Along the upper rim spilled a beautiful waterfall. The races cowered beneath the shadow of the harsh, jutting rocks that rose like spears from the earth. On the distant horizon, the rocks came together to form horrible teeth, and at the highest point, black fingers of rock curled upward toward the sky. Balls of blue-white fire, the size of human heads, rolled off each point of the creation.

The races shielded their eyes against the blinding Light. They screamed with fear as the flaming balls rolled toward them, easily penetrating the massive shield around them. Suddenly, both ascended back toward the Guardians. The balls of Light exploded just overhead, returning into the bodies of the Guardians who had breathed it out.

The undeniable scent of life filled the world: from the ice floes of the North, to the vast deserts of the South, to the vivid blue sky and the raging seas made by Sanctus's hand, to the majesty of the Guardians' creation risen from their sorrow and Light before the eyes of all living things. As *Darkness* fled, the hearts of the races bowed within them to the awesome power hovering overhead.

Most fell to their faces all over the earth, prostrating themselves while their hands raised in praise toward the powerful Guardians still glowing from the Flame within. The Elves of Light hung their heads in sorrow. The Astoni gaped with horror. Lorshin groaned as the Great Ones threw back their heads, drawing themselves up to their full height so that their wings blotted out the heavens as they roared with unbridled fury.

"Do they know what they have done?" Isentara whispered. Lorshin squeezed her hand.

"Enough!" Cadclucan shouted as he leaped from Firinn's pinnacle and descended in the veil of humanity before the races. His booted feet touched soundlessly upon the ground as his wings descended into arms. His midnight robe swept with a gentle rustling sound over the green grass as he walked, stopping only when Lorshin and Isentara were covered in his shadow against the sunlight.

Lorshin clung to his uncle's midnight robe.

Do not be afraid. Cadclucan whispered to their minds.

All across the world, one by one, the other Guardians transformed. Only their blue flaming eyes revealed what they really were, and those eyes shone with a bridled fury that no living creature had ever seen before. It surpassed even that which had caused *Darkness* to flee.

The earth never stopped quaking beneath their power; yet its full force was held in check by the Flame of mercy burning within their mighty hearts. It was a righteous anger without violence or guilt. It was glory without consuming force. It was all the power of the Light and none of the dark. Their power was pure, majestic, and beautiful even in fury.

Cadclucan's voice carried to the corners of the earth. "You worship us?" he shouted. "Are we gods that we should be worshipped?"

No one dared to answer. In the distant stronghold of *Darkness*, Sgarrwrath laughed.

"Sanctus gave you life! He gave us life too! We are Guardians! He gave us life with his Flame and made us able to wield it for his service, but this great power within us does not make us equal to him!" Cadclucan shouted. "Can you be so quick to forget? Can your hearts be so darkened that you cannot see the truth, even here in the shadow of Firinn's pinnacle?" He sighed a long, inhuman breath that rippled around him with the heat of his internal Flame. A perfect circle scored the earth around him as the grass shriveled.

All over the world, the same signs appeared on the earth around the silent Guardians. Their silence was as piercing as their words, cutting the races to their core. In slow progression, the races fled from before the Great Ones, returning to their homes to hide their shame until Lorshin and Isentara alone remained.

From the ice floes to the boiling deserts, every living thing held its breath as the Guardians remained too still. The earth and its inhabitants remained silent . . . waiting . . . for what they did not know. A storm rolled in as the hours passed. Rain poured in torrents from the thick black clouds that blacked out the Moon and stars; yet, the Light clung to the unmoving Guardians, shining brighter in their shadows than in any other place.

Lorshin shielded his eyes against it by pressing his face into the folds of Cadclucan's midnight robe. He shuddered, quaking as the earth quaked. For two days and two nights, the earth shook and the Guardians did not breathe.

When at last they stirred, the Guardians' breath lasted days without sun and nights without moon. It was impossible to tell the passage of time. How many days had been lost to their thinly veiled sorrow? How many nights had harbored their silent pain? How many raindrops had concealed their bitter tears? When at last the Sun showed his face, the Guardians thawed from their ridged stance. The birds burst forth with singing. The trees danced in the wind. The earth slowly exhaled, and the various scents of life sprang forth once more, but *Darkness* had spread a thread of corruption. Innocence was gone.

Cadclucan slowly turned. "We knew this moment would come," he said. His voice carried softly across the world. "All that Sanctus revealed in his Prophecy of Hope must be fulfilled, even this Sea of Sorrows! Though it breaks our hearts, the coming *Darkness* cannot be prevented. The One Whose Name is not Spoken will arise in many hearts to trouble the whole earth, and in that endless blackness, the races will call out to the Light once more!" He was quiet for a long moment before he spoke again with his mind, *Let the Light shine forth and awaken hope. Let Mhorag arise. Let the Promised come.*

Lorshin and Isentara crouched in the shadow of the Guardian. Their blue eyes burned dimly in the shadows . . . a single trace of Flame . . . a hint of the heritage that was both a blessing and a curse. They could not claim the perfection of the Guardian bloodline, no Samhail could—that had been denied them long before their birth. There was just enough Flame in them to light their eyes and that was all. It made them immortal, but never satisfied. They hungered for it, longing to fill their hearts and quench their thirsty veins. Within each life was a fingerprint of Flame that most never even sensed. *The curse of the Samhail* was not so much a bloodlust as it was the deprivation of Flame. Still, their ravaged hearts, beating slow and steady in their chests, felt heavier than they should have. They had borne many weights in their lifetime. Lorshin had seen his mother die. He had seen his father become the Heart of Evil, and through him Isentara had seen it too. They had endured this curse from birth because of their father's choice, but this time the weight felt too big, or perhaps they were just now acknowledging their own weakness.

"Must you go?" Lorshin asked softly.

Cadclucan glanced down at him. "To every season there is an added sorrow. Consider, nephew, the beautiful flowers of spring that wither in the heat of the summer sun; the trees that bring forth buds only to have those garments fall and rot upon the ground; the ground that freezes in winter locking up its bounty, but to every sorrow there is a purpose. There is always the promise. There is always Hope," he answered cryptically.

Lorshin shook his head. "I don't . . . I don't understand this. How can you think of leaving? We need you here to lead us!"

"This world has had us to lead them from the beginning," Cadclucan answered quietly. "Look around you, Lorshin, *Darkness* is everywhere and yet can anyone see it? They fight, but the One Whose Name is Not Spoken comes in many forms and they resist only in the ways that please them." He shook his head. "No, this world has blinded itself, and now they must face their choice."

"Not all have forgotten!" Lorshin cried.

Cadclucan sighed and the other Guardians with him. "I know."

"Will you leave those who still desire only Light?"

Cadclucan held out his hand to Lorshin. "Will you come out of the *Darkness*?"

Lorshin hesitated. He glanced toward his sister.

"In good times, the world grows and prospers, but it is in the *darkest* of times that all living things find what is really inside themselves," Cadclucan said.

Lorshin looked up into his uncle's piercing eyes. "I know what is inside me."

The Guardian smiled. "Do you, nephew?"

"Yes," Lorshin answered, but his voice sounded weak and less confident than he had intended.

Cadclucan searched his nephew's face. His eyes seemed to pierce right through into Lorshin's very soul. "You have nothing to prove here, Lorshin," he said after a long moment.

A flood of power crashed over Lorshin, causing the earth to tremble once more as he seized his uncle's hand and kissed it. "I have to," he whispered before releasing it.

Cadclucan nodded. "So be it, but remember, Lorshin, we are your family too. Call and we will answer." He looked pointedly at Isentara as he said this, as if he knew something neither of them had yet imagined.

She nodded as she and Lorshin backed into the safety of the forest.

The innumerable Guardians came together. Their soundless footsteps bound the rings formed by their power. Wherever their feet fell, water appeared, carving out a bitter memorial to their exodus. A dark vapor rose like eerily screaming wind in their wake—echoing the silent cries of their hearts as *Darkness* laughed again.

Cadclucan turned toward the sound. Fyrdung and Azolat froze on either side of him while the greater host disappeared in rapid flashes of Light. The brilliance of Bynthroenine burned upon the shadowy light of this new day.

"Do you feel it, brothers?" Cadclucan whispered.

"Yes," Fyrdung growled through clenched teeth.

"*Darkness* has grown stronger." Azolat looked at his brothers. "Arawn?" He breathed; the tortured sound of his twin's name came out in barely a whisper.

As if in response, a scream shattered the calm. Cadclucan's mind brushed Arawn's. *Pain.* It struck him like the blow of a hammer. He doubled over, groaning in agony. Dark shadows spread around his flaming eyes. *Despair.* The Flame in his heart burned more fiercely through his veins. Arawn's thoughts were tainted with *Darkness* that came unbidden into his mind, whispering. *It would be so easy to be free.* Cadclucan grimaced. His fingers curled into the earth as he struggled to find the will to face the horror and survive it. A memory of the future wriggled in the back of his mind—a warning . . . a promise . . . he could not tell, and he could not flee though the Dark One's time was near at hand. The choice before him—before all *the living*—might well be the catalyst to an inexorable path for the future, setting in motion the horrors that plagued his mind, but he still could not turn back. In silence, Fyrdung and Azolat gripped his shoulders and together they moved forward, setting the march of history and a new season in motion.

Darkness loomed before them—waiting, watching, *hungering*.

Not idle is Time; it rages on when all would have it stop. It strips away all that is held dear, and nothing can slow its advance, nothing can prevent it. Time . . . time brings forgetfulness; time breeds silence and despair . . . until no one can remember from whence it came or where it will go.

Chapter Two

EMPYREAN

The Kingdom, Beyond the Reach of Time

S creams rose from some distant place beyond the Light, a place distinctly separate and yet linked by one all binding cord . . . Flame . . . where **Darkness** breathed out its mindless despair. The blackness loomed so high it seemed to have no end just like the Light embroiled against it; yet high above the Sun and Moon, high above Light and **Darkness**, far beyond the weightlessness of space, the fountainhead of all Flame heaved forth from the zenith of the universe, and all these things fell away beneath his feet. What were they by comparison to his glory?

Flame was flying out away from him. Its blinding radiance poured from his snow-white flesh. With his hands, he braced himself against the sparkling outer shell of the Orb of Power. It rippled like water beneath his hands, yet it was as impenetrable as steel. Golden blood glowed out of the pale flesh of his hands, not following the course of any true veins, but swirling mysteriously up toward his heart. He sighed. His breath flew out to become one with the outer shell of the orb. Only air, draped in light veils of deliquescent crystal encircled him, satisfying his every hunger and nourishing every inch of his body with its cleansing flow while keeping him fixed in this secret place. This ever-purifying air was part of him—the very essence of life and perfection—constantly formed and renewed by his very breath! It was alive just as the fiery mask of his flesh lived through him.

Flame was gloriously reflected upon the liquid-steel wings of his breath, continuously flowing, changing, but impossible to fathom. Rivers of fire clothed the outer shell of humanity in icy wavelets of cerulean blue, heated ripples of white, and the pristine shine of royal purple. Violent heat and fierce cold existed side by side, entwined by the power of the mysterious Flame. Such was the depth of the Flame that neither the heat nor the cold rising from his naked flesh caused him pain. Flame came from within him, birthed from a deep place, making him the core, the perfect center, of all things. His every movement only made the Flame shine brighter, coruscating out of the orb whose sheer mass surpassed the highest mountains of Earth and the vastness of the oceans. His predominance and power filled the kingdom, setting it alight with the secret Source. Perfection swept out for miles upon miles, more wonderful than all the beauty of the universe below! All of it seamlessly woven together by this power . . . his power, yet he had never been outside this secret place. He dreamed; but he had never truly known joy or pain, fear or hope, peace or war, life with all its choices or death with all its tears and regret, though all were linked into his Flame. He had never been free!

He tried again to press through the barriers surrounding him. His efforts only made Flame shine brighter from every inch of his body; no matter how hard or long he struggled to escape, he could not break free, and time was endless. It was not measured here as it was in the universe below his feet. Existence was the first and only mark on the compass of the kingdom, and his existence was the heart of all existence. He wore himself out with fighting and sank exhausted to his knees. With his hands, he still braced himself against unbreakable walls. The Flame grew cold around him. Its violent heat banished to memory. He shivered, and the tongues of colored fire shivered with him.

Time flew by—days, weeks, years, yet he lingered on alone and unchanged, shackled by Flame and breath. He bowed his snow-white head against the orb. *Darkness* crept across the universe, sending bitter wails of death and despair, rising up into the perfect stillness all around him. He covered his ears against the cries of a broken universe. He squeezed his flaming eyes shut against the black, high-reaching void and sank down into the shelter of his strange, eternal sanctuary. In secret, he felt the Flame stir in answer to those horrible screams, and in his mind, if he concentrated hard enough, he could almost envision their answer. A Mark appeared behind his eyes, glowing with a faint golden Light. It curved like the waxing crescent moon, only tipped with a head and trailing a gleaming tail. Beneath this Mark, a face began to appear—snow-white skin, unnaturally flaming amber eyes, a lion's mane of snow-white hair, a beating crystal heart.

He gasped. His eyes flew open. That face gazed back at him, reflected upon the walls of his breath!

All around this vision, Flame flowed. The furthest reaching points were the tips of huge wings. A beautiful horse-shaped head crowned with a single iridescent horn appeared as the presence rose up with a noble cry. The glittering mane tumbled down the long neck. From the top of the head to the end of the long, thick tail, the massive body was made of Light divided into a covering of tiny, close-knit, scale like Flames. The outer edges were a royal purple fading into cerulean blue Flame and finally into the blinding white that shone brighter than the sun. He stood at the center of this Light shadow, a mixture of lion and youth and Guardian.

He shook his head, trying to clear it. This was nothing more than a shadow around a fixed point. He focused on that point with all his might. It was his reflection. Suddenly, the Flame threw him back into silhouette and the vision was gone. He sank down into his sanctuary with a soft whimper as his *Father's* voice whispered across the kingdom.

"There is still Hope," Sanctus said, but Arawn couldn't see it—not even in the glory of the kingdom. Oh, he knew the Prophecy as well as any other. *Darkness* had not taken that from him. Only his Flame and the heart that contained it had been left in the abyss. It was the emptiness; it was the scars left by that *Darkness* that made him tremble and fear. The Prophecy had never really given him much hope. He had been too blind to see it, too deaf to hear it, and too proud to admit he needed it.

Now, he was free in body, yet his mind echoed still with *Darkness*. The beat of his ruined heart thundered in his ears, seemingly closer than he knew it was. *Thud. Thud. Thud. Thud.* Flame rippled just out of sight. He could still feel it . . . foreign and wrong despite its familiarity . . . in the cavity where his heart had once resided. Blackness lashed out at him . . . that living blackness, foaming out its own shame; that hated thing, breathing forth its mindless despair, came upon him with memories he could not silence; for once he had been a part of the blackness, and it was still more real to him than the Light that had set him free! Arawn gasped beneath a blinding agony. His pale hands clawed at his chest as his body crumpled forward.

Sanctus was there, keeping him from tumbling back into *Darkness*. His gentle eyes held no condemnation, only compassion and, impossibly, understanding; but how could one so pure and powerful know agony?

"What have I done?" Arawn nearly screamed, collapsing into Sanctus's arms. He could feel the corrupted Flame!

Darkness laughed at him from the distance. *Does it hurt you, Arawn?* A mocking voice echoed through his mind. *Do you long for oblivion?* The Dark One was laughing.

Sanctus's hand filled the cavity in Arawn's chest and flexed like the pumping of a heart. "Enough," he said in a voice that demanded obedience. Light flared out around them, allowing Arawn to breathe easier.

When at last Arawn found the strength to look up, Sanctus was gazing down at him with unfathomable eyes. "Sanctus?"

Sanctus smiled. "Truth is always better," he said gently, "and it is time you remember what you forgot; it is time to reclaim what you lost and see what *Darkness* made you blind to for so long. In time you will be at peace, gentle *Guardian*."

Arawn cried out, "But—but I gave S . . . S." He choked on the words.

Sanctus smiled. "But you gave Sgarrwrath your Flame?"

Arawn nodded, unable to hide his grimace at the Dark One's name. "I gave him *life, power . . . everything!*"

Sanctus shook his head slowly. "Not everything, Arawn. You could not give him what you lost, nor could Sgarrwrath have taken it. It has always been out of his reach, and for that reason, it is his greatest desire."

"What did I lose?"

"Come. I will show you."

They journeyed as one to a secret place where none could follow. They moved in Light with a swiftness and power that defies description. Many great leaps and surges later, they stopped. Sanctus set Arawn on his feet. "Behold what was lost, Arawn."

Arawn stood frozen, his eyes fixed upon the orb before them. He vaguely remembered the journey he had taken with his brothers into the past. The memory played on the edges of his mind, just out of focus. The only bright spot was the Flame that fueled Sanctus's might. It coruscated out of the mammoth orb whose sheer mass explained why Sanctus had shed it from his person on the course of his ceaseless existence. Its volume exceeded even its size and was felt all throughout the kingdom. The lure of the predominance and power within explained why Sanctus had long kept it in this secret place. As it was, Arawn could not resist its pull and stepped into its shadow.

"Flame," he said softly. "Flame is what I lost."

"No, Arawn, look closer. It is more than Flame."

Arawn reached out his hand and touched the shining walls of the orb, studying them with his fingers. A cool stream of air flowed off the walls scented with power; there was no other word for it. Beneath his fingers came a pulsing beat almost like a heart, only somehow more fluid and simultaneously as hard as crystal. He could *see* it in his mind, this glowing crystal organ, casting wide, arcing rainbows in the Light, as it pumped pure, golden blood—the blood of neither Guardian nor men, nor any other race! He inhaled sharply, his eyes widening in alarm, at the vision in his mind.

Suddenly a hand appeared beneath his, pressing hard from within the shining walls of the orb without penetrating the barrier. The golden blood glowed out of the pale flesh of that hand, not following the course of any true veins, but swirling mysteriously up toward the heart like a subtle, dizzying tapestry of Light; from every inch came tiny shoots of white, blue, and purple Flame which were undeniable tokens of—Arawn slowly shook his head. Undeniable tokens of what?

Arawn.

A startled gasp tore itself from Arawn's throat as the magnetic voice whispered in his mind. He gaped in stunned silence at the orb, transfixed by the inherent sovereignty of the voice that called to him.

Arawn. A face appeared pressed against the orb's walls.

"It's alive!" Arawn said in a voice raw with terror.

Sanctus laughed. "Yes."

The beautiful face within the orb spiraled with the same golden designs the arm had and mirrored Sanctus's laugh with one of its own. Rich, childlike belly laughs pealed through Arawn's mind.

"What is it?" Arawn shrieked, jumping reflexively backward as if it had reached out and bitten him.

"You do not know?" Sanctus asked.

Arawn.

Arawn frowned. "Should I?"

"Yes."

Arawn. I see you.

Sanctus squatted down beside the orb. "Do not be afraid. Knowledge of *him,* the deep knowledge only a Guardian possesses. Here," he said, pointing toward his heart, "is what you lost so long ago. *He* is the Source, the living Flame."

"Mhorag," Arawn whispered as he dropped to his knees before the orb in long-deferred obeisance.

"A Flame unto Flame," Sanctus said gently, "such is Hope." He sighed. "Such is the Agony. Amidst these tears, a perfect will and plan will be born. He will be greater than the Light that nurtures him and the *Darkness* that hunts him . . . As I am so is he, flesh of my flesh, living Flame."

Left alone once more, The Source crouched in his sanctuary, listening as the screams continued to rise from the universe below. The undefined wailings of the broken constantly filled his ears as Time dragged on. Their incomprehensible pleadings and despair were no more than a noise before him. They had no meaning, no purpose beyond their *dark* portends, but he listened anyway, and when at last their tears were silent, he wept in their place. He wept for the life fading around them and for the agony it birthed in his heart.

His tears were no mere offering of compassion, but droplets of life that fell unseen, unheeded, and unwanted down into the universe. There amongst the darkening he left a stain all his own, and the irresistible pull of his power slowly ignited the Age of the Prophecy!

Darkness.

The Prophecy of Hope

Behold the signs here set forth by which all shall know the meaning of the two faces of the Guardian Moon, but lest despair take hold upon your souls here are foretold they whom our hope shall restore.

In the beginning, Sanctus brought forth from the void of His creation Nine grains of power, hence planted in the Light and the Stone of Existence plucked from his crown to give unbelievable might.

Father and Mother set on high, the diadems of Day and Night. Grains of Power there remain, but sacred stone concealed away. No Guardian shall harness their hidden might till Bynthroenine again has a king. Before that time is come, the mighty Guardians shall cling in unity to the Chosen One from a Colorless sprung.

The heavens will bleed. The Chosen One veiled in weakness shall be taken when the Heart of Evil is revealed. *Darkness* secretes through all that lies within its reach. Song of Guardians, fire and blood, Dark gift of power, Shadow and *Darkness* now combined seek power of a greater kind. A curse upon the Forbidden Kiss and the bestower's race.

The greed of Men will cause alliances to end. Sea of Sorrows, the portals shall be sealed. From ancient gift by Guardians given, song of haunting beauty takes flight, giving Evil might. The day of its creation shall be cursed when the secret of the Gemshorn is unleashed on the earth.

Crowned Head among the race of Men, who does not know his worth, within resides the hidden power that mortals ne'er possess. A battle rages for your unproven soul. Bitter, sorrowful, and in touch with Death, you must reach the end, where dwells the One naught of Humankind hath seen and bring Hope to the races once again. In the Guardian's seed no weakness shall prevail, but heed your mortal father's fate; traitors lie within your gate. This test you must endure in the frailty of Human form; but when it is past, your crown will last and you will be weak no more.

Great Guardians of this beware, danger lurks beyond your lair and will seek to bring great harm. A journey into stone awaits this One held dearest to your hearts. It shall be when *Darkness* covers all the earth, but do not fear, for Mhorag shall appear and silence the Gemshorn with his mighty roar.

A babe rests unknown in the womb of stone. Mhorag's seed none shall behold till the stronghold of Death is shattered from above. The One and her sleeping Guardians at once awake. Throughout all distance, the Guardian voices shall be raised in answer to Mhorag's call, and all shall fear the Guardians' might. Summoning stones shall be reforged as all creation for the Guardians call.

The catalyst of war must be reclaimed the Evil Heart to break. Grains of Power will revive to test the purity of all hearts once more, for soon Mhorag's armies shall converge behind the Nine; but take this warning, heed only the sign of the Guardian Moon set in the flesh by Sanctus formed, for *Darkness* is closing in on you.

Nine thrones of Light and Gold, Mhorag's seed, and the Circle of Power that you need to find the Treasure of *Darkness* born.

He of black and tortured soul calls forth the wraiths by *Darkness* sown, and when through Mhorag's fire he safely passes, Two Faces of the Moon unite. Then by the Stone of Existence unleash the power to bring *Darkness* into subjection to the Light and seal it by the might of Nine.

Chapter Three

CURSED

Fenachdra Willowbark used the small shard of a broken Styarfyre orb to light the way. Its eerie red glow bathed the mouth of the forest but did little to dispel the *darkness* creeping within. The Elfin Summoner sighed softly, ignoring the queasy feeling of unease churning in the pit of her stomach. Her new apprentice, a human girl by the name of Jysine, shivered close behind her.

"What is this place?" Jysine whispered.

"It is nameless. So much life was consumed here that long ago the name of this forest was purged from history and wiped from every map in all the lands in the hopes that no more would fall prey to the curse."

"The curse?" Jysine shuddered.

"The curse of the Samhail," Fenachdra explained gently. "In time, the children of Arawn were *tamed*, for lack of a better word, by the power, wisdom, and compassion of the Guardians with whom the Samhail enjoy a familial bond—though not equality." The Summoner sighed. "With the Guardians gone, those days of sanity may already be lost, yet if some civility remains in the Samhail, I must reach it." She took a resolute step forward.

"Do you really mean to go in there, Mistress Fenachdra?" Jysine asked in a hushed shriek.

"Yes," Fenachdra answered with an assurance she did not truly feel. "The races are gathering to Cartiman, to the Summoners, but without some link to the Guardians' themselves, I fear any attempt at alliance will fail. If we can reach the Samhail, their presence will bring a shot of life into this Resistance, for they, despite their curse, are of the Guardians' own lineage, as I have already said." Fenachdra Willowbark turned to look at her young apprentice. "I do not command you to come with me, Jysine. It is likely I will not make it out alive. *Darkness* has a stronger hold here."

Jysine shuddered, looking warily from the forest up to the Dianara Mountains in the distance and the *Darkness* sweeping down in thick living veils. "Why would anyone want to live here?"

"The Samhail live in seclusion for one reason, to preserve our lives." Fenachdra moved forward through the brush preceding the forest. She moved in virtual silence, drawing upon her heritage.

Jysine scrambled to keep up. She was not nearly so silent. "Don't leave me, mistress! I'm coming with you!"

The Summoner raised a hand cautioning her. Jysine fell obediently silent.

"Stay behind me, Jysine," Fenachdra instructed, "and stay close. The Samhail are nearby."

Jysine swallowed at the lump in her throat. "How do you know?" Her long pale fingers flexed around her shard of a broken Styarfyre orb. Her pale eyes uneasily scanned the forest. The glow of the shards made the deep shadows even more menacing. "I don't see anything."

"You won't. My senses are stronger than yours. Your human senses are too weak and the night belongs to the Samhail." Fenachdra moved forward slowly. Jysine shadowed her. "We are mere food to them, ripe for the picking." The Summoner shifted forward slightly and then back. "Shh." She stretched her hand out to stop Jysine's advance.

Jysine did not dare to break the silence. Their breaths already seemed too loud in the dark. Their heartbeats suddenly seemed too easy to track.

Mistress and apprentice crouched in the shadows with little hope of escape and even less hope of completing their task. Jysine glanced toward her mistress, an Elf hardened by war and loss, yet still possessing the eternal youth of her people. A twig snapped. Fenachdra shifted infinitesimally toward the sound, only to have it repeat from the other side.

"We're being hunted," she whispered. "Don't move." Fenachdra crept forward moving soundlessly.

"Mistress!" Jysine hissed.

"Quiet. Stay where you are!" Fenachdra said. "I'm going to see if I can make contact with one of them. They will be less likely to attack me. Elves are not as easy nor as tempting prey as humans." She spoke in barely a whisper. If it had not been for the glow of the Styarfyre shards enabling Jysine to read her lips, the apprentice would have missed them entirely.

Jysine obeyed despite the fact it was worse being alone. She was clammy with sweat within seconds. Every sound in the dark made her heart hammer more ferociously in her chest. Her eyes darted maniacally, trying to pick objects from the gloom. Her breath quickened, growing too loud for her own ears. Nauseating spurts of adrenaline coursed through her veins. An owl's hoot, a rabbit's dying shrieks, a whisper of grass in the night's breeze, her own spastic breaths, all of it came undone as her mistress's screams filled the air.

"Jysine, run!"

For one horrible second, Jysine was frozen. She couldn't breathe. Her heart even stopped beating, and then out of nowhere a feral growl rang in her ears. She whirled around onto her feet, fighting the shriek of raw terror that was rising in her throat as she came face-to-face with one of their bloodthirsty quarry: a girl of incredible beauty with deep brown hair that ran the length of her body, braided together with what appeared to be foxtails, and eyes that were fierce, dying blue Flames. It was too late to run. Jysine raised the Styarfyre shard out before her with trembling hands. "Stay back," she managed to whisper as she took a step back.

The Samhail maiden shifted forward ever so slightly. A gentle thread of honey floated on the breeze. "Do not be afraid," she said. Her eyes glowed with sincerity, compassion, and even sorrow.

Jysine's every breath was filled with honey. Where was the fear that had gripped her just moments before? Her arm grew heavy. The shard of the Styarfyre orb slipped from her hand.

The Samhail maiden smiled at her, showing perfect white teeth, as she took Jysine in her arms. "Forgive me, but you should not have come here."

Jysine whimpered.

"This will be over quickly. I promise."

Jysine whimpered again though it ended with a sigh of contentment. Her head rolled to the side. The huntress brushed the long blonde tresses back from her throat and those small white fangs, which barely stood out amongst those perfect white teeth, slid effortlessly into Jysine's throat to claim the trace of Flame flowing within the blood.

Abruptly the sense of calm vanished. The venom flowed in as her blood flowed out, poisoning her body as she shrieked in agony. Jysine thrashed against the huntress, trying to free herself from the vice of the Samhail maiden's arms, but it was no use. The huntress held her as effortlessly as a mother would her sleeping baby while Jysine's screams slowly dissolved into a childish whimper.

Suddenly, the huntress dropped Jysine with her own agonized wail. Her hands gripped the sides of her own head as Jysine fell. Jysine's body locked into a fetal position as she hit the ground.

"No!" Fenachdra screamed. She sounded so far away to Jysine's ears, yet the huntress whirled toward her and away from Jysine.

The huntress nearly screamed in agony as she leaned involuntarily forward into a crouch. Her lips curled back over her bloody teeth. A growl ripped up her throat.

"Mistress," Jysine groaned. Her eyes beheld only shadows.

Fenachdra Willowbark was frozen for half a second as a drop of Jysine's blood trickled down the exposed fangs of the Samhail maiden. Slowly the Summoner raised her hands. "Daughter of Arawn, I come in peace."

The huntress snarled.

"Do you understand?" Fenachdra took a slow step forward. "I mean you no harm. I am Fenachdra Willowbark, Summoner and true friend of Guardians. Do you understand? What is your name, Daughter of Arawn?"

The Samhail maiden wailed pitifully. "Isentara," she managed. Her hands framed the sides of her head as saliva and venom dripped in moist strings from her mouth. The closer Fenachdra came, the wilder the huntress' eyes became.

"Isentara, I come to honor the old alliances and beg you to do the same."

"You . . . shouldn't . . . have . . . come . . . here!" Isentara choked out the words. "Not . . . in . . . the . . . dark!"

"There was no time to delay," Fenachdra said softly. She was now standing within arms' reach of the Samhail maiden.

Isentara moaned. Her beautiful body was rigid, but her forbearance was lost in the insatiable hunger of her curse. A huntress once more, she growled, sinking lower into a crouch, ready to spring. As she bared her fangs, there was no mistaking the madness in her eyes. "If you had only come a few hours later," she said with a morbid smile as her restraint came unhinged.

Fenachdra saw the horrible surrender in Isentara's eyes, and she couldn't move. Her scream came out a mere horrified gasp.

In a split second, Isentara sprang.

"You should have left me," Jysine whispered, rolling toward the sounds heightened by the dark of night. Her eyes saw everything. The dark offered every spectrum of the rainbow, and those things that had been hidden from her human eyes by the dark suddenly burst out at her fresh and new. It was all so . . . distracting. In the distance, indigo-lined trees stood proud and strong in the shadow of a violet-hued mountain. A stream trickled softly through the emerald green plain. A blue moon hung low and full in the inky sky, and there beneath its glow stood a pale-skinned phantom staring back at her with haunted, blue fire eyes.

In a second, he vanished, and in the same second, Jysine heard her mistress' horrified gasp. Her eyes shifted back toward Fenachdra. Was her mistress' heart really beating so loud? Her head cocked to the side.

Fenachdra didn't flinch as the huntress sprang.

In the blur of movement, Jysine still saw the huntress plainly. She shimmered beneath the moonlight, the most beautiful sight ever seen, and Jysine had no words to describe her, but then her nostrils flared with the scent of something she had never smelled before. Her body's response startled her, yet she couldn't deny that she wanted to obey the impulse to claim the mouth-watering smell. Its source was easy to pinpoint when she gave herself over to the desire. She saw the pulse beating steadily through her mistress' veins. She could even hear the flow of blood, but it was not blood that caused her to surge up from the ground with a hissing breath. But if not blood then what? Her teeth gnashed together. Saliva flooded her mouth. Some part of her comprehended the curse that was rapidly taking hold. Every sensation struck her like lightning, searing through her, shocking her broken body back to life. There would be no human death for her, as the stories of her people claimed. She would not have to rise from her grave and feed upon the blood of the innocent. Her wounds were already healing. The venom was changing her into the very monster she had feared just moments before. While her mind still struggled to grasp these new realities, everything ran red with the scent of blood—no, she had been right; it was not blood but rather Flame! She could see it, smell it, even taste it in the air, and she wanted it! She had only to feed and the curse would be complete. It would never let her go. She knew that. The human Summoner, Jysine, was already gone never to return. She could feed and turn into the monster she feared or she could fight what she was becoming to find a new way—a way to live in peace with those she loved until either she or they were no more.

All of this played out in her mind within the moment it took her to rise and launch herself at the huntress. Out of nowhere, the pale-skinned phantom appeared. He glared at Fenachdra with those haunted eyes.

"You don't belong here," he growled as he caught the Summoner and threw her aside.

Jysine gasped, her focus shifted from the huntress to Fenachdra and back. "No!" she shouted, landing gracefully on her feet with a growl.

"You don't really want to kill your friend, do you?" The pale-skinned phantom asked in his beautiful, enchanting voice.

Jysine shook her head slowly. Her tongue licked over her dry lips that wanted to curl back over her aching teeth. She struggled to block

out the alluring smell, even the sound of it flowing in her mistress' veins from across the forest.

The pale-skinned phantom inclined his head to her. "Then you will not challenge me further, young one," he said. This was not a question. He spoke as one who was used to being obeyed and expected it. "Stay. I will deal with you in a moment."

Maybe it was the effect of the venom, maybe it was something more, but Jysine dropped to her knees before him, exposing her throat like an animal in submission, and she stayed there having neither will nor the strength to rise.

He swept past her to the crouching huntress where he kneeled and took the huntress's beautiful face gently between his hands. "Isentara," he said softly.

"Lorshin," she whispered in a pitiful moan. She looked up into his eyes as he brushed the dark hair back from her face. "I couldn't stop! I just wanted to stop, Lorshin! What is happening to us?"

"Shh." Lorshin pulled her close. "I am sorry, sister," he said quietly. "I shouldn't have left you."

"You didn't know," she said.

"I knew the *Darkness* was stronger. I knew the hunger would be stronger too."

"Stop." Isentara shook her head. "Please."

Lorshin lowered his head to rest it against hers with a weary sigh. "Go, Isentara. I will deal with this."

Isentara nodded and shot off into the forest as Lorshin rose. The leaves rustled in the wind. Lorshin waited until they grew still before he spoke again.

"Why did you come here?" he asked without turning.

"I followed my mistress," Jysine answered.

"The Elf?" Lorshin turned. His flaming eyes fixed on Jysine and then across the forest to where Fenachdra was standing.

"The Summoner," Jysine said softly, painfully.

Lorshin nodded. With a weary sigh, he turned back to Jysine. "Do you understand what is happening to you?"

She didn't answer.

Lorshin glanced down to see why she was silent and found her shaking all over. Her eyes were fixed mindlessly upon the Elf. Her mouth was hanging open, with her lips curled back over her teeth.

"What's happening to my apprentice?" Fenachdra asked, rushing toward them.

"She is not yours anymore," Lorshin said sternly. "She is mine, and she needs to feed." He glanced toward the sky where the first rays of dawn were creeping into view. "But not here." He scooped her up in his powerful arms. "You should leave."

"But I must speak with you, my lord," Fenachdra said softly.

Lorshin sighed heavily. His shoulders sagged in defeat. "Very well. Come then. We will talk, Summoner, once I have helped her."

Fenachdra nodded and reached out her hand to stroke Jysine's brow. Jysine moaned painfully.

"Will she live?"

Lorshin turned away. "She is a daughter of Arawn now."

*   *   *

A narrow path twisted its way up through the gradually rising land between the close press of trees.

"Will your people try to kill me?" Fenachdra asked as the whispering sounds of the forest encroached upon her mind, weakening her resolve.

Lorshin snickered under his breath. "What happened to that rash bravery that brought you here, Summoner?" He paused, not out of response to her silence, but to measure his own words and the truth of his answer. "My people are cursed, Summoner, as you well know, but to answer your question, no, my people will not kill you. We do not make a practice of using our visitors as food. Of course, not many would dare to come upon us in the dark." His words were a gentle rebuke. "A Summoner least of all."

His booted feet made barely a sound as he climbed a rocky crest of land. Even with his burden, he reached the top, breathing evenly with no sign of exertion.

"I could not delay," Fenachdra said, climbing up after him.

"Yes. So I heard." Any hint of friendliness that had been in his voice a moment before was completely missing now.

Jysine moaned.

Lorshin held her closer, warily measuring the light with practiced eyes. "Hold on, little sister," he whispered. "We're almost there." To Fenachdra he said, "We must hurry. She will not survive the dawn."

*   *   *

Fenachdra gasped. Her mouth hung open with mute surprise. The weird mass looming before them was actually, upon closer inspection, a soaring palace made of countless hexagonal, basalt columns. A matching door, engraved with the images of fangs over an orb of power and a scepter of justice, groaned open in front of them.

"Come," Lorshin commanded without a backward glance. "And follow me closely." He gave no other explanation, nor did he pause to ascertain her proximity to him. The dawn was hovering dangerously on the horizon. Birds were beginning their early morning songs. Their jubilant trills were warning calls to all Samhail that Night was to release his beloved Day from beneath the sky cloak. Lorshin sighed. It was his turn to have no time to delay.

Fenachdra Willowbark pulled her white Summoner's robe more tightly around her as she followed Lorshin into the dark hall. The doors closed behind them, sealing out the light so that even the eerie red glow of the Styarfyre orb shards was completely obliterated in the blackness. She couldn't see Lorshin in front of her nor hear his footsteps. She stumbled, over what she couldn't tell, but as she reached out blindly to steady herself, she caught hold of Lorshin's robes—at least she thought so—anyone or anything could be lurking there unseen. The overwhelming dark and the unexpected silence disoriented even her keen elfin senses.

Lorshin didn't respond to her touch, yet his pace slowed minutely as she quickly righted herself and pressed on.

They walked in pitch-blackness. Unable to tell the passage of time, Fenachdra focused on her vague impressions of her surroundings. There was not much to dwell on despite the dark that was far too reminiscent of the darkening taking place in the outside world, yet she did imagine a labyrinth built at some odd angle so that you got the dizzying sensation of the ground moving beneath your feet, always downward, making you wonder how much further you had to fall. She clutched tightly to the back of Lorshin's robe. The air was a weird mixture of stale, laced heavily by the scents of dirt and moisture, and the honey smell of the Samhail themselves. Slowly, however, the dark began to lighten. Weak light filtered down from above, and suddenly Lorshin's regal frame came into view.

Moments later, they stopped. A vast octagonal chamber spread before them, warm with candlelight. The whole chamber was ablaze with it. Guards outlined the room, and the central aisle where a blood-red carpet stretched up to the dais and one unoccupied onyx throne rose beneath a golden sun.

Fenachdra found herself standing on the outskirts of an opulent court. The walls were hexagonal basalt columns hung with red banners from yew poles. These walls, the black marble floors, even the onyx thrones were all carved with golden knot work designs that blazed in the light from above. Between the lines of fierce guards, the court was packed. Thousands of pairs of curious eyes fixed on her.

"The Summoner is our guest," Lorshin said, thereby casting his protection over her. His people bowed in acknowledgement as he turned toward her. "You stay here," he said, motioning to the very spot where she was already standing. His eyes held some unspoken warning. "I will return."

Fenachdra was fairly certain those guards would not let her enter the court unsummoned. She nodded her consent a second late. Lorshin was already moving rapidly out of sight.

When he returned, Jysine was no longer with him. Lorshin seated himself upon the throne and motioned Fenachdra forward. "You wanted to speak with me. So tell me, Summoner, why did you come here?"

Fenachdra Willowbark moved forward slowly. "I have come to ask you to honor the old alliances, to stand with the races once more against the *Darkness*."

"The Guardians are gone, Summoner. The old alliances mean nothing, and without the protection of the Guardians, my people cannot abide the light of the Sun, so why should I agree to stand with you?" Lorshin asked.

"Because not even you, Lorshin, Prince of the Samhail, want to be lost to the *Darkness* as your father was!"

Lorshin flew from his throne so fast and with such fury that Fenachdra didn't have time to react. His powerful hand was around her throat in a second. His fangs stopped not far from her face while his eyes seethed with anger. "Do not speak of him! Say nothing else about him for fear of what I might do!"

"My lord."

Lorshin's hand moved away from Fenachdra's throat. He took a step back and glanced back over his shoulder.

"Jysine?" Fenachdra gasped.

"My lord, may I speak?" Jysine said softly, gliding forward with elegance she had never possessed before.

Lorshin inclined his head toward her. "Speak, sister."

"I know, my lord, that you hoped these bloody days were behind you, but I am proof that they are not, and if the Dark One is allowed to spread his *Darkness* unchallenged, then these bloody days will never have an end. And your people," she paused, "our people will go on hating themselves for all eternity. You more than all the rest."

"What do you say, Isentara?" Lorshin said to his twin.

Isentara stepped from the shadow of one basalt column. "The young one is very brave and wise. I am closer to you than all others from the womb, and I tell you, Lorshin, that there is no dishonor and no betrayal in seeking our own eternal peace."

Fenachdra dropped to her knees and clung to Lorshin's hands. "I beseech you, Lorshin, Prince of the Samhail, stand with us!"

Lorshin pulled away from the Summoner. "Stop. All of you! These bloody days are not behind us, and rising up against the Dark One will change nothing!" He looked pointedly from Samhail to Samhail assembled there. "As for you, Jysine, you will learn what it means to be Samhail. I am master here! You can feel it in your veins. Isn't the curse enough, or would you have me risk the lives of our people so recklessly just so *they*," he said, making a wide sweeping motion with his hand toward Fenachdra and the outside world, "can go on lying to themselves that their feeble alliances will ever be enough to turn back the *Darkness*? The strength that held them together has been made void!"

"You must have hope, brother," Isentara said softly, resting her hand on his arm.

Lorshin snorted in disgust. "Hope? What hope is left? The Guardians are gone and we no longer have their protection!"

"The Prophecy stands," Fenachdra said gently.

"And the Sun still shines," Lorshin snapped. "A blessing for one is a curse for another. Don't forget that, Summoner, you'll live longer." His fangs flashed menacingly before he turned from them abruptly and stormed away.

"Lorshin, wait," Isentara said as her fingers slid from his arm.

"I need to think," he said. "See to our guest."

The Samhail bowed low as he passed.

"My brother will make the right decision, Summoner. You must have faith in that," Isentara said softly, yet she cast a troubled gaze once more in his direction. Something had changed in him . . . something had *darkened* beyond recognition, and it had not been long in coming.

Chapter Four

HALF LIFE

"My lord—"

"Not now," Lorshin said sternly. "Go. *Go!*" he screamed louder, his fist hitting the wall when his servant didn't move quickly enough out of the room. "Can't I have just one moment of peace?"

Chunks of basalt fell from the edges of the crater made by his fist and clattered to the floor.

"What was that about?" A familiar voice asked as the door creaked open, tearing through a newly woven strand of spider web that glittered ever so slightly in the firelight just moments later. The crackling, orange flames in the fireplace were the only light to penetrate the dark, windowless chamber. Not that it mattered, for the room's occupant could see perfectly in the dark.

Lorshin looked up, meeting his sister's delicately luminous eyes. They were the only specks of reality that held true for his troubled mind. Everything else ran crimson, like blood, and black, like the darkening taking place outside. The stench of hopelessness permeated the very air he breathed. "Nothing," he said evasively, turning his back on her and pacing away.

His sister let that answer pass as she walked slowly into the room. "I thought I would find you here."

A disgusted grunt came from across the chamber.

"Did you think you could hide from me?" Isentara asked softly. "Everything I am is you. Everything you are is me, or have you forgotten the half-life we share as twins of Guardian lineage, even cursed as we are?" she spoke in hesitation. "And why would you want to hide?" she finally asked in barely a whisper.

Lorshin didn't answer. Isentara came in equal silence to his side as he slouched, broodingly in a chair before the fireplace. She kneeled there beside him, leaning her head against his knee and gazing into the fire, waiting. The soothing sounds of the fire filled the long silence that stretched between them. The tension of those first few moments gradually dissolved into companionable silence—a closeness that they had enjoyed from their mother's womb, which had only grown stronger over the years. Isentara waited. All Lorshin needed was to know she was there.

"I'm sorry about before," he finally said when the fire had died and only the embers still glowed red. "I'm not sure why I reacted that way." Lorshin reached out and took her hand in his.

"What are you thinking?" Isentara whispered, glancing over at her brother.

"I was thinking how peaceful I should feel right now, and I was wondering why I don't."

"Do you regret staying? Do you wish now you had said yes to our uncle?"

Lorshin shook his head. "I don't feel anything. So how can I answer you, Isen?" he said, using her childhood nickname.

"I know you feel something, Lorshin," Isentara said softly, leaning her head on his knee once more, "because I feel it too."

"I feel lost! I have never felt so lost!" her brother growled and pulled away from her, rising in one fluid, angry movement to stand over her. "There! Does that make you happy to hear me say it? To hear me admit I am leading our people without the slightest clue as to what is right or wrong anymore! To know that my every choice could be the one that dooms us all! To know that I could end up hurting you worse than our father ever did! You of all people should know, Isentara, that some things are better left unsaid and undone or have you forgotten h—" His voice trailed off. Lorshin shook his head, unable to form those final words that would only hurt them both.

"Lorshin."

He jerked away. "Don't." He paced away. "Just leave me alone."

"I will not." Isentara rose. "And you would not really have me do so because that would be admitting you really do feel something more than lost!" She sighed. "If you will not allow yourself to feel, how can you be—"

"What more do you want me to say, Isen?" Lorshin interrupted. He glanced toward her, weary and defeated. "Do you want me to say that I am afraid because the curse is stronger and I feel so utterly out of control of my own body? Do you want me to say that I am completely torn apart inside? Do you want me to say that I can barely think of anything for the hunger burning in my veins?" His lips parted, slowly curling back from his sharp fangs as he hesitated, a grimace of pain faltering the desperate and angry flow of his words. He spoke again, but not as strongly as before. "Do I tell you that seclusion in this forest is absolutely essential, and yet to ignore the cries of the world—to abandon the alliances forged under the leadership of the Guardians is a betrayal of . . . of everything we are . . . of everything we have ever dreamed of! Do you want me to say I am loosing hope?"

"No, Lorshin. You only need to admit that you are not alone and that you do not have all the answers."

"How do I do that, Isen?" Lorshin reached out and pulled her forward.

"One step at a time."

He sighed. "What if I—"

"Shh." She pressed a finger to his lips. "I trust you, Lorshin," Isentara whispered as her brother embraced her. "You are stronger than you think."

"But I don't trust myself," Lorshin said even softer, his thoughts drifting to his father.

*   *   *

Fenachdra replayed the last moments of the encounter over again in her mind.

Lorshin snorted in disgust. "Hope? What hope is left to be had? The Guardians are gone, and we no longer have their protection!"

"The Prophecy stands." Fenachdra said gently.

"And the Sun still shines," Lorshin snapped. "A blessing for one is a curse for another. Don't forget that, Summoner, you'll live longer." His fangs flashed menacingly before he turned from them abruptly and stormed away.

Her memory focused on that last moment as he spoke those threatening words.

"Don't forget that, Summoner, you'll live longer."

She trembled as she remembered, but was that final glimpse of the Prince of the Samhail real or imagined? Had she really seen his eyes flash with *Darkness*? Or was this place playing tricks on her mind? Was the Dark One interfering, trying to quell the Resistance in its infancy? Or did *Darkness* already possess a far stronger hold here than she had at first expected?

"Mistress?"

Fenachdra looked up as Jysine called to her. The Styarfyre orb shard that she had been worrying between her fingers fell free. "Jysine."

"Is something wrong, mistress?"

"I am not sure," Fenachdra answered slowly. She leaned close to her apprentice's ear and whispered all her fears. "We must be vigilant," she concluded, drawing back from the trembling girl. "Speak of this to no one."

Jysine nodded mutely as she absentmindedly reached for the Styarfyre orb shard dangling from the cord around her neck. Perhaps it was foolish, but it made her feel safe as she glanced warily around the hall that suddenly seemed *darker* than it had just moments before, alive with shadows.

"No one," Fenachdra emphasized again. She too searched those shadows for any sign that her fears were true, yet she found nothing except the half-life of light and dark played out in the glow of flickering candle flames filtering down from above to create those same shadows that stirred between the basalt columns of the hall with a life seemingly all their own—just shadows—passing, harmless shadows. Even so, her skin crawled as if those shadows were gazing back at her just waiting for the right moment to strike.

*   *   *

It was hard not to doubt when thoughts of his father filled his mind. Lorshin crouched near the forest's edge, waiting for the sunset. A frown hardened his youthful face. Somewhere in that impenetrable black was his father, or at least he wanted to hope his father still lived. It was to this mountain, Rowlyrag, the highest peak of the Dianara Mountains, that his father had fled so long ago with his mother's lifeless body. Over the years, he had attempted contact many times and found only *Darkness*.

As he had been taught, Lorshin emptied his mind of all other thoughts. *Father.* He called louder. *Father, can you hear me?*

He did not notice the swirling shadow pause overhead.

Father. Father, can you hear me? the voice resounded in the dark. The blackness shifted toward the sound.

I knew the voice, or rather some piece of Arawn's cold, black heart did; but that part had been silenced on the day Light had carved out Arawn's heart and set him free. Barriers of *Darkness* surrounded the heart that was all that remained of Arawn in this world. *Darkness* was the answer. There could be no other.

Darkness flowed down. Rowlyrag shook with its force. Lorshin recoiled as it grazed his mind; however, the shadow shifted in the air, drawn to the pulsing mountain. For the briefest moment, it stood out between the fading sun and the abyss; then it was gone. Lorshin paid it no heed. His frown deepened. What had become of his father?

Chapter Five

DARK TIDES PREVAILING

C adclucan was alone, the last of the Guardians in a world slowly decaying before his flaming eyes. The Dark One's laughter seemed to snarl around him as he stood on the darkening plain, gazing at the borders of a nameless forest. He bowed his head; a haggard sigh escaped his lips. This last issue of breath released his power and true form. The Stone of Existence hung heavily around his neck, shining brightly in the *dark* as he spread his vast wings and soared into the sky.

He couldn't bear to continue looking at the world below as he soared overhead. Night was descending, hiding his beloved Day, in a gradual deepening of blue twilight; yet the stain of *Darkness* wriggled on the edges of the natural beauty, marring what had always been the soothing quiet of Night's advance. *Dark* tides would soon prevail upon the world, and they couldn't even see it—not really, not enough to know the truth, not enough to fathom the immensity of their need, not enough to heed the promise that had been set before them so long ago. Flame and knowledge stirred in his chest. Cadclucan sighed. His heart throbbed with recognition. The Flame in his heart answered the Flame above, shining brighter as it reflected its Source. Light clung to him, guiding him toward Sanctus's will while the whisper of the Light resounded even in the depths of the living *Darkness* slowly prevailing upon the universe below.

LettheLightshineforthandawakenhope.LetMhoragarise.Letthe Promised come.

*   *   *

The Borders of the Red Wood

A vast shadow passed over the Red Wood as the Guardian drew near. The kiss of moonlight glinted off the Guardian's emerald and gold scales mingling with the deepening blue-black of Night's descent and the gentle shine of the Light coming from within the Guardian himself. With massive wings that echoed like thunder as they sliced through the air, the Guardian flew rapidly away toward the West.

The archer drew his bow. The tip of his arrow was covered in pitch and set ablaze. His aim was high.

"Do it," his queen commanded in her gentle voice.

The archer loosed his burning arrow. It whistled through the air crossing the Guardian's path before plummeting back toward the earth.

Cadclucan froze in midair, seeing the orange glow of fire whiz across his path. His large head, shaped like a horse's, swung toward the Red Wood silently rising far below. From this height, those massive trees looked insignificant—like twigs, unworthy of even a second glance—and yet the Guardian smiled widely, showing two large rows of gleaming white, razor-sharp teeth. The arrow fell silently. Its flame snuffed out by the Guardian's breath as he laughed softly to himself.

He veered toward the Red Wood with a subtle shifting of his massive wings. His long, powerful tail made a wide sweeping motion that scattered the light of the Moon and stars into glittering emerald and gold shadows around his huge body as he turned himself upon the currents of the air. His wings parted the air before him as they swept back to rest against his body. He rapidly dove toward the ground, relishing the cool scent of the air rushing past his face and its gentle stroking of his scales, giving him buoyancy like one floating on water.

When the ground seemed to be rushing up to meet him, he thrust his powerful hind legs out as his wings erupted out of their folds to catch the current. His every movement was fluid and controlled. His talons curled into the fertile soil of the earth, but as his wings slowly descended, scattering light across the land, the veil of humanity overcame his true form, hiding him in plain sight. Only his eyes blazed, revealing him for who he was, a Guardian, a wielder of Flame.

Cadclucan shivered. In this new *darker* age, his human form was susceptible to the unseasonable chill that gripped the land. He pulled his midnight robe around him to stop the coolness from reaching his flesh, thankful for the warmth of the Flame burning in his chest, as the elfin archer stepped out of the Red Wood and took a knee before him.

"Great One, I, Laeginlast Thornecrowne, greet you on behalf of my people. We remain your true friends and the true friends of all

Guardians," the archer said without raising his white-robed head. "We hold to the ways of the Light. We keep hold of Hope."

Cadclucan nodded once. "The Elves of Light have always been true," he said softly, "and for that, you will dwell alone, hunted, as I am hunted." These final words he spoke sadly. His deep voice sounded as distant as the thoughts preceding his words—secret knowledge only a Guardian could possess.

Laeginlast Thornecrowne rose. "May I present my lady, Queen Maizie." He stepped back as four Elves, unremarkable in their gray cloaks, emerged from the Red Wood, carrying torches before them. They parted, letting another pass between them. She was striking in beauty; not even her gray traveling cloak diminished that. Her hair hung in long silken strands beneath a pearl diadem. The train of her long gown, the same color as moonlight and glittering like diamonds, whispered over the grass as she walked forward.

"Great One," Queen Maizie said as she curtseyed deeply. Standing silently in the shadows, her entourage bowed too.

Cadclucan smiled and lifted her gently until she stood erect, meeting his flaming gaze. "Please," he said, "there is no need for that. Tell me why you beckoned me here."

His eyes seemed to pierce right through her, unreadable and unfathomable, yet Maizie held his gaze, fearless of what he would find in her. He waited, and she struggled to understand why he said nothing; but the Guardian seemed intent on letting her speak what he surely had already read in her mind and heart. Queen Maizie reached up hesitantly and traced the dark rings under his eyes. His weariness looked to be permanently etched there.

He sighed, setting her free from his gaze when his eyes closed. Light still peeked out beneath the fleshly lids, ethereal and softly reminiscent of lightning.

Queen Maizie drew back uncertainly, yet she couldn't completely retreat from him. He still held her hands firmly in his.

Don't be afraid. His voice whispered in her mind.

Those gentle words instantly soothed her. "I offer you the peace of Loriath," she said.

"No place where I am will be safe," Cadclucan said. "The Dark One wants the Stone of Existence and I am its Guardian." He met Queen Maizie's gaze, willing her to understand. "The Gemshorn has been silenced for the moment. *Darkness* is waiting. The One Whose Name is not Spoken needs only one moment of weakness in one willing heart." His shoulders sagged with the burden of his words. "Let me go before the blood of your people is on your conscience and mine."

"Do you think we will turn our backs on you? Do you think we will falter at shadows? In the Light of Hope, what are these things? Loriath is strong. My people stand with you in Light and *Darkness*! Accept this sanctuary, my lord, and bless us with your presence. Rest in safety. Renew your strength for when the day of battle comes again and there is no rest left to be found." Queen Maizie stared at him in silence, squeezing his hands in hers. She wondered vaguely if he could feel the force she was using to hold him there—probably not . . . not unless he was reading her mind. She suddenly flushed, knowing exactly what wayward thought he would find there if he was. She liked his touch. She liked the feel of his hand in hers. Remembering her place, she abruptly dropped his hand.

This time he let her go, a knowing smile on his rugged face, yet the smile didn't reach his eyes or even touch the weariness written there.

Leaves were torn from the Red Wood by an eerie rush of wind. Birds roosting in the branches screeched and flew off in black droves. The Elves of Light tensed, holding their torches higher, but they could no longer differentiate between Night's gentle dark and the living *Darkness* that was slowly infecting the world. "My queen, we should return to Loriath," said one of the entourage.

"Wait," Maizie said. She turned back to the Guardian. "My lord?"

Cadclucan's gaze shifted back to her from the dark. "I will come."

The Elves of Light melted into the shadows of the Red Wood. Cadclucan followed having no need for the light of their torches to guide the way. A cool breeze blew around them. Only he heard the vile whisper riding upon its back.

Cadclucan. Cadclucan, I will find you. I will have the Stone of Existence. No matter where you go or how long it takes, I will prevail! I am the Evil that Devours. I am Sgarrwrath, the One Whose Name is not Spoken. I am the Heart of Evil and the plague spot from which all that is vile is sprung. I am the residue of Dullahan, and the corrupted Flame of Arawn. I am Darkness.

Cadclucan felt the Flame in his heart rise in answer, but its power was not his to wield, not this time.

* * *

Loriath, Kingdom of the Elves of Light

The Elves reached out to touch him as he passed. His hand, his hair, his midnight robe, his face, the heel of his boot, it didn't matter to them what they touched. He could see their hearts. He knew their thoughts. To have a Guardian among them gave them hope. Elves by nature abhorred the *dark*—even the natural dark that came with Night, yet they stayed in this world out of allegiance to the Light and he was a wielder of that Light.

Slowly and silently, Cadclucan passed through the throngs of Elves, letting that hope revive in their hearts. He would not tell them the things that plagued his mind. He would not speak of the long *dark* to come. By the time he reached the Guardian chamber in the heart of their kingdom, the weight of his burden had grown. In solitude, when the door to his chamber was shut and the Elves left him to rest, he let the veil of humanity sag beneath that burden and his true form rise in its place. He lowered his great frame onto the soft ground and curled into a tight ball. One yawn escaped his mouth, ending with an exhaled breath that was heard and felt throughout the entire world. Sleep pulled at his weary body as he laid his head in between his great paws and wrapped his tail up around it. The heartbeats of the outside world provided the soothing rhythm that lulled him into a fitful sleep. Guardian dreams were not dreams at all. They were truth. They were Flame. They were the present and the shadows of the future; and as Cadclucan dreamed, the signs of the Dark One's rising played out in his mind. He had seen this vision once before and now it seemed its time had nearly come.

He saw the faces of his brothers painted in blood.

Fyrdung and Azolat stood side by side wielding the Light. Arawn faced them. Darkness clothed him. His breath was black and his eyes dark.

Arawn was no more a slave to the Dark One. It was a fleeting memory that was soon displaced by something stronger. The war, the sorrow, his brothers—all had come to pass as he had seen. The memory of a vaster future still plagued his mind.

A storm was gathering all around him and at its eye was the cry of innocent blood rising from the heart of the earth. This blood was yet unshed, but the time of its shedding was rapidly approaching.

The earth was shaken apart by the black breath, and a fathomless Darkness opened before his eyes. Mountains fell and new rose in their place. These new mountains were the carcasses of the dead of every race and all manner of living things. Screaming trees were swallowed in the blackness. Water stopped flowing. The seas dried, and all that lived within lay suffocating beneath the boiling sun.

Father, Cadclucan thought as he gazed upon the sun. It ruptured into a thousand flaming balls before falling into Darkness.

Mother, he nearly cried out as the moon turned to blood and poured into nothingness.

"No!" he screamed as last of all he saw the Colorless rise, wielding the Flame that had grown dark until nothing was left save the void.

He knew that everything was nearly ready. Time rapidly approached the hour of temptation as the shadows thickened and he slept.

Darkness.

In the sky, high above where the Guardian slept, twin stars exploded . . . one flash of Light raining down into the waiting void.

Chapter Six

DEADLY ILLUSIONS

Rowlyrag, Dianara Mountains:

*A*rawn's heart was thirteen thousand years old, yet ageless. *Darkness* sighed and drifted restlessly around this newly claimed Heart of Evil. I needed someone capable of leading my army, someone worthy of wielding Arawn's corrupted power. I would not repeat the failures of the Guardian War!

Curse them all!

I shifted at the voice, which entered my black solitude. It was a voice I had never heard before, but the Heart of Evil beat more quickly. An image formed in my mind before the intruder set foot in the *Darkness*. A swirling vortex of shadow moved rapidly toward the mountain. *Arawn's* black heart caused me to know her at once for what she was. *So the Scarrow had returned from exile.*

Curse the Promised Ones! Curse the dragons! Curse them all!

I was at once lured from my meditations. I summoned the *Darkness* to my will and penetrated her mind. *Arawn's* corrupted voice echoed her cry with all the ruined power of his being.

The vortex dipped to the ground. I watched in silence through the eyes of my illusion as it rose up before him in a motionless pillar of shadow, but at its heart was the form of a person. Shadow was no more than a shroud. *Arawn* rose slowly, allowing the being to study him and access his power and his person.

I am Arawn, he said in his silent, yet powerful voice. He made a wide sweeping motion toward the mountain below their feet. *This is Rowlyrag, my kingdom, Souleater.*

"My name is Sithbhan." The voice from the shadow was cold and indistinct.

Arawn smiled. He sensed the menace that lurked within her. "Show yourself, Sithbhan. I mean you no harm."

A moment passed. Neither moved until at last the hood of shadow pealed back. The elegant and cold face of a young woman was revealed. Long, blonde tresses tumbled around her proud, angular jaw before delving back into the shadow. Tiny crystals that shone like starlight adorned her head and draped carelessly over her high forehead to rest above her left brow. Menacing hawk brown eyes fixed coldly on him, but she could not hide the wonder that drove them to rove over his regal body.

"How are we alike, Arawn of Rowlyrag?" Her voice was clear now, like the threatening howl of a winter wind.

Curse the Promised Ones, he said to her mind. *Curse the dragons. Curse them all.* He laughed. *I heard you before you heard me.* He took a slow step forward. "Tell me, what wrong has been committed against you?"

"I am one of the Scarrow, second of seven daughters, born of the union of Diastrilis, Lady of Light and Poulderon, Lord of Darkness, both immortals. My sisters and I are destined to die. Why must shadow fade when Day and Night are eternal? As you say, I am a Souleater, but that mask of life will not sustain me forever."

Arawn nodded thoughtfully but said nothing.

"We cause a little mischief, and legions of dragons," she spat out the word contemptuously, "banish us from their presence. Now I wonder through this world, a fading creature, with only desperate illusions and anger for comfort. Curse them all!"

"Yes, curse them, Sithbhan, but never underestimate the power of illusion. For example, when you eat the soul of your prey, you have the power to take on their form for a time, and only you know it is an illusion." *Arawn* circled her slowly. There was a menace in his movements. His manner was sinister, and it called to her. "Illusion, dear one, has sustained me for many years. In the beginning it helped keep my sanity, but now it is inseparable from who *I am*. Look around you. What is real? What is illusion?"

Sithbhan did not look away from him. Her eyes remained fixed squarely upon his beautiful face. "This mountain is real. You are real, Arawn."

"Am I?" He laughed. His blue eyes flashed like those of a wild man. "Do not be so hasty to trust your eyes."

She swallowed dryly. His voice had grown harsh and foreboding. Suddenly, there was a flash of black light that drove her to her knees.

Her pale hand shielded her eyes as it passed painfully through her. In its wake stood *Arawn*. His regal and ethereal beauty somehow remained intact despite the horrible changes that had come over him. She could see right through him to the beating, black organ that pulsed with the *Darkness* all around him and gazed out through his eyeless sockets.

Sithbhan shrank from him. Her instincts told her to flee, but her legs were frozen and useless beneath her. She felt his mind probe into hers, restraining her will. *Release me,* she screamed with her mind.

Laughter was the only response. Black and emerald Flames rose into his upheld hands. She could only watch in horror as he effortlessly exerted his will over the roaring blaze, hurtling it away from himself. The balls of fire rained down on her with searing heat and torrential force. Sithbhan wailed in excruciating pain. The fire ate her flesh, blistering, searing, and devouring.

His voice rose in her mind above the sound of her screams. *The fire isanillusion.Itstillsurroundsme.Lookbeyondtheillusionandlive!* His voice had become deep and angelic in nature.

Sithbhan fought the growing panic that erupted in her. "It is an illusion." She tried to look beyond the fire. It blazed higher and intensified. Her skin was blackening. "Look beyond the fire and live."

Arawn frowned. "Follow my voice, Sithbhan. Look at me. Look beyond the fire and live."

The fire was a wall around her. Swallowing screams of pain, she found a blur of images through the veil of heat. Though the smoke stung her eyes, she refused to close them. *Look beyond the fire and live,* she thought. *Follow Arawn's voice.* Through the wall of corrupted Flame and shadow she sought him, her only hope for survival. At first, he seemed a mere flicker of hope. She forced all other thoughts aside. Green-black fire blazed higher. The pain vanished as her desperation to survive surged as high as the flames. *There he is!*

She found him just as he said he would be. At once the fire was flung away from her as if she had raised a shield against it. With a wave of his hand, Arawn caused the flames to vanish and with them all evidence of their existence. Sithbhan gazed numbly at her own flesh. It was pale and cold as if the fire had never touched her.

"How is this possible?" she demanded breathlessly.

"Never underestimate the power of illusion, Sithbhan. You are fortunate you found me."

"What if I had not?" Her voice rose indignantly as she asked this.

"You would surely be dead," he replied with a nonchalant wave of his hand. "Illusion is one of the greatest weapons. Imagine an army of illusion that preys upon the fears of the races."

Sithbhan nodded. Curiosity and admiration at once replaced her panic. "How have you been wronged?"

"I will tell you." A weary sigh escaped his lips as he turned away from her. His movements were simple and regal, and with them Rowlyrag ceased to be a barren mountain. Columns of sculpted marble rose from the stone. Gold glittered like liquid over them, making a ceiling fit for the hall of a king. Flowers so dark they looked black and others of deep red grew up the pillars, connecting them one to another with arcs of treacherous beauty, for around each delicate blossom was a crown of menacing thorns. Even the ground beneath Arawn's feet was changed into an intricate and dizzying sea of tiny tiles. They seeped outward in a wildly colorful, circular, and unending design until Rowlyrag was completely dissolved into the illusion.

Curling streams of smoke bore the intoxicating scent of incense throughout the hall. Golden candelabras made the hall dance with light and darkness.

"Sit," he said, motioning to a chair that was beginning to materialize at the hall's center. The chair sat low to the ground on six legs, connected by what appeared to be the spokes of a wheel.

Sithbhan moved silently toward the offered chair. In the dance of light and dark, she was momentarily invisible, a shadow among shadow, until she sat in the light. Her seat was round, with a curving, three-paneled back, which, she noticed contentedly, was the perfect height and width for comfort.

"Would you care for a drink, perhaps?" Arawn asked with a slight motion of his hand toward the darkness beyond the illusion. "My servant Gnoll," he explained as a hideous form stepped into view.

It slunk toward her with a drinking horn, which was balanced upon its golden feet on his arched back. A strange white vapor rose from the gilt interior of the drinking horn, clouding the liquid contained within. Sithbhan took the horn with a questioning glance toward her host.

"Do not be afraid, dear one, drink. Refresh yourself. Rest your feet upon Gnoll's back. He lives only to serve. I will tell you what has brought me to this desolate place."

At once put to ease by Arawn's gentle manner, Sithbhan extended her feet over Gnoll's prostrate form and raised the drinking horn to her lips. The refreshing scent of cinnamon and cider filled her nostrils. Warm, sweet potion glided effortlessly down her throat, filling and satisfying, melting her senses as *Arawn's* story began to unfold.

"I was once the most beautiful of all living things," he said, turning to face her once more. "I used to walk in the courts of Sanctus, the Creator of all that is," he said, grimacing, "who exists beyond the bounds of time and space. I desired his Flame, and he threw me down. He gave the Flame to another. I should have received the honor, but Sanctus cursed me! He rose up against me!"

Sithbhan shrank from *Arawn* as his voice took on a hard, bitter tone.

"'The only powers you will know from henceforth will be fear, death, greed, hate, pride, war, and all things that should not have been but were bred of your very heart. Illusion will be your only comfort and silence your companion.' Thus, Sanctus passed his judgment. I was forsaken for the Guardi—" he said, grimacing, "the dragons and their Promised Ones. I have passed the long years here, surrounded by the desolate beauty of Rowlyrag. Using only illusion and those powers rooted in *my* very heart, I have created a wonderful kingdom for myself."

Arawn paused, letting his twisted half-truths and outright lies raise anger in Sithbhan's heart. His gaze turned upon her coldly. "As you have wandered the world, have you seen black mountains from time to time?" Without waiting for her answer, he turned away and continued, "I am certain you have. These Mountains of Difficulty have sprung up all over the world, but all find their source here, within the *Dark*. The Flame that surrounds me has no ending. It binds *my* heart to the mountains and them to me. I am the fire that spews difficulty into the world!" *Arawn* paused in his wild tirade and twisted slightly toward her.

Sithbhan swallowed dryly as his blue eyes, partially hidden by the wild mane of hair, fixed upon her. There was no mistaking the sinister glare that oozed from those eyes. *Arawn* sighed. He sounded tired and old as he spoke.

"There is but one power that I possess which no longer brings me joy."

"What power is that?" she asked hoarsely. She could not hide her curiosity despite the fear that suddenly gripped her like a vice.

"Death." *Arawn* turned on her. His vile laughter flooded her mind as he hurled a great ball of emerald-black fire at her once more.

Sithbhan let out a strangled cry and sprang from the seat. Gnoll cowered as the fire crushed her beneath it.

"Look beyond the illusion!" she whimpered childishly.

"No, dear one, no. This is no illusion. It is death. Take it into yourself, the way you take another's soul."

"I cannot!" she screamed.

"You must, or it will consume you!" Arawn said.

Sithbhan pulled the shadow around her. Her body straightened. The dark souls of her eyes flashed with determination. Using the shadow as a shield, she opened her mouth and inhaled deeply, drawing the fire and its infection into herself. Her lungs seared with the heat. The fire coursed through her body, burning and blistering. A snarl of agony distorted her features as the pain drove her to the ground. Her body curled and convulsed. Hideous moans filled the silence and tears welled in her eyes. "What . . . have . . . you . . . done . . . to . . . me?" she asked in agonized breaths.

"I have given you the power of death, but I must warn you, this power will not sustain you as it did me. No, when the pain passes you must leave this place and seek immortality, or else this power will accelerate your mortal life and consume you. If such were to happen, my gift would be for naught. When you have accomplished what I send you to do, you must return to me and I will teach you all that you must know about the power. I will teach you many other things as well."

The convulsions eased. "I . . . will . . . go . . . and I . . . will return . . . and . . . when . . . I do . . . I will . . . make . . . you . . . pay!" Even in her weakness, the anger was visible.

"No, dear one that would take more power than you possess." The Heart of Evil throbbed remembering the power that had cut it from the real Arawn's chest. *Darkness* churned. *Arawn* faltered as the illusion blurred into the black flood; for one terrifying moment, Sithbhan felt the weight of the dark.

The illusion reemerged a second later. *Arawn* laughed.

His laughter mocked her, but anger failed as her strength waned. Sithbhan struggled to her feet. *Arawn* reached for her. She recoiled from him and fled from his mountain. Through glazed eyes, she looked down at the world. The image was distorted and blurred. Shadow brooded around her. *I must feed*, she thought. Silently, she descended, the shadows swirling around her. She let their depth conceal her. A curse for *Arawn* was never far from her lips. She would do as he said, and then she would have her revenge. Sithbhan smiled. *I will have all his power!*

I let my illusion fade as I watched Sithbhan leave. "Follow her, Gnoll. See that she returns to me. She is a means to a greater end."

"Yes, master," the deformed creature hissed.

Chapter Seven

TEMPTATION

Lorshin crouched in silence at the forest's edge, gazing up at the Dianara Mountains. Rowlyrag had grown black. Night had once lingered on its face, but now Light never broke into the *Darkness* that covered it. A frown hardened his youthful face. *Darkness* was descending. With a sigh, he allowed his mind to retreat from the barrier of *Darkness* that had separated him from his father for so long, though he knew what lingered there was not his father anymore. Hunger clawed at his insides like a beast seeking release. His nostrils filled with the evening air. In that instant, he sensed the unnatural silence that had come unexpectedly around him.

At once Lorshin's instincts came alive. By this hour, the forest should have come alive with the songs of insects, the gentle passing of the deer, and many other such sounds heard at the coming of Night. His eyes glowed eerily in the dark. With a thought, his vision extended to take in the deepening shadows, easily penetrating their veil to see all that lay within their embrace. A shape formed in the shadows. Lorshin's fangs ached as the faintest trace of Flame filled his senses. Beneath the scent was another, the fingerprint of Flame that caused a lusty growl to rise in his throat, silenced only by the soft, feminine whimper of his chosen prey, yet he hesitated, not trusting himself. He clung to the trunks of the two trees between which he was crouching uncertain of the control he had over his curse. He cursed himself for coming this far alone. It would be so easy to become the monster again, to give into the all-consuming hunger, to surrender to the *Darkness* and become one with the unspoken fear of every race, but the *Darkness* was not yet so strong that it could take away his choice. So it came down to temptation and his ability to resist that temptation. The trouble was that the Dark One layered temptation upon temptation so that one could get trapped within their own defiance and fall just the same. He knew this. He had seen it happen with his father. He had seen it happen to his mother, and daily he lived with it clawing away at his own sanity.

The young trees groaned and creaked beneath the force of his iron grip. He squeezed his eyes shut to blot out the image. He breathed heavily through his mouth in the hope of ridding his senses of the appealing smell, but he could taste it thinly upon the air, and he moaned with disgust and desire as his fangs ached and saliva pooled in his mouth. Jysine was right; he hated himself!

A high-pitched scream shattered the silence and his resistance with it. Lorshin looked up with a predatory smile and slowly inhaled a long, telltale breath. In that moment, though he had barely moved, a life fell into his hands. He shifted forward quickly and silently, the most dangerous predator of the night hours. His heart hammered in his chest. Its wild beat seemed to fill the *Darkness*. Thud. Thud. Thud. Thud. The trees broke beneath his hands as he launched out of his low crouch. Thud. Thud. Thud. Thud.

Only then did he realize it was not his own heartbeat that he heard, but it was too late. The illusion was far too strong.

Darkness.

* * *

The wild boar crashed through the thicket. Its powerful tusks narrowly missed Sithbhan's leg. She screamed, though her lungs hurt from running. Her heart hammered in her chest. She tripped and fell. The boar was close. She could almost feel his hot breath, yet she couldn't find the strength to rise. She gasped for air. Would this be the end? She moaned pitifully; her eyes roamed wildly over the forest. The boar snorted and charged toward her. Sithbhan opened her mouth to scream. Only a squeak came out then the boar was gone. Dark Night descended before her eyes. Sithbhan slowly tested her body. Yes, she was whole. The boar squealed fiercely as she looked up in wonder into hungry, blue eyes. She gasped and recoiled.

"Are you hurt?" Two pale and powerful hands caught her.

The enchanted voice broke through her panic. She managed a nod. "The boar," she whispered.

"Gone."

"Where did you come from?" Sithbhan asked softly as she righted herself.

"Does it matter?" he asked. His hypnotic eyes bore into her, willing her not to question him further.

Sithbhan looked away.

"Why are you out here alone?"

She didn't understand the violence of his question. He was angry, but not at her. He was . . . she had no word to describe him, but her heart fluttered wildly in response to the livid gaze of his eyes.

"The Dark One is after me," she answered quietly.

He growled, "I will give you refuge." He leaned close to her. The trace of Flame hidden in her blood called to him, yet he resisted. It filled him with its rich, intoxicating stench. His mind touched hers. *I will not harm you.* He reached for her with tenderness unknown among so many of his people. To his eyes, she was a delicate flower of the night, with hair glistening like moonlight. Her hawk eyes fixed unwaveringly upon his face. There was strength in them that somehow distorted the frailty that hung over the rest of her body. A cadaverous hue was settling over her pale flesh. She felt cold and dead beneath his hands. Without thought, Lorshin bit his wrist, creating a life-giving flow; he pressed it to her lips. *Drink,* he commanded.

Will I change? Her voice rang with surprising strength in his mind.

No, he said to her mind. *The Immortal Kiss is forbidden by Prophecy.* He ignored the warning that echoed through his memory.

Sithbhan's mouth closed on the wound. His strength flowed like a stream of ripe wine down her throat before the wound closed without a trace. Strength extended from the trace of Flame to every corner of her body, peeling back the cloak of death, yet she could feel it coil and prepare to strike once more.

He lifted her from the ground and cradled her to his chest. Her body fit perfectly in his embrace. For a moment, his loneliness vanished. "You will stay in my house among my people until you are recovered. No one will harm you. I give you my word. I am Lorshin, Prince of the Samhail."

"I am Sithbhan."

He smiled as he headed for home, blind to the fact that in his arms lay *Death* and in the shadows behind him walked Gnoll, the servant of the Dark One. His offering gave her strength, but it was his kiss that could give her life. Sithbhan nearly laughed at the thought.

Darkness.

Chapter Eight

A PARASITIC LOVE

Lorshin laid Sithbhan on the velvet draped bed in his own chamber. He smoothed her hair back from her clammy brow. She smiled weakly, drawing in a raspy breath.

"Sithbhan?"

"I will be all right, my love," she said softly.

"My love?"

Sithbhan nodded. His eyes held hers with their hypnotic pull, but she couldn't read the emotion she saw there. It seemed some cross between doubt, pain, and sincere longing. *The Dark One's illusion was powerful indeed!*

Lorshin hesitantly brushed her cheek with his long fingers down to where the pulse beat abnormally in her throat. His mouth opened slightly so that she could just glimpse his fangs, and then his eyes closed; he shuddered and pulled his hand away.

Sithbhan caught his cool hand before it completely left her skin and pressed her face into his palm. She inhaled deeply, savoring the wild, wonderful moonlit scent of his cold, hard flesh.

"Sithbhan," Lorshin whispered her name. There was pain in his voice. He shuddered with the warmth of her breath, and he half-moaned, half-growled.

Sithbhan looked up with a question in her eyes. A tortured expression darkened his face. There was no denying the hunger and pain she saw there.

"This is wrong," Lorshin said through gritted teeth. "I am a monster." He rose abruptly, but still she clung to him with surprising strength for one with the look of death upon them. He had seen that look too many times before, and he knew his curse could make her live; yet it would make him hate himself even more! "I shouldn't have brought you here!" He pulled his hand free with such force that she fell off-balance back onto the bed. He sighed seeing the hurt in her eyes, and his voice softened. "Please," he whispered. "Let me go."

"Will I ever see you again?"

Lorshin backed away, shaking his head.

Sithbhan watched him in silence.

A heartbeat filled the silence. *Thud—Thud. Thud. Thud-Thud.*

Three steps back, he lost the conviction of his refusal. "Yes," he said softly. He hated himself for the weakness, but he couldn't refuse her.

"Sunset," Sithbhan said quietly.

He nodded and disappeared into the dark.

*   *   *

Fenachdra Willowbark was thankful for the sunlight even dulled as it was by the darkening. She couldn't shake the feeling that she was being watched, and it was not the eyes of the forest that made her squeamish now. No, there was something out there hiding, and it was neither the trees nor anything so welcome and natural. Of this she was most unfortunately certain. The stench of *Darkness* clung to the air.

The Summoner quickened her pace in response. She had no desire to be alone for long, and the Samhail would not come looking for her until sun down, if at all. Their prince refused to speak with her about the Resistance, and she had the distinct feeling that she was not really welcome among them anymore, though their prince had said nothing of the sort. For that reason, she stayed, refusing to be driven from Jysine's side. Cursed or not, Jysine was still her apprentice . . . her responsibility. She had ventured out into the forest alone only out of duty, as she had seen the messenger bird circling from the single window in her chamber (a luxury in the kingdom of the Samhail), and she knew the Resistance was calling.

A twig snapped behind her. The Summoner whirled around. The forest gazed back at her still and empty . . . too empty. Fenachdra scanned the forest again and found nothing amiss except for the uneasy feeling in the pit of her stomach and the chill running down her spine. She hesitated a moment more and then turned back to her trail. The trail was seldom used, being largely overgrown in places. At its widest point, the trail offered only enough space for one foot in front of the other, and even then it was riddled with broken branches and knots of root and stone. The obstacles did not slow her, thanks to the surefootedness of her elfin heritage.

Slowly, the forest began to thin and a clearing opened ahead. With a wary glance behind, Fenachdra stepped into full daylight and sang the tune that all Summoners' birds were trained to answer. The bird overhead answered with a horrible squawking that seemed out of place with its beautiful pale plumage and dove toward her uplifted hand. It alighted on her arm with grace, squawking with pleasure before taking the offered lump of meat. Fenachdra smiled. "Sorry I kept you waiting." She stroked the bird's chest affectionately before unlacing the strap binding the message to the bird's leg and pulled out a small roll of parchment. The message was written in code so that much could be said in a small amount of space. She sighed. The code would take time to break. The only thing that was immediately clear was that the common language had not been used to write it.

The Summoners were masters of all languages and routinely communicated with one another through various mixtures of those languages so that should any message fall into the wrong hands it would not be readily understood.

The bird finished his meat and flew from her arm up into a nearby tree. Fenachdra sang to him, another tune, one that instructed the bird to stay and wait for a return message. She clutched the message in her hand, out of sight, and ran back into the forest. Something was definitely following her now. She could hear it slithering and slinking through the underbrush behind and slightly to the right of her. Worst of all, it was humming the Summoners' tunes back at her, mocking her.

* * *

Velvet night bathed the forest. Sithbhan sat upon the summit of a distant hill, with her knees pulled up to her chin, waiting, listening, and hoping. Would Lorshin come tonight as he had promised? She had forgotten to breathe when she heard a light rustle of fabric in the shadows. His voice called to her.

"Sithbhan."

"You came!"

"Did you doubt it?" Lorshin said in his enchanting voice. He stepped out of the night into the pale moonlight.

She smiled.

He took a hesitant step toward her. "I'm not sure I should have come," he said softly.

Sithbhan's breath caught in her throat as his long fingers brushed her cheek. She caught his cool hand before he could pull it away and pressed her lips to his cool, pale flesh.

Lorshin drew in a rough breath. His body instantly tensed.

Sithbhan clung to him. "Stay. Please." There was no masking of the desperation in her voice.

"I can't," he groaned.

"You will let me die? I—"

Lorshin shook his head. "Don't," he said, placing a finger to her lips. "We can never be what you hope. This," he paused, "this is all we will ever have." He pulled free. His movement was fluid and powerful.

She tried to hold onto him, but the power of death was heavy in her chest. He was too strong. She fell forward. Her hands hit the ground. She cried out as something cut her hands. In the dark, she could not see what it was, but she felt the hot, sticky flow of blood. A trace of Flame released into the air.

"Sithbhan." His voice was tense. It rang in her ears before she even registered the pain.

She looked mutely at her hands. "I . . . I'm all right."

"Get away from me!" Lorshin shouted.

She looked up with hurt in her eyes into those mad, blue eyes glowing from his beautiful face. His mouth was open. Saliva and venom dripped from two gleaming white fangs.

"Run!" he growled. His hands gripped knots of stone protruding from the ground. "Go," he moaned. The stones were cracking beneath his grasp.

Sithbhan remained frozen. Her bloody hand was stretched out toward him.

The stones were crumbling. He fell forward with the shattering mass. The fragments were ground to dust beneath his hands. When there was nothing left, he dug his fingers into the earth. "Sithbhan," he cried.

Her hand glided through his hair.

Lorshin cried wildly. Her touch was a lightning strike of desire, hunger, and pain. Before he could stop himself, he had her in his arms, crushed to his chest with his fangs on, but not yet piercing, her throat. Bones snapped with the violence of his grip. She let out a strangled cry that sounded oddly like a shout of anticipation, and then, thankfully, he was flying away from her having been wrenched away a mere fraction of a second before it was too late and he could not resist claiming that fingerprint of Flame flowing in her veins. Panic overpowered the hunger as the scent of clean air filtered through.

Isentara's face appeared over him as he landed in a crouch. "Lorshin? Can you hear me?"

He was breathing heavily, but he could feel the sanity slowly returning. "Yes. Thank you," he groaned. "Sithbhan?"

Isentara frowned. "She's alive. You didn't infect her."

86

Lorshin nodded. He could hear her heartbeat now, but he didn't dare to touch her again. He could not trust himself to go near her with the intoxicating scent in the air.

Sithbhan whimpered, reaching out to him.

He took a step back. "Forgive me," he whispered.

Isentara glared down at her. "If you care about him at all, you should leave," she said before bounding away after her brother.

Sithbhan moaned. Lorshin was gone, and a part of her went with him. She felt nothing. *Darkness* was closing in around her. Neither pain nor fear reached her there. Without him, it all meant nothing. Death was near, but it did not have her yet!

Thud. Thud. Thud. Thud.

Darkness.

*   *   *

Fenachdra bent over the parchment in the light of a single candle. A clean piece of parchment and a well of ink sat on the table beside her, and with the feather quill ready in her hand, she laboriously studied the coded message. The complex configuration of the symbols had her completely absorbed. She didn't even look up as the door to her chamber opened and Jysine walked in.

"News from the Resistance?" Jysine asked.

Fenachdra nodded without looking up. "I cannot read most of it yet. This first line is easy enough. It's in Elfish, my native language."

"What does it say, mistress?" Jysine asked, coming to stand beside her.

"Summoner Fenachdra Willowbark."

Jysine laughed. "That's all?"

Fenachdra smiled. "The rest of this is written in a mixture of languages. It will take some time to translate."

"Perhaps I can help you, mistress. This curse came with some benefits."

"Such as?" Fenachdra glanced toward her apprentice.

"The Samhail speak many languages. It is a gift handed down through the Guardian bloodline, and it survived the curse." Jysine smiled guardedly at the Summoner's shocked expression. "No need to train me now. It's all up here," she said, pointing to her head, "already."

"I am sorry I brought you here," Fenachdra said softly.

"Don't be." Jysine's smile faltered. "You are right. The Resistance needs the Samhail, and I want to be a part of it!"

Fenachdra nodded. "Very well." She slid the coded message over to her apprentice. "I would be glad for your help." As Jysine set to work, the Summoner rose and stretched. "It is so easy to lose track of time here. Is it sunrise or sunset?"

"Day approaches," Jysine answered as her hand simultaneously flew across the page and the feather quill scratched out words on the page. *Be forewarned.*

"How long have we been here?"

"Four days." *The Scarrow have returned.*

Fenachdra read the words over Jysine's shoulder. *Assume they stand against all who love the Light. Remember the Prophecy.* The Summoner read aloud, "'Shadow and Darkness now combined seek power of a greater kind.'" She gasped.

Jysine scratched the final words onto the page and handed it to her mistress. *Races gathering at Firinn, urgent that we hear from you.* It was signed, *Master Okx, Summoner.*

Fenachdra sighed. "We must push the Prince for an answer."

Jysine nodded. "I will speak to his sister, Isentara. She will help us. I am sure of it."

The Summoner nodded. "If only we could be as sure of his answer." She paused. "There may be another problem."

"What?"

"I heard something in the forest today, and I smelled its foul stench."

"What was it, mistress?"

"I wish I knew." The Summoner sighed. "But you can be sure the Dark One is not far behind."

*　　*　　*

Sithbhan awoke in darkness. How long had it been? Her mind cleared slowly. "Lorshin?"

"I am here," he said softly.

"Come here." She stretched her hand toward him in the dark.

He laughed bitterly. "Do you want to die?"

"I trust you," she said weakly. When he didn't show himself or answer her, she gave voice to her dark secret. "I want to be with you." Her voice trembled. "Forever."

She heard his sharp intake of breath. "You have no idea what you are asking!"

"I am asking you to make me yours." Sithbhan threw aside the covers pinning her to the bed and rose slowly to her feet.

"No. Stop," Lorshin whispered as she took a deliberate step toward him. She could plainly see the panic in his flaming eyes. "Do you love me?"

The heartbeat pounded in the silence. Thud. Thud. Thud. Thud.

A series of emotions crossed his face: pain, sadness, fear, and loathing. The beating of the seconds brought with it a change. "I love you," he said almost mindlessly.

Sithbhan stepped into the circle of his arms.

For a second, his mind cleared. The scent of her was distracting. He recoiled. "But I can't."

"Shh." Sithbhan pressed a finger to his lips. "My love."

"You take all my will," he whispered against her hair. His lips moved down the line of her jaw to claim her cold, bluish lips.

Chapter Nine

MADNESS

"My lady." Lorshin bowed low to Sithbhan before offering her his arm. The lighted court was packed with Samhail whiling away the last of the daylight hours each as they would, breaking their entertainments only long enough to acknowledge their prince as he passed. For the lady at his side, they had only veiled looks and no words.

Isentara stepped out from the throng, blocking her brother's path. "I must speak with you," she said, ignoring the glare of her brother's companion.

Lorshin smiled. "Of course." He leaned to whisper in Sithbhan's ear, making her giggle, before he released her. He watched her walk seductively away before turning back to his sister. "Leave us."

The Samhail obeyed quickly and silently. When they were alone in the court, brother and sister stood silently staring at one another.

"You needed to speak with me?" Lorshin asked.

"Yes. It has been five days and you have yet to give the Summoner an answer."

Lorshin nodded, but he was gazing past Isentara, not really listening at all.

Isentara frowned, glancing slightly back over her shoulder just enough to see her brother's new little *pet* slip into the shadows and vanish. A chill ran down her spine.

"Who is she, Lorshin?" Isentara asked in a hushed voice. "What do you know of her? Why was she in the forest? How has she gained your trust and affections so quickly?"

"Why does it matter, sister?" Lorshin asked.

"Because I don't trust her."

"Why?" Lorshin turned on her. "You have no reason not to."

"Lorshin, I feel it inside me. Something is wrong. You have never not listened to me before!"

"I am listening to you!"

"But you're not hearing me!" Isentara shouted back. "You haven't spoken to anyone but her in days, Lorshin! She is like a leech sucking you dry!"

"Stop it."

"No, Lorshin, because the Summoner has received a warning from the Resistance! She says—"

Lorshin growled. He slammed Isentara against the basalt column, cracking it with the force of his blow, as his hand closed around his sister's throat. "You forget your place, sister," he said. "As for your precious Summoner, she can leave if she does not like what she sees."

"Can't you see? You have changed! Sithbhan is changing you!"

"Whose side are you on?"

"Yours, brother, always yours, except where right is against you."

Lorshin threw her aside with an animalistic roar and such preternatural force that she flew across the room and smashed into another basalt column before dropping into a crouch as chunks of rock fell around her. "Do not make me do this! I am master here, not you!" he shouted. "Do not think to tell me what is right! You are mine! You will not challenge me!"

Isentara cried out but the pain came from her heart, not her body.

Lorshin grimaced. He felt her pain as his own. Some things lingered from their Guardian heritage, whereas others had been denied them by the curse. The bond between them, for instance, was more intense for they were twins . . . two, but one at their very core, like all Guardian twins. He sprang to her side with the grace and majesty of a wild cat and lifted her in his arms. "Forgive me," he said softly as he gently reached up to brush her hair back from her face. Sanity had returned to his eyes, but the madness was still there in the shadows.

Isentara caught that hand and pulled it to her heart. "Promise me something."

"Anything, sister," Lorshin whispered.

"Promise me that I will not lose you as we lost father, and I will say no more, my lord." She lowered her eyes as a slave before their master.

Lorshin groaned. Never had she done so before. They had been equals all their lives.

Isentara's long, dark brown hair fell thickly around her face as she bowed and kissed his hand.

Lorshin sighed. "I—" He sighed again, closing his eyes. "You know that is a promise I cannot make. What if I am not strong enough to keep it? What if I have no choice?"

"You are choosing."

A moment passed in silence. He opened his eyes and met her tortured gaze.

"Isentara?" he whispered.

"Do not force me to watch your fall." Isentara rose silently, letting her hand linger a moment longer in his before she walked away.

"Isentara," Lorshin groaned, but she was already gone, leaving him alone in the dance of dark and light that filled the chamber, not all of it natural.

A scream erupted from his lungs. He bowed forward and beat his fists on the ground. "What do you want from me?" he screamed to the emptiness and silence all around him. His arms crossed over his head as he rocked on his knees, weeping bitterly. "Haven't you taken enough already?"

Thud. Thud. Thud. Thud. Thud.

The candle flames went out and all Light with them. Lorshin lifted his head slightly as his own words whispered back to him distorted by the *Darkness*.

"Isentara?" he whispered.

"Can she quiet the madness of your heart, Lorshin, my love?"

"Sithbhan?"

"Can she ease your burden with her love?"

Lorshin rose slowly.

"Can she fill your bed?"

Sithbhan rushed into his arms. "Take me, Lorshin! Make me yours! Don't let them tear us apart!"

"What are you talking about?" Lorshin asked softly.

"Can't you see?"

"See what?"

Sithbhan ran her hand through his hair. The scent of her filled his senses . . . intoxication and the ripeness of death.

Lorshin groaned. "Stop. Please."

Sithbhan pressed herself to him. "Bite me."

Lorshin looked up in shock. "Are you mad?"

Sithbhan laughed. "No, you are. You know what you smell. You know what you desire. You know what you fear."

Lorshin shook his head, staggering back from her embrace. "Why are you doing this?"

"You already know, and if you would stop running from it, we could be together. Forever. I love you."

Lorshin couldn't deny that he did know. The cadaverous hue of her flesh was the evidence, but it was his memories that spoke to him more loudly. He had seen that look as his mother had died beneath his father's hands so long ago. He had seen that look as his father fled with his mother's lifeless body. He had smelled it as his father bled with *Darkness*. He had tasted it in his victims who had not survived the madness of his unrelenting hunger for Flame. Death.

Sithbhan took a step toward him.

Lorshin staggered back. "Stop."

"Then you are prepared to let me die? To let the Dark One win?"

Lorshin shuddered.

"It doesn't have to be this way," Sithbhan whispered, pressing herself against him. "You can prevent it!"

"It's forbidden." The sane corner of his mind was screaming at him to release her and run the other way, but he barely heard it. Madness filled his eyes.

His name was a moan on her lips. "Lorshin." Her cool hands moved lovingly on his face, guiding his gaze to hers. "Make me as you are. Let us be together forever." Sithbhan pressed her pale lips to his. She parted his lips and let her tongue flick across his fangs. A drop of Flame's fingerprint fell warmly on his tongue.

Lorshin's eyes closed as he fought to imprison the desire, the madness, even as a shudder of pleasure ran through his body. "It is forbidden," he said weakly, yet he leaned in dangerously.

"I will die," she pleaded. "Make me as you are, my love." Sithbhan panted madly.

Lorshin shuddered. His head dropped to her neck, and his mouth opened revealing his sharp, white fangs. His breath fell hot upon her.

"Yes," she moaned. Her hands gripped his shirt, holding him with unexpected force.

He hesitated, and then the madness overwhelmed him.

Thud. Thud. Thud. Sithbhan's cry of victory echoed in the rapid spiral of the heartbeats and the decay of all illusion. Thud-Thud. Thud-Thud. Thud-Thud.

Lorshin recoiled as his world crumbled before his eyes. He found himself alone, far from any source of refuge and solace. Helpless and vulnerable, he faced the unknown. All around him, the shadows thickened, waiting for that one, least expected moment to send heavy, suffocating *Darkness* crashing down upon him. Fear's icy hand clawed its way down his spine. He trembled. From deep within him came a rush of heat, surging upward from the gut, as simultaneously all strength drained from his body. His lungs refused to draw a breath. Pressure built in the pit of his stomach, nausea rose, the stench of vomit filled his nostrils, and then only cold, raw terror remained.

Darkness.

I laughed, and the mountains quaked, spewing their tortured fires down over the thick nameless forest. The Samhail screamed, horrible bitter screams of fear as my *Darkness* came, yet I had no intention of destroying them. They were far too valuable for that.

Chapter Ten

AMARANTHINE

*D*arkness.

 That living blackness foaming out its own shame; that hated thing breathing forth its mindless despair poured down upon them in a great black tide.

"You cannot leave me now," Sithbhan whispered, but it was his father's ruined voice he heard in the *dark*, in his mind, as she rose in shadow before him.

Lorshin shook his head. It couldn't possibly be real, that voice from her mouth. His eyes widened with alarm. *Could it be?* His every instinct was screaming at him. *Illusion—the greatest weapon of the dark!* "No," he gasped as he staggered back. His voice echoed through the bounds of the chamber. He turned wildly to seek escape as the basalt columns began to tear themselves apart. Chunks of falling rock barred his path.

Sithbhan's maniacal laughter made him pause. "Don't you see, my love," she said, "I had to do it! Now I will never fade." Her wild laughter sent chills down his spine. "I am undying Death!"

"Lorshin!" Isentara screamed as she ran toward him from the shadows. "Take my hand!"

Lorshin hesitated, staring as *Darkness* bled from Sithbhan's eyes, confirming his fears. "Do you think the Dark One gave you power?" he shouted. "He made you a slave!"

"Lorshin!"

He reached for his sister's hand as that *Darkness* lashed out at him. Their fingers brushed. *Darkness* yanked him back. He fell. His face scraped painfully open on the debris. "Go," he groaned as his nails grated over the stone, seeking purchase.

"I won't leave you!" Isentara said. "Help me!" she screamed desperately when her fingers slipped off his.

"Get her out of here, Summoner!" Lorshin shouted as *Darkness* yanked him another inch away.

"No!" Isentara screamed, thrashing wildly against the two pairs of hands that took hold of her.

"You cannot help him," Fenachdra said in her ear. "It's too late for your brother now!"

"No!" Isentara wrenched herself free, sending the Summoner sprawling on the ground.

"Hold her, Jysine!" Fenachdra shouted as Isentara strained to reach Lorshin's hand once more.

Isentara gave a jubilant cry when her hand, against all odds, gripped that of her brother, but inch-by-inch his hand slipped out of hers.

"You have to leave me, Isen," Lorshin said when only their fingers still touched.

"Never!" Isentara wailed.

"I will not force you to watch me fall. Go."

"No," Isentara whispered. Her knees buckled.

Lorshin's fingers slipped out of hers. "Then close your eyes, sister," he said as the *Darkness* dragged him another inch away from her.

Isentara squeezed her eyes shut with a horrible scream as the *Darkness* swallowed Lorshin in its depths. She couldn't breathe. She couldn't even form a coherent thought, and the horrible silence lingered until it was painfully shattered by Jysine's terrible shrieks. Isentara looked up to see *Darkness* encircling Jysine's waist; she gasped, reaching for her friend as the *Darkness* yanked her away too.

"Run!" Fenachdra said, throwing herself between Isentara and the *Darkness*, raising the Styarfyre orb shard in her hand. "The Resistance needs you! Run for Firinn's pinnacle!"

The Dark One laughed. *Darkness* reared and crashed down over her with the full force of its black fury. It swatted her aside like a pesky fly, but the mere second of her stand was enough for Isentara to run!

Isentara ran. She couldn't see for the tears blinding her eyes. Her breath came hard in her lungs, choked by that place inside her heart that was cracking apart. She heard the screams of her people as *Darkness* swept out to claim them. She could hear the crackle of fire and the shrieking groans of the forest. Worst of all, she could hear that horrible voice calling her name.

Isentara. Again, this time with her father's voice. *Isentara.* Again, worse still, this time with Lorshin's voice. *Isentara.*

She leaped over a log that was enflamed and blocking her path. She could smell the burning and feel its searing heat. All around her she could see a blur of forest all enflamed, yet she couldn't stop, nor could she stop the tears wrenching from her eyes as the sting of *Darkness* breached her heart. Worse still, the light of the sun loomed on the forest's edge, scattered into a billion tiny droplets by her tears, yet made no less threatening by their division. Her heart clenched in her chest. For one horrible moment, she gave in to the terror—not the terror of Death and *Darkness* that chased her, nor of the flames that fell all around her, but the terror that she had forgotten how to hope when hope was all that was left to her now. Isentara broke free of the forest before fear could trap her. If hope failed, she would give herself to the Sun, but *Darkness* would not have her!

Instantly, she felt the Sun's fire deep inside her, rippling out through her chest, weakening her. *Darkness* was coming, ripping its way through the blazing inferno at her back. An open plain spread before offering no sanctuary for miles. She didn't have that long, yet she fixed her eyes on the rocky slope rising on the horizon and pushed herself harder, faster toward its shade. The burning was inescapable, crippling. She stumbled, sprawling face first on the ground and continued to claw and crawl desperately forward. *Darkness* swept in, besetting her on every side. It slowly advanced, torturously delaying the inevitable, relishing in her panic as the sunlight continued to burn inside her. Smoke was beginning to rise from her flesh—the smoke that came with the intense heat that would precede the deadly flames that would turn her to ash. She squeezed her eyes shut. Her preternatural screams pierced the horrible silence . . . a silence that had already devoured all she had ever loved and held dear. She was beaten so why didn't it just take her? Why did the Dark One wait? And then through the chaos she sensed the subtle change beginning; the Dark One sensed it too, and it stopped *Darkness* in its tracks.

She wasn't burning anymore. The pain had vanished. Its weight had been completely lifted from her. Even the air seemed lighter and yet full of unseen power. Her ears filled with the rush of wings. She looked up into eyes of blue Flame, shining mysteriously out of a cool, glowing, white mist that completely encompassed the *Darkness*.

A spasm of hope seized her heart as she watched the glow become stronger and more defined. The ghostly silhouette of nine trees broke into view, and out of that glittering haze a figure emerged, hooded and cloaked in a midnight robe that left only those eyes of blue Flame visible. Isentara stretched out her hand toward the vision.

"Lightwielder!" the One Whose Name is not Spoken shrieked. A gagging sound came from the *Darkness* as if it was being strangled as it shook all over. "Wretched dragon!"

The Guardian spoke and his voice held a not-so-subtle threat. "Let her go."

Darkness shifted at the sound of that voice, measuring the power flowing upon it. Even Isentara could sense the newness of it. She shivered as the Dark One spoke.

"Who are you to command me?" the Dark One mocked. "I have seen more years than you."

The Light shone brighter as the Guardian pulled the hood of his cloak back to reveal his short cropped, slightly spiked hair and that ageless, perfect, and impossibly human face. On either side of his neck, he bore a birthmark. On one side was the waning crescent moon and on the other was the waxing crescent moon—symbols of the Prophecy . . . of Hope. "I am Ylochllion, a Guardian of the Prophecy, tested and proven in the days of the Guardian War, and I am not alone." His words were slow and deliberate, each one a warning and a threat.

As he spoke those words, eight more Guardians, hooded and cloaked in their midnight robes stepped into view. They appeared one by one through the glowing mist like phantoms and drew back their hoods, letting the Dark One taste the power flowing off them.

"I am Eithne, a Guardian of Prophecy, tested and tried in the days of the Guardian War, and I am not alone," the first said. The same marks adorned her neck. She was long and lean, her face sweetly expressive in a way that made Isentara shiver; her hair was a thick satiny veil draping her bony shoulders that should have made her look harmless but didn't. She wore a gown of snow-white and gold brocade beneath her robe. Its elegant folds whispered over the ground as she moved.

"I am Scrymgeour, a Guardian of Prophecy, tested and tried in the days of the Guardian War, and I am not alone," the second said. He was big all over, packed with muscles, like a bear packs on fat for the winter. The weight of power grew stronger at his appearance, but despite the visual menace he represented, there was gentleness about him, hidden within that perfectly sculpted face, framed by the tawny mane that fell carelessly around it. Still his mouth was set in a hard line, and his nostrils flared in subtle warning while his stance clearly indicated he was ready for a fight. He too bore the marks on his neck as did those who came after him.

"I am Gara, a Guardian of Prophecy, tested and tried in the days of the Guardian War, and I am not alone," the third said. She was fleshy, with pouchy chipmunk cheeks, yet this in no way lessened her presence or altered the innate beauty and perfection of all Guardians. Her pixie hair was violent red, with darker streaks of brown coming from the roots. The power flowing off her was sharp, flamboyant even, and her brilliant, wide smile begged for the Dark One to just make the wrong move.

"I am Llacheu, a Guardian of Prophecy, tested and tried in the days of the Guardian War, and I am not alone," the fourth said. He stood out from the others with short brown hair and a thin growth of hair on his ageless face, but he was sinewy with muscles—not so visibly as Scrymgeour, but enough so that his very presence would make even the bravest warrior falter. The Dark One, however, merely laughed even as the weight of power made the earth begin to tremble.

"I am Cairistiona, a Guardian of Prophecy, tested and tried in the days of the Guardian War, and I am not alone," the fifth said. The resemblance between her and Llacheu was remarkable. Both were of medium height, both were strong, and both had full lips set in a look of permanent disapproval. She had an ever so slightly lighter shade of brown hair fixed in an elegant chignon on the back of her head and a smooth complexion giving her a less imposing presence until you felt the power rolling from her.

The Dark One snarled as the earth shook more violently, and the Light pressed around him.

"I am Orain, a Guardian of Prophecy, tested and tried in the days of the Guardian War, and I am not alone," the sixth said. In size he was somewhere between Scrymgeour and Llacheu with long frosted hair that in no way implied age—it was more like a layer of ice on a frozen lake in the moonlight and was very startling in that it even glittered like moonlight ice. His flesh was as pale as newly fallen snow with a markedly exotic lure, and his appearance both eased Isentara's anxiety and simultaneously enraged the Dark One though the power flowing from him did not seem any more remarkable than that which had preceded him.

Darkness writhed in upon itself, moving like a flame beaten down in a wind. A gap slowly began to form as the living blackness cringed away from the Guardians. It was not yet wide enough for Isentara to escape, and she was not sure she could even get to her feet with the ground shaking as it was.

"I am Tlachtga, a Guardian of Prophecy, tested and tried in the days of the Guardian War, and I am not alone," the seventh said. She was small and extremely petite, yet her appearance was the most startling and uneasy to take place on the border of the misty Light. Perhaps it was that she was both more beautiful and simultaneously more unfathomable than her companions. Her hair was as long as she was tall, parted in the middle and hanging in extremely thick, semi-frazzled obsidian locks.

In the center of her forehead was a ruby fixed in a diadem of diamond droplets that hung down past her angelic face. Her lower, full blood red lip was pierced with a tiny silver ring, and the right side of her body, from hairline to toe, was besmeared with red, Guardian runes—at one with her lily white flesh. She wore a fitted black leather cuirass and matching pants beneath her midnight robe, virtually identical to the ones worn by Ylochllion, only smaller. Her eyes were touched with an iridescent hue in the midst of their endless blue Flames that was unsettling, as if she could see what others could not, beyond even the scope of other Guardians, even while everything else about her implied delicateness. She winked at Ylochllion as the Dark One first mocked her presence and then thought better of it, backing off even further with a low, hideous snarl.

Ylochllion smiled back at her brilliantly, his eyes full of adoration as the eighth and final Guardian stepped into view.

"I am Uchdryd," the Guardian said, letting the name hang between himself and the Dark One a moment longer. "The Son of Azolat whom you failed to conquer and corrupt in the days of the Guardian War." He spread his hands to indicate the others. "And I am not alone."

Nine Guardians stood side by side, masked by their human forms. Only their eyes revealed them for what they were.

Isentara shuddered. These were not like other Guardians. They were wilder, fiercer, and seemed far less human than others of their kind even in the veil of humanity.

Their supernatural voices combined into one, yet within that one, all nine were heard. "We are the nine Guardians of the Prophecy."

"Then you know that this girl is mine by right of Prophecy!" the Dark One growled.

"No," Ylochllion said. "You have no claim to any who would forsake *Darkness.*" Until he spoke, his brooding presence could have been completely overlooked, his power masked by the power of his companions. His strength was subtle, surprising, unexpected, less pronounced. It did not define him, though he was tall, even lion-like in his presence, with a regal, golden frame corded with muscles.

"Release her," the Guardians of the Prophecy said as one.

"Never."

"Consider carefully, Dark One, whether your power can withstand ours," they said; all nine now stood upon the brink of the Light. Their power flowed, unmasked, all around the *Darkness.* "Release her or feel its sting."

Vile laughter rang from the *Darkness* defiantly.

Ylochllion sighed. "You have won a great victory today, Dark One. Will you now accept defeat? Will you turn from the void?"

"Never!" the Dark One wailed.

"Then what is one life to you?" Ylochllion asked softly, his eyes fierce. He stepped out of the glowing mist, still more an angelic vision than the dark-robed human he appeared, and walked toward Isentara with his hand outstretched to meet hers. "Isentara, princess of the Samhail, daughter of Arawn, will you come out of the *Darkness*?" He stopped a short distance away from her.

Isentara met his probing gaze. "Yes," she said softly through her tears, "yes."

"Then take my hand."

Isentara shuddered. Her frantic gaze shifted from his onto the snarling blackness all around him.

Ylochllion crouched down onto her level, unbothered by the enemy brooding at his exposed back. "Isentara," he said gently, waiting until she looked at him. "Saying the word is not enough. You must act upon your conviction. You must take that step of faith."

She nodded mutely.

The Guardian rose in a fluid, graceful movement and held out his hand to her once more. "Will you come?" His voice diminished in volume until it whispered only in her mind. *Do not be afraid.*

Peace dripped with each glorious word into her heart. Isentara locked eyes with him, letting her fears fade, letting everything fade except those amaranthine Flames that held all the promise of deliverance. She rose feebly and took a step toward him, her trembling hand stretched out to meet his.

The Dark One growled. Tendrils of *Darkness* crept out on every side toward Isentara like a huge dark hand.

Ylochllion whirled. His true form erupted from the veil of humanity in a flash of brilliance that made the *Darkness* shriek. His huge bronze paws hit the earth with a crack-like thunder that sent fissures through the ground in visible gaping lines, separating himself and Isentara from the encroaching blackness. He blazed beneath the Sun, bronze and silver striped from head to tail, a menacing giant with Flame gleaming on his breath and talons churning the earth. Gone was the subtle strength of his human form; in its place was a fierce creature whose massive frame was banded with cords of muscle. "Wrong choice," he said. His voice took on an added edge of power that up until that moment had not been on display. He roared, stamping the earth yet again with his massive feet as his wings beat the air, driving the *Darkness* back.

The other Guardians of the Prophecy shed the veil of humanity. Flame poured from their nostrils, rending a path through the shrieking *Darkness.*

The earth moved violently beneath them, obedient to the Guardians' power. Isentara scrambled to mount Ylochllion's back but slipped off her protector's smooth impenetrable scales and fell under his feet. He reared to bring them down again. Isentara cringed, squeezing her eyes shut, as she let out a blood-curdling scream that was sure to be her last.

* * *

Cartiman

A piercing wail echoed eerily over the land, through the encroaching *Darkness.* The circle of bonfires could not hold it back; even in the heated orange light, the sound and the blackness shrouding it made the flesh of all living things crawl. An uneasy gathering of Summoners stood frozen in the light, gazing mutely into the *dark.*

"A Banshee wails," one among them whispered.

"Her cry foretells Death," another said.

"Is there no hope then?" another asked pitifully.

"We should return to our homes!" another shouted. "This is foolish. If we rise, it will be our deaths the wail foretells!"

"We are dooming ourselves this night and all Races with us!"

An aged Summoner hobbled forward from the throng. A hush settled over them as the races watched to see what he would do. The Summoner pulled a golden hilted dagger from his belt with a shaky, age-spotted hand. "If we are to survive this *Darkness,* we must rise as one against it, as the Guardians taught us!" He slashed the blade across his hand, letting the blood flow down before them all. "Let us pledge a bond by blood oath. Let neither *Darkness* nor illusion divide us. Let us rise through *Darkness* with wrath! Let us fight with fury for hope, whether unto life or unto death! Let us never be broken! Let us never surrender! We stand enslaved to the Light!"

Another haunting wail shattered the silence, and with it the Darkening War began.

Darkness.

* * *

"It is over now." Ylochllion's voice filtered down through her screams. "You are safe."

Isentara opened her eyes to the Light. She lay on golden earth, gasping for breath through her sobs. Nine behemoth trees, as pale as the first rays of dawn, encircled the vast expanse, growing out of the never-ending Light. She didn't question how she had come to be here. She knew in whose presence she lay. The nine Guardians of the Prophecy, in their human forms, stood around her, with eyes shining from the Flame within. Even in their soothing presence, she could not silence the convulsions of grief that wracked her body, curling her in upon herself and strangling her cries so that she could barely breathe.

Ylochllion came to her side. His midnight robe swirled the Light as he walked, stirring the dewy golden-white brilliance into a radiant halo over his whole being. He kneeled beside her, taking her pale face in his hands. "The dark time is not over yet," he said softly. "There will be more suffering in the days to come. It is the price of the choice. But in the end . . ." His voice trailed off as Isentara looked up into his eyes of blue Flame and whimpered.

She drew in a raspy breath as tears spilled from her eyes into his gentle hands. An echo of her pain flashed in his eyes and then softened into compassion. He rested his hand on her bowed head. "Your strength will return and your hope with it, but for now, be at peace." The Guardian lifted her in his arms and carried her through the unbroken canopy of the trees, following the tangle of roots through the Light to the bound hooves of a shining mountain. Water rolled in pure, crystal falls down the shining mountain to feed the land stretching in Light farther than the eye could see.

Ylochllion lowered her beside it. "Drink," he said softly, wiping the tears from her eyes. "It will help." He squatted silently beside her as she dipped her hands into the cool, clear water.

Isentara lifted the clear fluid in her cupped hands, watching as it gathered the Light.

As she raised the glowing water to her lips, Ylochllion turned his head to meet her gaze. "Welcome to Bynthroenine." The water passed her lips, releasing her from the stain of *Darkness*, filling her with the amaranthine Light and all its promise. Power washed over her. Her knees buckled as Light whispered around her. *Let the Light shine forth and awaken hope. Let Mhorag arise. Let the Promised come.*

"Rest now and be at peace," Ylochllion said softly as he lifted her in his arms.

Her mind drifted as the Nine Guardians of Prophecy floated forward on the Light.

Chapter Eleven

DRIFTING

Nameless Forest

*D**arkness.*
        Fenachdra had felt the full force of its black fury. It had
dashed her into trees and rocks. The pain searing through every inch
of her body left her drifting somewhere between unconsciousness and
reality—where she could feel everything and resist nothing. With a
bloody hand, she groped for the shard of the Styarfyre orb around her
neck. Its eerie blood red glow did little to dispel the *dark* that seemed
to have opened and swallowed everything in black. The trees had
ceased their screaming. Their desiccated husks still stood over the land,
sheathed in black Flame, but there was no more life within them to be
devoured. The earth all around her had become a wasteland of thorn and
despair, yet where she lay *Darkness* had not taken hold. Not yet.
        The Summoner tried to pull herself upright only to be overcome by
a wave of dizziness that sent her drifting once more. She couldn't tell up
from down, or Light from Dark. Her world was insubstantial, dissolving
into its own self and reforming just before drifting away into nothing.
Her mind screamed at her. *Void! Void! Get up, you fool! Run!* But it
was impossible. Her long fingers groped across the hard earth as she
painfully dragged her battered body forward. Thorns dug deep into her
flesh, breaking off as they buried themselves nearly to her bones. Still
she struggled forward with a fool's hope, hour after hour, one torturous
inch at a time, leaving a telltale trail of blood in her wake. She hoped
Isentara had escaped. She hoped that somehow she might escape too,
though she knew she would not escape whole. Screaming for help would
do her no good. There was no one to hear for miles in any direction, and

she would not give the Dark One the pleasure of her despair. If Death claimed her, so be it, but if life was granted to her, she would use every second of it! Either way, she would not falter now! "Sanctus, give me strength!"

I am here.

The voice broke gently from the shifting **Darkness** up ahead.

Fenachdra froze. Her blurred vision made it nearly impossible to see the figure that had appeared out of nowhere. "Sanctus?"

If that is who you desire. The figure drifted forward, lightening on the edges but still a dark figure cut from the **dark**, like a mirage.

There was a chance that this was all in her mind, yet there was something seductive about the way in which it drifted forward, and the voice—the voice was not alarming in any way, it was a welcome sound in the midst of an eerie silence. She no longer felt alone so how could this be a bad *thing*?

Something in the back of her mind told her she should be afraid, but she wasn't. The disturbing truth was that she couldn't *feel* it. Even the pain that had wracked her body just seconds before was now strangely numb—so numb that she couldn't even form a coherent thought of the warning in the back of her mind, so numb that she failed to consider the very real danger that could be upon her. Fenachdra extended her bloody hand toward the mirage with a deranged smile on her lips. "Sanctus. You came for me."

Yes.

She looked up into eyes that drifted away into nothing. A second of panic seized her just before the figure grabbed her hand. In place of a scream, a contented sigh passed between her lips. Fenachdra sagged against *him* as he lifted her from the ground. "Take me to the Resistance," she whispered before losing consciousness. When her eyes closed, the figure faltered, carrying her forward upon a mass of *darkness*.

It will be my pleasure. Corrupted laughter drifted through the black into nothingness as it swept out across the land, darkening everything in its wake.

* * *

Bynthroenine

Floating on Light that is how Isentara felt as she awakened from a deep, blissful sleep. She remembered, vaguely, being rocked to sleep by its ceaseless flow, by the power living in everything that made up this land, by the whispers of Guardians and their Light. These captivated her mind, holding it back from less pleasant memories—memories of *Darkness*, of screams rising from earth and tree, of the mountains falling in a hail of emerald-black fire. Her heart contracted violently as those memories broke through with the threat of still worse memories. *Lorshin*.

A wave of peace washed over her. Isentara looked up into blue flaming eyes flecked with gold. "Uncle Fyrdung," she whispered. The Guardian stood before her in his human form, surrounded by the Nine Guardians of Prophecy all lounging in their true forms upon crystalline stones.

Her uncle smiled gently as he opened his arms to her. "Come."

With a strangled cry, Isentara leaped into his embrace. His arms closed around her in a way that seemed to hold her together even as she broke into a thousand pieces. Over and over again, she gasped her twin's name between horrible sobs. "Lorshin. Lorshin. Lorshin . . ."

"To all things there is a season, Isentara," Fyrdung said gently, "but seasons change."

"How do you know?" Isentara whispered through her tears.

"Because I believe the promise, and deep down so do you." His eyes bore through her into the depths of her drifting soul. "A new day will dawn when lives will no longer be held in such cruel balance, and only Sanctus knows what blessings that day will bring." *Do not despair.* His voice drifted into her as the Light did. *Rest. Let the Light strengthen you once more. You may yet see Lorshin again.*

Chapter Twelve

In Cruel Balance

The doors of Cartiman stood wide open. Fear was everywhere, but it was not yet rooted within their hearts. The chamber was full of Summoners—young and old—waiting for the armies of every race to converge upon this spot. I could hear them coming. All clung to an unspoken hope that the Guardians would rise, willfully choosing to ignore the very sin that had driven the Great Ones from these shores! For to acknowledge their guilt, they would have to acknowledge that they were alone, and then what hope would they have? I smiled to myself. Already their choices were bound to the deep corruption flowing before me, and they called it *Hope*! The Summoners were different.

Fenachdra stirred as I laughed. Her eyes fluttered open, forcing the black to take shape once more. The illusion was strong. All who looked upon it would see what they wanted to see. *Sanctus, or a Guardian, or some other desire.* Just enough to draw them in. I could take my time with the races, but the Summoners were a different story. Even with broken shards, they were too near to power to remain alive. They held too much influence—even more so than the Samhail, though few could see it by looking at them—and even in a world of *Darkness*, they could not be bent to another purpose. They were slaves of Light, bound by blood and oath. An oath could be broken perhaps; but once bound by blood, always bound, surrendering free will to the wielders of power and Light, dangerous even in the cruel balance of this hour, and what better way to stake a claim to this universe than to destroy the Summoners with the very seed of Guardian?

Fenachdra gazed up into the eyes of the illusion. Even in a daze, she seemed to sense something was wrong. She moaned pitifully, swatting at the illusion with her blood-caked hands. I painstakingly reigned in the

Darkness. I had to be careful. To strike too soon was to leave them with a chance, a mistake I could not afford. It was the same mistake that had cost me one of the Samhail.

Saveyourstrength. Thevoiceinstantlysoothedher. *Wearenearlythere.*

"Sanctus?"

Shh. A glowing finger touched her lips.

"I thought you were a trick of the Dark One," she mumbled as she drifted back toward unconsciousness. "But now I see, hope lives."

He chuckled sweetly in response, even as the void flashed in his eyes. *Hope.* The word twisted bitterly in my mind. Hope was even more dangerous than the Summoners. Hope was a *need* most foul and bewitching.

Darkness.

* * *

Cartiman

It was hard to take that final step into the domed sanctuary, which still reeked of Guardian breath. Though vacant of their presence in all other ways, Cartiman held a certain nauseatingly reverent atmosphere. Its closeness to Firinn was no doubt to blame for the locked-in sense of holiness that nearly made me gag with revulsion. Illusion faltered as I bridled—if I had possessed a real body my cheeks would be bloated holding back vomit, but this was a mere hiccup in the formless black. *Darkness* reclaimed control over itself before any of the slaves of Light could sense the deception walking among them. The doors swung closed with an ominous groan drawing the attention of the Summoners a mere second too late for their warning.

We stood facing each other—the Summoners and my illusion—in the involuntary silence of this moment. *I* watched a play of emotions cross their faces—shock, unbelief, and finally a mad frenzy of hope. Instantly, they clamored around me, trying to touch the midnight robe of a Guardian! Begging to feel the power of the Light once more!

I knew what they saw, and it was best if they did not have a chance to look too deeply. A distraction would move things in a more suitable direction, and I was thankful I had thought to bring the broken Summoner who hung so limply in the arms of my illusion. They did not even seem to notice her, so enamored were they by what they believed they saw. Herein lay my advantage for as long as it would last. If they started to question what they saw, my strike would come too late, and in this place, among these prey, time was against me. Once they were gone however . . . I smiled to myself and dropped my unconscious burden unceremoniously on the floor before them.

Your friend is badly hurt. The Dark One nearly had her. The voice was not perfect for a Guardian, whose voices were the most beautiful and powerful of instruments, but the Summoners' horrified gasps were directed at the Elf's body at their feet, not at the false speech entering their minds.

"Fenachdra!"

She is alive. Barely.

"She had gone to the Samhail. What of them? Is there any sign?"

I would not worry about the children of Arawn if I were you. They are . . . consumed. A half-truth, of course. The Samhail were indeed lost irrevocably to the Resistance, but they were very much alive, slaves now to the *Darkness*.

"Remember the oath," a weak voice said from the shadows as the Summoners whispered one to another uncertainly. Silence fell at the sound of it. The *whack-whack* of a walking stick on the floor was broken in rhythm by the creaking of ancient bones as a Summoner hobbled forward. It was clear as the Summoners tipped their heads at his approach, he was the eldest among them and the leader. By the looks of him, he could have been the first Summoner ever to live, as old as the beginning, older than the power of Death. Perhaps it was possible. The Summoners enjoyed a closeness to the Guardians through the Styarfyre orbs that may well be responsible for such unimaginable longevity in one who was quite obviously a mere human. Light had untold power.

I could remember only one other human that could compare—*Laphair, the human wife of Arawn*, now gone, as soon, this one would be gone when the time was right. My illusion remained intact as it drifted a few steps back from the man . . . an instinctive response—nothing more, as it was clear not even this wizened slave of the Light suspected deceit. None of them wanted to *see* it, so blinded were they by this thing called *Hope*.

The ancient Summoner came to stand in the midst of the lesser Summoners who were floundering uselessly over the broken body of their comrade. "Remember the blood," he said.

A silent snarl twisted the lips of my illusion. Fists clenched at its sides, holding back the fury.

"We Summoners have stood on the edge of despair many times before and we have never fallen!" The walking stick made a sharp rap on the floor. "We will not fall now! We are slaves of the Light, not twisted creations of the *Dark*. Light was given by the great god himself. It was not bred of nothing in the stillness before time as *Darkness* was!"

I glared through illusion at the Summoners. The old man's words were not entirely true, a fact that was of little consequence, but I hated them just the same, for now the memory of failure pierced my mind—

The Kingdom, The Beginning of it all:

Sanctus sat upon his throne, gazing over his kingdom. On his silver head, he wore many crowns. His eyes burned with fire. His regal garments were as red as blood. Power and life belonged to him alone. How long he remained this way only he will ever know; but at last he stretched out his bright hand and carved out of the nothingness a deep place. Into the black foundation of the universe, he set a great pinnacle and called it Firinn, Truth. This was his footstool, for it rose up beneath his throne. In that hollow place, he next fashioned Dullahan, the first of all living things, with his word.

Dullahan was a huge white hound, with shining rubies for eyes. They cast great arching bows in every direction. His fur was a flowing mist that filled the empty spaces of eternity. He could run mile after mile and not grow weary. He could sing and never thirst. His howling songs echoed through the passage of eternity like a chorus of chimes. Thus Dullahan was with Sanctus long before anything else was made. Together they trod the ever-lengthening miles of eternity.

Though he was magnificent and strong, Dullahan could not equal Sanctus, and there was none like him. He suffered alone, in secret, from a consuming sadness. He hid it deep inside himself and caged it there. Slowly, it darkened the beauty of his existence until the glory of his beginning was overshadowed.

Finally, Dullahan bowed himself at the feet of Sanctus and was silent. He did not move nor even lift his head. How much time passed he could not tell, for time was not measured then as it is now. Only when he felt that all hope was lost did Sanctus ask for the secret he kept in his heart.

"Dullahan," said Sanctus in his mighty voice, "what troubles you? Give me your petition, and I will grant it to you, even to half of the kingdom."

Dullahan gazed into Sanctus's gentle glowing face. "Great King," he began, "I ask only for a companion of my own."

Sanctus frowned. "I am not enough, Dullahan?"

"Forgive me the weakness, Great King, but no. There is no one like me."

Sanctus nodded his head. He knew the truth of the matter. Only truth could be spoken upon the pinnacle. "I will do as you ask, Dullahan, but you must promise to wait patiently and without question while I do my work."

"Will it take long?"

Sanctus smiled. "I was in no great hurry when I made you. Your equal must have the same care and workmanship. Now, do you promise all that I ask?"

Dullahan bowed his head in between his paws. "I do," and in that moment, he spoke truth.

"Then rest, and when I return, you shall have your request." Sanctus rose out of his throne and journeyed to a secret place where none could follow. He moved in Light with a swiftness and power that defies description. Many great leaps and surges later, he stopped.

There was the Flame that fueled his might. It coruscated out of a mammoth orb, who's sheer mass explained why Sanctus had shed it from his person on the course of his ceaseless existence. Its volume exceeded even its size and was felt all throughout the kingdom, though never beheld. The lure of the predominance and power within explained why Sanctus had long kept it in this secret place; yet the time had come to take the Flame upon himself once again. In it was contained the capacity to create order and perfection out of nothing. Sanctus stretched forth his bright hands and embraced the Flame. The orb that had been compounded by time without end enfolded Sanctus in a royal garment, the like of which has never been seen to this day.

Sanctus's promised return brought Dullahan to his feet. The garment was so bright that Dullahan resisted the urge to cover his face with his tail. Sanctus paid him no attention, however, as he set to work. Dullahan watched with excitement, dancing first one way and then the other. Mile after mile, he danced back and forth, as Sanctus worked in silence. Slowly, Dullahan's dance turned to pacing, and then to nothing at all. He surveyed Sanctus's work, hoping for a glimpse of his promised answer and found only the same empty patch of universe that Sanctus had carved long ago.

"My best work," Sanctus said as his hands flew over nothing.

Dullahan turned and walked away. A new feeling settled inside of him, one that was previously unknown and for which he had no name. It came with an uneasiness that hardened the tendons of his body so that he could not rest—neither body nor mind.

Sanctus was good and faithful. He rested upon truth. Surely, his promise could not be false. Then again with power so great, Sanctus could do as he pleased. *Didn't Sanctus say that I would have his answer upon his return?* Dullahan thought. *Hasn't he returned and done nothing?*

These questions and the nameless emotion fermented into another more terrifying and unknown than the one before. His breath turned black with its boiling onslaught. The first of these new emotions was a weight that crushed his soul and a storm inside him that wanted to lash out, to destroy. He could not rise through the oppression enough to do so, that is, until he lifted up his head and gazed upon the Flame. In his heart, Dullahan desired it and another new emotion revealed itself. He surged to his feet and stalked toward Sanctus.

I will wield the Flame. Its power will be mine!

Each though preceded a footstep.

I will be greater than Sanctus. He will grovel at my feet!

Sanctus turned, his work forgotten. "Dullahan, what have you done?"

Dullahan growled, showing his sharp, white teeth. "I am Dullahan no more," he said. Black breath poured from his mouth. "I am Sgarrwrath." He stalked forward. His giant paws shook the pinnacle. There was no lie. He spoke only the truth.

"Dullahan, stop!"

"Dullahan was weak. I have made him strong! He is your slave no longer!" The black breath poured from Dullahan's mouth, a living thing as he leapt toward Sanctus.

In that instant, *Darkness* took root. It appeared in his eyes as they turned pitch black. "You do not deserve the Flame. Give it to me!"

"Your name will never be spoken again." The Flame surged around Sanctus burning more brightly than it ever had before.

Dullahan's padded feet landed softly, scattering the invisible dust of creation with oozing *darkness*. Light came out of nowhere, transforming itself from insubstantial spectral energy moving at the will of Sanctus to something frightfully untamed—a strangely translucent Flame that he could *feel,* not measured by the screams of nerve endings in his flesh, but by the weight within his chest that radiated out through veins and sinew leaving its *scar* (without a wound) somehow raising the infection from its bed into visible mounds of excess tissue upon the surface of his flesh. His eyes widened as he watched his flesh start to cave in beneath the corruption. Suddenly, he was standing alone in existence—though he knew Sanctus stood before him—he remained alone; Flame enveloping him, clinging to his body, seeping up his nostrils, sending shivers of power sliding into the darkest niches of his soul. He hesitated mid stride. His white paw raised, and a whine rising from his uplifted mouth. Some primal instinct told him he should be afraid, told him he should even run, yet *Darkness* whispered in the back of his mind, craving, hungering for this entity that imprinted itself upon every fiber of his being—an electrical shock that manipulated everything to its will! Dullahan shook his head trying to clear it; another whine rising as he found he could not shake off the cords of Flame. He rubbed at his muzzle with his misty, white paw, continuing to whine—the sound reaching excruciating pitches as he tried futilely to free himself from the hold of power. His ears flattened against his head; he pulled against the power trying first one way and then another—remembering when the Kingdom had been his playground—remembering this power cradling him always and for the first time desiring to escape its presence. Fear came upon him so fiercely that his body convulsed and his very bones shook within him.

It was then that he discovered he was not alone within this expanding spark that was burning ever brighter. A specter passed before his face— the backbone of the Flame it seemed to him as his white hair stood on end! His ears pricked to the sound of a strong heart; the mighty rhythm was alive inside his own flesh—in bones and muscles—its shaking pulse somehow holding him and everything around him together. Dullahan's keening cry rang hauntingly through the Light. His great frame shook all over as he tried to stand against the weakness invading his legs—the dim piece of his mind that was still sane wanted to bow in submission; the darker part merely brooded. The heartbeat of existence made the Flame and power more substantial, changing it into an entity not merely a force. Childish laughter rang hauntingly in his ears. The sound broke all around him, a roaring wind with flashes of light whiter against the blackness of his breath.

The harder he struggled the deeper the power delved; gagging on Flame, Dullahan sought to gnaw his way to freedom. In the span of a single heartbeat, his mouth closed upon substance, his teeth tore into unexpected flesh and his eyes beheld the Source. Their eyes met; they two alone: one with eyes bleeding *Darkness* one with untamed eyes of burning amber. Though both stood still, Dullahan could not quite make out the form of the being before him. He felt flesh but he tasted Flame, and his eyes filled with burning gold and bone. The presence ignited, all flesh consuming into a golden blaze. Breath continued to stir his fur but the sound of it had faded into silence beneath the screaming of strange pinpoints of Light that streaked away from this Source of glory, racing into the nothingness below as if startled from his side by a nameless dread.

Held in the hypnotic stare of those amber eyes, Dullahan could not move. His body went limp; even the grip of his teeth upon the fleshly substance of the great golden inferno relaxed though he did not—could not—draw back.

"Can you truly be more worthy?"

A voice delved into his mind. Dullahan trembled within its grasp.

"Shall you be more just than He who made you, Dullahan? Do you think yourself to be more pure than the hands that fashioned you of nothing?" Pain entered the beautiful voice. "Though I see plainly what has taken root within you!" Flame flowed more furiously outward. Horror and knowledge filled those burning eyes. "Sgarrwrath," the specter breathed the unspeakable name as Dullahan's fangs ripped free of his flesh.

Furious growls rumbled through the *dark*.

Flame struck Dullahan where *Darkness* lurked and cast him down into the hollow of the universe. The force of the Flame broke through him. His deafening screams filled eternity as he fell. His body broke upon the deep. A howl issued from his mouth droning down into one last breath of black despair, and it covered the deep in its void. His flesh split open to the bone releasing Sgarrwrath, the beginning of *Darkness* into the empty bowl of the universe. There *Darkness* took a mirror of life all its own from one drop of golden blood and filled the spaces between the bones of Dullahan's rent carcass. No corporeal substance remained yet Sgarrwrath the Source of Darkness *lived*.

Darkness . . .

"*Darkness* had bred itself in the holes carved by Dullahan's choices so long ago when Flame's Source, the prize of the universe was revealed and the universe was yet unformed. There is still hope!" the ancient Summoner said, concluding the rest of his unheard tirade, but those final words poured like acid on my open wounds.

"There will be no Hope!" I screamed.

The Summoners turned to gaze upon my illusion with shocked eyes, never suspecting to see it crumble into *Darkness*. They didn't even scream as the black exploded around them, twisting the walls of Cartiman in upon themselves and flinging the remnants away. The *dark* descended around them until Night, and his gentle light was lost in the swelling void. My black breath crept around them, sealing every possible escape. The shards of the broken Styarfyre orbs glowed eerily from around the Summoners' necks as *we* gazed at each other—the strategic maneuvering of pawns on a chessboard, yet I had played this game before with far greater opponents than these.

Darkness came in a mushrooming cloud, blacking out the universe from before their eyes.

"Stand firm!" the ancient Summoner commanded. "Do not falter! Stand firm!"

I laughed. My black breath sent corrupted Flame down upon him, melting him where he stood. The Summoners, instantly and utterly consumed with terrors, scrambled to escape from me; behind the emerald-black Flame came Death and with her the enslaved and ever hungry Samhail.

"Feast upon them!" I roared.

Death stretched her scythe over the Summoners as *my fury* broke forth from the cruel balance that had so long held me at bay. Here I would make my everlasting statement of glory! Here I would give warning to all who chose to stand against me! This was my Time against which no Light would stand!

Darkness.

Chapter Thirteen

Travail

*D*arkness—always *Darkness* so thick that it felt impossible to even breathe. It pressed in so hard that it was impossible for Lorshin to separate himself from its vicious restraints, impossible to tell where one stopped and the other started. He crouched in the midst. His eyes darted maniacally from side to side, desperately looking, longing for an escape, a glimmer of Light, a spark of hope, something . . . anything to hold on to even as he felt the *Darkness* contracting around him. Piece by piece, he was losing himself. Slowly, painfully, *Darkness* was poisoning him, making any glimmer of hope into an empty promise. Is this how it had been for his father all those years ago?

The scent of Flame and blood was everywhere, impossible to ignore, stirring his unnatural hunger, keeping him on the edge of madness, adding torment upon torment to the endless void, but oblivion never came. The more he resisted, the stronger his bonds became. Lorshin screamed mindlessly as he suffered the pangs of toil. His mouth hung open; his lips curled back from his aching fangs; foam overflowed his mouth making him look rabid—a monster. His worst fear was becoming a reality, a living nightmare from which there was no awakening. He had no hope.

In the distance of his memory, he could see Flame, blue and bold, as it cut through the black. He could hear his uncle's voice whispering from that unreachable point, mocking him . . .

"In good times, the world grows and prospers, but it is in the *darkest* of times that all living things find what is really inside themselves," Cadclucan said.

Lorshin looked up into his uncle's piercing eyes. "I know what is inside me."

The Guardian smiled. "Do you, nephew?"

Everything about that memory caused him pain. He would give anything to go back and change his choice on that day. He would do anything to stand in the shadow of a Guardian once again, to see the Sun, Urgilis the Father of all Guardians, and feel the warmth upon his flesh without fear of burning, safe in the unconditional love of a *family* that nurtured him despite the curse; yet how could he stand against what was inside of him? How could he fight when the hunger consumed him, turning his will against him? How could he silence the vile voices plaguing his mind, trying to twist him to the will of the Dark One? How could he hope when all hope had vanished in *Darkness*?

How long had it been? Hours? Days? Weeks? Months? Years? Lorshin set himself to the extremely difficult task of focusing on his surroundings. Surely there was some tiny fissure in the black that could be manipulated, but wherever he turned, there was *Darkness*—always *Darkness*. From somewhere behind him, footsteps resounded in the abyss. Phantom breaths filled the dark, falling hotly upon his neck. Voices rang out all around him so faintly that they barely seemed whispers. They came from within and without spreading confusion in their wake, and then quite unexpectedly another voice wove its way into his hearing.

"There is still Hope."

Darkness screamed all around him in defiance to those words. The contraction released. Lorshin drew in a ragged breath. He shifted forward as the outside world was cast into a luminous gray cloud before his eyes. He could just make out a blur of figures in long robes, and that was all. His hands reached out automatically toward them—impulsively without a single coherent thought in his mind—he just knew that out there was some remnant of Light! *Light. Life. Truth. Freedom. Hope. Cure.*

"Stand firm!" one of the figures in the gray commanded. "Do not falter! Stand firm!"

Lorshin froze. There was fear in the man's ancient voice.

Darkness laughed. The black breath rushed out past Lorshin's shuddering frame pouring corrupted Flame down upon the figure, dissolving him where he stood. "No!" Lorshin screamed too late.

The robed figures were instantly and utterly consumed with terrors. They scrambled to escape as behind the emerald-black Flame came Death and with her his own enslaved people.

"Feast upon them!" the One Whose Name is not Spoken roared.

Death stretched her scythe over the robed figures. Lorshin felt the command deep within his heart. He cried out with *need* as he was thrust forward upon one of the terrified prey. His quick eyes took in the girl's every detail. She was young—very young, with bright golden curls and innocent blue eyes. The shard of a Summoner's stone hung around her neck. Where his hands gripped her too roughly, bruises were already forming. He could smell the blood that formed them beneath her skin and worst of all he could smell the fingerprint of Flame that fueled his hunger. Taking her would be so easy . . . his head dropped till his fangs rested just over her frantic heart.

"Please," she said in a whisper. "I know you are stronger than this."

Lorshin hesitated, "How?" Agony contorted his face and his voice.

The girl stroked his cheek, gently, without fear. "Because you have eyes that burn with Flame. You are the seed of a Guardian despite your curse."

Lorshin staggered back, dropping her onto the ground. "Run," he groaned as a convulsion seized him, and he doubled over in pain.

"You mean to defy me?" the Dark One hissed through the black. "Then you will taste the unprotected dawn!"

The girl stood frozen, her eyes wide with horror as she watched.

Lorshin struggled forward on his knees to push her aside. "Run," he moaned as *Darkness* peeled back, slowly, tortuously.

The Guardian Father burned low on the horizon. Death gazed down on him with lust. Lorshin sank his fangs into his own flesh to keep from crying out. The screams came from his people and filled *Darkness* on every hand. Lorshin twisted toward the first glimmer of Light, bracing himself for the pain that was coming, knowing that its end could set him free . . . forever.

Chapter Fourteen

FLAME'S BECKONING

M iles of Light moving at invisible speed, at least to weaker eyes, burned golden-red across the distance. It scattered into a thousand colors, most too rare to bear a name. Neither tree, nor mountain could stop its advance. They greeted the first rays of dawn, as a long lost friend, for it seemed that the darkening had been turned back—an illusion that would soon render itself powerless.

Natural instinct commanded him to fear where others gloried, yet Lorshin could hear the Flame's beckoning. *Let the Light shine forth and awaken hope. Let Mhorag arise. Let the Promised come.*

He faced his impending death with euphoria, rising up to meet the Light that would destroy him instead of cringing back into *Darkness*. Light burned with greater Flame than he had ever hungered for. He had never imagined such sustenance, as was embodied in all Guardians; his curse had forbidden it up until this moment—a moment that could wipe all other moments clean. Flame was indescribable as it delved beneath the surface of his base instincts. Lorshin could smell it, a rich untamed fragrance that had no name other than power. He could taste it, a wild nectar caressing the air, flowing across his fangs, the one organ that allowed him to sense the Flame in a way few others could. There was no blood to corrupt and distract from its scent. Lorshin shuddered near ecstasy as the Light invaded the deepest recesses of his flesh in intense ripples. There the sensation changed, slowly at first, into a warning. The internal tremors lengthened into the pricks of a thousand needles and thrust into the center of his being, snatching his breath away.

LettheLightshineforthandawakenhope.LetMhoragarise.Letthe Promised come.

A continual undercurrent of need now breached his meager defenses, crippling him where he stood. Heat intensified, laying siege to his cursed heart. Light tried to quicken the reservoir of Flame within, to burn away the bonds placed upon it by a god. It burned hotter when the bonds held. He wished now to quell the arousal that had caused him to evacuate his base instincts, yet he couldn't find the strength though he grappled with his paralyzed senses for the will to escape.

Darkness laughed at his mute screams till smoke began to rise off his flesh, and then the black breath oozed around him once more, cutting off the flow of Light before it ignited. The two forces hissed against each other before *Darkness* quieted the abstruse[1] veins of sunlight flowing down from the Guardian father's aloof Flame.

Darkness—always *Darkness* that living blackness foaming out its own shame that hated thing breathing forth its mindless despair thickened the air around him; Lorshin drew in a ragged breath, yet even the darkening could not completely expunge that taste of unadulterated Flame, neither could it undo what the seconds of Lorshin's defiance had allowed. By drawing the Dark One's fury upon himself, Lorshin had made a way for the Summoners to escape to the shadow of Firinn's pinnacle where the powers of *Darkness* had not yet taken a foothold, the living dragging their wounded and dead with them.

Darkness.

* * *

Bynthroenine

The Nine behemoth trees grew from the Light, visibly rooted in the Grains of Power. The trees formed an unbroken canopy above and below, and though they stood out against the Light, its brilliance was not broken. Rather, the pure, blinding radiance filled everything, shining brighter in the rich blossoms adorning every branch, kissing the fruits that glowed like pale, blue fire, and pouring over the rough tangle of their massive roots, all within a vast unbroken circle. The roots gathered through the Light to entwine higher and higher, binding even the crown of the Shining Mountain. There, accessible only by wing or magic, a vast cluster of bluish stone protrusions dominated the plain of sky and Light. Their great-shouldered silhouette rose mysteriously through the

---

[1]   Abstruse: remote from ordinary minds or notions; difficult to be comprehended or understood

120

Light that set the low hanging clouds aglow and gave the stones their otherworldly aura beneath the burning sky. These stones marked the very heart of Bynthroenine's vast, elaborately sculpted expanse, and from its center came the waters that fed the land.

Within the huge circle, another took shape as the Guardians came, hooded and cloaked in their midnight robes, silhouettes against the glory of the Light. Their blue flaming eyes burned with the Light, shining out beneath their hoods with subtle power. Beneath the Flame of their eyes what was hidden just moments before emerged through an apparent fracture of root and brilliance that was nothing more than a trick of the unified Light. The Grains of Power floated to the surface, moving freely through root and splendor, baring upon them the Vrogandak. This book, formed of innumerable crystalline tablets that bent and fractured the Light into a flowing waterfall of colors making the brilliance burn, contained all the memories of the Light, all the histories of the Ages, all the hope revealed by Sanctus, all the promise of the future, all the mystery of the Flame flowing through the hearts of the Guardians back across time to the Source! Here was the knowledge of rising. Here was the pure law of the Light and the throne of the Promised King who was Flame and Light! Here was the hidden name of power, a name revealed only to the Guardians, beyond the high name of Mhorag, beyond the mystery of the Flame and yet an intricate part of both . . . a unifying of Hope, Prophecy and power of elevated supremacy, equal to Sanctus himself. *The Empyrean.*

The Guardians spoke softly, reverently. Their hushed, yet powerful voices flowed as one upon the Light, the key to unlock the book. "Let the Light shine forth and awaken hope. Let Mhorag arise. Let the Promised come."

Their voices bathed the crystalline cover. In the flow of power, glowing words smoldered across the surface—words of memory and hope. The seals broke open, and the book unfurled like a glorious flower, round and round, becoming a mirrored reflection of the universe—from the highest stars to the bowels of the earth and everything in between. They beheld the present through the memories of the past while threads of the future trickled up just beneath the surface of their vision from the endless foundation of the Vrogandak. Past and future together formed an ensign over the whole, that, in the glow of the Guardians' eyes and the swirl of colored Light, was etched with the Prophecy of Hope, handed down to a world afflicted and ensnared by *Darkness.*

The words of Prophecy burned with Flame, a reminder of the Source they all served, felt distantly even in the most fragile and insignificant of all living things under their protection, searing in the power beating from their own hearts. Unbound by time, this ineradicable core of existence had long been beheld as if through a darkened glass—a whisper of Hope, a word, a dream, a hidden promise. The Prophecy had thrust the Source into the realm of an incurable need, but in the silence and *Darkness*, this need dissolved into pain. Some surrendered into bitterness. Some clung desperately to unseen hope, yet the Flame still burned . . . beckoning, calling to a world that had all but forgotten the Source for the oblivion and unfeeling destruction of the One Whose Name is not Spoken, blind to the offering of life.

All the Guardians were assembled, but only the nine Guardians of the Prophecy stood within that circle of standing stone around the mirrored universe on the height of the Shining Mountain. As all watched, Tlachtga shed her midnight robe and crouched down beside the mirror. Her gaze fixed upon Ylochllion as she placed her hand upon the crystalline surface. Ripples spread across its fluid face like the water flowing down the mountain from its mysterious depths. Light flowed up through her fingers into the runes, covering one side of her body, causing them to shimmer with the wealth of its precious and closely guarded secrets. It spread to glow in the two faces of the Guardian Moon visible upon the throats of the other eight standing protectively around her, connecting them to her vision.

Tlachtga exhaled a long, slow breath, softly glowing with blue Flame. The air grew heavy, and the faces of the Nine Guardians of Prophecy grew troubled as something stirred in the high water of Time. Light and *Darkness* seared through their minds, dragging painful, shuddering gasps from their lips and bloody tears from their brightly flaming eyes. In the fury of the opposing forces' clash, the vision broke upon them. A waxing crescent moon around which a Guardian draped appeared with blinding force behind their eyes, and then *Darkness* struck. The retreating tide of Hope and Light faded, draining the strength from the Guardians who beheld it in silence, and yet the vision held them, pulling its life from theirs.

Malicious laughter crept up through the waters. The power of the Guardians rose in answer. Visible veils of blue Flame poured from their flesh, swelling out to contain the encroaching black. A heartbeat drowned out every other sound; it consumed the present as its rhythm beat out the past. The beat rang in opposition to the melodious noise of Guardian heartbeats pumping in unison with the rushing of Flame. Their hearts had burned with it since the beginning of measured Time. Flame was *life*, power, and beyond simple understanding, stretching out from some distant point to encompass everything! Through the Flame's icy blue inferno, the Guardians watched the past play out. The past started with Flame (oceans of it) and Flame with its unseen Source. Many memories lingered in the annals of Time between the two points; histories of every race and living thing combined to form a past that connect into the Guardians themselves.

Arawn's story was familiar to them—a family heritage, a sadness and a warning. Memories of Light and *Darkness* blurred into one as they looked deeper. Choices already made formed the past, but similar choices formed the shadows of the present and echoed in the vapors of the future, inseparable from the brooding forces that held their minds transfixed. Slowly, *Darkness* filtered in. The black breath fanned the Flame, separating and dividing the perfection until only a residue of its original glory remained.

Yet the distant past preceded a greater black breath rising to consume their vision. The only Light remaining to them was breathed in the silence to break the shields that had held the *Darkness* at bay for so long. The heartbeat pounded in their minds louder, stronger, and more defiant by the second.

Darkness oozed slowly through the air, circling on the farthest horizons of the universe, creeping in by subtle shadows around the Guardians whose heart flames burned more brightly in answer, shining out through them to form a bubble of lighted power all around them. Bloody tears were pulled from their eyes as their vision swept like a fierce and majestic tide across Time. They gazed across oceans and deserts, seeing the brokenness of all living things. Each droplet was a gift to the fallen, but their power could not undo the past.

The past continued to move rapidly forward—darkly and chaotically back into reality. The Guardians growled, their power growing with their ragged breaths and rapid heartbeats. Water burned beneath Tlachtga's hand—*Darkness* enflamed—and when she opened her mouth to speak, it was the Dark One's voice that filled the tense silence of the present.

"I walk this maze of moments, and I see no grand weaver's design. I see a tangle of raveled threads—fragile hope. I see that which must be rent apart for the void to come. I see each tiny Flame bathing the splendid wounds of the universe, exposing the sickness creeping slowly in."

Guardian voices mangled by the *Darkness* whispered mockingly through the waters repeating the words that had broken the shields of the universe.

Truth to expose the defilement of all hearts
Righteousness so that all may know their unworthiness and sin
Justice to satisfy the wrath of he who was forgotten
Mercy to hold back destruction, for the Promised will come in the appointed time.

Grace to all who will remember there is still hope.
Peace, for even in Darkness you are not forgotten.
Joy, for your hope shall come and Light shall shine forth once more to
all who will but call in true humility!

The Guardians tensed against its violent onslaught as the Dark One sought to twist the power back upon them. Tlachtga convulsed with its irrepressible malignity. Those ancient Guardian runes burning on her flesh offered no relief from the black hole gaping open before her.

"I see the fine line between these Flames and mine. I see the undoing of Light. I see oblivion. I see greed. I see sadness. I see pain. I see ruin. I see . . . Death . . . and this is just the beginning." The One Whose Name is not Spoken laughed through Tlachtga.

Tlachtga's eyelids fluttered down breaking her gaze from Ylochllion. He staggered back with a laborious inhalation as the vision released him. The crescent moon symbols on his throat faded back into their gentle glow. One by one, the other seven Guardians of Prophecy were released from the vision, but Tlachtga did not raise her head. Her body curled in upon itself.

"Tlachtga!" Ylochllion shouted.

Her heart fluttered in response to the voice of her beloved even as his cry faded into nothingness. The Dark One dragged her deeper into the cocoon of blackness and the runes of her flesh burned darkly. She screamed. Her screams floated in silence. The black hole sucked her breath away, the vision feeding upon the life within her. She couldn't tell up from down, present from future, Light from *Dark*, reality from vision. She was falling, drowning in Time.

"Tlachtga!" Ylochllion shouted again. He lurched forward, his hands stretched out toward her.

Scrymgeour caught him from behind, holding him back with an iron grip. "Wait. The Dark One has grown stronger," he said uneasily, "to reach through Time and touch us."

The Guardians of the Prophecy nodded in agreement.

"And he has cut Tlachtga off from us!" Ylochllion growled, writhing against the restraint.

"Perhaps he will betray himself to her," Eithne said softly. "Sanctus knows we could use the intelligence that knowing the Dark One's mind would bring."

Ylochllion growled even more fiercely. "Such knowledge would torture Tlachtga all of her days! She would never be the same. I won't allow it!"

Gara placed her hand on her brother's shoulder before he could wrench Tlachtga back from the water. "Wait. We don't know what interrupting the vision could do to her. Real evil can lurk in the most innocent of places."

"We don't know what leaving her in the vision will do to her!" Ylochllion said. "We are stronger together! She is alone!" He shook his sister off. "I won't do that to her!"

Uchdryd raised a hand to block Ylochllion's path. "Tlachtga is strong, proven. She can withstand the entity bent on consuming her. To wrench her free could hurt her more than the fight itself!"

"Heed the Flame in your heart," Llacheu said.

"The love you have for her must not outweigh the will of Sanctus," Cairistiona said softly. "He placed those runes upon Tlachtga. He gave her the ability to see what others cannot."

"Tlachtga will return to you," Orain said. "Wait. Heed the Flame."

Six stood against him.

"Listen, brother!" Scrymgeour said, his grip tightening from behind.

Eight Guardians of Prophecy listened as the song of Guardians flowed up the mountain from the host, filling everything below. Ylochllion grew still. The glory of the Guardians' voices bathed him in peace. Flame stirred in his heart.

"*Darkness* has not grown so strong that it can withstand the power of a Guardian's voice," Scrymgeour whispered to his brother. "Call to her. Guide her out."

"Tlachtga."

Darkness.

Chapter Fifteen

TIME YET TO COME

Tlachtga.

A beautiful voice penetrated oblivion. Light streaked down in blue-white Flame from a point high above her. Tlachtga drew in a ragged breath. "Ylochllion," she whispered. Hope surged in her heart.

The Dark One laughed from the writhing blackness all around her. "The world is dying," he said in his twisted voice. "*Life* returns! Behold my power!"

An icy chill ran down Tlachtga's spine. She could feel the eyes of the One Whose Name is not Spoken upon her, and she immediately sought to shed the veil of humanity, but the power was frozen within her. She shivered, not from the bone-chilling cold, but with the knowledge that this vision belonged to her enemy. Shades of choices yet unmade appeared in the black. Tortured screams filled the dark. The undefined wailings of the broken filled the abyss. Their incomprehensible pleadings and despair seared through Tlachtga's mind. They had no meaning, no purpose beyond their *dark* portends, but she could not silence them. The Dark One's revelation was too strong in this place, beyond her control. Never before had she found so much *Darkness* within the waters of Time! Then again, never before had the shields been broken.

Thousands of ghostly hands grasped for her. A sickening feeling welled up in her stomach, overwhelming everything else.

"You call this life?" Tlachtga shouted into the dark, fighting the nausea that was choking her. Bloody tears dripped from her eyes, down her pale cheeks into nothingness. The vision shook violently around her.

The Dark One hissed in pain.

Tlachtga. Tlachtga. Tlachtga . . . Cords of Flame descended around her with the layered voices of her people.

The Dark One's hiss turned to laughter. "The void comes. Time stretches before me with infinite possibilities. Light has separated itself from the world. Though Day and Night still keep their passage in the heavens and the Sun and Moon maintain their silent vigils, emptiness has torn through all of creation with the Exodus of the Guardians. The void will come first to their hearts and then to completion! Hope will crumble from within!"

Darkness stretched, testing its newfound freedom, spitting contemptuously upon every thread of Light it encountered, dampening the Light of each tiny Flame though the Dark One couldn't put them out.

"The time is nearly at hand when I will arise, and Death will go before me to bow the entire world to my command."

Darkness churned impatiently.

"You will fail!" Tlachtga said.

"And who will stop me?" the Dark One asked mockingly. He twisted the whisper of the Light back upon her. *Let the Light shine forth and awaken hope. Let Mhorag arise. Let the Promised come.* "You serve what you have never seen, but *I* have seen. *I* know! *I* have been consumed. *I* have burned, and it is *I* who will arise from the ashes! Your Prophecy will fail. Light will be undone and *Darkness* will reign supreme!"

Tlachtga backed toward the cords of Light, away from the Dark One's raging. "Do you think it will be so easy?" she asked softly. She caught hold of one cord of Light and climbed toward freedom. "Do you think destroying life and goodness is enough to stop the Prophecy? Do you think you can prevent the Coming? Do you think the Source will fall so easily? Do you think you can mount the heavens and take *him*?"

The Dark One laughed. "I think you have *seen* but do not understand. This is a story that begins in a universe descending into the void. Light has become a rumor. The Prophecy of Hope has been relegated to the land of dreams and the Guardians with it. *Darkness* rises." (Laughter resounded in the depths of the abyss, cracking like thunder against the lingering threads of Light.) "Yes, I can wait for the poison to spread and darken every heart. I can wait for hope to die from within. Even you are not immune!"

Darkness lashed out, but the Guardian was already beyond reach, breaching the surface of Time, back into the present, safe for now in the secret realm of Guardians and Light where it could not follow. As Light and *Darkness* touched for one brief second, the strange Mark appeared like sunlight on thick, white ice . . . a waxing crescent moon around which a glittering Guardian draped. The flash was blinding. The Dark

One screamed. *Darkness* recoiled back upon itself, brooding in silence and solitude and corrupted Flame.

Darkness.

*   *   *

"Tlachtga!" Ylochllion caught her in his strong arms as she sagged forward with a shuddering breath. "Tlachtga!"

The other seven Guardians of Prophecy stood around them in tense silence as the moments passed. Slowly the runes on Tlachtga's flesh lightened. Her eyes opened, and she lifted her hand from the waters.

"Are you all right?" Ylochllion whispered as her face cleared. He wiped a bloody tear from her eye.

She nodded, clinging to him. "I have never . . . felt . . . seen such . . . *Darkness* as was there."

"What did you see?" Eithne asked.

"*Darkness,*" Tlachtga said softly. "A time when *Darkness* is life and Death is hope."

"A day we must hope never comes," Uchdryd said quietly.

The others nodded in agreement.

"The Prophecy stands," Ylochllion said. He lifted Tlachtga to her feet. "Come. We have seen enough for now."

Tlachtga smiled slightly at the protectiveness in his voice, but that smile quickly turned to a grimace of pain. An intense cramp started in her lower body, growing with rapid intensity until she was doubled over in agony. Blinding white fire burned behind her eyes. "Something's wrong," she gasped before Light took her from them into a vision all its own.

"There is still Hope," Sanctus said, but Tlachtga, like Arawn before her, couldn't see it—not even in the glory of the kingdom. Oh, she knew the Prophecy as well as any other. *Darkness* had not taken that from her, but the *Darkness* she had seen so far surpassed the vague impression she had gleaned of it before; now she was free in body, while her mind echoed still with *Darkness.* The beat of Arawn's ruined heart, carved out by Light and left in the dark, thundered in her ears, seemingly closer than she knew it was. *Thud. Thud. Thud. Thud.* Flame rippled darkly just out of sight. She could feel it . . . foreign and wrong despite its familiarity . . . the dark Flame matched the weight of the Flame in her own heart. Blackness lashed out at her . . . that living blackness, foaming out its own shame; that hated thing, breathing forth its mindless despair came upon her with visions she could not silence. Tlachtga gasped beneath a blinding agony. Her pale hands clawed at her chest as her body crumpled forward.

Sanctus was there, lifting her from *Darkness*. His gentle eyes held no condemnation, only compassion and, impossibly, understanding? "Enough," he said in a voice that demanded obedience. Light flared out around them, allowing Tlachtga to breathe easier.

When at last she found the strength to look up, Sanctus was gazing down at her with unfathomable eyes. "Sanctus?"

Sanctus smiled. "Truth is always better," he said gently, "and it is Time you see what the Dark One has forgotten. It is Time to know who you serve and believe what *Darkness* has never known. In time you will be at peace, gentle *Guardian*. All that I show you, you must carry back to my people. You must hold to Hope in Time of *Darkness*. Sgarrwrath will grow stronger still."

Tlachtga nodded, unable to hide her grimace at the Dark One's name.

Sanctus shook his head slowly. "What I offer has always been out of his reach, and for that reason it is his greatest desire. He saw it once, and lust for it gave him life."

"What did he see?"

"Come. I will show you."

They journeyed as one to a secret place where none could follow. They moved in Light with a swiftness and power that defies description. Many great leaps and surges later, they stopped. Sanctus set Tlachtga on her feet. "See what no Guardian has seen before in life."

Tlachtga stood frozen, her eyes fixed upon the orb before them. Tlachtga could not resist pull of power and predominance coming from within and stepped into its shadow.

"Flame," she said softly.

"No, Tlachtga, look closer. It is more than Flame."

Tlachtga reached out her hand and touched the shining walls of the orb, studying them with her fingers. A cool stream of air flowed off the walls scented with power; beneath her fingers came a pulsing beat almost like a heart, only somehow more fluid and simultaneously as hard as crystal. She could *see* it in her mind, this glowing crystal organ, casting wide, arcing rainbows in the Light, as it pumped pure, golden blood— the blood of neither Guardian nor Men, nor any other race! She inhaled sharply, her eyes widening in alarm, at the vision in her mind.

Suddenly a hand appeared beneath hers, pressing hard from within the shining walls of the orb without penetrating the barrier. The golden blood glowed out of the pale flesh of that hand, not following the course of any true veins, but swirling mysteriously up toward the heart like a subtle, dizzying tapestry of Light; from every inch came tiny shoots of

white, blue, and purple Flame which were undeniable tokens of—
Tlachtga slowly shook her head. Undeniable tokens of what?

Tlachtga. Egrontallas.

A startled gasp tore itself from Tlachtga's throat as the magnetic
voice whispered in her mind. She gaped in stunned silence at the orb,
transfixed by the inherent sovereignty of the voice that called to her. Her
hands moved over her abdomen as something fluttered inside her at the
sound of the strange name. *Egrontallas.* She looked down, cradling her
arms for the infant that appeared there. Her own unborn child looked up
into her eyes with knowledge. He smiled.

Tlachtga. Egrontallas. A face appeared pressed against the orb's walls.

"It's alive!" Tlachtga said in a voice raw with terror as her eyes
drifted up from the child in her arms to the orb.

Sanctus laughed. "Yes."

The beautiful face within the orb spiraled with the same golden
designs the arm had and mirrored Sanctus's laugh with one of its own.
Rich, child-like belly laughs pealed through Tlachtga's mind. From the
child in her arms, she felt an answering flutter.

The infant she cradled reached out to touch the orb of power with a
wide, inhuman grin.

"Mhorag," Tlachtga whispered as she dropped to her knees before
the orb.

"A Flame unto Flame," Sanctus said gently, "such is Hope, such is
the Agony. The child you carry will be his Guardian. Soon the Promised
will come."

"When?" Tlachtga asked.

Soon, but not yet, Sanctus whispered to her mind as the vision slowly
faded.

Chapter Sixteen

DARKNESS

Loriath, Kingdom of the Elves of Light

A t last awakened from his long sleep, Cadclucan stood in his human form high in the kingdom where Night's embrace was the strongest. His dark, wavy hair whipped fiercely around his face in the unnatural tempest breathing blackly from the East. Light whispered against it. *Let the Light shine forth and awaken hope. Let Mhorag arise. Let the Promised come.* The whisper rose from the land and played in the Red Wood. Loriath, the magnificent alabaster and gold city hidden within the vast Red Wood, had grown quiet with the coming of Night. Its native occupants had retreated to their elaborate halls where Night did not cast his shadow. Elves by nature abhorred the dark hours and spent them in chambers of artificial light.

Cadclucan stood beneath the moonlight and watched in silence as it was slowly eclipsed. A pale, red hue came over the face of the moon as the shadow of the earth passed between the Mother and Father. The eclipse would pass as surely as the sun would rise, yet to watch it brought great sadness into his heart. *In the times before*, when *Darkness* was virtually unknown, his parents had given themselves for the races. Sanctus had honored them greatly by placing them so prominently in the heavens to crown Day and Night. Father was called the Sun and lit the world with his fire. Mother was called the Moon, and she reflected his father's Light into the dark of Night. Their children, those called Guardian, received immortality, but the cost was great.

He pushed those thoughts aside as he walked the golden bridge between the red giants high over the rushing river beneath. His long, midnight robe blended with the night and moved soundlessly about his muscular frame. Around his neck was the Stone of Existence. It captured every possible glimmer of Light and made it alive. Light gathered to it and returned in streaks of pale, blue fire. Even the whisper of the land was drawn to him with the Light that bore it. Absentmindedly, Cadclucan touched the cool stone. So much pain and so much power had come from this stone. It was the key to everything. Only one could wield it, Mhorag, the Great Guardian King of Prophecy. His heart echoed the whisper. *Let theLightshineforthandawakenhope.LetMhoragarise.LetthePromised come*. Until that time, he was the stone's keeper. Father had given it to him. Sanctus had led him to this place. Everything was changing. In his memory lurked the future, haunting his every footstep.

He knew what *Darkness* was. He had called it brother until the withered black heart had been carved from Arawn's chest. Now *Darkness* hunted him and the objects of its desire, all the while spreading its corruption into the hearts of the races, enslaving some with its pestilence, crushing most. It grew with each conquest. The land beneath its rule withered and died. Anguish and despair replaced life, and the crushing black would soon hold captive both Day and Night. Hope was already faltering in its presence. The very word seemed a thing out of time.

Emptiness surrounded Cadclucan. All that he had loved was lost. His heart ached with a hope that he dared not to trust. Sanctus was silent; he was alone with a weight larger than he could bear. His way was hidden from him. The will of Almighty Sanctus was not clear, though he knew that he could not stay among the Elves indefinitely. He feared what such silence could mean. Had the power of *Darkness* already grown so great? Was the course of the future already set in stone?

The whisper of cloth on the golden bridge and the smell of lilacs broke into his troubled thoughts. Cadclucan knew the identity of the Elf at once. He could count the beats of her heart with a single thought, yet he could not escape the strange, light-headed feeling her presence brought on him. *Maizie*. He liked the way her named rolled through his mind, vanquishing his troubles for one brief moment. A smile played on his lips even as uncertainty pricked his heart.

"Great One."

With a sigh, Cadclucan released the stone. He knew from her reverent words that she was kneeling. With a flourish of his dark robe, he turned and fixed his unnatural eyes on her. She was a flaxen-haired beauty whose snow-white skin was delicately arrayed in a gown as green as the newly budding leaves of the great trees around them (a thing out of season and due to his presence alone). A sleeveless gold, samite robe, whose train spread around her bowed form in perfect folds, overlaid the gown. A diadem of pearls crowned her head. Cadclucan's hand moved over its smooth surface and trailed over her silken hair to the baby-soft skin of her face. He lifted her head. She averted her eyes.

"Maizie," he said softly as he took her hand in his.

The elf maiden did not resist when he helped her to her feet.

"Why do you insist on kneeling in my presence?" Cadclucan demanded gently. "Why do you persist in calling me Great One? You are more than your title, Queen of Elves, and, like you, I have a name."

"You already know the answers to those questions and more, my lord. I am not worthy to speak a Guardian's true name. If it pleases you, I will use the name my ancestors gave your kind." She paused. "Baculus," she said to test the name on her companion.

Cadclucan flinched at her gentle voice. *Baculus. Power symbol.* A shadow of sadness passed through him.

Maizie saw it in the Guardian's eyes and gently smiled at him.

As quickly as it had come, the shadow passed. He raised her hand to his lips. "So be it," he answered before softly kissing her there. Upon releasing her, Cadclucan turned away. "You are not with your people tonight. They will miss you."

"Will you join us, Baculus?"

"Not tonight."

Maizie quietly walked to his side. "Something troubles you, Baculus."

Cadclucan was silent for a long moment. The whisper of the Light echoed in the wood but rang clearly in his mind. *Hope?* It seemed such a long time since he dared to dream of the dawn of hope! He gazed at the sky. A crack of light appeared as the earth shifted and his Father met his Mother once more. The burst of light was weak, but it still seemed as if his parents were smiling down on him. At last he spoke. "It is my burden to bear, Maizie."

Maizie placed her hand on his shoulder. "You are not alone."

He didn't answer. A companionable silence settled between them. Her closeness made his heart somersault. The weight of trouble was not so great with her at his side, yet *Darkness* lurked on the horizon. It was not the darkness, which belongs to Night. At its heart was the One Whose Name is not Spoken.

*　　*　　*

That living blackness, foaming out its own shame that hated thing, breathing forth its mindless despair crept out from me, slowly, secretly designing itself to the veiled longings of every living thing. I would come neither as the impenetrable black of the abyss, nor as fear, nor as pain, nor as any other hated thing. When they found themselves alone, helpless, and vulnerable, I would come baring their desires in the palms of my unformed hands, with promises dripping like honey from my lips, and in time, they too would come to *Darkness* and despair within my embrace. (Laughter echoed once more through the gloom, rising toward the heavens.)

Down in the *Darkness* I plan, knowing that my time will come. I am Sgarrwrath, the One Whose Name is Not Spoken. I am the Heart of Evil carved from Arawn's chest; I am the Plague Spot from which all that is vile is sprung. I am the residue of Dullahan, the first of all created beings, and I am the corrupted Flame of Arawn. I am *Darkness*.

Put aside all that you know or think you know. Your reality means nothing within the *Darkness*, where illusion breathes. Do not imagine yourself immune, for what Light do you possess that could ever penetrate oblivion?

Can you wield the Flame? Have you ever beheld its Source? I think not. How can you know what it is to be consumed, to burn, in the presence of Flame's Source? Even the Guardians, in whose hearts Flame burns, who breathe and wield its power, have never seen its Source nor harnessed its full potential. They are content to serve the Light; but I have seen! I know! There is nothing I desire more in the entire universe than the unseen Source whose immortal Flame has burned since before time began.

Long have I dreamed of it, this mystery so beyond compare. Long have I craved it, above every other thought, above every desire, above even this horrible—glorious—void in which I exist. Always it is the one thing that has been denied me, maintained beyond my reach, but now I am linked to it! Flame! *Life. Power.* I see now it is not *everything* I hoped for. It alone is not enough to stop the wretched Prophecy. It is not enough to cover the universe in the void; still, what does the Light have more than I? Truth? The Chosen One? A promise? If I can just get my hands on the Stone of Existence, hidden somewhere in this vast universe, and the Gemshorn made from Arawn's talon, lost in the final great battle of the Guardian War, these too will fall! Then who will stand against me? Who will deny me my victory?

Yet as I waited, I watched, and as I watched, I couldn't help but wonder what other secrets the Light had left behind. What had I missed? What actions of the Light had escaped my attention? What new *monster* awaited my destruction? Despite my advantage, despite the hollow shields, the Resistance took shape. The races and the Summoners emerged from their homes, gathering once more to Firinn, despite the fact that no *Guardian* would rise to their defense this time. This was my time.

I walk this maze of moments, and I see the undoing of Light. I see oblivion. I see greed. I see sadness. I see pain. I see ruin. I see . . . Death . . . and this, my friends, is just the beginning.

Light flashed. A Mark appeared, blinding in its radiance and power, a waxing crescent moon around which the form of a young, glittering Guardian draped.

Darkness.

Remembrance

Each new thread of time finds its beginning from an ending.
For some, this leaves wounds that never heal.

Chapter Seventeen

TOUCH OF DESTINY

The Times Before, In the Days of the Great Exodus

Guardian eyes could see what others could not. A stain poured down against the current of the *Darkness* as if the universe itself was weeping, but these were no ordinary tears. Light was being wrung out of the universe as the darkening spread; power was draining away in its wake, yet these tears left scars within the black tide, scars that reeked of life, life that consumed—consumed, not in destruction, but as if all things were subservient to it and therefore could not resist the pull of its power.

Fyrdung felt the burning of this power deep inside his heart, and it stayed him, momentarily, upon the edge of the great cliff. Flame wanted to rise. It wanted to sear through the *Darkness* and set souls alight; yet he knew it was not his Flame to wield—not this time. He, with all his power, was not strong enough to do what must be done. He could not be the cure for a world descending toward the void. No Guardian could.

Such power—such unadulterated Flame—belonged to only one, the highest of all, the predominate life! He himself was a mere echo of this living Flame who was the Source. No Guardian had ever beheld the Source, yet all knew it at the very essence of their being. The very core of all that they were was but a link to the fathomless supremacy of the Source! Fyrdung sighed softly.

The One Whose Name is not Spoken laughed. His laughter spread like a blackened roar across the weird silence of the universe.

Fyrdung's midnight robe blew wildly around him. His honey-colored mane flailed uneasily upon the black breath whipping past him, but the Guardian stood firm high on the rugged cliff. The darkening crept upon fitful skies over the angry sea. Waves beat violently against the rocks beneath his feet. Foaming white spray crashed over him again and again. Over its mighty voice, he could still hear the faltering beats of every heart of every race. Fear was in their hearts, but it was not fear that would set them free. "Only when your souls are troubled, will you know agony," he said softly. "Only when you know true agony will the Promised come, and he will come! The Prophecy will stand! All else will fall! One day the holy fire of the Source will be poured out to be Hope and Cure for all living things, to break the Curse that is upon you now and to restore you to all that was lost! The Curse and the Cure have the same *Father*."

Darkness hissed around him where it encountered the Light of his breath and the glow of his heart Flame.

Fyrdung turned toward the sea. He rose up on his toes and spread his arms toward the heavens. "May your hearts be set on fire," he whispered to the world as he leaped from the cliff and dove majestically toward the sea. As he descended, the Light spread out from his heart, transforming him from the guise of humanity into his true form an instant before he sliced through the surface of the water and disappeared into its depths.

The sea pressed down on him. He felt its weight as no other could, for he was its Guardian. He was bound to the water as to no other living thing in the universe outside the Source. He knew its sorrows, its pains, its joy and laughter. He knew its anger, its love, and its every unspoken desire. The swirling currents pulled at his massive frame, finding no purchase on his smooth, sparkling scales. Fyrdung could feel it trying to hold onto him. He could hear every droplet of water pleading with him to stay, but *Darkness* was creeping even into the deep. An ache settled in the Guardian's heart as the dingy streams slowly polluted the sea, darkening its natural beauty. Its stain moved against the currents, oozing down toward him—the only Light in these dismal depths.

Fyrdung spiraled downward; his powerful tail smashed through the black tendrils as if they were nothing. The *dark* hissed and sizzled all around him unable to touch the Flame glowing out of his heart. Virtually at one with the water, he dove with great speed oblivious to the violent pull of desperate currents down beyond the deserted reef, down beyond the colorful anemones, down through a maze of subterranean caverns, down into the bowels of the sea—a place so deep that no other living creature could survive there. Here the flow of the water changed and even its smell shifted, turning from fishy, salty brine to pure slightly frigid water. In the Light of flaming, blue eyes, the divided currents were plainly visible—one natural, the other wholly unnatural glowing with its own fragile Light. The latter was a gurgling spout whose water swirled backward over a gaping hole. On the other side of that hole was home. *Bynthroenine!* This was but one portal to the secret realm, and soon it too would be sealed. The Guardian wove his way sinuously through the tangle of jagged, fire red rocks that circled the portal. Home called to him as it called to all who could not abide the **dark**. The azurite charm hung around his neck, ready to open the door before him.

Suddenly, unexpected screams shattered the silence, filtering down from high above his head. Fyrdung's massive body whipped around effortlessly. With his talons, he perched upon the firestones. His fiery gaze turned toward the surface. The specks of gold in his flaming blue eyes sparked like sunlight in the deep. Nothing could stop his vision from reaching its heights, not even the bleeding stain.

A flash of blinding white Light bleached the universe. A new era dawned. The Sun rose on the Eastern horizon, crowning Day, but the Light of the Guardian Father seemed dim. An unholy gloom hung upon the Sun's face, a bitter reminder of the sin that cast its shadow upon every race. The darkening spread upon drops of sunlight across the hollow shields of the universe into the far corners of the earth, grimly awakening the inhabitants of the world. Darkly luminous spheres erupted from the East, pounding the earth from above and below. The sea churned wildly, bombarded by these luminous spheres as the water tried to free itself. The violent struggle whipped the sea into a whirlpool in which a host of galleon ships were caught.

Humans. The Guardian listened to their panicked cries. In that moment, he heard the plea of their hearts and the Flame stirred powerfully in his chest. Fyrdung launched himself from the firestones, shooting back toward the surface. His snorted breath issued power through the water, making its depths tremble at his presence. He could not ignore the Flame rising within him or the destiny that touched the deepest corners of his heart. Somehow, someway, for some purpose that was not entirely clear, he was connected to these humans and they in turn were intimately connected to the Prophecy . . .

LettheLightshineforthandawakenhope.LetMhoragarise.Letthe Promised come.

Darkness.

Part Two

of the Arising

Laid in Ashes

The Long Guardian Silence in the Days of the Darkening War

"Time passes even in this *dark* place.
And where is my hope?
Lost. Silent."
—Arawn, in his days of *Darkness*

Chapter Eighteen

Whispers

Present Day

Trin Thibodeaux crossed his arms over his chest and watched incredulously as his mentor "Benoit" (almost definitely not the old spy's real name) raised the oversized spyglasses to his eyes in a rather pointless effort to see through the *Darkness*. Not that there was anything to see! *Darkness* was everywhere—breathing—whispering.

There had always been whispers. Indecipherable breaths beckoning from distant places with the promise of newness and adventure had tempted Trin as a youngster. Of course their lure had always been tempered with the security of Faedom. The outside world was proving to be far different than his imaginings! Knowledge of the outside world was much like a flower coming to bud after a long winter to find that there was no more Sun to warm its petals, no fertile soil to hug its roots with nourishment, and no appreciative eyes to admire its delicate beauty. In other words, it was depressing!

"This is just great!" Benoit said sarcastically. "We are two days behind schedule!"

Trin frowned. "How can you tell?" He looked pointedly at the *Darkness*.

Just then a gurgling pop preceded a flash of brownish-yellow illumination that seemed to lift the *Darkness* upon its back and heave it away. Trin gaped openmouthed at the scene. He couldn't explain the sensation that came over him. The entire world faded around him; even the warning call of his mentor was garbled as he was inexplicably drawn toward this strange phenomenon. Suddenly, he was falling. He panicked.

He groped for a handhold and found only air. His shrill scream was cut abruptly short as he landed face first in a questionable substance.

Benoit stood above him laughing.

Apprenticed to the finest spy in all Faedom, Trin had expected to throw off the shackles of his parents' quiet life for the thrill of adventure, yet this was not what he had bargained for! Needless to say, all sense of glory had departed from him! He would quite literally give *anything* to see the borders of Faedom once more, to sit under the shade of the trees of Ougashade, watching the dance of silver dust as his people darted to and fro, and pretend that he had never seen all that he had seen these past days. Forgetting would be his primary occupation, since changing the past was out of the question. He struggled to free himself, sputtering as he fought to right himself.

He muttered angrily under his breath as he struggled with the stinky substance. Benoit flew unhindered toward their destination, completely ignoring him. It was so unfair! His mentor was as wide as he was tall, virtually circular, with frazzled antennae distinguishing his head from the rest of the lardy mass and two wilted wings hanging dejectedly from his back. His arms and legs stuck out at sharp points and looked far too small for his body, and yet he flew ahead not even slipping on the questionable substance oozing up through the spongy land in which Trin himself was unfortunately wallowing.

Trin gagged. "Please tell me this is not what I think it is."

The master spy turned to smile at him condescendingly. From behind the spyglasses with hugely oversized lenses, his eyes slanted down to fix on Trin. "Stop being so morbid," he said in the common language with a heavy accent.

"Oh it is, isn't it?" Trin whined as he struggled to free himself from the bubbling brown stuff only to get sucked further into its stinky depths. He gagged on the toxic vapors rising from each popping bubble.

"Yes," the master spy said with a shrug, "this is Gnome Waste, but that is quite beside the point. Have you looked around you recently?"

"Uh, hello!" Trin exclaimed sarcastically. "I'm covered in Gnome Waste and you ask me if I've looked around me recently! Are you blind?"

The master spy shook his head. The annoyance was on his face quite visibly now. "Trin, you are so busy wallowing in the muck you can't see what is right in front of your face."

"It's not my fault. This stuff is—"

"I don't mean the Gnome Waste. I mean your attitude. You are so busy being miserable that you are missing something important!" The master took a hold of Trin's arm and pulled him out with a gurgling pop.

"Now look," he commanded as Trin flung the brown icky stuff left and right.

"I don't see anything," Trin whined. "I don't see why we have to come here. Gnomes are gross!"

His mentor made an exasperated sigh. "Gnome Waste is highly volatile in its natural state. In the olden days the mini explosions of the gases here caused a lot of superstition among the races. Few would venture so far into Gnome territory. The Gnomes preferred it that way." Benoit laughed as Trin gawked at him in disbelief. "I've never met a more hotheaded lot than Gnomes. The only thing they care more about than their privacy is money, but don't think you can buy their loyalty. Oh no, as simpleminded as they may seem, they are in fact quite cunning—murderous even if they see cause—and if they do, well, let's just say bog muck makes an excellent grave."

Trin could clearly see the dead things now—rotting limbs and worst of all Fairy wings churning in the waste of the most disgusting creatures he could think of. "Please, get us out of here."

"All in good time," Benoit said a little too nonchalantly for Trin's liking. "Gnomes are not warriors, but they do a great service for the Resistance. The Gnome War Effort, or the GWE as they call themselves, makes Gnome Waste into bricks, and each brick provides a day's worth of precious illumination to the Resistance. Light is the one substance that seems to have any effect on the Dark One and his servants, and while Gnome light is nothing compared to the stories I have heard of Guardian Flame, it is the best we have and it does seem to slow the advance of the void."

"Not much," Trin grumbled.

"No, not much," agreed his mentor. "Still, I have been hearing whispers." His voice sounded almost wistful as he spoke those words.

Despite his sour mood, Trin felt his curiosity perk. "Whispers? What kind of whispers?"

"I can't be sure. It could just be the talk of weary soldiers dreaming for home and peace."

"What do they say?" Trin asked, his curiosity growing.

"I hear tell that one of the Samhail has been seen walking free. It is said she is still under the protection of the Guardians and Darkness cannot touch her, just a rumor, but combined with the talk of Light—real Light mind you, not the Gnome light—" Benoit shrugged. "It gives me reason to wonder."

"Light?"

Benoit nodded. "It is a substance you have never seen. Nor I. There are few living who have seen it. We Fairies have the memories of its magic, and it is worth more than all the treasures of all the races combined!" He shrugged. "But as I said, I can't be sure and I am not convinced that these whispers are true. Until I am, we must not speak of them. Do you understand, Trin, my boy?"

Trin shook his head slowly. "No."

"My reason is very simple. Hope would be a great asset, but false hope would be our undoing. The Resistance would crumble from within, and then the meager offering of Gnome light would fail and the void would conquer us all. Our enemy will stop at nothing to destroy us. We must not give him an opening of any kind! Now do you understand?"

Trin nodded. "But I still don't see why we have to be *here*."

His mentor looked at him as if he was missing something obvious.

Trin groaned. "We have to carry this stuff?"

"We have to keep the supplies flowing. A spy's work is never done. Now try to keep up, and mind your footsteps."

Pop! Pop! Pop! Pop! Pop! Out of the bursting brown bubbles Gnomes emerged into the brownish-yellow illumination. At first only their green mushroom hats were visible floating upon the muck. Then a hint of red appeared like the stems of mushrooms, followed by tiny humanlike heads and bodies that were clothed from head to toe in shiny, bright orange garments from which the waste just rolled off. All looked remarkably alike in their uniforms, with no distinctions one from another as they whispered back and forth.

"Thieves. Thieves."

"That one took Gnome Waste without pay."

"Make him pay."

"Tear his wings off."

"Feed the Waste!"

"Skuttlebug."

"Skuttlebug."

The Gnomes chanted in hushed voices; their fists made plop, plop, plop sounds in the muck as they spoke. "Skuttlebug. Skuttlebug. Skuttlebug. Skuttlebug."

Gurgling pops drifted up from the depths of the muck as the bubbles grew larger and larger and the Gnomes' chanting gradually grew louder. "Skuttlebug. Skuttlebug. Skuttlebug!" Together they drifted swiftly through the muck after the intruders.

Trin glanced warily over his shoulder but couldn't make anything out of the murky illumination. Whatever had come over him before was missing, replaced with an uncomfortable feeling in the pit of his stomach.

If anything, the illumination was disturbingly unnatural. Maybe it was something your eyes had to become accustomed to. The whispers did seem louder than they had just moments before though. A chill ran down his spine as he whipped back around to speak to his mentor. "Do you hear that?"

Benoit nodded his old head; the movement almost made him look like he was bowing, swelling him out at the sides before he resumed his correct shape. "Whispers," he said gravely. "Nasty things, whispers, never know if they are good or bad. Deceptive."

For once, something his mentor said actually made sense. Trin shuddered. "Can you see anything with those glasses?"

"Shiftings in the *Darkness*. Nothing to trouble yourself with now, my boy, but soon, I fear, we may have to split up."

"What? What do you mean?" Trin asked uneasily, his former anxiety momentarily pushed to the background.

"I mean," Benoit sighed in exasperation, "we are already two days behind! The Gnome light of multiple fronts will be going out because their stock of bricks is depleted. All the advantage will be turning to our enemy and more lives will be lost to the black unless we make haste!"

The whispers drifted closer becoming more distinct. "Skuttlebug. Skuttlebug. Skuttlebug!"

Benoit frowned. "Gnomes," he said in a hushed voice, "closing in fast!"

"What does that mean?" Trin asked in a whisper of his own.

The old spy shook his head.

"Skuttlebug. Skuttlebug. Skuttlebug!"

Before either of them had a chance to react, a horrible *something* exploded through the surface of the muck. It was brown and oozing, brightly veined all over its round body. Squid-like tentacles served as its arms and legs propelled it masterfully out of the muck, simultaneously knocking Trin and his mentor off their feet and keeping them pinned to the ground as the Gnomes drifted nearer.

"Skuttlebug. Skuttlebug. Skuttlebug!"

Its tentacles had no fleshy feel like those of a living creature but rather felt metallic in nature and uncomfortably warm. Every few seconds, steam spouted from a small porthole in its rear with a whooshing sound.

"It's a machine!" Benoit shouted.

"I prefer magic!" Trin shouted back as he struggled against the tentacles. "I thought the Gnomes were expecting us!"

"They were! Two days ago!"

"Is this normal?" Trin asked.

148

"This has never happened before!"

The Gnomes climbed up out of the muck, looking quite disturbing and alien in their orange muck gear and mushroom hats. Gnome Waste dripped from their hats as they swarmed around the prisoners. They were still chanting as if that one word explained everything. "Skuttlebug! Skuttlebug! Skuttlebug! Skuttlebug!"

"We come in peace!" Trin squeaked.

"You come to steal!" the Gnomes answered together.

"No!" Benoit shouted. "We come on behalf of the Resistance. We are expected." He pulled against the restraints enough to jingle the money purse at his side.

Instantly he was dropped from the iron tentacle that had trapped him. The old spy motioned toward Trin. "My apprentice?"

"Thief!" the Gnomes said. "Skuttlebug. Skuttlebug. Skuttlebug!"

Trin screamed as the machine jolted to life once more and crawled toward the muck.

"Wait!" The old spy smiled. "Release him and I will let you have your choice of payment for the Gnome Waste we take." He produced a second sack vastly larger than the first.

The Gnomes whispered one to another.

"What!" Trin squeaked.

Benoit winked at him.

"We will choose," the Gnomes finally answered. The machine dropped Trin, who landed with a painful thud on the ground.

"Agreed," Benoit said, "on one condition."

"What condition?"

"You accept all payment as final. No going back on your word."

The Gnomes whispered one to another. Even as they debated amongst themselves, their eyes kept drifting back to the two sacks in Benoit's hands. At last, they answered, "We will choose."

Benoit nodded. A single Gnome drifted forward and snatched the larger of the two sacks from the old spy's hand. Another produced five cases of Gnome Waste Bricks. Trin and his master took them and backed quickly away as the Gnomes huddled around the large sack.

"Run," Benoit said.

"What was in that sack?" Trin asked as he obeyed.

"One gold coin and a lot of silver dust!"

"Aren't you afraid they won't do business with the Resistance anymore?"

Benoit shook his head. "No. They love money far too much for that."

In the distance, the Gnomes screamed.

Trin and his mentor laughed as they safely broke free of Gnome territory. Benoit slowed.

"We need to split up. Take one case and go to the Summoners at Firinn's pinnacle. Speak with Master Esarian and give him all the news we have gleaned thus far. I will take the rest of the Gnome Waste to the Races in the greatest need. I will return to Firinn as soon as I can."

"But master—"

"There is no time to waste. Do as I say. Run with all haste and do not look back!"

Chapter Nineteen

A FRAGILE RESISTANCE

Cartiman, Year 1090 of the Darkening War

B lack stained the golden fragments of the Counsel domes that were strewn along the ground like dismembered limbs left on a field of battle. Here the Dark One had thrown down his gauntlet, and all that remained of Cartiman was a riddled carcass of marble and gold. Its splendor was undone, replaced by the neglect and erosion of time. The ruins of the Guardians' marble thrones still hovered like fragile white phantoms above the land in the constant near *dark* of a bitter Age. They heaved into sight and then melted back into the dismal tapestry that cloaked the land. A Resistance scout darted from one point to the next in bitter silence as a boisterous, howling wind echoed across the withered plain, masking the sound of weary footsteps. Like a shade following some timeworn path, the figure advanced. A residue of silvery dust and small white clouds of exhaled breath were the only evidence of life.

The snow-dusted path rapidly receded behind the cloaked figure till Firinn's pinnacle loomed overhead. Its spotless heights were lost in the black, and tonight a hoary mist through which a haze of pearly Light still shone overcast even its tiered column. The Summoners rose from the shadow of Firinn as the scout stopped. Their torn, white robes, stained with blood and black, testified of the unending struggle of this Age. The broken shards of the Styarfyre orbs glowed an eerie blood red in the *dark*, and the Summoners' gaunt, beleaguered frames gave evidence of the *want* that was breaking them all, one by one.

The crops had failed. The water had become undrinkable. The remaining resources were scarce, and so the Summoners sacrificed themselves to give the races a chance to fight. Power lingering faintly in the shadow of Firinn's pinnacle kept them alive, but that thread of life was fleeting at best, diminishing with each passing of Day, for no Guardian was there to renew it. Of the ten thousand Summoners who had a will to fight in the first days of the darkening, only a handful remained. Some had fled, living now as recluses with the shame of their cowardice, but most had died unnatural deaths, their bones littering the ground around Firinn. Those few Summoners who still remained were all children—one from every known race. They had carved ancient, Guardian symbols on their foreheads to ward off the temptations and illusions of the *Darkness*; still, with each death, the Dark One grew stronger and the Resistance faltered. These days, some found it easier to give up than to fight; one by one, the strongholds of each race were crumbling into *Darkness* and the Summoners were powerless to prevent it. Hope was being wiped out with the very blood of those who clung to it! Something needed to change soon, or there would be no turning back from the void.

The scout stood just within the eerie glow of the Styarfyre orb shards. Clouds of silvery dust enfolded him in rising and falling puffs with his constant twitching. "I am Trin Thibodeaux. I bring news for Master Esarian," he said in a whisper.

A single human Summoner stepped forward. His shagged sandy blond hair framed his childish face—a face so ghostly pale because he had never known the pure light of the Sun, dominated by hollow, gray eyes that had seen too much and a mouth that had never known how to form a smile. He had never known the ways of the Light, yet here was a boy who had lost so much and still had hope, though it was nothing more than a dream—not even his own dream. He didn't know how to begin to dream! He clung to the dream of his father and grandfather. No, more than that, it was the dream of another Age, handed down. "What is this news, friend? I am Master Esarian," he said softly.

Trin hesitated. His luminous green eyes widened at this revelation. One so extremely young bore the weight of so many upon his shoulders! Never had he suspected such a thing—though he could not shake the images of young and old falling side by side on the field of battle. Not even though he, himself, had become a scout!

"Trin Thibodeaux," Esarian said with surprising authority, far beyond his years. "The Darkening War will not wait for you. What is your news? Lives may right now be hanging in peril!"

The scout squatted down beside the map roughly carved into the slabs of gray stone surrounding Firinn. "There is no sign of the Dark One himself though his *Darkness* is seen on every front." Trin indicated the map. "The Sylph send word that despite appearances the condition of the air is stable. They are holding their own against the *Darkness*. The Merar have lost another waterway. They have fallen back to the River Scarlen and beg reinforcements. The Giants are moving to help them. The Dwarves report that their weapon stores are nearly depleted and have proved ineffective against the advance of incorporeal *Darkness*. They request permission to return to the Ice Floes of the Far North to make more and perhaps develop new weapons for use in this war."

Master Esarian squatted down as well. "Can our lines hold if the Dwarves retreat?"

"Our lines already falter on every front, Master Esarian. The Fauns, Trolls, and the Astoni all report heavy losses. The Humans report that two more of their kingdoms have been lost."

"No entire races have been lost?"

Trin Thibodeaux was silent for a moment. His thoughts had drifted to the same place that Master Esarian's no doubt had. *The fall of the Samhail.* Slowly, he shook his head. "No. The Shee have been pinned down, but my own people have gone to aid them with all the speed gifted to us by the Great Guardian Fendore," the scout sighed softly. "We have lost contact with the Elves of Light, but to the best of our intelligence, they are still safe behind their magical walls, though we have been unable to reach them."

Esarian considered this news; his face betrayed nothing.

"What are your orders, master?" Trin asked.

"Spread word among the Resistance. Have everyone fall back to Firinn. Now go with all speed. There is no time to waste!" Esarian turned and walked wearily back into the shadow of Firinn's pinnacle. He melted into the background and the other Summoners with him.

That living blackness foaming out its own shame; that hated thing breathing forth its mindless despair whispered through the air. Trin Thibodeaux trembled. If only he could outrun the *Darkness* as easily as he could outrun everything else. The scout ran as hard and fast as he could. His legs became nothing more than a blur of movement and silver dust as he shot across the world baring the message of the Summoner.

* * *

Darkness.

Always *Darkness.* I smiled as I relished its black embrace. This time the universe would have no escape. My time had come at last! A time when the world would be swallowed by cruel, all-consuming blackness, a time utterly devoid of Light, ruled by *Darkness* as ne'er was seen before!

My quarry searches for relief, but they will find none! I swear it upon Arawn's withered black heart, carved by the Light from his chest and left here in the *dark* with a life all its own and a Flame gone black! *Darkness.*

Chapter Twenty

A Kiss Says it All

The blackened heart of Arawn rested upon the top of the intricate ivory pillar that rose majestically between two ivory thrones. A wide circle of ivory pillars spread around them, bearing a domed roof upon their heads. The roof was adorned with vividly colored tiles making a detailed portrait of two enraptured lovers. They were set against a backdrop of cloudy blue, black, and gold twilight. Upon one hand, a blazing sun kissed their naked flesh, and upon the other, the cold silvery moon cast its haunting shadow over them.

Gossamer veils filled the gaps between each pillar. Most hung free to play in the breeze, but two had been tied back to reveal the beauty that lay without. Sithbhan stood between them, gazing out in quiet wonder upon the thick forest of monstrous trees standing in quiet tranquility. A meandering stream flowed among them on its determined course. The crystal clear water gurgled as it splashed over rocks forming tiny, white waterfalls. Emerald moss grew upon felled logs by the stream's edge, and boldly colored autumn leaves blanketed the ground. The water's soothing sound mingled with the song of birds in the treetops and swishing leaves in the breeze. Squirrels chattered happily as they scampered to and fro in search of nuts. Everything was peaceful here where nature ruled supreme. It was a place too perfect for words, yet not all was as it seemed.

At the forest's edge, the pale light of the rising sun broke against the trees, dividing the darkness with faint rays of gold. The Dianara Mountains rose proudly, and in the distance, other great cliffs towered regally and veils of water poured from the heights, but beyond the cliffs was shadow. The whole place teemed with mystery. The very trees seemed to breathe with memories and desires of their own, but the desires were *dark*. Sithbhan breathed deeply. Nature's rich, intoxicating scent filled her nostrils. It was an ancient scent, yet ageless; constant, yet unpredictable; beautiful, yet often fearful and deadly.

Sithbhan looked into the treetops. A smile of sheer pleasure graced her blackened lips. "Lorshin!" she called, her voice suddenly sounding like the howl of the winter wind.

The stillness was shattered as the treetops began to stir with the bitter cries of thousands of angry, yet unseen captives. A shrouded figure moved in the treetops above her and crept slowly forward to squat upon the canopy. Others like him propelled forward against their bonds in agitation. The shadows were ignited with the dim glow of their blue eyes, which fixed upon her unwaveringly. Sithbhan laughed, basking in the hateful gaze of the slaves.

"Come here, Lorshin," she summoned him softly with an enticing curl of one, long, pale finger.

Lorshin rose from the treetops with a great bound. His abundant, black robe billowed out behind him as he propelled downward through the air. The robe's sizeable, black hood flew back from his head to lay upon his back. The wide, flowing sleeves ballooned with the upward rush of air, yet his extended arms remained concealed. His body never faltered from the course he had set, despite the distance through which he descended. Lorshin landed moments later with supernatural grace and power upon the soft earth. The long, lean fingers of a dirt-caked hand brushed lightly upon the ground.

Sithbhan smiled sweetly at him. "I thought you might enjoy seeing your home again. Do you remember, Lorshin, my love? This was how I saw it that night when you brought me here all those years ago. Only a few things have changed."

Lorshin straightened. His shaggy, brown hair, matted with grime and ash, shrouded his face. A strip of plaited hair extended further than the rest to drape his right shoulder and brush the collar of claws that hung over his chest. His blue, fire-tinged eyes glowed from behind the mask of hair with the fierceness of a predator. "You forget, Death, that you, like I, are a slave here. True illusion belongs to the Dark One, not you. I can see through your illusions, for I gave you immortality's kiss." His voice mercilessly tore into her mind. His hand extended. The ruined black heart that had once beat in his father's chest rose from its place into his hand at his silent summons. "It is from this that your powers come! You are nothing outside the *Darkness*!"

Sithbhan frowned as he covered the heart with his ample sleeve. The illusion faded, leaving the wastes naked before them. Gone was the sweet innocence that had exuded from her. In its place, she stood both fair and fearful. Her skin was devoid of color and warmth, though in all other ways it remained unblemished. Her long hair oozed with the *darkness* around her, flowing in long silken strands beneath her dark, thorn-twined crown. A thin veil of shadow lay over the whole and framed her angular face. There was an air of evil in her blackened eyes that could make the heart quake with fear. Shadow clothed her, yet beneath those shadows her seductive, hourglass frame could be faintly seen. She was shadow, and yet separate from it. The shadow seemed to feed on the evil ambitions of the *dark* as the ruined, but still beating, husk of his father's heart fed her power. In her hand was a great, double-bladed scythe of fire, the implement of the Dark One's ancient gift.

In place of the forest was *Darkness*. Nature's thrilling scent had been vanquished by the sickly, sweet stench of Death. Sithbhan smiled wickedly as she took her place in one of two vacant thorn-covered thrones that had appeared. Swirling emerald-black Flame rose to form a footstool beneath her feet. "Lorshin, you should know the illusions are as real as the observer perceives them." As she spoke the taunting words, she extended the scythe of fire toward him. "Behold."

Darkness lent itself to her will. The Heart of Evil, which still beat in Lorshin's hand, began to quiver. In an instant, he saw the illusion she had prepared for him. *Darkness* engulfed his mind before slowly fading into the forest that had been a vast and wondrous playground in his childhood. A well of sadness flooded his soul. He stood powerless against the force of the attack. Lorshin saw himself as he had been two thousand years before.

"Remember?"

Lorshin groaned helplessly as he watched Sithbhan press her pale lips and seductive body to his. He felt each sensation as if it was real, wanting her as he had wanted her then . . . "No!" he screamed, casting the Heart of Evil away from him, causing the vision to fade from his mind.

Simultaneously, Sithbhan extended a pale hand lifting the heart through the black to its place upon the pillar of shadow. The forest illusion returned to conceal the vile lair. Lorshin turned his face and raised a trembling hand to the strand of plaited hair. A mournful groan escaped his lips. Death smiled knowingly at him as the *Darkness* laughed.

"You saw your failure, my love?" she asked. She did not try to conceal the mocking tone of her voice.

Lorshin raised his head. His unruly hair fell back from his youthful and unblemished face. "I will bear the shame of that day for all the long Ages of my life, Sithbhan."

"You loved me once, and I loved you. I love you still, though your heart has proved to be untrue."

"My heart? You betrayed me!"

Sithbhan smiled as her blackened eyes roved his body.

His human appearance was alluring to look upon, even covered with the dirt and grime of two thousand years of slavery, yet it was no mere human that stood before her so proudly. He was Samhail. A race cursed to roam the night, immortal save in the sunlight, since the first was conceived in the ill-fated union of Arawn and Laphair. He was a prince among a race known for their mysterious and ageless beauty, ferociousness, strength, agility; their perfection exceeded only by the Guardians themselves. The Samhail were feared for their voracious hunger. Lorshin was the embodiment of all such perfection.

Sithbhan rose from her throne. Her feet made no sound upon the earth as she strode toward him with a seductive sway of her body. Her pale hand ran the length of his angular jaw and down his long, sleek neck. She delighted in touching the succulent skin of his muscular abdomen that was left exposed by his open, ground-length robe. Lorshin inhaled sharply at her touch. His body stiffened. She laughed and let her fingers play at his hips.

The mystery of the Samhail lay deeper than their outward appearance. Only Lorshin's blue fiery eyes hinted of its existence as they fixed upon her coldly. Here were the eyes of a Guardian fixed in the body of one who was not, nor ever would be, ranked among the Guardians, his ancestors—forever an outcast of the powerful bloodline, cursed to haunt Night's long lonely hours by Arawn's fall, enslaved to *Darkness* by one fateful choice. Lorshin's eyes shone with a wealth of memories and knowledge, possessed by all of his kind, from the beginning of their history; so it would be until the end. These memories were both part of, yet separate from, the aura of sorrow and malice that emanated from him. She, too, possessed them, but their meaning remained hidden from her. Perhaps it was because she alone was free from their curse. Being Scarrow, she was sprung from the union of both light and dark. Day's light had no more power over her than the dark of Night.

Like she had conquered their curse, she would conquer love. With *Darkness*. It was time he bowed to her will once more.

"Lorshin, what does the future hold?"

"I do not know what the future may hold. Nor do you, Death."

A wicked smile curled her lips. "You are mistaken, my love. I do know what the future holds. One day I, Sithbhan, will rule the future of all races. And you, Lorshin, shall sit at my side as king!"

Lorshin snorted with disgust. "Who told you that? The Dark One? He lies, and even if by some strange chance he speaks truth, I will never submit! Give that honor to someone who desires your affection!" Lorshin spat the words. His repulsion at her declaration was vivid in every word.

Sithbhan howled, "You will wallow at my feet for such insolence, slave! It will be the only existence you will know!"

"Why do you think the Dark One even allows you to exist, Sithbhan? Do you think you are any better than the One who gave you the power of death? You call me a slave. How are you any different?"

She turned to face him. Lorshin saw the challenge in her blackened eyes. His raw, cracked lips parted, revealing his sharp, white fangs in a hiss of defiance even as the shadowy chains materialized about his wrists and dragged him to his knees.

"You forget your place, slave," she taunted.

He turned his face away from her. "I have not forgotten, Death," he said. His deep, sad voice echoed faintly throughout the forest illusion. "You have."

"I thought perhaps that these two thousand years would have broken you of your stubbornness! You enslaved your people by giving me immortality's kiss, yet, since that time have I not cared for you and them?" She motioned upward into the shadows as she raged. "Does the **Darkness** not feed and clothe you? Does it not house you beyond the light of the Sun? All I ask for in return is your love! Am I not good enough for Lorshin, the slave Prince of the Samhail?"

Silence was her answer. He wondered if she could even hear, as he did, the slips in her speech between herself and the Dark One.

Angrily, she circled him. "'Tis true, I possessed your love by trickery, yet you did love me!" Sithbhan's cold hand glided through his hair and down his jaw to his sturdy chin. She forced him to look at her as she spoke. "You did love me, Lorshin."

His features hardened into a glare. "My love for you turned to malice when the illusion faded and my people were enslaved!"

Death frowned and withdrew her hand. The hurt his words had inflicted was evident in her voice. "I did not force you to kiss me. You have only yourself to blame."

Lorshin looked away.

His downcast gaze neither pleased nor made her sorrowful. She loved him. Why couldn't he see that? She had power at her disposal, but without Lorshin, she was incomplete. Slowly, she circled him. He shivered as her hand glided gently across his back.

"I am not as cruel as you would make me, Lorshin," she said softly. The Dark One's voice overlaid her own, but she didn't notice. The chains of shadow receded from his wrists.

Slowly, he rose. His cold gaze fixed upon her angrily, yet when he spoke, his voice had softened. "How are you then, Sithbhan?"

"Alone. All who should have loved me betrayed me. Love? What is love, Lorshin, if death and destruction have no part? Only the Dark One ever embraced me!"

"Well, there is *his* heart carved from my father's chest!" Lorshin said coldly.

Sithbhan's voice suddenly sounded burdened by years of pain and suffering. "I did not always want such power. I feared the *Darkness* like those around me feared it." The shadows billowed and threatened around her as she ranted. Sithbhan turned to face him, an evil smile upon her black lips. "In time these Promised Ones will fall and *I* will rise in power. All Races, both mortal and immortal, will bow to *me*! Someday even Sanctus will worship *me*! Death and destruction will seize their day and conquer it just as they once conquered love and will do so again!"

With the last sentence, the vile mask of the Dark One's voice was lifted. Lorshin winced as if he had been struck. Would he be tormented forever?

Sithbhan looked upon him with mock contrition. Her hand gently caressed his cheek. "Forgive me, my love," she said. "I meant no offense."

He frowned but did not withdraw. *Let the Dark play its games*, he thought. *I will play too and this time, I will conquer. My people will be free again, and I will have my revenge.* "How will you defeat the Guardians and the Promised?" he asked simply, revealing none of his thoughts to her. Her thoughts were not safe, tangled as they were with the One Whose Name is not Spoken, but his, at least for now, were sheltered.

"*Darkness* is most instructive. From Arawn's heart, it gleaned many things. Did you know that the Guardians gave powerful gifts to the races? Some of these gifts were very powerful indeed and were meant for good. In the wrong hands though, they could be dangerous weapons. The most treacherous of all is the Gemshorn, given to the Calianith by your father against the will of the great Guardian counsel. When played by a master, the haunting melody could only be compared to the voice of a Guardian raised in song. Each time the instrument is played, its song grows stronger, whether for good or evil depends upon the player. Under Arawn's tutelage, its power for evil became great, making it the most powerful and deadly of all the gifts ever given!"

Lorshin frowned. *The Gemshorn!* The name struck terror in his soul. What could he say? He knew of this instrument. He knew of its power for evil. He had beheld it with his own eyes centuries ago when Matwyn had led the Dark One's forces in a war against all living things.

Sithbhan laughed wildly. Again her voice was lost within the Dark One's. "I will find this Gemshorn and exploit its power over even the Guardians themselves! I will have my revenge!" A glimmer of sadness flashed in those blackened eyes. "Will I still lack what I most desire?" She spoke for herself once more, but the implication of her words mirrored darker things. "Will you deny me your love, Lorshin? Love me, and I will make you equal in my kingdom! My power will be your power, and my knowledge will be your knowledge. We will be one."

Lorshin recoiled. "There is nothing you can offer me that will make me desire you!"

"Are you certain?"

He hesitated to answer.

Sithbhan leaned in close so that her lips brushed his ear. She whispered so lowly he had to strain to hear her, as if she sought to keep something from the ever-pressing blackness. "What about your twin?"

Lorshin's face twisted in anguish. "Isentara?" he whispered his twin sister's name. He saw his sister as clearly as if she were there beside him, cowering in the moonlight as *Darkness* pressed in upon her. Whether his mind had melded with Isentara's or whether it was a vile trick prepared by the *Darkness* itself, he could not say. His mind was clouded. "She escaped."

"She has left the realm of the Guardians," Sithbhan whispered. "Even now their protection over her is beginning to weaken. She begins to feel the *Darkness* around her. It is only a matter of time until she is taken."

"No!"

"I can help her, Lorshin."

"How?"

Sithbhan smiled. "Be one with me and I promise you the Dark One will spare her this fate."

Lorshin shuddered inwardly at the thought of ever again being one with Death, yet the bond of blood was already between them. The blood bound them together for all eternity or at least as long as both drew breath. The bond of blood was even stronger with Isentara, for they had shared the same womb. He knew her pain. He felt it growing stronger with the passing seconds. To defeat *Darkness,* he needed Death to trust him.

Wise Ones, hear me and be merciful! I am in desperate need of your guidance. Do not leave my people to drown in this Darkness! Come to me!

He guarded his thoughts from her. Sithbhan must not know of his silent plea. A weary sigh shuddered from his body. The eyes of his people glowed in the *dark*. Isentara's face was fixed in his mind. He could see the tears in her shining eyes.

Slowly, he raised his finger to Sithbhan's lips. "Keep your promise. Free my sister, and I will be yours. Beg no more, Sithbhan." Lorshin smiled at her gently, hoping she did not sense his betrayal else the Dark One would sense it too.

Her dark eyes looked upon him, completely enraptured by his sweet words. If there was deception in her promise, at this moment, he could not sense it. She stepped closer.

The game had begun. Lorshin smiled and lowered his mouth toward hers.

"Let this be a token of my promise," he whispered. His mouth moved over hers in a kiss that was filled with the deep passion of lovers long separated but at last reunited. The simple kiss deepened further, taking on an edge of *darkness*. Lorshin staggered back, trembling, as he broke free. The beat of his heart raged in his ears. Thud-Thud. Thud—Thud. Or perhaps it was the beat of the Heart of Evil. He couldn't tell. Thud. Thud. Thud. Thud. His mind was screaming at him. *This is a game! A game I cannot afford to lose. I do not love her! I cannot!* He was still shaken when Sithbhan drew him back into her possessive embrace and descended the great stairway, concealed by forest, into the unknown abyss.

Wise Ones, hear me!
Darkness.

Chapter Twenty-One

RUMORS OF LIGHT

Near Odiam, a Border Village in Isear, a Kingdom of Men

A serpentine chain of children, linked at the hands, ran across the open, green plain. They lashed fiercely like a whip in the faint evening light. Squeals of delight surrounded them as a young, fair-skinned boy was knocked off the end.

"You are out!" the eldest shouted. His dark, hard features seemed reminiscent of a stone. Kinjour's deep, brooding eyes fixed on Cait, who now occupied the end position. Black hair cascaded from her head and draped wildly around her delicate face. Her large dewdrop eyes gazed back at him excitedly. Her small frame heaved from the exertion of their game, yet she glowed with anticipation. Kinjour flashed her with his wide, toothy grin. "Think you can keep up, little sister?"

Cait scowled indignantly at her brother. "You'll see, Kinjour!" She stuck out her tongue at him and grabbed her friend's hand. "Hold on tight, Goldya."

Goldya nodded. Her thick blond hair shined silkily in the light.

Kinjour laughed and took off at top speed, running against the wind that flowed darkly visible from the East.

Their whip lashed violently, trying to break Cait from the group. Laughter filled her ears. Her lungs strained to breathe as her muscles propelled her forward. The wind stung with a hint of the coming winter as the group turned sharply. Her grip loosened.

"Goldya!"

Cait was caught by the wind's numbing force. Her fingers brushed with that of her friend, and then she was torn away from the group. In the seconds before her imminent fall, her stomach fluttered upward. Giggles erupted and resounded across the open plain. She almost felt as if she was flying, and then she landed with a hard thud on the ground. Her well-used silk dress tangled around her limbs, a splash of shimmering scarlet on the darkened border of the land.

Moments later, Goldya was at her side, still reeling with the thrill of the ride. A streak of gold flowed around her as she too landed with a thud in the rolling green grass. Blindly, she extended her hand toward Cait. Their fingers fused together. In the distance, they could hear the others playing still but did not try to rejoin them. The girls lay on their backs, gazing up at the silver-tipped clouds.

"Do you think someone will ever want us?" Cait whispered.

Goldya shrugged. "Being an orphan isn't so bad. We have each other." She squeezed her friend's hand. "And Kinjour watches out for us, doesn't he?"

Droplets of rain dislodged from secret compartments in the clouds and plummeted toward the earth.

Cait smiled. "Yeah." The few scattered raindrops masked her tears. They lay side by side in companionable silence.

Slowly, the clouds shifted and stretched, breaking in thick billows to make designs upon the vast canvas of the sky. Dragons, an ocean full of whales, and giant turtles sprang to life before their eyes. The black wind followed after them, chasing the designs away toward a well of open sky. Rising up in the center of that open space was a vast and beautiful palace.

"I'd like to live in a house that grand," Cait said wistfully.

Goldya giggled. "We're orphans, remember? Anyone living in a house that grand wouldn't want us around!"

"How would you know?" Cait asked.

Goldya rolled away, over onto her belly with her feet crossed in the air behind her. "I just do, okay?" Her voice was sad and guarded. Her eyes misted with tears that she wiped roughly away.

"Goldya?" Cait crawled back to her friend's side.

Goldya smiled instantly. "Come on." She hopped to her feet and pulled Cait up after her. The little girls skipped hand in hand up the steep hill, not paying much attention to their surroundings. Suddenly upon the hill's crest, a sparkle of silver caught Goldya's eye. "Cait, look!" she shouted, motioning excitedly toward the valley.

Cait looked the direction her friend pointed. Miles beneath them in a maze of ancient trees, a streak of silver was moving from point to point in the *dark*. "What is it?" she whispered.

Goldya shrugged.

Cait withdrew, putting a safe span between herself and the darting silver figure.

Goldya smiled slyly and reached for her friend's hand. "Come on. Let's go see it!"

Cait shook her head. "No." A quiver of fear was evident in her voice. "We should go back. We shouldn't have come so close to the border!"

"I don't want to. I want to see what it is."

Cait frowned. "I'm telling Kinjour. Kinjour!"

"Cait!" Goldya exclaimed in objection.

"Kinjour!" Cait shouted frantically. "Kinjour! Kinjour! Kinjour!"

Before his name faded beyond hearing, Kinjour appeared beside them. "You called?" he asked with a dramatic bow and a tussle of his sister's hair.

Cait pushed his hand away. "Stop it," she said sharply.

Kinjour's face hardened. "What did you want, Cait?"

"We saw something. Look." She pointed back toward the crest of the hill.

"This better be worth it. I was winning that game," Kinjour said with a roll of his eyes. He ran up the hill, not even getting winded by the climb. "Where? I don't see—" He stopped abruptly. A gasp escaped his lips.

"What is it?" Cait and Goldya asked simultaneously, one out of fear and the other out of curiosity. "Is it the Abwyd?"

Kinjour flashed them with a mischievous grin. "Well, we are near Odiam. The village lies just over that hill." He motioned to the right. "There is not much to see there, only a simple cluster of houses that sit smack on the edge of the borderland. Most are so ragged they are barely standing. Their residents have been hardened by life nestled between *Darkness* and Light and have gone quite mad."

The girls shivered.

"Bitter seasons have left them with nothing, yet they eke out an existence from their volatile surroundings. There is a graveyard there, bearing testimony to the danger of their changeable, forgotten corner of the nation. More lie in their graves than live. No worse danger rules there than the Abwyd, a horrible *dark*-born beast that roams the borderland, poisoning everything around it. No crops will grow—even in fertile soil— where the Abwyd crawls. At sunset, it will begin as it always does."

"Kinjour," Cait whined. "Stop it!"

Her brother laughed. "You started it. You know that thing can't possibly be the Abwyd. The Abwyd blends with its surroundings."

"Well, what is it then?" Goldya asked impatiently.

Kinjour hesitated only a moment. He was not one to admit his own ignorance, at least not when an adventure was at stake. "Let's go see."

"Kinjour! It could be dangerous," Cait objected. "The Abwyd's lair is—"

"So? That's the fun of it, Cait," he said with a grin.

"But it is getting dark," she pleaded, "and the Abwyd comes out at night."

"Go back to the orphanage if you want," Kinjour said with a dismissive wave of his hand. "I'm going down there."

"Kinjour!" Cait half-shouted, half-whimpered as her brother started down the other side of the hill.

Goldya stood poised on the crest. "You coming or not, Cait," she asked glancing back. "It will be fun. You'll see."

"I—I don't know."

"Come with us, Cait. Please?" Goldya said.

"Together?"

Goldya nodded and extended her hand. Reluctantly, Cait walked back up the hill to accept it.

"On the count of three," Goldya said.

Cait nodded. Dread flooded her senses as her friend slowly counted.

"One. Two. Three."

They ran down the hill. Kinjour glanced back at them. He grinned excitedly. "Last one down is a rotten egg!" he shouted back to them before taking off at top speed.

"No fair!" Goldya yelled back. She released Cait's hand and sped after him.

Cait's fear was lost in the excitement of the game. Her laughter flowed around her companions as she sought to overtake them both. The air rushed past her as if she were flying! She surged ahead.

"Oh, no you don't!" Kinjour yelled. The deep laughing words fell hotly on her neck. His strong hand closed around her waist and pulled her back. Everything faded as she struggled against him. Lost in their fun, neither noticed the strange cloud of silver dust turn toward them.

Goldya screamed. She tried to stop, but it was no use. She was moving too fast, and the hill was too steep. Kinjour freed Cait from his grip and raised his arms defensively over his head. This too was of no use. He was already too close to the darting silver figure. Cait clung to him. Goldya crashed into them, and all three hurtled through the air, smacking squarely into the cloud of silver dust. They were shocked beyond words when they impacted something hard, and it fell beneath them with a shout of, "Bonjour!"[2] followed by a "Humph! Ooof!"

---

[2]   French. Means: Hello!

The three children landed silently and abruptly in a tangled heap on top, but unharmed, as the silver dust rained down around them.

The thing beneath them moaned and groaned, shifting restlessly.

Cait and Goldya screamed and jumped away. "What is it?" they wailed, clinging to each other.

"I'm not sure," Kinjour said, rising to his feet. "I've never seen anything like it." He nudged the moaning form with his foot. It flopped like a dying fish and moaned even more pitifully. "Whatever it is, I think it is alive." Kinjour took a wary step back as it began to raise itself up from the ground. "Stay back," he said in nervous warning to the girls.

Cait and Goldya screamed again as it jerked its head up from the ground. Its head was cocked at an odd angle, and a snarling grin was on its lips. Greenish antennae, standing out from a furry brown mop, twitched from its head. Its ears pointed long and sharp, slanting back from his gaunt, sharply planed face on a head that at first looked far too big for the body it governed, but as the body unfolded itself, the impression faded slightly.

"EW!" Goldya squealed. "Squish it, Kinjour! Squish it!"

"I don't think it is a bug, silly," Kinjour said. "It's too big."

"Well, what then?" Goldya shrieked, clinging to Cait as they peaked out from behind Kinjour to get a better look.

Kinjour shrugged. "Don't know, but it sure is weird looking."

In the end, it stood as tall as a scraggly shrub, muttering to itself in a language the children could not understand, as it beat the grass and dirt off its clothes, which were green and red and woven entirely out of what appeared to be some kind of moss stitched together with a substance that looked remarkably like spider web. Silver dust puffed up with its every blindingly fast movement.

All three children stood as still as statues, watching openmouthed as it continued to shake and beat itself. All the while a strange trilling sound filled the air. Cait leaned around her brother more. Her eyes widened.

"Are those . . . wings?" she whispered hesitantly.

Suddenly it turned toward them. "Who wants to know?" It snapped.

Cait and Goldya shrieked, ducking back behind Kinjour.

"Don't tell it anything!" Goldya whispered.

"Don't even talk to it!" Cait nearly hissed.

"What are you?" Kinjour demanded, ignoring them.

"Don't you mean, who are you?" It asked indignantly. "I am not an *it*. I happen to have a name and a very good one too!"

Kinjour folded his arms across his chest and narrowed his eyes.

It raised its hands in response. "Fine. Fine. Have it your way. My name is Trin Thibodeaux, and I am a Fairy," he said emphatically.

"A Fairy?" Kinjour asked, his voice questioning the sanity of that answer. "There is no such thing."

Trin planted his hands on his hips. "Oh yeah? What makes you such an expert on the subject?"

Kinjour shrugged. "I've never seen a Fairy."

Trin laughed. "Until now, genius," he said before conking Kinjour on the head.

"Now see here—" Kinjour started to object, but before he could finish, Goldya darted out from behind him and kicked the Fairy in the shin!

"Take that you filthy bug!" she exclaimed.

"I am not a bug!" Trin wailed as he hopped around on one foot. "I am a Fairy!"

"Wait!" Cait exclaimed, jumping out from behind her brother. "Maybe he's telling the truth!"

Kinjour and Goldya froze, waiting anxiously as Cait crept forward. She reached out her tiny hand and stroked the small wings folded along Trin's back. One wing nearly covered the other, like a cricket's wing, only they were bright in color and had markings similar to those of a peacock's plumage.

Trin stood still with his one leg hoisted up, yet a strange almost purring sound came from his throat as Cait stroked his wings.

"Are they broken?" Cait asked gently. "Can you fly?"

"No." Trin smiled. "They aren't meant for flying."

"What are they for?"

"Decoration mostly," he said laughing, "ladies love them!"

"Now I know he's lying." Goldya said. "Everyone knows that Fairies can fly."

"And that's assuming there is such a thing as a Fairy," Kinjour muttered.

Trin tisked softly, shaking his head. "I never said I couldn't fly. I only said my decorous appendages were not for flying."

"Huh?" all three children asked at the same time.

Trin muttered under his breath in the foreign language, lowering his foot. Finally, he sighed. "I'll show you," he said. "Watch closely now or you will miss it." With that, he took off at a run. Within a second, he had disappeared, leaving only a cloud of silver dust behind him. In another second, he was back. The trail of silver dust made a wide, circular path behind him.

"How did you do that?" Goldya asked.

Trin Thibodeaux flashed them a triumphant grin. "A Fairy secret," he said with a wink.

Cait giggled, and even Goldya smiled. Kinjour frowned.

"Fairy or not, you have the stink of *Darkness* on you," Kinjour said. He drew a small knife from his belt. "I don't want any trouble from you. You're under arrest."

"For what?"

"Spying."

"Spying!" Trin's mouth fell wide open with disbelief.

Kinjour took the opportunity to tie a rope around the Fairy's hands and sheathed the knife. "I'm taking you to the An Taoseach."

"Spying!" Trin exclaimed again, incredulously, as Kinjour started to march back up the hill, pulling the rope behind him.

Cait and Goldya scrambled to keep up.

"Are you crazy? You can't take him to the An Taoseach!" Goldya screeched. "You're only an orphan! They'll never let you in the palace!"

Kinjour set his mouth determinedly and walked faster. "I'm going to be a knight someday."

"Don't be silly, Kinjour," Goldya snapped.

Cait slipped her hand into her brother's. "I believe in you," she whispered, "but what will happen to us?"

Kinjour squeezed her hand in response. "I'll take you with me. I won't leave you behind. Not any of you." He looked pointedly at Goldya, who smiled sheepishly in answer.

"Spying!" Trin exclaimed again, but as he looked up, his objections were silenced, for there upon the crest of the hill was a sight he could not comprehend. *Darkness* burned away. "What is it?" he asked in an awed whisper.

The children looked at him in surprise.

"What? The light?" Kinjour asked.

"Light?" Trin breathed the word. "This is Light?" He staggered and clawed his way toward the rosy glow peaking over the top of the hill. He collapsed on the top, raising his bound hands to shield his sunken eyes. "It's so bright! Is it always like this?"

The children laughed.

"No, it gets much brighter," Cait said through her giggles. "It's nearly nighttime now."

"Nighttime?" Trin gasped. "We heard rumors, but we never—I never—thought . . . I mean the *Darkness*, it's—"

"I don't think the Fairy has ever seen light before!" Kinjour exclaimed softly as words failed his prisoner.

The children fell silent, staring at Trin in wonder.

Chapter Twenty-Two

ABWYD

Odiam, Isear

"Stay close to the fire," the old woman whispered to what was left of her family. Of five children born to her, only one remained. The rest were fodder for the graveyard. Her one remaining child lay sick with fever from last night's attack. The old woman's husband stood over them; his one good hand held to a broken pitchfork, which was their only defense beyond the fire, and a poor one at that. Sunset was upon them. The Abwyd was stirring. "Be watchful," she said to her husband as she pressed a cool cloth to her daughter's brow. "One of my children will live to have children of her own!"

A high-pitched screeching pierced the uneasy silence of the twilight, sending shivers down their spines. The old man jerked restlessly from side to side, sensing the unseen danger somewhere in the green-black. "Stay back, you devils!" he shouted.

"Shh," the old woman said soothingly. Her daughter moaned.

The fire made the brooding shadows skitter in its light as another haunting cry echoed across the deep rolling hills. Like the wind, the cry echoed around them, with no discernable point of origin.

"Mamma. Papa. Do you see anything?"

"No," the old woman whispered. "Nothing."

"But I can feel it watching so that my skin crawls and my very bones seem to melt," the old man said. "It could be anywhere."

Just then another screech rose, this time closer than before, adding a foreboding warning to his words.

"Hush now," the old woman said sharply. "No more talk of prowling demons, lest you bring it down upon us!"

"The Abwyd is not a demon, mamma. I saw it with my own eyes. It is—"

"It nearly killed you," the old woman interrupted. "A demon it will always be!" she sighed. "Now please, no more talk unless you talk in prayer."

"What are words against that thing?" the old man grumbled. "The only thing it understands is blood and death."

The screeching grew louder.

"It smells easy prey," he whispered.

"No, Papa. It let me live."

"The poor child's out of her mind with fever. She doesn't know what she is saying. She doesn't remember," the old woman said softly.

Her husband nodded his gray head. "Quite mad she is, but—"

The old woman shook her head. "No false hope, husband. You will dig your own grave."

They huddled together in silence. Waiting. Theirs was not the only such fire outside the door of a broken house. Theirs were not the only whispers that had filled the twilight, but now all was quiet, the air was heavy with smoke, and the sky was veiled by Night. Just beyond the fires, invisible in the black, the Abwyd moved, slithering through the *dark*.

* * *

The purple hues of twilight faded into a luminous blue that slowly darkened before Trin's uplifted eyes; even this darkness was light by comparison to all he had ever known. Moon and starlight scattered across the heavens; their light paling as his gaze moved toward another far more pleasing light, but there was no explanation for this light—no circled orb, no fire's flame, no assigned orbit or fixed point—that his eyes could see. He could not bring himself to speak a word as he gazed upon its distant, ever-present splendor. Its scent filled everything in this land. It had no heat, as a fire's light would. It had no feel of sunlight. No smell of smoke or dawn on its iridescent back—he was beginning to feel a tingling inside of him as if the air he breathed was made of this wondrous sight for which no remembered story of his people had a name, and yet deep in his heart, where the light touched, he sensed . . . something; he just couldn't comprehend the rush of suffering, the thrill of agitation, the piercing sensation of need that had him fanatically shaking all over, laughing and weeping all at the same time.

Trin was well aware of the human children gazing at him as if he was mad, but he had no time to care for his vanity in their eyes. He had no time to care for anything! Light existed in this world of

Darkness! Countless generations had not fought and died in vain! Their blood did not cry unheard in the heart of the earth! Not now, not that he knew beyond any doubt that the rumors were true! As much as he wanted to stay here, he knew that he couldn't—not when his brothers and sisters, both in flesh and sword, were dying out there in the black abyss! Death was the dream of many. In reality, few really died; most fell as the Samhail had into *Darkness* never to be seen again—at least not to be seen as they had been, and this was the real torture of the Darkening War . . . He shook his head trying to clear his mind of the morbid images that sought to vanquish the glory of the Light before him.

Barely composed and still shaking uncontrollably, he searched through the gray sack slung over his head and shoulder. It hung low enough that he could still easily reach inside with his bound hands. His movements were blindingly fast and contained within furious puffs of silver dust. Only the tinkling of glass tubes betrayed his work as he pulled the specimen bottles into view.

"What are you doing?" Kinjour asked.

Trin ignored the boy, as he muttered to himself in his foreign language. "Air," he said as he waved the first specimen bottle in the air before quickly replacing and sealing the cap.

The children leaned closer, curious now, it seemed.

"Terre,"[3] Trin said as he struggled with vibrating fingers to dig a sample of the soil into the second specimen bottle.

"What's wrong, Trin?" Cait asked in a soft voice.

Trin ignored her too, though she was the only one of the three that seemed willing to believe him. "Leger,"[4] he said as he scooped some of the glittering embers, invisible to human eyes, from the ever-present Light. Once capped and sealed, he placed the first three specimen bottles back in his pouch and lifted the fourth and final one. "Eau." [5] He looked all around as he muttered to himself before suddenly taking off over the next hill where the black smoke of fire made it impossible to tell the division between this land and that of the Dark One, except for the lingering scent of Light.

"Odiam is that way," Goldya said.

"Wait!" Cait shouted.

"The Abwyd's lair is that way," Kinjour yelled, "and you're still under arrest!"

---

[3]   French word: earth

[4]   French word: light; having illumination

[5]   French word: water

Trin didn't even indicate he had heard them though he had, in fact, and was also well aware that they were pursuing him. He just didn't have time to care! A tiny stream flowed on the other side of the hill. He collapsed on its bank and thrust the remaining specimen bottle into its cool bed. The children arrived just as he was sealing the sample of water.

"Now see here!" Kinjour said sternly. "I've had about enough of you, bug—Fairy—whatever you are!" His dagger was in hand.

Trin placed the last bottle back into his pouch and lifted his face with a sheepish smile. "Calm down," he said. "No harm intended." He glanced toward the *Darkness* a bit impatiently. "I have to go."

"What don't you understand about, 'You're under arrest'?" Kinjour asked annoyed as he reached down and took hold of the rope, simultaneously sheathing his dagger.

"You're the one who doesn't understand," Trin snapped. *"I have to go."* He emphasized each word as if each made up its own sentence.

"On your feet, you stinking bug," Kinjour snapped, jerking hard on the rope.

Trin scowled. *"I am not a bug!"* he said, yanking back on the rope as hard as he could, throwing Kinjour off-balance. "You are!"

"Cait! Goldya! Help me!" Kinjour exclaimed. His face clearly showed his surprise at Trin's sudden outburst and unexpected strength.

Trin saw his opportunity and sprang to his feet, but he couldn't resist taking one more look at the Light. It was enough opportunity for Cait and Goldya to just grab hold of the rope; it was not enough to stop him from acting upon the decision he had made. With a sudden burst of speed, he shot down the steep hill toward *Darkness*. The children managed to keep a hold on the rope as he flew. Their screams echoed across the hills.

"Stop!"

"I knew you should have squished him!"

"I'm going to be sick!"

"You're under arrest!" all three shouted between choking, mouthfuls of silver dust, only to be drowned out by a horrible, sustained screeching that could be just one creature.

Trin skidded to a halt. The children crashed to the ground behind him. "Abwyd," Trin breathed in a quivering voice.

"You know about the Abwyd?" Cait whispered.

Trin nodded. "There are hundreds of them. They serve the Dark One. They guard his borders and eat the flesh of all who dare to withstand him."

"This one does not fear the light," Kinjour said.

"No, they wouldn't. They are completely blind, you see. The dark cannot sustain them when they are young. They have voracious appetites at birth. As larvae, they must feed upon good earth. There is none left in the realm of the Dark One, which is why they plague your borders," Trin whispered. "There is only one way to prevent them from poisoning the earth of your land. Wherever they lay their young, you must burn it. Tell your king this. It is the only way." He suddenly stiffened. "Shh."

"What is it?"

The children's gaze was riveted upon the eerily churning **Darkness**.

"Shh." Trin glanced at them. "Don't even move." He mouthed the words without making a sound.

The children froze, but they couldn't see anything. Kinjour itched to reach for his dagger; he forced himself to remain still—as still as a stone—as the first sounds of passage reached his ears.

Darkness.

* * *

"I'll be glad when the sun comes up," the scout said softly as he rejoined the beleaguered band of border patrol soldiers, breaking their tense silence.

The soldiers agreed in hushed voices. All had endured months of hard service, but come sunrise their replacements would arrive.

"One more night in this wretched hole."

"Be sure it is not your last!" their captain said sternly. His scowl made the scars on his face stand out. "Stay focused." A hush fell at his words. "I want something to show for our time here, for all our comrades who died here," he sighed. "I want the Abwyd's carcass. Tonight!" He motioned toward the fields and hills with his torch. "The peasants have their fires lit. It's out there somewhere. Find it!"

"It likes the fields," the scout said, "and we will never see it in time."

"Then burn the fields," the captain said fiercely.

"But the peasants—"

"Now!" the captain said in a tone that left no room for discussion.

"That's not the Abwyd," Kinjour said in a whisper as fire erupted across the fields.

"Soldiers!" Goldya exclaimed. "They can't find us out here or we'll be in big trouble!"

"Shh," Trin hissed, clamping his dirty hand over her mouth. His wild green eyes roved the darkened hills. His tubular green antennae twitched this way and that feeling for what his eyes could not see.

"Get your hands off her!" Kinjour shouted.

"Are you mad?" Trin nearly growled. "Do you want the Abwyd to strip the skin from your bones? I am trying to keep you alive, you stupid,

stupid human! So why won't you listen to me?" His voice rose into a shout that ended with him abruptly slapping his hand over his own lips.

"My brother is not stupid," Cait whispered. "Be nice."

Trin scowled. Kinjour flashed his sister with a playful smile.

"Now see here," Kinjour began in a reasonable voice, "I already told you, that is not the Abwyd. You are clearly overreacting."

"Overreacting, am I?" Trin said with a mocking smile. "Then what do you call that?"

An ominous shrieking echoed through the hills and burning fields. The children clustered together, eyes wide with terror. Kinjour drew his dagger, but Trin wasn't paying attention.

The Fairy stomped his foot in aggravation. "Humans are all the same!" he ranted. "You see only what you want to see. You never listen!"

"Oh, and Fairies are so perfect, are they?" Kinjour demanded.

Another shriek, this time dangerously close though still out of sight, silenced Trin's sarcastic answer.

"We can talk about this later," Goldya whispered. "Right now I think we should—"

"Run!" Cait screamed.

"No! They sense—" Trin did not get to finish. Kinjour grabbed the rope and yanked it, pulling the Fairy behind him as the shrieking Abwyd lurched from the blazing inferno of a nearby field.

*   *   *

Odiam, Isear

The old man looked down at the old woman who kneeled by their fitfully sleeping daughter. "The Abwyd has found its prey," he said.

She nodded. "We live another night."

The elderly couple smiled at one another as the Abwyd's shrieking moved off in the distance and the pounding hooves of the soldiers' horses pursued after it. It was hard to feel sorry for the one who would die when it meant that you and yours would get to live.

Darkness.

Chapter Twenty-Three

WALKING IN DARKNESS

This path was a dangerous one. Isentara knew, but how could she not take it when Lorshin might be at its ending. She could feel him in the *Darkness*, unable to answer her silent cries, yet pleading with her not to abandon hope. The *Darkness* was vast—far more vast than she had ever known it to be before—and her twin . . . the other half of herself from the womb . . . was lost in it. He could be anywhere. He needed her. All of her people needed her, so she could not turn back from the void. She could not heed the warnings of the Guardians and stay in the Light. No. She would walk in *Darkness*, clinging to her amulet of protection, and hope to find the lost before its power waned, and she too was lost.

Ruins of Rowlyrag

No illusion cloaked the depths of the ruined mountain. Lorshin shuddered despite himself, as its secrets were made known to him. Sithbhan said nothing as he entered but stood back allowing him to digest all that he beheld. A smile of wicked pleasure graced her lips.

A massive, cavernous hall spread before him. Its moist walls gave way here and there to blackened pathways and uncertain outcomes. Upon closer inspection, Lorshin glimpsed shadows of life within that foretold all was not as it at first appeared. The strangeness of it caused Lorshin to pause and study the blurring black images.

"Amazing, is it not?" Sithbhan asked. Her soulless, black eyes glinted with amusement. He was indeed interested in *her* work.

"What are they?" Lorshin momentarily forgot his game as he studied the black chasms with fascination.

"They are portals, my love."

He swallowed dryly. No further explanation was needed. They were doorways of Death, a direct route for *Darkness* to enter a single kingdom or a single life. Numbly, he passed them by: Fairy, Shee, Dwarves, Men . . . on and on they stretched, one for each kingdom of the world, until at last he came to one that revealed nothing though he could feel the blackness pressing in upon this portal stronger than at any of the ones before. *A kingdom where Darkness has no power!* Instinctively, Lorshin knew its name. It could be no other save Bynthroenine, the secret realm of Guardians, ruled by the Chosen One whom few had ever seen. It came as no surprise that this was the one kingdom into which the evil and the blackness could not pass at will.

"Someday that portal will be opened," Sithbhan said, her voice cloaked in *Darkness*.

Lorshin did not answer as he passed through the end of the hall where the stalactites and stalagmites formed dark arches, the pathway narrowing sharply before widening once more into a second chamber. *Darkness* filled its immeasurable expanse. His footsteps faltered on the brink of the lair. Did Sithbhan notice? He couldn't be sure as he searched himself for the will to go on. He did what he must to survive in the hope that one day his people would be free. Lorshin forced himself to take the step across the threshold. Death followed. He sensed her unnerving presence and felt her icy breath on his back. At that instant he knew that if any of them were to be free, he had to stay focused. Sithbhan he could fool, perhaps, but the Dark One could sense deception as easily as breathing. If he faltered even for a moment, all would be lost.

Lorshin passed, as quickly as he dared, from the second chamber into the third, barely allowing himself to think as the black was made deeper (if such were truly possible) by the addition of blackened stone and thick sulfuric vapors that hung like tapestries around a trickling pool. Dark stones formed uneven stairways on either side of it, joining together before rushing away into an even narrower path with an even more uncertain destination. He tried not to look down as he climbed the narrow stairway, which he realized halfway up it, was all that separated him from a fall over a deep precipice into the nothingness below.

With each step, Lorshin braced himself against the suffocating odor and the aura of evil growing more intense around him. He was all too aware of the *Darkness*. Its crushing weight slowed his footsteps. Sithbhan walked at his side in silence. She seemed to absorb the evil into herself, yet like the shadow, the evil was still separate from her. The evil was greater than she, and his father's withered black heart gave it even more power. He could not help but wonder, as he mounted the final steps, whether Sithbhan even knew how the *Darkness* wielded her. He suspected that some part of her did know. He immediately regretted this train of thought as he was forced to fight the overwhelming sense of pity and sorrow that gripped him. He had to remember that ultimately she was inseparable from the evil, possessed by the power of Death. If any good had ever been in her, it had died long ago . . . consumed by the *Darkness* she had taken into herself.

Lorshin forced his thoughts aside, sighing heavily. He must stay focused on the game at hand. He was playing against evil itself, and it would likely consume him too before the end, but maybe his people would have a chance. *Wise Ones, I beseech you. Come to me.* Sithbhan's icy hand on his shoulder startled him.

"My love, come with me," she commanded softly.

He forced a smile, though he was unnerved by both her touch and her dark, completely unnatural, and lusting gaze. If Death sensed his turmoil, she said nothing. It seemed she was content to possess him and his pretense of love. Her cold, pale hand curled around his and drew him after her. He had no choice but to follow, though every fiber of his being screamed for him to run. This was for his people. This was for Isentara!

Sithbhan guided him to the great chamber that lurked just out of sight. This room had been altered from its natural state, yet there was no taste of illusion in the air. A single structure dominated the room: a circle of ebony pillars entwined with golden serpents that supported a domed roof. Lorshin silently wished this structure had remained invisible. Four of his kind stood huddled together in a distant corner, bound by chains of shadow, waiting to serve their dark mistress in whatever manner she commanded. Summoned by his presence, each met Lorshin's gaze. There was an unquestioning trust visible in their eyes for the brief moment they looked upon him. His heart ached with sadness. *I am the Prince of the Samhail, no matter how unworthy I am of such a distinction. My people trust me. I cannot fail them again. I will not!*

Lorshin stood motionless for a long moment, trying to silence the inner quaking of his spirit. His heart pounded in his chest. Its beat rang deafeningly in his ears. Sithbhan's cold hand glided up his shoulder. He flinched as she spoke his name.

"Lorshin, my love."

Out of sheer force, he turned to face her. "Sithbhan," he numbly acknowledged her.

Death studied him with those blackened eyes. He forced himself to hold the gaze, to reveal nothing, to bury it so deep that in time he too would likely forget. She smiled coolly. "Come, my love, I have something to show you." The beckoning curl of her pale finger danced before his rigid face.

"What will you have me see, Sithbhan?"

"The last of the Calianith."

Lorshin frowned, sudden panic rising within him. He quickly forced it aside. "How can that be, my love?" he pried innocently. "I was at the final battle of the Guardian War when the alliance of the races joined the Guardians to face the Accursed race of which you speak, and Matwyn, their leader, chosen by the Dark One himself. They were all destroyed. I saw it with my own eyes!"

"Not all," she answered with a dark, pleased smile. "One survived, and she knows the art of the Gemshorn. A lot has changed in these centuries of your servitude, my love. Many wars are raging, but the Gemshorn remains silent, lost. Soon *I* will release this pathetic creature to reclaim the Gemshorn, and *my* power will grow. *I* will become more powerful than the Promised!" Sithbhan roared with maniacal laughter that was not her own.

Lorshin shuddered fearfully at the thought. *Wise Ones, hear me!* "Show me the Calianith," he said softly.

Sithbhan grew silent. Her eyes fixed on his face, but he could no longer meet her gaze. Averting his eyes, he waited. "Come," she said at last.

He followed her to a distant wall of black rock. At her touch, a secret panel opened, revealing a dimly lit room in which stood a large, man-sized cage. Inside this prison crouched the Calianith maiden. Surely, this accursed creature was nigh six thousand years of age, yet she looked to be just a child.

"The Calianith are not immortal, but they age very slowly."

Lorshin nodded. All this he knew. Silently, he studied the maiden. There was a feline quality to her movements as she shifted forward. Her evergreen garments rustled like leaves in the wind, but the movement threw the stench of her flesh into his face—mold and rot and blood. His stomach churned.

"Play us something," Sithbhan commanded.

Lorshin stiffened. He could almost hear the laughter in her voice as the Calianith raised a bone instrument to her lips. His gaze never strayed from the deep red of the Calianith's eyes. The song she played was familiar, yet weaker than he remembered, powerless except for the memories it brought to his mind. He recoiled from the sound.

Sithbhan laughed at his obvious disturbance and leaned close to him. "Just think," she whispered, "how powerful the Gemshorn will be!"

Lorshin frowned. No words could justly voice his torment. The Dark One's plans were further along than he had known, and he saw no way to catch up without giving himself fully into Death's hands. Her dark, impatient eyes fixed upon him. What could he say? "What makes you so sure this Calianith will serve you, my love?" he asked at last.

"*I* spared her life. In exchange for her assistance, *I* clothed her wounds in the emerald-black Flame that binds to the Heart of Evil. With it she can defend herself with a power no mortal can comprehend. *I* have given her the means to take revenge upon all those who killed her people." Sithbhan stroked his cheek gently. "Except for you, my love."

Lorshin stiffened. "And my people?"

Death frowned. "Yes, them too, my love," she conceded with a careless flip of her pale hand.

"And my twin?" Lorshin pressed.

"*I* gave my word, didn't I?"

Reluctantly, he raised his hand to touch Sithbhan's face (an attempt to keep her, and thereby the Dark One, off-balance, nothing more). Death melted into his touch. Despite the disquiet of his spirit, he leaned down to her. His lips softly, passionately kissed her as the weakened but strangely disorienting song rang around them.

Was it the song, remembered or otherwise, that suddenly made him long for Sithbhan? He could not answer his own question, yet he could think of nothing else save having her.

Darkness.

* * *

The world was much changed since her last memory of it. Isentara's eyes were transfixed by horrors she could not even begin to fathom. Her raw breaths came too loudly in this place, causing a strangely disembodied feeling as if she had fallen out of Time, but not even her breaths could cover the silence. The silence mirrored the emptiness inside of her. She wondered if any of it was real or if this was some illusion birthed in *Darkness*. It would be easy to lose herself here if it were not for the amulet around her neck.

The charm was simplistic in nature, but its rough design harbored a powerful Guardian rune that repelled *Darkness*. Still, the silence marred the feeling of safety the rune was intended to give. She had been warned, before leaving the realm of Guardians, that its power would be assaulted and, in time, broken by some unpleasant element of this grotesquely shrouded world. Even the trees, once proud, free roaming and alive, were themselves now standing frozen and quiet, trapped deep within themselves. Old friends lost to the silence infecting earth and air. Silence was merely the wound however. Oblivion was the end, and between them was unimaginable *Darkness*.

She dared not even whisper her twin's name in this place for fear she would find him as silent, or, worse, that he would not know her, trapped like the trees within himself—oblivious to everything even the silence. Isentara forced herself to take another step, her heart panging in defiance to these bitter possibilities. No silence could match the silence already inflicted upon her. There had never been a moment of her life spent in such loneliness. Even apart from Lorshin, she had known no silence, linked as they were, her twin and she, but now only *Darkness*, only despair, only her own muffled footsteps to break the portentous monotony of silence.

Was Lorshin out there, somewhere, being driven mad, as she was by this silence? Was he hoping she would find him or was he really gone, never to return from the *Darkness* as their father before him? Was she really alone, the last of her kind, forever?

Lorshin rolled away from Sithbhan with a sigh. It was not a sigh of satisfaction but of irritation. He had given himself to her, and he had enjoyed it! Where had the hatred, that ate his soul now, been when he needed its *strength* and determination? He could feel her beside him. Her delicate frame fit perfectly against him. Disturbingly so.

A sudden rush of panic jolted him from the gold-draped bed. His spirit was more unsettled than it had been before. *I hate you, Sithbhan, with every fiber of my being, and yet there are times . . .* He buried the thought deep inside himself. *Focus on the hate.*

The Calianith still played her erotically beautiful song. Each note hurt him and drove his senses wild. One or the other, either the song or the memory tried to control him but did not have the power. He could envision all too well what the Gemshorn could do and knew its song would be hard to escape. He shook his head, trying to clear it. At once the music ceased.

Lorshin looked toward the open passage. From the cage, the Calianith leered at him with her greenish lips parted to reveal catlike teeth, smaller and less powerful than his own.

"Samhail," she crooned softly, "lover of Death."

He scowled remembering the crimes of her race. "Calianith," he replied coldly, "accursed one."

"Accursed? I will be the mistress of the Gemshorn. You are a slave," she spat.

"Mistress, you say? I walk free. You dwell in a cage. Death spared you to possess your talent. You are a pawn, nothing more—replaceable, as others could be found to do the work the Dark One has set before you—disposable, as all the rest of your kind. You will never know true freedom again."

"No, Samhail. I will not be ruled by Death or the Dark One who governs her," the Calianith whispered. Her luminous red eyes met his.

Could it be that enemies understood one another?

"I am Zrene, daughter of Caruk," she said.

He hesitated, "I am Lorshin, Prince of the Samhail."

Both stiffened as Death's voice rang from the shadows behind him. "Lorshin is my husband."

He frowned. The chains of shadow formed about his wrists, drawing him back to her. How much had Sithbhan heard? His mind raced wildly. Her pale arms encircled him like a vice. He didn't struggle, though his lungs burned for air. Sithbhan's breath was cold against his neck. Her body taunted him. Frantically, he sought for something to distract her.

"When will you free the Calianith?" Lorshin focused on his question and her answer. He forced himself not to think on either his past sin or his strange yearning for her.

"Soon, my love, and then *my* game will truly begin!"

He felt himself being drawn further in her possessive embrace as Death concealed the Calianith once more. Sithbhan's voice caressed him, reviving the buried desires.

"Come, Lorshin, teach me more about love," she said huskily.

The Prince of the Samhail took a deep breath and turned into her embrace. He could play the lover, but for how long? His head lowered toward hers. When would play cease? How deep into this double life could he delve before it consumed him? How long before his **need** for her became too great and his allegiance faltered? Where did the game end and reality begin? He exhaled softly. The cleansing breath soothed his troubled spirit and gave him some semblance of control. Their lips met. Shadow completely enveloped him. The future of his people rested heavily upon his shoulders. In this game, he had to be the master, no matter the cost. *Wise Ones. Please hear me!*

Silence.

Darkness.

Chapter Twenty-Four

DREAD

*D*arkness.
     That living blackness, foaming out its own shame that hated thing breathing forth its mindless despair churned restlessly, sensing *something* beyond its borders. It could not shield me from that *feeling* of dread that stirred in the Heart of Evil.

What was that smell? My nostrils burned with a scent too glorious and pure to be of *Darkness*, but not pure enough to be one of the ghastly Light wielders returned from their secret realm of Light. What was that taste that made me gag in disgust? What was that hidden from my sight? What power withstood me if not one of my ancient foes? How? Why was it just now revealed when the world stood upon the brink of the void? What did I hear whispered beneath the screams and the screeching? Dare I listen? Dare I press in upon this mystery and expose myself to the unknown? Or do I content myself with only half a dominion? There really was no choice—not for me.

I had to know. I had to hear. I had to see.
Darkness.

Borderland, Near Odiam, Isear
     Kinjour risked a glance back over his shoulder as he crested the hill. "I thought you said this thing was blind!" he shouted to Trin.

"It is!"

"Well, it's gaining on us!" Kinjour snapped.

The Abwyd was so close upon his heels that he could see its pasty white eyes bulging too large and useless from its green, praying mantis face. Its pointy legs jabbed the air violently as it screeched. He could smell its putrid breath and see thick brown drool hanging from its horrible teeth as it lurched forward with its slimy wormlike body that blended into the fertile soil.

"I tried to tell you—" Trin shouted as they started running again, "the Abwyd senses movement! You'll never out run it!"

"And you think you could?"

"You're not listening again!" Trin shouted. He planted his feet, skidding to a stop. "That is so annoying!"

Kinjour ran until the rope pulled taut, completely ignoring Trin. He tripped, falling face first on the ground. "Now see here, I—" He pushed himself up, looking back in time to see the Abwyd leap right past Trin who was standing absolutely still with a mocking smile on his face.

"No way!" Kinjour exclaimed as he whirled around into an upright position.

Trin cringed, closing his eyes and shaking his head as the Abwyd tackled Kinjour before the boy could even defend himself. He peaked out of one eye to survey the carnage and found the Abwyd and Kinjour wrestling in a rolling heap of failing limbs and jabbing feet. Trin's mouth gaped open in astonishment despite himself.

"A little help here, please?" Kinjour said as the Abwyd knocked his dagger from his hand and he held back the pointy green feet from his face.

"You have to help, Kinjour!" Goldya shouted to him.

"I think we already established that he won't listen!" Trin said. "No one wants to listen to the Fairy-bug thing!" he said, indicating himself with overly dramatic flair.

"Guys!" Kinjour shouted.

"Quit being such a . . . such a . . . oh, just do something!" Cait screamed.

"Fine! But you have to promise to let me go."

"What?" Kinjour shrieked.

"We promise. We promise!" Goldya and Cait exclaimed.

"Not you," Trin said. "He has to promise." The Fairy looked pointedly at his captor who was just barely keeping the Abwyd off him. "What's it going to be, human boy?"

"I promise! Now get this thing off me!"

Trin smiled condescendingly at him. "I believe I already told you, but of course you were not listening."

"Trin!" all three children whined at the same time.

He sighed, "Just let go of the Abwyd and hold very, very still."

"That's it?" Kinjour asked, his voice rising.

Trin shrugged. "Or you could keep trying it your way." His smile was gone, and his voice had taken on an edge. "Because that's working so well."

Kinjour held his breath, closed his eyes, and let go.

The Abwyd shrieked angrily, jabbing him with those pointed green feet over and over again until Kinjour was sure he would have bruises from head to toe, yet he forced himself to hold still and endure it. His lungs screamed for air. He didn't dare to draw a breath. Suddenly, he felt the ground shake. *Horse hooves*! His mind exclaimed.

"Soldiers," Goldya whispered.

The Abwyd reared, feeling it too. It shrieked ominously. A glob of yucky brown drool pulled loose and fell with a plop onto Kinjour's face, making him gag. The weight of the Abwyd's wormy body came down full force on his abdomen so that he couldn't breathe, but its attention was no longer on him alone. It jabbed the air blindly, with its feet seeking the movement that dominated its senses. Horses circled. Their mounted soldiers armed with torch and sword stood in stark silhouette against the night. Their captain's slow, appraising glance took in the whole scene, missing nothing—not even the small dagger lying just out of Kinjour's reach.

"Boy, when I tell you, roll to your dagger," he said.

"You mean to use the kid as bait?" one of the soldiers whispered.

"Quiet," the captain said, but it was too late. Kinjour had already heard. He didn't respond as he was still struggling to breathe and hold perfectly still all at the same time. Truth was he had never felt so close to fulfilling his dream of knighthood as he did at this moment, and for that reason, he couldn't feel the proper fear!

The captain turned slowly in his saddle to address his men. "Dismount. Slowly. No sudden movements. Draw the Abwyd off the boy and then hold," he said in a hushed voice.

Kinjour knew the instant they made their move, though his eyes were still firmly closed. The Abwyd rushed off him with another ominous shriek.

"Now, boy!" the captain called.

Kinjour drew in a ragged breath and rolled. The Abwyd whirled toward his movement oblivious to the soldiers who stood like statues in an arc around it. Kinjour's hand closed over the hilt of his dagger, giving substance to his courage. He scrambled up onto his knees as the Abwyd lurched toward him.

The captain signaled his men.

Kinjour held his ground as the Abwyd towered over him.

The soldiers moved in with painful slowness upon their prey. Kinjour slowly rose to his feet; his eyes were fixed upon the captain. The soldiers used their torches, setting the Abwyd ablaze. It roared and screamed, thrashing all around. The captain nodded once toward Kinjour, who sprang toward the creature's exposed heart as it reared back. His blade sank up to the hilt in the slimy flesh. The captain pulled Kinjour free as the Abwyd folded in upon itself, a mass of oozing flesh and flame.

"I want the carcass! Put out that fire!" the captain shouted. He shoved Kinjour aside as he barked orders to his men. "Hurry up! Careful! It belongs to the An Taoseach!"

Kinjour fell to the ground too weary to object. Goldya, Cait, and Trin gathered around him silently. The girls stroked his feverish brow while Trin gazed silently toward the blackness looming below. He muttered a bitter oath in his foreign tongue, knowing he could never run beyond the reach of the vacant hunger of that stare.

Darkness.

* * *

Here was no ordinary thing. I couldn't bear it even wrapped safely within the borders of my own *darkness*. This was not of Flame, neither Light nor *Dark*, but something new . . . something that I had not anticipated and could not yet comprehend—something much like a dream that a dreamer did not want to lose, but at the same time, one that the dreamer didn't dare to hope for either, wrapped up and tucked away in a special, secret place only the dreamer knew. But who was the dreamer and what was the dream? I burned as I had before the Source so long ago, but there was no lure of predominance and power here, no presence that surpassed all presence, no reason I could *see* for the dread coiling within the Heart of Evil—nothing beyond the unknown cause of the torments clawing at my other senses: the stench of purity, the sound of Light tinkling softly down from Moon and starlight, the taste of ancient Guardian breath undiminished by the void, and above all the *feeling* that I was missing something. It was a *feeling* that had plagued me since the Great Exodus, pacified for a time by the darkening, yet never vanquished. For this *feeling* I had no name. It went beyond mere dread into something deeper, darker, and more consuming than anything I had felt since the *beginning*. Something akin to the lust that had birthed me forth only fermented into something wholly unrecognizable. Now, as then, I wanted this thing beyond my reach, yet I feared it. There was no denying this fact.

This was *someone* else's dream, and what was the use of a dream unless . . . Still the scent of humanity promised an easy victory. What did they know of dreams?

Dreams were the culmination of all Light and *Darkness*, harnessed together within all of creation—the nethermost doorway to each individual soul that was the region of choice, the tainted heart lurking within all life, so easily manipulated into fodder for the void. Dreams had always been within the reach of my domain. What were they more than illusions? The unknown plagued my mind, and then I heard it—the whisper, too faint at first to be understood . . . a breath sighing inaudibly from the earth, felt like a voiceless wind. It mounted slowly out of solemn, deathlike silence, rending the air with a pandemonium of whispered voices, echoed by nature's muted cry.

LettheLightshineforthandawakenhope.LetMhoragarise.Letthe Promised come.

"No!" I screamed, but the whisper didn't stop. It continued to mount in blatant defiance to my will. Nothing had withstood me this way since the days of the Guardian War. *Darkness* hissed, unable to deaden those words rising more and more and more, one upon another upon another, upon another around me.

LettheLightshineforthandawakenhope.LetMhoragarise.Letthe Promisedcome.LettheLightshineforthandawakenhope.LetMhorag arise.LethePromisedcome.LettheLightshineforthandawakenhope. Let Mhorag arise. Let the Promised come . . . I screamed, but my screams meant nothing, because in that moment I looked up and I *saw*, and all *Darkness* with me, those horrible burning shadows.

Darkness.

Chapter Twenty-Five

A STAR COMES FORTH

Two forces stood deadlocked against each other. Light and *Darkness*, entrenched in bitter equality and silence, waited, but for what? From the unfathomable height and breadth of the Kingdom, the Source watched with eyes that felt they had seen too much already, ageless and eternal, he gazed from the solitude of the Orb of Power—Breath and Flame and existence—where the passage of Time meant nothing.

The universe, a seemingly endless black expanse of spiraling galaxies, revolved around itself, or rather, in reality, revolved around the invisible pull of his power. Sun and Moon, a maze of perfectly aligned constellations, and rotating planetary systems, appearing to hang independently in space were in truth held in place by his existence alone, maintaining their courses in restless confinement on the magnetic currents of his Flame that had been drawn upon by Sanctus so long ago to create everything that was, that is, and that one day will be. It filled the emptiness like dust grains coated with ice. This afterglow of power dissolved slowly into invisibility, but would never cease to be.

Further within this vastness, seasons of Time played through their courses, once consistently governed by Light, but now disrupted by the shifting of *Darkness*, breaking the intended balance of the seasons (this being in those regions where *Darkness* had not completely overcome the natural workings of the world). Only one place stood free of this corruption, forged in the midst of burning shadows standing boldly against the *Darkness*, growing strong and brazen with the passage of Time. From this height, the glow of power splintered into every spectrum of the rainbow—most notably the invisible ultraviolet, shining like a weird star from the heart of the universe like an X indicating the spot of a buried treasure. But whose treasure was it?

Strange though it was, this point of freedom, far distant from his own little sanctuary, pulled more fiercely into alignment with him than all the rest of the universe combined. It was his tears for the screams of the rest of the universe that had set the shadows aflame and bathed this land in its own miraculous dawn, though no one heeded this estuary of hope save its own inhabitants, and they blindly so. Time brought forgetfulness even there, and what should not have been forgotten was lost to legend. The Source continued to watch in desperate wonder as the universe turned through its courses. He alone never changed, yet the pull of power intensified day by day till even he was on the verge of burning. His hands pressed harder against the walls of his breath; the agony of these moments intensified in every fiber of his being, from the molten, golden blood spiraling visibly beneath the surface of his flesh toward its bed in his crystal heart, to the dance of colored Flame and the liquid steel of his breath, to the cast of his once amber eyes now inflamed with the same indescribable liquid gold of his blood.

The Source moaned and all Flame with him. Focused beams of living Light erupted from his burning eyes with a nameless hunger. The Orb of Power seemed to swell while he himself felt diminished, as if a change were coming that he was not certain he was ready to face. It was just a feeling, yet his gaze remained fixed, unwaveringly, upon the spot where the unnatural star beckoned with the same nameless hunger, almost as if he looked upon a reflection of himself deep, out of focus, and incomplete upon the darkened mirror of the universe. *Impossible. Terrifying. Mysteriously captivating.* What did it mean? Why was it there, and why could he feel it in the very core of his being?

Darkness.

* * *

An aura of decay hung heavily over Firinn—once the height of all glory, the footstool of Sanctus, it now soared forlorn, decrepit, and forgotten through the *dark* abyss. Its towering pinnacle ascended like a pale spike of pearl stone against the *darkness* that was alive with timeless anger. The echoes of the Dark One's growl surpassed even the wind's piercing wail.

The Summoners rose from their beds upon the base of Firinn with awe as the earth and the stones roared against it—a chorus of lamentation that haunted the world, dripping down like rain even from the black bound peak of Firinn. The voices of earth and stone bled with ancient sorrow, as through the unyielding *Darkness* a far distant halo of burning shadows broke into view. *Darkness* brooded in silence all around its vast circle. Though the luminescence lay upon its borders, it offered no real hope to the Dark One's prisoners beyond the fragments of hope still hidden in their memory, stories handed down from Ages past, myths, legends, nothing more. It burned out of the endless sea of black and back into the abyss, yet its weak light seemed to confirm all the whispers of the forgotten Ages, still more dream than reality, but it was enough, for the moment.

Master Esarian ran forward, casting off the burdens of his mind, and gripped the cool stone of Firinn determined to see, if he could, what lay beyond those burning shades. If there was any truth to be found, the legend, he had so far ignored, told him he would find it upon Firinn's pinnacle. He would not allow himself to think of the difficult task before him lest the fear of it would keep him from the revelation he sought. Perhaps this was a test. Perhaps the *Darkness* had broken him. Perhaps this was indeed a trap, yet he had served others' hopes and dreams since birth and he had to know once and for all if this fight was in vain. His own history was inseparable from the *Darkness*. For eight years, *Darkness* had taken their toll upon him. Born a Summoner, to Summoners, he had never known anything else. His mother, he had been told, fell in *Darkness*—a warning tale designed to make him fear the very substance that cradled both his waking and his sleeping. Her name was never spoken, and so she remained more a figment of myth than reality. His father, on the other hand, brought with him many unpleasant, but quite real memories. Memories Esarian kept by sheer force in the shadows of his mind. He had never known a life beyond the shadow of Firinn. The first three years of his life he had been reared upon the legends of forgotten Ages. He had heard the stories of a Time when Guardians walked among the races, when Light was a thing of beauty not a vacant hope. He had heard of the time the Dark One came to power, how he had scattered the old Summoners to the winds, and even those who had stood against the Dark One had in time ultimately abandoned the Resistance to the hands of younger more inexperienced Summoners for the sake of their own lives—some scarred to the point of madness. He had seen firsthand the ravages of Death and *Darkness* until only children remained, confined to Firinn and a thread of power that lingered—a mere hollow fragment of the glory his ancestors had imagined. For all eight years of his life, he had known nothing but this war. For three of those years, he had been its commander in chief by mere fact that he was eldest among them. Yet what more did he have to give? He knew nothing but *Darkness*, nothing but despair.

"What are you doing?" one of the Summoners whispered.

Esarian wasn't sure who had spoken. All the Summoners gazed at him completely dumbfounded.

"I . . . need . . . to . . . see," he said between ragged breaths of both strain and desire as he pulled himself higher.

"Are you mad?"

"You will fall to your Death!"

"And if not, only *Darkness* awaits!"

He ignored them.

Firinn seemed to be helping him. Footholds appeared where he had expected to find none. As his hands sought higher perches, the stone complied. Its smooth pearl surface that he had rested against all his life now offered him strength, rough places to grip, and even pockets of moisture to cool his brow and quench his thirst. The pinnacle, however, never seemed to get any closer though the Summoners appeared smaller inch by inch and finally disappeared altogether in the black fog below as if the pinnacle too was testing him and the desires of his heart, almost as if it wanted to know he was true before it revealed the truth.

The air was heavier. It was harder to take breaths. Perhaps it was the *Darkness* fighting against him. Perhaps it was just the weakness of his body, wasted as it was by the poisonous breath infecting everything around them. But the burning in his chest grew stronger inch by horrible inch of his climb. His hands and his feet dripped with blood, the flesh worn out with use, yet he pushed higher, refusing to look down, only looking up toward the unattainable pinnacle. It was impossible to tell the passage of Time, and the feeble brownish glow of Gnome light did not extend this high. Even the normal, eerie red glow of the Styarfyre orb shard around his neck was faded, offering no comfort. His body throbbed with agony, yet he pulled himself higher. Suddenly, it gripped his mind that this was what Hope felt like—agony, yet expectation; violence, yet mercy; consuming, yet yielding to outside choices; hunger that could never be satisfied until the object of Hope was achieved, no matter how hard or long it might be. So long as those who sought it remained steadfast in their purpose, Hope would never fail. This was why, though Ages had brought forgetfulness, the Summoners held to their stories! This was why he had been abandoned in the shadow of Firinn as his parents willingly faced their deaths for a dream! As soon as he embraced this realization, he tumbled forward onto Firinn's pinnacle. There he found a bowl of stew, a chunk of bread, and a large golden chalice of fresh milk—almost like an offering of welcome from an unseen host.

Esarian, too weak to take another step, crawled toward the nourishment. How long had it been since he began his ascent? Did the other Summoners think him lost to the void? Was he? Was this all a dream or worse, a trick? His bloody hands closed around the chalice. It felt real enough, but then again, the Dark One's illusions could feel real too. His mind grappled against itself as whispers flowed around him until his hunger overcame his hesitation and the pangs of his stomach became unbearable. Only then did he lift the chalice to his parched lips and drink deeply of the offering. Nothing happened, so he took a bite of bread and then a bit of stew before finally setting aside his fear completely and devouring the meal in its entirety. No food had ever tasted as this. Some childish corner of his mind imagined he had never truly eaten anything in all his eight years. For a time, he quite forgot his purpose, relishing in this dreamlike bubble above the world. Only when his fingers and the dishes were licked clean and the dishes had vanished as mysteriously as they had appeared did Esarian awaken enough to find himself changed. His wounds were gone without a trace. His flesh bore a healthier tinge, and even his breaths came easier, though the height was great enough for the air to have thinned considerably. He crept toward the edge, remembering the burning shadows and what had lured him here. Fear sent chills down his spine. What if he found nothing? He tried to convince himself it wouldn't matter, but the truth was it did matter. It mattered so much that he would rather fall from this pinnacle to his death than look for Hope and find it did not exist. This sudden revelation made him hesitate. He had come seeking Truth, and it seemed the first truth he must face was his own. Other children had guides. He was alone, and for the first time he felt that caged pain—sorrows pressed down out of want for survival, yet it was this *Darkness* that was devouring him. He watched it rise as he released it all with deep, shuddering cries . . . the memories that held him captive.

All his memory hinged upon a single moment. The moment that had transformed all the stories of his ancestors into just that—empty dreams—truth wrapped in legend, buried in myth, told and retold, transforming with each telling into something darker because the *Hope* it shrouded was buried further away, removed from the dreamer by Time and silence. He had resisted this memory for over half his life, yet it came now, unbidden, from the shadows . . .

Everything was *dark*, as it always was. His father stood before him, screaming mutely with some long-forgotten horror painting his gaunt and weathered face, and then, it happened . . . his father pitched forward and was falling.

Desperate screams filled the silence. "Hold on, Daddy. Please hold on." A little child crashed through the black and fell upon his father's still form, pounding on the unmoving chest with his tiny fists as he tried to beat the life back into the fallen man. "Daddy, please be okay. Daddy! Please don't go, Daddy!" he said, hope dying in the sound of his own voice.

All the Light went out. His breath caught in his throat as he buried his face against his father. His one wish was to go too. His lungs hurt from not breathing by the time the arms of some faceless Summoner wrapped around him. Clinging to his father as those foreign hands pried his fingers free with strength he could not resist. His mind and body rejected the touch, dead weight in unwanted arms that lifted him away from his father and pulled him close.

"Breathe, Esarian," said a woman's voice. "It's over. The Dark One's gone. You are safe." Her warm lips brushed his tear-stained cheek as she rocked him. "Come on, child. Your lips are turning blue. Breathe," she whispered.

He felt her breath upon his face as she whispered to him, just a breath . . . a breath that had shattered everything. He drew in a ragged breath, laced with the perfume of this woman's flesh and found no comfort in it. The first nagging pains of loss came from deep inside, and he clenched himself against them from the inside out. Everything seemed so much darker than it had before as if his world had lost its color, yet he continued to breathe in and out, in and out. No hope. No dreams. Just empty, unfeeling air. What was the other anyway? Words . . . just words . . .

Those memories were faded, scattered, and fragmented by time, but the pain was not. It was new, almost alive as it came to torment him, yet by some merciful happening, it was not allowed to take hold. Rather it was forced away almost as if a shield had been raised against it. Immediately, the earth shuddered, knocking him back, as the stones shouted with the awakening of memory far older than itself. Time slowed, and all creation waited in deathlike silence as a swell of wind lashed furiously around the great pinnacle. Voices whispered to him from its depths in unison, with a host of strange Lights dancing upon it. Esarian imagined figures in the mist carrying those translucent Flames of semi-ghostly blue and white. Before these phantoms, the erosion of time held no power. Firinn stood firm as all else faded into nothingness, leaving only a mound of bones laid bare, far below, in the unformed earth. A pool of liquid gold—almost burning it seemed—rippled through the *Darkness*. It easily washed over him while the phantoms beat an ominous rhythm upon the ground.

Esarian drew back with sudden apprehension. A small cry escaped his lips as the burning gold slowly pealed back even the crust of his

192

weakened, if somewhat improved, body to reveal the smooth, succulent flesh of a young boy—untouched by the unnatural hardships of this Age. The voices resounded in his head as this *dream* held him there, frozen and incomplete.

"Do you wish to remain lost between two forever?"

The question was an unusual one and not easily answered. For if this was indeed a dream, the question's answer could be a trap. Dreams were but a fraction removed from illusion, and illusion brought the *dark*, its master. Yet if his answers were to be found then the question must be answered. Esarian considered this as the dancing Flames glowed demandingly before his eyes.

"I have faced many things and suffered many pains to see this war ended and all Races walk free, yet I know not what I seek for myself," he answered cautiously.

"That is not the answer to the question that was asked." The voices made the Lights shine more brightly though they broke gently around him . . . no longer threatening in nature. "You are seeking, what, you do not know, but come. Look deeper and you will know."

"What will I see?" Esarian asked, both curious and wary at the same time.

"For one upon Firinn there is but one answer."

Esarian leaned forward. "And that is?"

"Truth." The voices drifted away into utter silence, and the Flames parted before him, igniting the eerie red glow of the Styarfyre orb.

Esarian crawled cautiously toward the edge once more. The wind, blowing softly, carried the lingering scent of oblivion upon its back, making him question once more whether this was a dream or reality, but the Flames held constant, hissing against the encroaching gloom. Dark heaven receded like a curtain gradually drawn open, and across the miles, his weak, human eyes glimpsed the same burning gold suspended in the earth. It crowned the borders of *Darkness* with fire and flowed like water, each droplet shining like a weird diamond in the night (a star perhaps, for no other explanation seemed fitting, yet it was like no star ever seen or heard of before). It seized him once more, and his hand stretched toward it, ignoring the danger of the edge; so desperately did he want to touch it.

It dawned on him suddenly that he should be plummeting to his death, yet he was not. The Flames seemed to be gazing expectantly at him now. He could hear the whispering once more.

Truth to expose the defilement of all hearts
Righteousness so that all may know their unworthiness and sin
Justice to satisfy the wrath of he who was forgotten

Mercy to hold back destruction, for the Promised will come in the appointed time.

Grace to all who will remember there is still hope.

Peace, for even in Darkness you are not forgotten.

Joy, for your hope shall come and Light shall shine forth once more to all who will but call in true humility!

Each Flame manifested, leaving its brand upon his forehead before draining away. Esarian found himself alone, scarred, and yet somehow complete. No longer did he fear to dream. The Flames had burned all that away. As he looked down at himself, he saw that he too had been made new. Only his white robe, stained with blood and black, and the Styarfyre orb shard remained as evidence of his former self—wasted and ruined no more. A new voice drifted down from the heavens on visible puffs of air.

"I am Sanctus," the voice said. "One who seeks is always found. It is I who has chosen you. Remember this and be strong."

As the god spoke, Esarian trembled, but when silence returned, he found the boldness to question the heavens. "May I see you?"

"In time," Sanctus said. "The time is not now. The place is not here. There is much work for you to do. You are the Firebrand, the mouthpiece of he who is Promised, he who will come."

"Tell me of the burning shadows."

"They are his, and he will fill them," Sanctus said softly.

"When?"

"That answer is not for you. Remember the Prophecy. Remember and be strong. Much *Darkness* is yet to come." The voice drifted away, and the black descended as the light was extinguished.

Esarian stood upon Firinn's pinnacle, gazing upon the distant burning shadows. He could see them clearer now. Light came—a single Flame—falling from the apex of the universe, through space, tumbling down to earth where it seemed to break to pieces, filling the wounds and burning against the *Darkness*. These splintered fragments—each their own blue-white Flame—were but linked to the greater Light (the sheen of gold) that carved a hole in the borders of the *Darkness*. A rain of Light. A rain of power.

Hope was no longer the dream of his ancestors. It was his *purpose*, and he would see it through so long as Sanctus gave him breath. Maybe it would not come in his lifetime, but someday. He would preserve its dream for his own children and for those he led; and if called upon to do so, he would gladly give his life for its sake. Truth had indeed set him free.

Darkness.

*   *   *

That living blackness foaming out its own shame that hated thing breathing forth its mindless despair coiled around itself, attempting to keep me blind to the horror shining before me, but it was no use. The shine of that earthbound *star* could not be ignored for all my will and *Darkness*. I tested the air with my nostrils. The scent of Guardian lingered there, but it was faded, almost gone after so many centuries of silence, as all Guardian scent was faded, for they no longer walked within this realm—not since the days of the Great Exodus. I dared not draw any nearer. The Light was strange. No Guardian Flame, no Guardian breath had caused this, at least not alone, and my senses could not detect a source. This was not wholly unexpected. Guardians were mere servants after all. No, this was something greater, but not complete—a promise long forgotten—an expected coming, but a coming of what? I couldn't pinpoint the cause of my unrest. The Flames breathed forth by my departing enemies still lurked in the earth, but they did not explain what I saw now.

The strange light held no power of its own, almost like it was a shadow, a reflection perhaps, that seemed to emanate from no single source but hung over the land as a burning gold mist darkening to crimson as it clashed upon the borders of *Darkness*, which could not penetrate the wide berth of this land—land and a kingdom I had no knowledge of until this very moment. It reeked of humanity, yet no human had concealed themselves from me. Who, if not the Guardians? Why, if this was not a plot of the Light? When, if not in *my* Time? What was the secret? How had it been kept from me for all this time? *My time!*

I growled defiantly, "The void will come!"

Darkness.

Chapter Twenty-Six

THE FIREBRAND

Darkness watched, waited, a breathing, preying creature coiling upon itself and those it held prisoner. Round and round billows of black breath swirled, growling and snarling as it blotted the burning shadows from their sight. The Summoners watched in silence, unable to feel even the slightest yearning for the return of the distant, strange light. With the descent of *Darkness*, the Gnome light flickered back into view, and they found comfort in its brown glow as they too waited. Its weak glimmer—not far removed from total blackness—contented their troubled souls, silencing the questions of their minds before they were totally formed. They felt safe here now in the shadow of Firinn, in the black as they waited for Esarian's return.

No one in all the remembered stories of Ages past had ascended Firinn. It was said that only a Guardian by wing or magic could attain its pinnacle and meet with the god who once rested his feet upon it, and they only by right of the Flame burning in their hearts that linked them to their creator. So the stories said, yet the Summoners though they could recite the stories, had long since stopped embracing them. They fought now only because they had not yet embraced the *Darkness* either. (The stories of their parents were still too fresh in their memories for it to take hold, but one day, as all the rest before them, these Summoners would fall or flee or die. Of this the Dark One was certain, though they, themselves, were too blind to see it.) Firinn was a smooth obelisk standing against the black, but its meaning was clouded in doubt and forgetting like the Summoners themselves.

"How long has it been?" D'Faihven asked in a whisper. She was the tallest of the Summoners being of the Giant race. She limped forward on her broken foot.

"Too long," chirped Nulet, the smallest of the Summoners being a Poeth, a rare race, seldom seen, and therefore often declared extinct.

Their whispers went largely ignored by the other Summoners from whom they stood a few paces apart. Esarian was their dearest friend.

"He is no doubt dead or corrupted," Orlok snapped, overhearing their whispers thanks to the supersensitive hearing of the Dwarf race of which he was part. "Esarian was stupid even to try!"

Nulet whirled around his tiny hands balled into fists while his hair burned like a rupturing volcano (a place uniquely suited to the fiery Poeth).

"What?" Orlok said defensively. "Everyone knows it was crazy to go up there."

The other Summoners nodded in agreement.

"Oh yeah!" Nulet shouted.

"I say we vote for a new leader," Orlok snapped. "Esarian isn't coming back."

"I'll rip your ears off!" Nulet shouted, flying forward with lightning speed. "I'll tear you all to pieces!"

D'Faihven hobbled forward, her head down like a charging bull, to pluck Nulet from Orlok's nose where his teeth were sunk in. "Stop it!" she said. "Stop it, all of you!"

Orlok thrust his pudgy hand out wildly and caught her in the middle of her three eyes, momentarily blinding her as she continued to crash forward. The dwarf knocked Nulet off his nose a second before he saw her falling. His startled cry was silenced beneath her.

"Get off me!" Nulet shouted from the bottom of the pile where he had been thrown. He pushed them up with obvious pleasure.

"Sorry, little buddy," D'Faihven said, extracting herself from the dangle of limbs. "Did I hurt you?"

Nulet hopped free with a wide smile. "No. I'm small and mighty like an ant!"

Orlok grumbled as he pulled himself free.

The other Summoners had lost all interest in the tussle of their companions. Orlok joined them, still grumbling, and holding dramatically to his bleeding nose. His complaints, however, were silenced in mid-sentence as Esarian dropped to the base of Firinn.

"Esarian!" Nulet and D'Faihven, the giant choosing to hop precariously on one foot to keep from being slowed by the broken one, exclaimed together as they rushed forward.

He gave them a guarded smile (one not free of trouble or fear, but closer than ever before) as he walked forward to embrace them.

The Summoners gathered around. Their faces were masked with uncertainty as the bravest reached out to touch the strange scars upon Esarian's forehead. Though he had not borne the evidence of wounds when he left them, they looked years' old—no longer angry wounds as they surely must have been to leave their marks so deep—yet they showed no signs of fading either. They were etched upon his pale skin almost as if they belonged there, no more alarming than the ridges on the skin of the fingertips, but there was something about them that held the Summoners in rapt silence around their master.

Aware of the *Darkness* harboring its master, Esarian beckoned them into the shadow of Firinn once more. The trace of power he had felt there now seemed hopelessly weak. He feared the slightest push of the *Darkness* could shatter its pocket of safety, yet for the moment it held giving them Time to plan and prepare. Esarian whispered to them all that he had seen and heard and felt up there above the world. He did not know what came next. He did not know if they would live or die, but his story was closer than all the rest. His story brought strength, and when it was told, the Summoners melted back into the shadows of Firinn.

Some time passed in silence.

Nulet sighed, "The scout should have returned by now."

D'Faihven placed another brick of Gnome Waste upon the fire.

Orlok nodded as they all listened to the crackle of the flame. The former quarrel between them was already forgotten. "Do you think he has been lost?"

"The scout may be alive. Fairies are like cockroaches."

"Not exactly, Orlok," Nulet said with annoyance, "but I do agree there is a chance he is alive."

The Summoners whispered one to another, making no decision one way or the other.

Esarian sat cross-legged in their midst. The brands on his forehead tingled, uneasy with the *Darkness* pressing all around them. *Firebrand.* The voice whispered back through his memory with callings all its own. He could not tell what it called him to, and so he remained silent . . . waiting for some undeniable sign.

Darkness.

Chapter Twenty-Seven

BOUND

Borderland

Trin Thibodeaux shuddered inwardly as the *Darkness* grew silent. There was no comfort in its silence, but a perspiring of dread, fear, and anger that would build within its confines, as pressure builds in the earth, deceptive in its muteness until a rupture begins. Only it would not be lava that exploded from this volcano. His eyes fixed with wonder upon this thing called Light—still shining bright, though Night was well upon the land. Its allure captivated him again, pulling him into itself, yet he felt sure that this Light was a portent of worse things to come. As he gazed upon it, however, his heart could not maintain its fear, and he found that he wanted to believe the whispers of promises handed down from *the times before*.

So distracted was he by these private thoughts that he failed to notice when the soldiers ceased their frantic work of trying to save the Abwyd's carcass from the fire and remembered the rest of their quarries.

"What about them?" one of the soldiers asked gruffly, invading the private meditations of the Fairy.

From the tone of his voice, Trin wondered if these humans had even noticed the *Darkness* screaming upon their borders. His quick eyes took in each of the soldiers hard faces, taking note that such faces could harbor many secrets and that perhaps they felt more, heard more, than they were willing to show. The fire was out, and what was left of the Abwyd had been carefully wrapped and loaded onto a packhorse to be taken to the palace . . . a place Trin would have loved to see in this land of wonders if he only had the time, which he did not . . . the Resistance was waiting.

The captain glanced down at Trin and the children disdainfully as if they were dung that he had stepped in and now had to laboriously scrape from his shoes. His face told a different story now that Trin had singled him out from the rest. This was a man hardened by *Darkness* so that he felt nothing and cared for no one but himself. "Arrest them. Bind their hands together. Lead them behind the horses."

Trin sighed dramatically, his gaze shifting to Kinjour who lay delirious with fever; some of the Abwyd's drool had no doubt gotten in his mouth, and the girls kneeled in a mothering hover on either side of him. "Not again!" Trin exclaimed.

"On your feet!" one of the soldiers said as he came toward them.

"On what grounds do you do this?" Trin asked defiantly.

"In the name of the An Taoseach," the captain said as if this was the beginning and end of any possible objections.

"Oh! That just explains everything!" Trin snapped in exaggeration. "I am on a mission of great importance. I have no time for this!" His antennae twitched furiously as he shook from head to toe with pent-up rage.

"You're not human. What are you?" The captain rode forward till he towered over the Fairy.

Trin nearly growled, "Here we go again. I am not a *what!* I am a *who!* I have a *name!*"

"As of right now, you have a tongue also," the captain said fiercely, "but that could change."

"I'd like to see you try!" Trin shouted, rocking up onto the balls of his feet so that he came within an inch of the horse's nostrils.

The horse jerked back nervously, sensing the *Darkness* that still riddled his clothes with its stench.

"Shh," Goldya hissed and elbowed him hard in the side. "Are you trying to get yourself killed?"

"*Ow!*" Trin turned on her with squinted eyes and stuck out his tongue.

"You're welcome," Goldya whispered as the Fairy rubbed his bruised side.

The captain sighed as he slowly turned his horse.

"Please, sir," Cait cried when a soldier yanked her to her feet and roughly tied her hands, "my brother is sick. He helped you! Why are you arresting us?" Her little voice broke in the perfect spot to make even the hardest heart falter.

The captain glanced back at her. "You children are out after curfew." He jerked his head toward Trin. "As for that one, I don't like the look of him."

"I arrested him too," Kinjour moaned softly.

"You?" the captain said with mockery.

200

Kinjour nodded. "He has the stink of **Darkness** upon him. I thought him a spy, but now—"

"There you have it," the captain interrupted. "You are not only out after curfew, you are associates of a spy. Your lives are in my hands."

"You mean the An Taoseach's hands, don't you?" Kinjour said weakly. "Isearian law—"

"Cooperate," the captain said loudly over the children's objections, "and things may go well for you. The An Taoseach is merciful. Resist and I assure you I will not speak for you in his presence!"

"You think of yourself too highly," Kinjour said, moaning as the soldiers lifted him. "You are nothing compared to him."

"I do not think this one is strong enough to walk," one of the soldiers said.

"*Nothing*!" Kinjour cried.

"He sounds strong enough to me," the captain said coldly. "Bind him with the others."

"Nothing!" Kinjour said again.

"And you are even less," the captain spit on the ground, "orphan."

"I know what I am," Kinjour said quietly. "Just as he will know what you are."

"Gag them." The captain turned his back to them.

"*Nothing*!" Kinjour screamed again before the gag was in place. Deliriously, he kept mumbling the same word over and over again as the soldiers led them toward the capital, and the one who ruled all the land bathed in Light.

Chapter Twenty-Eight

CALADRIUS

Nithrodine Castle, Isear:

T he physician turned toward the small window before which stood an elegant table. His eyes glimpsed the *Darkness* pressing upon the far borders of the land. This chamber was high enough within the palace that all the land swept away beneath it obstructing nothing. He bent and washed his hands turning the water, in the ivory basin, red with royal blood. He didn't look up from this task as the door opened; the Mydrian bodyguards scattered almost invisibly through the chamber straightened, only one person would be entering this chamber unsummoned—the one over whom his instructions held no authority. "Do not be alarmed, An Taoseach," the physician said with a shake of his aged head as he dried his hands on the towel offered to him by the servant girl. "The danger is past. Queen Keliah's fever has broken and the bleeding has stopped," he hesitated, turning his full attention toward his master. "My lord, I fear it falls on me to tell you yet again that the baby was lost."

Armahad sighed, nodding once. Four times he had heard those words. He was numb to them and the pain they brought. His nod was a dismissal as his full attention turned toward the shadows dancing with firelight. A huge veiled bed filled that entire side of the vast chamber. He approached it silently, drawing back the thin veil before sitting on the side of the bed. His wife stirred as his weight pressed down on the mattress. Keliah smiled weakly as he took her hand and raised it to his lips, kissing her gently. She was so incredibly pale, he felt certain her life was a miracle.

"Why can't I give you a child?" she whispered.

He smiled gently, glad for the numbness of his heart in this moment. "You're alive, my love." His fingers brushed lightly along her cheek, wiping away her silent tears. "That's all that matters."

"Hold me."

Armahad shifted around beside his wife as the door closed, signaling the physician's departure. Keliah tucked herself into her husband's arms, nuzzling into his strength as he stroked her sweat-dampened, golden hair.

"Tell me the story," she said weakly.

He stiffened slightly. "Which story?"

Keliah lifted her head to meet his gaze. Her pale, trembling fingers reached up to touch his stubbly face and the glowing Mark that was not darkened by the two days of growth on his smooth, regal face. She saw plainly enough the worry that had kept him from rest these last two days, and she loved him more because of it. Slowly, her fingers traced the waxing crescent moon and the figure draped around it, sparkling like natural diamonds in its own Light, which surpassed the red glow of the fire and yet diminished none of his own natural features. "You know which story," she said softly.

Armahad caught her hand and pulled it down into his. "I don't want to make you cry."

"Please, Armahad," Keliah said, looking down. "Please tell it to me. Just once more."

He sighed, pulling her close. His lips pressed against the top of her head as she nestled against him. Moments passed in silence as he hesitated and she waited. When at last he spoke, his voice was soft, heavy—weighted by memory far too old to be *remembered* by the living.

"Our house—the Royal House of Caladrius—from which all rulers of Isear have come, has a noble history steeped in legend, and we who will wear the crown are marked, forever bound to the myth. My forefather, Nudhug, was the first to bear the surname of Caladrius and the Mark that has passed to every firstborn son in direct line of descent since that moment. He was not born marked as all have been since his day, but rather he was scarred and that scar was the gift that started it all or so the stories say." He smiled to himself.

He pulled the blanket over his wife as she shivered. "Nudhug was born long ago in a land so distant its exact location has been forgotten. All that is remembered is that in the midst of the great strife in that land, Nudhug heard a mysterious cry, power unlike any power he had known, beauty like no music he had ever heard, and it awakened something inside of him that he had never felt before. Others heard the cry and abandoned their homeland to seek it out. Nudhug became their king, leading them on the great journey that left them outcasts among all races and kingdoms of Men, having no shore to call home. They became nomads, wandering across unknown lands and seas until at last they ventured forth upon the greatest sea of all."

Armahad spoke the next words softly. "When they were in the midst of this sea, a flash of blinding white Light bleached the universe. A new day dawned. The Sun rose on the Eastern horizon, crowning Day, but the light seemed dim. An unholy gloom hung upon the Sun's face. The darkening spread upon drops of sunlight across the universe into the far corners of the earth, grimly awakening the world. Darkly luminous spheres erupted from the East, pounding the earth from above and below. Everything they touched disintegrated, leaving nothing but poisonous, blackened waste behind it to contaminate the water, the crops, the air, even the people! The sea was boisterous, fighting against them at every turn. Hundreds lost their lives in its forbidding chaos as our people battled the elements for the very survival of our race. Doom seemed the only likely outcome of this adventure, yet when all hope seemed lost, the sea gave forth an unexpected treasure."

"Don't stop," Keliah said softly when Armahad hesitated.

His troubled brown eyes searched her face. She looked away, afraid of what he might see there and waited, knowing he would not deny her.

"A great white *bird* came from the formidable depths, it is said. Its head was shaped much like a horse's, only bigger, and its feathers were unnatural, strong and sharp like blades of steel, yet different. Its huge body was covered all over with diamonds harder than stone, far more beautiful and as smooth as scales. Its eyes were pools of blue fire tinged with gold. Its wings blotted out the sun, and water parted before the thrashing of its massive tail while its cry silenced every other sound. Its cry was like the cry that had drawn Nudhug and his people from their homeland. Our people called this *bird* Caladrius, for it was the cure to all their troubles. Caladrius brought our people to this shore. We were a small people then, weak, but that was all to change, as it is written in the chronicles of the An Taoseach."

Armahad stroked his wife's hair, curling it between his fingers as he gazed into the fire through the thin veil around the bed that bore the royal emblem, a Caladrius. His next words came unwillingly. "Caladrius was a powerful being whose footsteps shook the entire earth and whose voice exceeded any instrument with its beauty and any weapon with its power. Some say it was a merciful and righteous winged protector. Others speak of its ferocity, saying it was a breather of fire. Either way, Nudhug made a deal with this creature, ensuring that the throne of this new kingdom would not depart from his house and that one son would never rise against another. Thus, the troubles that had once plagued his homeland would not follow him here. No one would usurp the crown or step to power over the corpses of their predecessor. Nudhug was given a sign that was first carved on his own flesh by Caladrius and then appeared upon that of his firstborn son. The Mark of the Caladrius has appeared on the flesh of the trueborn heir at birth ever since. Nudhug's line would never fail. In exchange for this promise, Nudhug pledged his fealty and that of his ancestors to the great *bird*. The deal was sealed with fire and blood. Where they met, the Shrieking Stone erupted from the earth, an enduring monument to the first Isearian An Taoseach, Nudhug—who took the name of Caladrius as his surname. Nudhug was blessed and all our people through him. Every marked son is blessed and the House of Caladrius is long enduring . . ." he said, stopping with a sigh. "We alone have Light in this *Darkness*."

"And one day, the seed of the great *bird* will return to this strong kingdom to claim the loyalty owed to him," Keliah said softly, "to fill the womb of the last wife of the last human An Taoseach."

"So it is said." Armahad held Keliah tightly as she wept. "You see, my love," he said softly, "we too will be blessed. In time, these tears will be forgotten. The line of Nudhug cannot fail."

Keliah met his gaze. "How do you know?" she asked. Her tears watered his fingers.

Armahad didn't answer. He wasn't given the chance. The door burst open just then and a guard rushed in.

"An Taoseach!"

"Yes?" Armahad unwillingly looked away from his wife. "What is it?"

"Forgive the interruption, my lord, but riders approach!"

Armahad nodded, glancing back at Keliah.

"Go," she said, squeezing his hand weakly before releasing him.

"This will wait?" he asked softly.

"Yes, Armahad Caladrius." Keliah smiled, but the smile didn't touch her eyes as she leaned back against the satiny pillows.

He bent down to claim a kiss, and then he rose and walked away. Keliah turned her face into the pillows to muffle her bitter wails, one hand pressed hard against her vacant womb, the hope in her heart dying by fractions with each passing.

* * *

Trin went slack in the grip of the soldier responsible for bringing him in. All weapons had been confiscated at the gates of the royal palace, and even the ropes that had bound the prisoners were forbidden beyond that point. The captain had assigned each of his soldiers to a prisoner while he himself had been assigned an official escort who carried an unknown number of blades within his long, flowing, black coat, which was fitted deceptively to his burly frame. More escorts followed behind them, armed equally as well. Each boasted a similar black coat fitted so that the weapons concealed within were virtually invisible. All wore black leather cuirasses and matching breeches; gold rings encircled the necks of some, badges of rank and honor no doubt, while all wore blood-red bands upon their forearms and black fabric masks around their faces, covering all their natural features except for their hard, ever-watchful eyes. The sight of these warriors did not seem to upset Kinjour or the girls in the slightest. In fact, he detected a slight smile of pleasure on Kinjour's face though he could not understand why. The captain and his soldiers seemed uneasy. Trin was not sure how he should feel himself. Fear was to be expected. Awe was too, after all the splendor of those outermost gates surpassed everything he had ever seen before, yet he felt something more. He just couldn't pinpoint what it was exactly. However, this feeling grew with each footstep as the grandeur grew around him. His eyes could scarcely take it all in, and he was sure he missed most of it by the time they finally stopped.

Soaring architecture made him feel extremely small. This new chamber was somewhere in the heart of the palace, he was sure—it had taken a long time to reach, though he had seen no other door or passageway except the one that had led them here from the gate—and here it seemed that invisible doorways swept off in either direction by sheltered passageways fit for walking and over these were an elevation of rounded galleries that reeked of importance. The chamber was a masterpiece of white and gold contrasted by polychrome ornamental marble tiling and painting, made bolder by the crystalline mirrors lining the far sides of the gallery above, catching the light of a thousand crystalline chandeliers proudly baring their countless flames throughout the vast chamber. More darkly clad warriors, their faces covered, stood like statues beneath the arches, behind the pillars, everywhere Trin's quick eyes dared to look, a hundred at least probably more. His eyes nearly bulged from his sockets as he took in this glory, so he couldn't understand the captain's reaction a second later.

"Why are we stopping here? I asked to see the An Taoseach!" the captain said.

Their official escort turned and looked at them with hard, unsettling eyes. "So you shall, but the hour is late," he said firmly, but not unkindly.

"Take me to the An Taoseach."

"The An Taoseach has retired for the night," the escort said.

"Who are you? Do you know who I am? I am Captain Manarc of the Border Patrol Guards. I bring news, prisoners, and gifts for the An Taoseach," the captain said, trying to push past the man.

The escort pushed him back. A hint of authority leaked into his voice. "I am a High Captain of the Mydrian, the An Taoseach's personal bodyguards and I say that your news, your prisoners, and your gifts can wait for the An Taoseach's pleasure." His hand shifted minutely toward one of those weapons concealed beneath his coat. "Try to pass me again, and I will see that you never stand in the An Taoseach's presence. Is that understood?"

Captain Manarc raised his hands as if in surrender and took a step back. "Has the An Taoseach at least been told we are here?"

"I would not have brought you this far into his own private residence if he had not been informed," the Mydrian said.

"And we are not to be received at court? We are to be received here in this vestibule?" Captain Manarc's face and words were full of disdain.

"The hour is late," their escort said. "You await his presence here. If he chooses to honor you, he will come above. Wherever his presence is, you will find all the glory and authority of his official court, and by right of Isearian law, you will behave as such. Protocol dictates that you do not speak unless spoken to, do not look at him unless commanded to do so, do not attempt to approach him unless summoned, and remember your place even if these permissions are granted or you will surely die." His words fell ominously from his lips as he turned his back on them once more. "You are no longer free men. In his presence, you are slaves as are we all."

Trin shuddered. Behind him Kinjour smiled like a fool.

Several tense moments passed in silence, but before his fear could fully take root, their escort straightened abruptly and shouted, "Hail the An Taoseach of Isear!"

"Hail!" the Mydrian shouted, coming from the recesses in every direction. Their numbers swelled into the thousands as another approached upon the western face of the gallery.

Trin was shocked to hear the voices of women in their host, but the one that came after it quickly overshadowed this shock. The presence of the An Taoseach was beyond startling to Trin, for he thought up until this moment that there were no greater wonders in this land than what his eyes had already beheld. Everything about the ruler of this land screamed of majesty from his ornaments: a golden crown rimmed in jewels encircling his head; a wide, equally adorned, gold belt that encircled his bare, finely toned abdomen; golden bands extending from wrist to forearm and a shimmering white-gold garment starting under the belt and extending to his feet; to the regal manner in which he walked; to the Mark upon his face that reflected the Light so that his face glowed, hiding most of his own features, bringing a god-like feel into an already humbling chamber. The scents of myrrh and frankincense permeated the air to mask the stench of the peasants.

The An Taoseach stopped in a section of the gallery, as it rounded toward the east that offered the most shelter from the blazing light of this chamber. (Perhaps the gallery was wider there, hinting once more of the secret passageways leading off in every direction.) His face dimmed, allowing Trin to make out his smooth, freshly shaven features. The An Taoseach's eyes met his with equal wonder and curiosity. An aura of goodness flowed down with his gaze. Trin gaped in wonder, remembering too late that they had been instructed not to look upon him unless commanded to do so.

"Who are you? Where do you come from?" the An Taoseach asked, holding Trin's gaze with his own.

Trin twitched from antennae to toe with a mixture of fear and excitement.

Captain Manarc bristled with shock. "He is my prisoner, sire. They all—"

Their escort shoved him aside. "The An Taoseach was not speaking to you, sir," he said as he simultaneously grabbed Trin and pushed him forward. "When the An Taoseach speaks, you must answer," he said, his voice kind once more.

"I-I-I," Trin stammered. "I am Trin Th-Thibodeaux, g-g-great King," he managed with some effort.

"And are you my captain's prisoner?" the An Taoseach asked kindly.

"Not for any crime on my part," Trin answered, looking down.

"Is this true, Captain?"

"Sire, I believe him to be a spy and these orphans," he snarled the word, "I caught outside after the curfew you, yourself imposed upon the borderlands!" Captain Manarc said defensively.

"I know my own laws, Captain," the An Taoseach said.

"I beg your Majesty's pardon," Captain Manarc said with a less than worthy bow to his king. "I bring gifts—the Abwyd's carcass." He waved one of his soldiers forward with the burden. "I have served you well, great King."

"Please, sire," Cait said, struggling against the soldier that held her.

"Let the child speak," the An Taoseach said before any of his men could silence her.

"Please, sire, my brother is very sick! Will you help him?"

"He was poisoned by Abwyd drool, sire," Trin spoke up quickly, "while trying to help your Border Patrol put a stop to the creature."

"And you still arrested him, Captain?" the An Taoseach said, a hint of unbelief coloring his voice.

"I-I-" Captain Manarc stammered.

"You think I am best served by such unmerciful actions, Captain?" the An Taoseach asked. "I would choose rather to honor those who serve me than to punish them. Take the boy to my physician."

"May we stay with my brother?" Cait asked quickly.

The An Taoseach nodded once.

Several of the Mydrian who had escorted them into this vestibule bowed and motioned for the children to follow. Trin watched in silence as they disappeared beneath one of arches.

"But sire!" Captain Manarc objected.

"You have earned your rest, Captain," the An Taoseach said. "You and your men may return to your homes." He dismissed them with a wave of his hand. "As for this visitor," he said, motioning toward Trin, "bring him to me. I will speak with him. I believe he comes on a mission of great importance."

"He has the stink of *Darkness* upon him," Captain Manarc said angrily.

"Yes. I know," the An Taoseach answered in a voice that silenced all objections. "All the more reason to understand why he has come. Bring him." With that, the An Taoseach disappeared back the way he had come and the black-clad Mydrian receded after him in every direction.

Trin was seized from behind. He let out a startled gasp and was carried away in the tide of black. Passing beneath the arches of the vestibule, he saw the network of passageways, veins of a living organism, exactly as he had suspected running out from this antechamber into an unimaginably large and extravagant home. Mydrian guarded the entrance to every one of these passages, and in the midst stood a huge fountain, sheltered within a cove of stone and marble with open gardens, each as vast as the vestibule itself, on either side. The outer walls were visible along the borders of these gardens so thick and strong that the guards posted there rode in golden chariots. The walls tapered back higher and higher until they fit snugly against the palace itself, disorienting until Trin considered the possibility that the palace spiraled around itself, higher and higher. He remembered his first glimpse of this fortress, before the opulence and Light had shoved it from his mind, and recalled how it had towered above the land so that Firinn, the pinnacle that was visible the world over, was blocked from view—a nearly impossible height and width to fathom even with the *Darkness* working against his vision. Waterfalls flowing from some invisible source rushed down from the great heights on either side of the fortress, with the pinnacle of the fortress built over it, and disappeared before reaching the lush green valley sweeping away in every direction. The lowest gates, barely remarkable beyond their intimidating size and dismal portents, had led to another gate only slightly larger than the first. It in turn had brought them to a hub of activity, an entire farming community occupied by peasants, and animals dominated the first level of the fortress, a restful place full of simple pleasures and hard work that seemed far out of place in such a structure that spoke of domination and military might. A single dirt road had given way to a third gate, bigger and more intimidating than the ones before it. This third level was a full-blown city complete with markets and merchants of every variety, but it was less inviting, being completely encapsulated in fiery stone. Navigating its maze of over-infested streets was difficult, to say the least, and he shuddered again at the memory. Fairies did not like such confined places. Other levels had followed, blurring now in his memory, but every echelon of society had been represented from slave to magician, to warrior, to nobles both high and low. The final gate, made of some rare blue stone his eyes had never seen before, ornamented with crystal spikes in the form of a great sparkling creature—an image that nagged at his memory of stories of old—had given way to this captivation. From here, he could see the waterfalls crashing down from some point still high above him.

He barely had time to marvel at the beauty of it. The Mydrian were efficient, bustling him into one closed-in passage lit only by the torch carried by a slave before them. The Light he had begun to grow accustomed to was snatched away and he faltered. The Mydrian guard held him upright, barely pausing to let him adjust to the dim surroundings. A stairway of unremarkable and uninviting stone—too narrow for comfort—spiraled upward. An occasional arrow loop broke the monotony of the stone walls and let in a faint glimmer of the light beyond, and then suddenly it opened out upon a gold-encrusted terrace overlooking an entire forest growing naturally within this palace; the waterfalls were within reach, forming a sparkling curtain between the terrace and the forest below. Passageways broke off from the terrace toward the east and toward the west, with walls closing back into semi-natural stone tunnels. More light entered here from larger windows, and more Mydrian stood guard in natural coves of the rocks, remarkably easy to overlook for all the marble statues, each a masterpiece in its own right, bearing basins of light upon their heads, hands, or feet that decorated the walkway. His escort marched them toward the west. A single doorway denoted the end of this lighted tunnel, the walls closing in around them once more with unwelcome gloom as they mounted another spiraling stairway this one much longer than the first, with even fewer arrow loops to let in the light. The smoke from the torch made Trin cough for lack of ventilation, and when he thought he could bear it no longer, the stairway gave way to a court of such opulence it made the vestibule pale by comparison.

The court was ten times larger than the vestibule, at least, and was sanctified by the same excess of light—a welcome sight after the stairs. The walls were made entirely of crystals, cut like oblong gems and fitted together seamlessly with an almost cavernous feel except for the light. Flaming chandeliers of crystal hung from the high ceiling, their reflections bouncing like ringlets of light between the walls and across the marbled floor etched with its own ornaments of pure gold. Mydrian lined the walls on either side of him, bringing an air of intimidation to the glory. Trin slowly realized that he must be coming close to his destination and the presence of the An Taoseach. The court gave way to another, equally adorned so that except for the doorway that separated them, they could have been all the same room. Abruptly, he was ushered through a hidden doorway, contained behind a section of rather solid-looking crystalline wall that opened by a key, carried by his Mydrian escort, inserted into a narrow crevice that would be entirely missed by untrained eyes. The passage ran between two walls on a straight course and opened out unexpectedly through a small door fit into the hearth of a stone fireplace. A fire blazed too close for Trin's comfort, as he was ushered through this opening, which disappeared behind his escort as the stone slid back into place, leaving no evidence of the door's existence. The whole of this palace it seemed was built to confuse and disorient any would-be assassin, and the Mydrian seemed a virtually innumerable host that navigated these secrets with expert ease and not a small amount of intimidation for all who beheld them. Their king was protected and adored beyond any king Trin had ever heard of before.

To say that they had entered another chamber would not be entirely true. The secret passage led into an entire network of chambers of which the room with the fireplace was a small, virtually insignificant part and its rather dismal beginnings gave way to greater secrets. A court, nearly twice the size of the last, greeted his eyes. The great interior height, round and pushing higher in the middle to a window that let a flood of golden light fill the room, made him feel hugely insignificant. A grand fountain dominated the exact center of the court, bathed in this light that made every droplet of water glimmer as it poured from the mouth of a huge winged sculpture: finely crafted of crystal, highly detailed with intricate scales from its vast head, shaped much like a horse's, to its massive tail forming the border of the fountain as it coiled around a vast body; sapphire eyes touched with gold gazed from the creature's uplifted face, and its talon-clad paw was thrust above the geyser of water bearing a golden crown. The water rained down, over the statue, out of its bounds, rushing through a circular opening in the floor, feeding, Trin realized with awe, the very waterfalls he had glimpsed before.

"What is this place?" Trin breathed as he was drawn toward the lighted water.

His escort caught him from behind. "The palace was built around the only pure water source left in the world. It is pumped up to this fountain, from the deepest foundations, where it shoots from the mouth of Caladrius," he spoke the name with reverence, "and nourishes our land. Only the Royal House of Caladrius may drink directly from the fountain." He warned.

Trin nodded his head mutely and forced his gaze to shift away from the light. The court was encircled by columns of blue marble supporting golden statues of kings bearing the weight of the world on their shoulders as they supported the vast stone arches framing a complete rectangle of lighted corridors above. More Mydrian guarded this suite of interconnected rooms attainable only by the grand stairway, etched like the floor and the ceiling with intricate and ornate, gold swirls, sweeping up from the court and branching to the left and to the right.

His escort followed the line of his gaze. "This is the Head of Nithrodine. You are being afforded an unheard-of honor," he said softly, yet his voice still managed to echo. "Outside of the Mydrian and a few highly regarded servants, no Isearian has ever set foot within this court or in the rooms above. No stranger has ever seen so much, and I tell you now, one wrong move and this will be the last thing you ever see."

"What is up there?" Trin asked in renewed wonder.

"The private chambers of the Royal House of Caladrius."

Trin's mouth gaped open, his words choking in his throat before they could form, as the escort took hold of him and ushered him toward the stairs. The network of corridors he had glimpsed from below seemed far more impressive as he drew nearer—growing in his sight into an impossible labyrinth shooting further back in a multitude of directions as if it were built into and all around a range of mountains. Perhaps it was if the deepest foundation harbored a water source capable of producing the waterfalls he had seen. His first glimpse of this place had not done justice to, nor given rise to the knowledge of its sheer vastness, and he could think of no plausible reason for this beyond the obvious skill of ancient architects and a land whose layout, and frankly its very existence, was a mystery!

They mounted the steps in silence. His escort steered them from the landing up the left fork, past a line of Mydrian to a doorway covered by a heavy, purple velvet curtain. His escort stopped abruptly, holding him firmly by the arms. "Remember what I said," the Mydrian warned as he drew aside the curtain and pushed Trin through the door. The curtain fell back into place, leaving Trin suddenly alone.

Only a low burning fire in the fireplace lighted the chamber. Trin waited for his eyes to adjust to the sudden near dark of the room. Gradually he made out the shape of the room—mostly round, but squaring off on both ends. The walls were painted blue with crisscrossing stripes of darker blue, bound along the base by low, wide marble benches overlaid with bright blue, velvet cushions tasseled in gold. Discarded works of fine lace and embroidery lay here and there upon the surface. In each of the four corners, the marble came a little higher, making sharp, angular columns topped by golden candelabras, their white candles unlit at this hour. Between these columns, at the far end of the room, hung matching blue velvet curtains tied back with golden cords to frame a wide but short barren hall ending in a heavy oak door that stood propped open. More light filtered out from beyond its wide berth. Except for the faint crackle of flames in the fireplace, the rooms were utterly quiet. He crept closer. Lingering traces of perfume and exotic spices filled the air. His restless twitching intensified with his anticipation.

The innermost room was a maze of pale gossamer veils, blowing in the wind of countless open windows, and elegant pillars rose to a dizzyingly high-vaulted ceiling. Hulking Mydrian (they seemed bigger perhaps because of their surroundings) stood like silent shadows in a room dredged by shadows. Light and dark danced, lovers that could never quite touch. The room was large, extending further into the palace labyrinth than he had anticipated. This room, like the palace itself, seemed to wrap around itself, growing larger and larger until he lost himself in the dance and forgot what he was looking for—if he had ever really known.

He could lose himself in the light and never look back. He couldn't help himself! The darkness here held no fear in his heart; it was powerless while the light was ceaseless, the food and water of the soul. He could not get enough.

"You may approach." The An Taoseach's voice broke the silence with a magic all its own.

Trin froze.

"I am sure you were warned not to, but please, come closer. No one will harm you now that I have spoken." The An Taoseach appeared like a phantom from the maze of windblown veils.

Trin glanced up into his shining face, opening his mouth to answer, and was instantly struck dumb once more by his presence.

"I must terrify you," the An Taoseach said softly.

"No," Trin choked out the word. "I mean yes," he said in a rush, remembering he stood before a great and unknown king. He lowered his gaze, but his eyes wouldn't stay down. They kept drifting back to the Light reflecting off the man's face. "I mean I have never seen anything, sorry, anyone like you."

"There are no men in the *dark* land?"

"Many," Trin answered. "I meant, you are not like other men, great king."

The An Taoseach smiled, spreading his hands. "I can bleed. I can die, like all men," he said gently, "but you are right. I am not like other men. I, like my forefathers before me, have been set apart from other men. My face shines with another's Light. I age differently. I know things I shouldn't know, and for all this, common men will not even meet my gaze, yet I am just a man, prone to the same weaknesses, subject to the same *Darkness*." His voice was heavy with unrevealed burdens and sadness. He fell silent, turning his face away toward a distant section of the regal maze. His youthful brow creased with worry.

Trin couldn't help but wonder what lay beyond his sight, what drew the concern of such a noble king so entirely that he would hold court in his own private chambers with a complete stranger. Despite his curiosity, evidenced in the constant twitching that had built nearly to the point of convulsions, Trin would not allow himself to move forward uninvited. The Mydrian were everywhere! Their stillness was unsettling, yet their eyes were ever watchful. He could feel them boring through the shadows, measuring his loyalty against their own, questioning his presence in their land, ready to throw themselves around the king at the first hint of danger! He tried to control his twitching, certain that his constant movements were unnerving to these armored statues of men, but his efforts were in vain. The An Taoseach looked back at him, and the Light struck him once more.

"Come," the An Taoseach said, motioning him forward. He turned and disappeared into the maze of veils.

Trin followed in silence. Quite abruptly, before he had even begun to suspect its coming, the maze of pillars and veils opened, the room squaring off before him. Crystal chandeliers hung down from gilt fixtures. Their white candles were unlit, but a fireplace was built into the interior wall. A great roaring blaze filled its wide, ornate mouth. The light from the windows and light from the fire banished the shadows, ending the dance. This section of the vast chamber seemed to be a chamber all its own, though there had been no doorway or other division. Even with its ornate features, it held a more intimate feel than the rest of the palace he had seen.

The An Taoseach approached the far side of the room where curtains cascaded down from a huge golden crown. The curtains were dark except for the ghostly white beast, these men called Caladrius, emblazoned upon its surface.

Trin felt forgotten and out of place as he watched the king draw aside the curtain.

"Keliah, are you awake?"

"Armahad," the soft voice of a woman came from inside as a pale hand reached out to touch the An Taoseach's.

The An Taoseach took that pale hand in his and lifted it toward his lips. "We have a guest."

"Someone is here?"

The An Taoseach kissed her hand. "Yes, my love. I must speak to this visitor, but I did not want to leave you alone for long."

Trin crept closer until he could peek past the opening in the curtain to see the woman shrouded within. He half expected her face to shine like her master's, but it didn't. She lay upon a huge bed, looking so frail he expected Death to materialize before her eyes at any moment. Her face was pale—too pale. Her eyes were red and swollen from tears. Sweat lay clammy on her skin. She looked scarcely able to lift her head—a wretched piece of humanity, yet the An Taoseach looked down upon her as if she were the most beautiful jewel in all the world and she looked at him with equal admiration.

"Who is he?" she asked weakly.

"His name is Trin. He comes from the *dark* lands," the An Taoseach said. He lifted her so that she sat upright on the bed, tucking silken pillows behind her with gentle hands so that she would not fall over. "What he is, well, that is a different matter."

She smiled at his touch. "From the *dark* lands, Armahad?" True curiosity gave strength to her voice.

"I am a Fairy, great King. I come from the Resistance, my lady, for whom I am a scout," Trin answered them.

Keliah looked at him in wonder. "So not all in the *dark* lands serve the Dark One?"

"No, not all serve the Dark One, but the *Darkness* grows stronger every day. The Resistance falters," Trin said. He wasn't sure why he was revealing so much, but he felt compelled to continue. "I was sent to spread the word for retreat, but then I saw Light and I couldn't escape from it! No one remembers Light, my lady. It is a rumor, a whisper, I myself heard and rejected. If I was not seeing it now, I still would not believe. The Dark One will win very soon I fear if things continue as they are."

"Retreat you say?" the An Taoseach said, studying him closely.

"Yes," Trin answered. "Retreat. *Darkness* is breaking through our defenses. We have no weapons against it. One by one we are falling."

"Where will you run?"

Trin shrugged, a hopeless gesture. "To Firinn. To the Summoners, but their power is broken. Retreat only delays the inevitable. The Resistance falls." He hung his head dejectedly. "We have no hope of a Cure."

"Perhaps," Keliah said slowly, "you do."

Trin looked up into her eyes. She silently gazed up into her husband's eyes.

The An Taoseach gazed down at her in silence.

Chapter Twenty-Nine

THE KNOWLEDGE OF DESPAIR

*D*arkness.

That living blackness was, as Sithbhan said, the fount of knowledge—the knowledge of despair. Lorshin crouched in the corner of her deserted lair just beyond the dismal hall of portals. His chin rested on his knees as he considered her words, his life, and the choice that brought him here. His price. With Death gone to weave her vile work in the world, he was a slave to his thoughts as deep and troubled as they were. How had he come to this? His father was gone, lost in the *darkness* for more years than Lorshin cared to remember, having fallen prey to his choice just as Lorshin was prey to his. His mother was dead at his father's touch. His people were slaves, and he was bound by inescapable guilt. The forest of his childhood had burned. The Dianara Mountains were corrupted shells of their former beauty. His life was a tangled web of sin, deception, grief, and pain. *Darkness*. On top of it all, he was the lover of Death. *Darkness* had given him only sorrow and illusion, and he wallowed in it! He had let Sithbhan in. Slowly, he was beginning to understand, and it scared him beyond measure. *Wise Ones, hear me!* His heart pleaded within him for the thousandth time, yet he doubted his cry could breach the *Darkness*.

Lorshin leaned back against the stone wall. His thoughts drifted beyond *Darkness* to his twin. Isentara. She was his only link to life outside. He couldn't help but wonder whether she still enjoyed the kiss of daylight on her flesh, thanks to the protection of the Guardians. A single thought could connect his mind to hers, yet he did not call out to her lest he find her hunted by *Darkness* despite Sithbhan's promise.

"Lorshin, my love." Death's eerie voice startled him from his thoughts.

He looked up in time to see her emerge from one of those distant portals. To which kingdom and race it connected, he did not care to know. Sithbhan stepped into the Dark One's domain in a fury of shadow. The portal solidified with her passing. No doubt another soul simultaneously turned to dust. Chains of shadow formed around his wrists and lifted him into Death's embrace.

"What is wrong, my love?" she asked, at once aware of his troubled gaze.

Lorshin forced his thoughts aside. "Nothing," he said softly. The single-word answer sounded unconvincing even to his ears.

Sithbhan smiled like a fool as he lowered his mouth to her neck. His fangs grazed the flesh, igniting her desire and driving suspicion from her mind. His kiss said it all. In it she imagined his love. The way she felt beneath his hands, the way she made him hunger for more than just the trace of Flame buried in her flesh, the way she looked into his eyes, it all left a stain upon his soul. Though he could not escape the sudden longing of his heart, there was also a darker motive to his affection. One day he would be free of her until then she must trust in the kiss that bound them to his despair. *Wise Ones, please! I beg you! Hear me!*

* * *

Isentara crouched in a clearing—a border of burning shadows that broke the veil of *Darkness*, letting the light of the moon filter down. Trees rose around her like black giants. *Darkness* watched from its mighty stronghold. Her body glistened with a cold sweat in the dim light. Her lips moved frantically as one in great need, but no sound escaped.

She clutched to the amulet around her neck. Its three crescents pressed sharply into her small fist as she held them to her lips. The *Darkness* seemed to close in around her, yet she remained protected in a circle of light. Something moved out there in the dark. She felt its foul breath on her flesh. It was waiting, she knew, for the power of her amulet to fade, and then it would enslave her. Somewhere in the dark were her people. Somewhere in those depths was her twin, yet she feared to lose herself in the abyss in order to find him. Why didn't the Guardians come to her whispered pleadings? She had glimpsed hope. Would there be none for her people?

"Lorshin." His name was no more than a whisper from her lips that was lost in the dark.

Lorshin.

The Prince of the Samhail heard the faint call drawing him. *Sister.* He sought her with his mind. For a moment, the distance melted away. Their minds and hearts connected. *Isentara, I am here.* She was a glimmer of Light to his tortured soul even as he sank into Death's embrace.

Isentara reached for his voice. "Lorshin," she said stronger.

He felt the black breath that pressed in around her. He saw the *Darkness* rising. *No!* he cried inwardly. His hands tightened around Sithbhan like a vice.

Isentara gasped, but she was invisible to him as the *Darkness* of his vision threw him back, rending Death free. Its black mask fell over him. Its weight was like an anvil crushing him beneath it. Isentara's screams were all that remained of their connection. Lorshin recoiled with his hands pressed to his ears. Were they his twin's screams? Were they Death's? Or were they his transformed by some illusion?

Sithbhan kneeled beside him. She cradled his head to her chest. "My love begins to understand," she said softly. "The *Darkness* is greater than us all. Submit to it and gain its power, my love, before it drives you mad."

"Lorshin?" Isentara whispered. She had felt him, surely she had! "Lorshin?"

Silence filled the *Darkness* all around her.

"Lorshin!" she screamed. "Lorshin!"

*   *   *

Lorshin stirred. Death's bed was cold and empty except for him. How had he come to be there? The last thing he remembered was Isentara's screams. At least, he thought they were hers. He massaged his throbbing temples. *Darkness* had come between them. Even now he could hear its corrupted voice in the recesses of his mind. The Prince of the Samhail shook his head, trying to free himself from its grasp.

Lorshin, my son. The voice broke through the barriers he had raised in his mind. *Come to me.*

He resisted. *Darkness* compelled him. Lorshin felt himself rise from the bed and ascend through *darkness* to the Heart of Evil. His hand trembled as it reached toward the beating source of his torment, yet he was powerless to resist the invisible chords that drew him.

Son. The *Darkness* took shape before him. His father's pale face materialized from the depths.

Lorshin shuddered. "You are not my father."

Laughter resounded from the dark. *But I am,* came the response. *I am perfected.*

Lorshin shook his head. "No, you are the monster that devoured my father's heart."

Darkness shifted around him. Black mountains soared on every side. Their number was so great; he could not tell how many there were.

"Enough!" Lorshin shouted into the dark, but the vision held him.

I am your father. Arawn gave me his heart and his Flame. The Flame binds Sithbhan, the Calianith, even these mountains and all illusion to me! I control them all. You and your kind are enslaved to Death and therefore to me! Surrender, and I will show you all secrets, my son.

The Prince of the Samhail forced his hand to release the throbbing heart. It took all of his strength, and his fingers felt like stone. "Never!" he yelled.

At once the vision faded. *Then you are nothing to me but a slave!* The weight of *darkness* drove him to his knees. Perhaps it was an illusion meant to break him, but the black voice suddenly sounded very much like his father's—as it had in the forest during the Guardian War, as it sounded in his memories.

"Father!" His scream was a reflex that echoed in the deepest regions of the Dark One's domain, filling it with his emptiness and despair.

Darkness pressed him to the earth. He cowered in a broken heap on the cold stones. His entire being screamed with groanings that could find no other utterance, did the Guardians hear? Little by little, he grew numb till Death's hands lifted him from beneath it.

"My love," she said softly. Sithbhan cast her shadows around him. "Is it so hard to surrender?"

Vile laughter flowed from the Heart of Evil. *Soon enough, my son, you will be mine as will all the universe. Every choice bares a price. I am yours. Embrace me!*

Lorshin recoiled into himself and turned his face into Sithbhan's embrace. Was there any choice left to him? Inch by inch, *Darkness* carved into him with its knowledge. Inch by inch, it hollowed his soul. He didn't want to admit it, but he was slowly, painfully loosing himself. Was despair the end or the beginning?

Darkness.

These things must come to pass. I still have Hope,
and I have given it to all my creation in the Guardians,
in the Prophecy, in the choice.

—Sanctus

Chapter Thirty

AFTERGLOW

Three days and nights he awaited the An Taoseach's answer. Long hours spent anxiously pacing the spiraling halls of the palace until the grandeur became a cage. Trin's constant twitching intensified into near convulsions. These "episodes" made the humans nervous—long sheltered as they had been from the other inhabitants of the world, some of whom where far stranger than a restless Fairy. He felt guilty for causing their ill ease, yet each minute brought unknown cost to the Resistance. How much blood was already on his hands for this delay?

Running would have helped if he had dared to venture forth into this awesome kingdom—which he did not, mostly out of fear. He had never felt so twisted and torn in all his life, a life spent and validated until now by the helter-skelter flights of a Resistance scout! He couldn't breathe within these splendid walls, but he feared losing all that they contained, a hopeless condition for one who finally felt hope, which was the very cause of this restlessness. These conflictions were no more desirable than that which awaited him beyond—an abyss whose only exit was Death. Here was Light, shining like the sun even at midnight while coiled powers bound the borders (a thick burning strand between health and harm) and one marked with purpose ruled supreme. Trin had never known anything to compare. These hours wrung the stink of *Darkness* from him and replaced it with the breath of Light, filling his being with hunger so intense that to pass the time immobile was unthinkable; to leave now was foolish; to stay was both selfish and imperative, which left him only one option—twitching—to sober the long hours and keep himself sane.

The more he tried to name his hunger, the more restless he grew. His hunger was as coiled in his belly as the borders were coiled in burning

222

shadows. All was bound to the An Taoseach who was like a hinge on a door—an absolutely essential presence in the grand scheme, but it was not all about him either. The great king was merely a servant upon whom the greater plan moved. Secrets cradled a hidden point of power that birthed it all forth.

His tangled thoughts were impossible to unravel even for himself so how could he hope to make the Summoners understand? The world was changing. Rather, it was forcing him to change as it would force them all to change.

One day felt as long as a year. The sensation, strangely enough, was not that different than living in *Darkness* except that he could *see* the passage of time, which somehow made it feel longer. Three days felt like an eternity, yet when they were passed, they seemed but a blink of the eyes.

Even now, as he ran in the *Darkness*, a blur of speed and silver dust, he could feel the afterglow of that land. The glory of the An Taoseach was not his own. The Light of that kingdom was not its own. Both had a source outside of itself. He could almost fathom the stories of his ancestors now. Guardians would have such power, surely. Trin sighed to the wind, and the wind sighed back carrying upon it the sound of a thousand whispers . . . whispers of hope, whispers of dreams, and whispers of dread.

Glancing back, Trin could no longer see the Light or even the burning shadows. They had vanished behind the darkening of this place, yet Light clung to him like a glowing mist, making the air all around him sizzle with the white fire of lightning. It was a shield pushing through the black tides that sought to waylay his message. The Fairy scout pushed against the blast of coiling fury. Rather than slow him, the weight of his proof and the An Taoseach's answer, a letter written by that royal hand to the Summoners, gave wings to his feet that sliced the blackened air in twain to carry him through. Time was short, and he carried *hope*. Surely, he did.

Darkness.

Sprawling trees heaved into sight and then melted back into the black. In defiance of the season, ancient evergreens drooped beneath the weight of long, pointed icicles resembling deadly teeth prepared to cleave flesh from bone. Screams echoed over the frozen earth—a world swallowed by cruel, all-consuming blackness, a world utterly devoid of Light, ruled by *Darkness* as ne'er was seen before. Trin suddenly felt very alone, far from any source of refuge and solace. Helpless and vulnerable, he fought his way through the unknown. All around him, shadows thickened, waiting for that one, least expected moment to send heavy, suffocating *Darkness* crashing down upon him. Fear's icy hand clawed its way down his spine. He trembled. His lungs rebelled, refusing to draw a breath. Pressure built, nausea rose, the stench of vomit filled his nostrils, and then only cold, raw terror remained.

Trin pushed himself harder, faster, flying like a phantom in the night. White clouds of exhaled breath from a larger cloud of silver dust were the only evidence of life in this wild and wasted region of the *dark*. He fixed his eyes upon Firinn and ran with all his might.

* * *

Firinn

Esarian was changed. Firinn's vision had changed him. While the Summoners paced around Firinn as the screams intensified in the *dark*, he sat with his eyes closed, embracing the silence . . . the peace . . . of his own soul. The fire that branded him had burned everything else away. It had freed him.

"I think we must consider the possibility that the scout is dead," Orlok said angrily.

Esarian opened his eyes but said nothing.

Some of the Summoners murmured in agreement.

"Oh, yes?" feisty Nulet asked. "And what proof do you have?"

"That he is weeks late!" Orlok answered. "What proof do you have that he isn't?"

D'Faihven ran between them. "Not again!" she exclaimed, holding them apart with her outstretched hands. "Esarian, help!"

Esarian rose from his cross-legged position. "No fighting amongst ourselves," he said simply, "it's what the Dark One wants."

"Is that all you have to say?" Orlok demanded as he lowered his clenched fists.

"What more would you have me say?" Esarian asked. "That the races flee before the *Darkness*? That it is their screams we hear? That the scout is dead or is even now coming to us? I know only what you know, Orlok. The scout is late. *Darkness* prevails, and we are the last line of defense! If we give up," he said, shaking his head, "if we, who are the leaders, give up, how will this Resistance stand?"

"How will it stand with us, Esarian?" one of the other Summoners asked. "*Darkness* grows stronger with each passing day!"

"What do the brands tell you?" D'Faihven asked softly.

"That even in *Darkness* there is hope," Esarian answered with a slight smile. "There is Hope," he said more firmly, "if you will just believe!"

The Summoners considered his words in silence. No one knew how to answer him because no one knew how to believe anymore.

Nulet gasped, "Look!" He pointed toward the ruins of Cartiman and the approaching cloud of silver dust. "A scout!"

Trin Thibodeaux skidded to a halt as Master Esarian strode forward to meet him.

"What news?" Esarian asked, skipping the pleasantries of welcome and curiosity.

"The races flee before the *Darkness*," Trin said to the horrified gasps of the Summoners. "There is only one source of refuge for us now."

"Where, Trin? Where can we go for refuge?" Esarian asked.

The moment he was waiting for came sooner than he had anticipated. Trin opened his pouch and produced his evidence. "The whispers are true. There is still Light in this world." He opened the first vile. "This is the air of that land." He poured out the thick opalescence contained within upon the stones at Firinn's base. The substance crackled like flame as it scattered the *Darkness*.

The Summoners gasped as they breathed in pure air—cleansed entirely of *Darkness* for the duration of his offering of evidence.

Trin pulled the second vile from his pouch. "This is the earth of that land." He poured it out upon the stones. Dark fertile soil almost seemed to glow against the veils of *Darkness*. Its rich scent filled the nostrils of those who had only ever smelled wasted earth, giving strength to his evidence. He didn't wait for the Summoners to respond to this evidence but produced a third vile. "This is the water of that land." He poured it out upon the stones. It glimmered with gold and washed all *Darkness* away from its path.

"Impossible," Nulet whispered.

"A land of wonders indeed!" D'Faihven said.

"Sorcery," Orlok grumbled.

The Summoners whispered one to another uncertainly. Esarian said nothing.

Trin took the final vial from his pouch. "Light," he said simply as he opened the vial. The glittering embers contained within burst into Flame—blue, royal purple, white, and finally to burning gold—the afterglow of this Light.

The Summoners drew back with horrified gasps, whispering now out of fear.

Esarian met the scout's gaze. "Tell me of this land."

Trin pulled the scroll from his belt. "Isear is a kingdom of Men."

"A kingdom of Men?"

Trin nodded. "I would not believe it myself, sir, if I had not seen it with my own eyes. Light, the likes of which I have not seen, shines out from the heart of their great kingdom! *Darkness* does not touch them! It looms on every hand but not over them!"

Esarian's frown deepened. *Burning shadows?* Is this what his vision had been foretelling? "How can this be? Humans? How can humans hold back the *dark*?"

"I know of only one way," Trin said quietly. "The old way. The way of our ancestors."

Esarian shook his head. "What do we know of these Isearians?"

"Almost nothing. Their history is a closely guarded secret, but their land is vast. Their kingdom surpasses any other human kingdom, and their king is the noblest of men, commanding unfathomable loyalty from his people. The Dark One cannot reach them! I bear in my hand this token of their king's sovereignty and this letter penned by his own hand in my presence as the last of my proof!" Trin offered the scroll to the Summoner.

Esarian took the scroll, studying the wax seal. The seal curved like the waxing crescent moon, only tipped with a head like a Guardian's and ending with a tail also like a Guardian's. "I have never seen a mark like this one before."

"Nor I," Trin said quietly, "but the Isearian king bears the same Mark upon his face, only it shines brightly with golden Light."

Esarian broke the seal and unrolled the parchment.

To those who have so nobly resisted the Dark One:

I regret all the years of my forefathers' silence. We should have ended our separation from your plight long ago. I deeply regret the lives lost due to this cowardice. I have heard many great things concerning your bravery, loyalty, and love of freedom. Should you ever need a friend, Isear is open to you.

Armahad Caladrius, the An Taoseach of Isear.

The seal was repeated beneath the king's name.

Trin leaned forward. "Is it as I think, Master Esarian? Could this be the work of a Guardian?"

Esarian shrugged. "You know as much as I."

Trin nodded, trying to hide his disappointment and failing miserably. "And what of the Isearians?"

Esarian considered the question for a long moment. "Perhaps we should let this king—this Armahad Caladrius, the An Taoseach of Isear—come speak for himself. For all we know, this could be a trick of the *Darkness*, but here at Firinn he could speak only truth." The Summoner crumbled the letter and threw it to the ground. "I say, let him prove his friendship here before us all or die!"

Darkness.

Chapter Thirty-One

A BLESSED DAWN?

Dark dreams weren't like other dreams. They were stronger—harder to escape—virtually impossible, for one held hard in its grasp, to distinguish from reality. Somewhere between waking and sleeping, Lorshin felt the onslaught of *Darkness*. He rose up semiconscious from Death's bed, drawn by the black grip toward an unknown ending.

The lair was much changed, lost in the illusion. Dark, bleeding stones rose to his sides and back. Cobwebs hung from the invisible ceilings hanging heavy with their dead creators. The stench of rotting flesh filled the *darkness*. Maggots were crawling everywhere beneath his feet, more numerous than the dust. Bodies lay scattered upon his path in various stages of decomposition. Wind blasted through the dismal scene over the gaping mouths of the dead, filling the black with ghostly screams.

Isentara's face flashed before his eyes. The screams combined into one.

This flash of thought jolted Lorshin out of the lingering remnant of troubled rest, a rest that came only in Death's absence. Isentara often broke through the veil of *Darkness* in these rare moments but never so intensely as at that moment. He saw her there in that place he had thought a dream. Blood streamed all around her from some vicious battle—not yet swallowed by the earth. The wind was caught in her long, dark hair. It tried to pull the thick strands from the leather bands that encased them midway down her back. Her eyes glowed in the dark of his mind. Fangs flashed. She was falling. He reached for her, his heart clenching with the same agony that held hers. Shades of Reality snarled in the blackness, circling her. Anger rose inside of him. His own fangs flashed with the heat of his rage.

"Sithbhan!" he roared, forgetting she was not present. Hadn't she promised him his sister would be safe? She would pay for this treachery.

The One whose Name is not Spoken laughed. *She is not here.* His father's ruined voice attacked his mind. *I am. I can help you.*

Lorshin's head jerked to one side like a wild cat that faced a predator stronger than itself. A low growl rose from deep in his chest. He answered with his mind. *Leave me alone!*

Laughter in the *dark* greeted his defiance. Power, outside his own, drove him toward the brooding hall of portals and the return of the vision the beast had prepared. He tried not to look, but the *Darkness* compelled him.

Isentara, he whispered with his mind. "Isentara!" he screamed.

* * *

Darkness circled her camp. Her freshly laid fire kept it at bay, but it could not silence the screams filling the black. Isentara crouched near the fire pit, trying to ignore her grotesque surroundings. She heard the Dark One circling. Footsteps resounded in the abyss. She could hear his snarling in her mind. Her trembling hands clung to the crescent amulet around her neck. With the growing *dark*, its power was weakening. The longer she stayed outside the Light, the weaker it would become. Eventually, it would leave her defenseless against the Sun and the *Darkness* would either claim her or let her burn. How could she go back? Even if she wanted to, the portals were sealed and only a Guardian could open them to her. Why would she want to? Hadn't the Great Ones abandoned the races to the power of the *dark*? Wasn't her own flesh and blood lost to it without hope? So why did she deserve hope?

Isentara.

"Lorshin?" Isentara looked around her.

"Isentara!"

"Lorshin!" Her hand raised toward his invisible cry as it lifted her from the brink of surrender. Every instinct told Isentara she should flee, but she hesitated. A feeling deep inside called to her, promising that this road was the answer to all of her questions and whispered prayers.

Lorshin saw her move. He reached for her. "Sister." The portal kept them apart. Without Death's presence and the Dark One's will, it seemed the doorways were nothing more than mirrors.

"You cannot save her, Lorshin." *His father's* voice interrupted. "Not without me. The Shades of Reality are under my control. It is true I cannot reach her, yet it is only a matter of time. The choice is yours. Do you surrender or does your twin pay the price, which for you is worse than losing your own soul?"

The Prince of the Samhail growled. His fists smashed against the portal as he tried to break through and reach her. His body was heaving with the weight of his sorrow and rage. He beat the petrified doorway, but it would not break. Ripples, similar to those that appear on the surface of water when a rock is thrown, radiated across the solid plane.

Darkness laughed. *Yes, fight me,* it whispered to his mind. *It makes this all the more fun.*

Lorshin sank to his knees, his hands still lifted to Isentara. The *dark* descended on him. His tough outer shell was bowed, nearly broken. A tortured soul was left exposed. Blood and *Darkness* flowed with his tears. Another blister formed on his heart. The vision faded. His sister was lost. "Let her go!" he screamed.

His father's voice answered, "You know the price." The *dark* lifted. Lorshin fled.

*　*　*

Remnants of Rowlyrag

He ran from the bowels of *Darkness*, to the crumbling height of Rowlyrag. His tormentor did not follow. Lorshin stood upon the peak of the blackened mountain, encircled by the shroud of *Darkness* that had long ago been cast upon him by his choice. With the barren wasteland far below—speared through by the charred pillars of his ancient forest home—and only the vastness of the darkly clotted heavens before him, he could see across the horizon to the distant burning shadows and just glimpse the slowly rising light of the sun beyond the *Dark*. For someone, somewhere this was a blessed dawn. The sun's golden rays skipped across the distant treetops of the outside world, dipped into the rolling valleys and rode upon the back of the life-giving waters. Its light danced among the wispy waves of blackness pressing hard against those burning borders and created hues of purple, blue, and crimson against the coiling backdrop of conflicting powers. Though he had beheld the Sun in Ages past, it seemed new, growing in splendor before his long-denied eyes. It no longer held power over his body—not while the Dark One kept him.

The beauty reminded him not of what he had but of what he had lost. The sin was his alone, yet he had been freed of the curse—by treachery and desire—while his people were bound by him to *Darkness* and to Death. Upon the sunlight, he had sworn oaths understood by all his kind though never spoken lest Death discover their intended defiance and the Dark One through her. Lorshin gazed upon the sun unblinkingly. He could still fight the *Darkness* all around him so long as there was something to hold on to.

Lorshin.

The corrupted voice called from every direction. Part of him wanted to surrender. He closed his eyes, willing his own beast to be silent.

"So long as the Sun is in the heavens, I will not be consumed by *Darkness*, neither heart nor soul. I swear it," he said in a hushed and unwavering voice.

Lorshin.

The voice was right there on top of him. He half expected to see the Heart of Evil hovering in front of his face when he opened his eyes. Instead, there was *Darkness*, then fire, and then Death.

"What do you swear?"

Lorshin forced a smile as the grip of terror seized his belly and tried to rip it from his body. Her approach always brought the same sensation over him, though the feeling faded more quickly now. He feared its passing. Chains bound his people, but he was in danger of being consumed. *Wise Ones, please hear me!*

"What do you swear upon the sun, my love?" Sithbhan asked once more.

Lorshin forced himself to look toward the sun lest she see the lie in his eyes. "I swore that my love is like the sun," he said softly.

"Your love rises with promise only to fade into the dark?"

"Even Night reflects Day's light, Sithbhan, or have you forgotten the eternal dance of your parents upon the heavens? You are my eternal night, and there my love is renewed," Lorshin said softly, his eyes never flinching from the sunlight, hoping Death did not sense his heart's unfaithfulness to the words that dripped like honey from his lips.

A lustful smiled curled Sithbhan's dark lips. Chains appeared on his wrists, drawing him into the circle of her arms. Lorshin stiffened. Her pale hand glided gently across his back. The seductive movement of her hands was like a soft, ravaging kiss. Her other hand guided his face downward till his eyes met hers. He swallowed dryly. What if his eyes betrayed him? A Scarrow could read even the deepest and most well-hidden desires by searching the eyes, and he had no strong defense against her at this moment. Her touch clouded his mind. If she saw the lie in his eyes, however, she said nothing about it. Her eyes closed as quickly as her mouth reached his.

The passion of her kiss shook him. Lorshin pulled away. A wealth of emotion welled up inside of him. He should hate her. In many ways he did, yet part of him cherished her.

Sithbhan followed. "I know your soul, Lorshin. I know you." For a moment, she changed. He looked through *Darkness* to the Heart of Evil and the illusion of his father. Her voice deepened and became the foul, black breath. *Do not resist the part of yourself you fear,* the voice whispered in his mind. *Come to me.*

Just as quickly, the illusion faded and he was alone with Sithbhan. He looked at her. The momentary fear faded. It seemed he was Sithbhan's one weakness and likewise she was his. Her dark, hypnotic eyes drew him back into her cold embrace, though every fiber of his being screamed in objection. *Wise Ones, I beseech you. Please. Will you not hear me?* In the back of his mind, he could still see the rotting carcasses of his vision. Nausea twisted his gut; he swallowed back the bile and forced himself to stay in Sithbhan's embrace, revealing nothing. Inside, he trembled; outside he was as still as stone.

The black breath swelled around them, obliterating the distant dawn, yet it waited to strike. Its prey was not ready. The catalyst had to be perfect. *Darkness* had to seem like an escape from the turmoil of his soul. The hold of Light had to be broken. It had already faltered but not enough, not enough for surrender. *Darkness* brooded.

Lorshin knew its presence. He felt it as if it flowed in his veins. The Wise Ones and the Light were so far away, a fading dream that he wanted to hold on to, but it was still slipping away. Was this the price of his choice? Would Sanctus be merciful? He covered his face with his hands and wept. No one noticed, not even Death. *Darkness* veiled his pain.

"Lorshin." The black voice caressed his senses. "I can give you peace. Surrender to me, Lorshin."

The prince resisted. His lips moved soundlessly, speaking the language of the Guardians.

"That will not help you, slave. You belong to me! I am your only escape!"

The weight of *Darkness* pressed around him, snatching his breath away, crushing him beneath itself. He held it back with all the strength he possessed. His heart ached as the attack lingered. A wave of dizziness left him feeling weak and disembodied. Was he still, somehow, in the grip of the illusion? A cry was wrenched from his lips. Bloody tears ran down his face. Death caught him when his body pitched forward, and he nearly fell.

"My love!"

Darkness released him with a malignant laugh.

Lorshin sagged against her. He had no strength left with which to lift himself upright. Each attack left fresh blisters on his heart, and this had been the worst of all. His eyes closed with exhaustion.

Darkness—I watched and waited. The stage for my greatest victory was nearly set. What could disrupt my plans now?

Fear writhed in my *Darkness*. Remembrances of burning shadows and strange markings tempered my *joy*. They were not like my illusions. I did not control their beginning, their purpose was hidden, and I could not fathom their ending. The need for answers waylaid my plans as I drew my *darkness* around me to give substance to my unformed frame. It was time I paid the Resistance another visit, to glean their knowledge, to divide their fleeing forces, to usurp the remnants of their hope!

I am the One Whose Name is not Spoken. I am the Heart of Evil and the residue of Dullahan. I am the plague spot from which all that is vile is sprung. I am *Darkness*. I am fear; I am dread; I am despair. I am Sgarrwrath, and this would be my blessed dawn. This was my Time!

Chapter Thirty-Two

BEHOLD, THE MARK!

Nithrodine Castle, Isear

Queen Keliah, bedecked in all her royal apparel, leaned against the ornate balustrade of Nithrodine's lowest terrace. "Please be careful," she said to her husband as he pulled on his gold encrusted helm.

His white stallion pranced majestically beneath him, ready to run the miles set before him. Armahad turned the stallion toward the terrace. "Do not be afraid, my love," he said gently. "Mydrian, ride with me." His band of assembled bodyguards cheered in response. "And we are led by one who has roamed the *dark* regions all his life." The An Taoseach nodded once toward Trin, who seemed uneasy with this delay. "I will return."

Queen Keliah nodded, though she continued to worry her lip with her teeth to hold back the tears brimming in her eyes.

"Take care of her for me," Armahad said to the queen's special attendants.

"We will," Kinjour said in a very grown-up voice as Goldya and Cait peaked shyly out from behind him.

"The Resistance awaits," Trin interrupted. "We must go."

Armahad rose in his saddle, stretching his hand up toward the terrace and his wife. Keliah leaned over the balustrade to grasp it. "I love you," he said.

"And I, you, Armahad Caladrius."

He kissed her pale hand and then withdrew, turning back to his quest as the tears broke down his beloved's cheeks. "Lead on, Trin Thibodeaux. To Firinn!" His stallion reared excitedly before flying away.

A half-second later, if that, the Mydrian host followed, arching him in a protective shield.

The excitement of their quest diminished when they passed beyond their own borders of burning shadow. Armahad and his guards were forced to slow their chargers to a slow walk for the blackness pressing in around them. Their eyes had never beheld such *Darkness* that forbade them to even see their hands in front of their faces. The chargers whinnied suddenly terrified; horses that would fly into the heat of battle were now guided along by the soft coaxing of their equally terrified riders.

No creaking of bough, no song of bird gave evidence of life. Only horrible whispers broke the otherwise eerie silence. Even the horse's hooves seemed to whisper over the infected earth.

"Light the torches. Box us in. No gaps," the Mydrian High Captain whispered uneasily from the An Taoseach's right hand. "Tie the horses together if necessary. And be quick about it."

His orders were obeyed as if he had shouted them.

"Is something wrong, Captain?" Armahad whispered.

"Just a feeling, my lord," the captain answered his master and charge with an incline of his head.

"There is nothing to be afraid of here," Trin said.

"I will trust your judgment, Captain," Armahad answered, putting more stock in his guardians than in his guide. His trust for the Mydrian had been earned by centuries of history and yearly trials that spoke volumes for their worth.

"This region is abandoned," Trin continued.

The Mydrian swung in their saddles, left, right, left again, flinging their torches out and around, frantically searching the *dark*. The smoke of their torches rose against the black ceiling and, denied escape, spread out to oppress the air.

"It keeps its secrets well," Trin said, before running ahead to scout the path. His trail of silver dust, sparkling dimly in the light of the torches, stained their trail until the flames died beneath the oppression of their own smoke.

They continued on in slow progression, finding their way by sheer determination. Trin stayed close to the humans out of necessity. If they were separated, he might never find them again! The slowness, however, was unbearable, and his restless twitching returned.

Slow hours dragged into even slower days, possibly weeks. The passage of Time was uncertain. *Darkness*, impossibly, seemed to grow thicker and deeper till it clung to their limbs, to the hooves of their horses, to their very breath, resisting their advance through its abyss. The disembodied whispers grew into screams—echoes perhaps of some long-ago battle—perhaps something more sinister, waiting to make them its prey. Trin led the humans not by the straightest path he knew—not the one most traveled, but one that offered little *natural* obstacle to their blinded senses, one that would give them the best sense of the Dark One's corruption, one that had been specifically ordered by Master Esarian. This path was a test to see if a greater path might truly be before them. If these strangers who had never tasted *Darkness* reached Firinn without turning back, it would be a sign to all races, a sign the Resistance prayed for, that hope was not lost.

The Mydrian had drawn their swords, nervous of the *dark* and its cries. They kept close to their master in a suffocating array all around him.

"Protect the An Taoseach," their captain said in a hushed voice over and over again. "No gaps."

"What is this place?" the An Taoseach whispered.

Trin didn't answer. He was forbidden to tell them what lay ahead.

"We are lost," one of the Mydrian whispered. Murmurs of agreement passed through the ranks.

"This *creature*—" Trin turned to scowl at them for those words, "is leading us into a trap."

Another whispered, "We should turn back while we still can."

"What is the captain thinking? It is foolish to allow the An Taoseach to risk his life so. We should drag His Majesty to safety this instant!"

"Quiet," the captain said sharply.

Trin smiled as a hush fell through the host. "We are not lost, great king," he said to the An Taoseach, "and this not a trap." He motioned into the distance. "What do you see, sire?"

Human eyes were not meant to strain against such *Darkness*. Armahad broke into a sweat with the effort.

"I see nothing . . ." he said, "no, wait! I see . . . something . . . I cannot make out what it is, but it rises in a pale sliver from the *Darkness*."

"Firinn, Majesty," Trin said. "The pinnacle that is visible the world over and the spot where I lead you to meet with the Resistance. You may turn back if you wish. No one will stop you. The choice is yours."

Armahad nodded his helmed head once. "Lead on."

Trin made a deep, twitching bow. "I know a place where we can rest."

* * *

236

Darkness—that living blackness gathered to me—a leg of *greed*; an arm of *fear*; an eye of *lust* . . . a body framed of *anger, hatred,* and *despair* with a head of *pride* and *ambition,* and bowels of commingled *defiance, wrath,* and *dread.* Together they formed a body, but not of solid flesh and blood, not held together by sinews and bones, and therein lay my weakness. I needed a vessel for that—a fleshly nest for the Heart of Evil to contain all the power I now possessed by virtue of Arawn's fall. Once I thought Flame would be enough, but Sanctus had never intended Guardian Flame to reside without a body. Flame was a living substance in and of itself, flying where it willed though always linked to its Source. To assert full control over it, I needed to bind it. Strange that the Flame's true strength should lie in its weakness and not its strength, but if Time had taught me anything, it was that I could achieve anything by simply giving myself over to the lust that had first opened my eyes so long ago. Obstacles still lay before me. I needed the Stone of Existence to release more power and unify myself—my formless *Darkness*—with this vessel I had yet to claim. Lorshin was far stronger than his father had ever been! I needed the Gemshorn and one truly worthy of wielding the power of the Guardian's voice. I needed all of this before I could ever hope to bring my dominion to completion! Plan upon plan, waylaid by distraction, but soon all would be set right. The Resistance would fall once and for all and with it the Prophecy. With the Prophecy out of the way, everything else would fall easily into place.

I laughed. Soon—very soon—I would lay claim to the Gemshorn hidden somewhere in the vast universe. Zrene, the last of my Accursed Race, would find it for me; Death would lay my enemies low; Lorshin would bow his knee and lead my armies to victory; the void would be complete! I told myself this as I stepped out of my sanctuary into the world and fixed my gaze upon Firinn, momentarily forgetting all else.

Darkness.

* * *

Silence fell quickly upon them. The weary wayfarers feared it more than the screams that had been their constant companions for an untold number of days. Armahad leaned forward in his saddle to address their guide.

"Trin? Where is this place of rest?" he asked wearily. The dark rings under his eyes were deep, permanent things now. Sleep was impossible in this place. The lack of it pulled at all of them. Mydrian sagged in their saddles, barely able to keep their heads from resting on the back of their animals. Horses stumbled over nothing, and yet they couldn't sleep. Even Trin's footsteps were dragging and his twitching was ended.

"Lesser men would have run mad by now," Trin said. His words came in a mumble as he rolled his eyes incoherently toward the An Taoseach.

"What?" Armahad whispered, too unsettled by the silence to speak louder. "What are you talking about? Where are we? Where may we find rest?"

"Not here," Trin whispered. "Only there." With these words, he pitched forward, tumbling over his own feet face first upon the ground. His wings twitched once upon his back and fell limply around him.

"Stop!" Armahad shouted, jerking the Mydrian from the brink. Their swords came up almost in unison as their heads popped up. The An Taoseach reined his horse to a stop, and immediately the Mydrian followed suit, feeling the command through the cords that bound their mounts all together and through the High Captain's raised fist, a silent command to halt. Their unified force stopped just inches from Trin's body, lying unmoving across the path. Armahad dismounted and rushed toward the Fairy.

"Is our guide dead, Majesty?" one of the Mydrian asked.

"Quiet," the High Captain snapped as he too dismounted. "Stay alert."

"Trin's heavier than he looks," Armahad said in a strained voice as he struggled to roll Trin over without success.

"It is this place, An Taoseach," the High Captain said quietly as he bent to help his master. Together, with some effort, they turned their guide over. "I know what I said to them." He jerked his head toward the Mydrian host as he continued, "But, sire, we really should turn back."

Armahad kneeled beside Trin. "He's alive!"

"Majesty, listen to me," the High Captain said tensely in a hushed voice. "I am sworn to protect and defend you, but not just you. I am sworn to protect and defend the Mark! The Royal lineage! The House of Caladrius of which you are the last! You have no heir. We must turn back!"

"Captain," Armahad said harshly, but softened. "Your words do not fall on deaf ears, my friend. My own mind tells me to go back, which is why I press on. You are sworn to a task—a noble one, and so am I," he sighed. "Does my word mean nothing? If we turn back now, what will they think of the glory of Isear? We are blessed, Captain. Let us bless others who have known only heartache."

"Your word and your presence are everything, Majesty," the High Captain whispered.

"Then are you with me, Captain?"

The High Captain nodded once, leaned forward, and kissed the royal emblem emblazoned upon the breastplate of the king's armor and swore his oath. "My life, my liege, is in your hands and at your service to death and beyond, for Mark and for Throne I give my blood and my will, for An Taoseach and Crown I swear allegiance and give my children as I was given and my ancestors before me to honor, to obey, to protect the Deepest Foundations and sacrifice all for the Caladrius." He spoke the royal name in a reverent breath.

"Come, Captain. Help me."

Armahad took Trin by the arms, while the captain took him by the feet. Trin moaned softly.

"We'll put him on my horse," Armahad said. "I can walk for a while."

"No, sire. It is too dangerous," the captain objected quietly. "If we do this, I will walk before us. You will stay in the midst of the Mydrian. Give me your word on this, An Taoseach, and I will say no more."

Armahad inclined his head once in assent. The An Taoseach's horse balked at the Fairy loaded upon his back, but a few gentle words soon set the faithful horse at peace. Armahad mounted the captain's horse with ease while the captain took the lead with caution. Footstep by footstep—a monotonous rhythm to ease the silence, the humans pressed slowly forward through unfamiliar land.

Slowly, the *dark* shadows lengthened, drifting enough to lessen the oppression upon them. Silence lingered. Sleep remained evasive, yet Armahad felt his spirits lifting. Out of those shadows a citadel, long in ruins, emerged. Ancient mud brick buildings, crumbled now, had first dominated this plain, and as they fell, new had been erected. Layer by layer, the remaining ruins had risen upon those that had come before it.

"An Taoseach." The captain turned to address his king. "I think we should take advantage of this shelter."

Armahad glanced up at the ruins. "Do you think it is safe, Captain?"

The captain answered honestly, "I doubt we will find safety anywhere within the *Dark* lands, Majesty, but we must rest, and this place will provide a measure of security the open road will not. I have another reason, as well, my lord." He said quietly so that only the An Taoseach could hear him now, "Our supplies are depleted. There may still be things of use to us in there, forgotten by its former inhabitants. There may be a well. We need water."

Armahad nodded. "Lead on, Captain."

The new course led them off the main path onto a narrower trail that forced them to divide their unified force into one single-file train. They lashed the horses together with the single lead tied around the captain's waist so that none would stray blindly into *Darkness* and be lost. Shadows were thicker here, visibly moving—almost breathing—blackly away in a cauldron of unbound seasons. The trail twisted up through the layers of ruins toward the citadel that became less inviting the closer they climbed. Skulls emerged from the muddy trail. Bones protruded from the foundation of ruins—fragile relics that would surely deteriorate if light or air were ever allowed to touch them. Even in decomposition, the faces of these dead where twisted by whatever horrors had come upon them in that moment. Mouths hung wide in silent, eternal screams which were heard now only by the eerie wind flowing over them as the long shadows grew longer, moving away.

Armahad ignored the unsettled feeling in his gut. His lifted spirits had been dashed to the ground as soon as they had found their wings, but he said nothing. A feeling meant nothing in this place. Feelings lied while the need was too great to ignore.

The citadel wore its signs of abandonment like a warning, complete with decomposing corpses draping its broken walls. Rotten flesh paved the trail, squishing ominously beneath the feet of the horses. The smell was impossible to escape as the very air, black and clotted as it was, reeked of blood.

"I see a well, Majesty!" the High Captain called breathlessly. He dropped the lead rope and ran through the carnage to the circular stone pit. With eager hands, he lowered the bucket by means of the wheel mechanism rigged over the well's mouth and raised it up again. He took his own cup from his belt and dipped it into the cool liquid, tasted it, and then returned to his king. "Drink, Majesty."

"Him first." Armahad nodded toward Trin.

"Sire, please, think of your health."

"Him first," Armahad said again. Trin had not stirred since they placed him upon the horse.

"As you will." The captain bowed before turning his attention to Trin.

No sooner had a single drop of water touched his lips, Trin jerked upright in the saddle suddenly, angrily, knocking the cup away. "Water! Yuck!"

"Have it your way," the captain said, returning his attention to his master. "Please, drink, sire."

Armahad reached for the cup.

"No!" Trin shouted, launching himself from the horse's back at the An Taoseach.

A single, unified shout rose from the Mydrian. The captain tackled Trin, dropping the cup in the process. Trin hit the ground with a hard, painful thud and twisted around to face the points of a thousand swords; a thousand more surrounded the An Taoseach.

"You would attack my king," the captain said fiercely, "while I am at his side?"

"Don't drink the water!" Trin said with equal ferocity.

"You may not drink water, Fairy," the captain said, "but we humans need water to survive!"

"Not this water," Trin said.

Armahad dismounted. "Let him up."

The Mydrian stood aside as he passed through their midst. Their High Captain withdrew last, scowling in response to Trin's smirk as the latter rose, dusting off grime and filth from his clothes.

"Trin, speak plainly," Armahad said with all the authority of his rank. "Why should we not drink this water?"

"Look around you, great king, what do you see?"

"The carnage of a great battle."

"Yes, but who was the enemy? Look closer," Trin said. He motioned to the two nearest corpses. Flesh hung in rotting ribbons from their bodies, bodies that were locked together in bitter struggle even now.

"Look at the dead!" the captain exclaimed. He shoved Trin hard. "Look at the living!"

"Enough, Captain!" Armahad said fiercely. "I will hear this."

Trin smiled smugly and continued, "They were once allies, great king, driven mad by the water."

"I tasted the water, Majesty," the captain whispered, "there was nothing wrong with it."

"And therein lies the trap," Trin answered.

"Sire, forgive me, but if you listen to him, you are the traitor! We have not slept, we have not eaten, and we have not even had a drop of water to ease the burning of our throats! There stands a perfectly good well full of water, and you would allow him to forbid us a drop! Well, you will not keep me from it!" He raised his sword before the An Taoseach's face.

"Captain!" a Mydrian shouted, thrusting his blade between his commander and his king in time to intercept the blow with a horrible clash. "Stop!"

"Out of my way!" the captain shouted.

Two big Mydrian tackled the captain from behind, wrestling him to the ground as the others hovered in weary vigilance around the An Taoseach. The captain screamed, writhing in muscled fury beneath his opponents until a blow to the head knocked him out. They bound the captain's hands and feet with quick efficiency before dropping with exhaustion beside him.

"He tasted the water," Trin said quietly.

All eyes turned toward him.

Trin continued, "You must understand, the Dark One turns us against each other! He does not fight openly and honestly. He uses illusion, trickery, betrayal, need, and . . . hope," he said dismally. "Do not fall prey to his evil, my lord. You who have known light must show us there is still real Hope!"

"My captain is right, Trin," Armahad said softly, "we need water."

"There is none," Trin answered sorrowfully. "There is none. Not until we reach Firinn."

"How far?"

"That depends."

"On what, Trin?" Armahad asked with uncertainty.

"On you, great king."

*　　*　　*

Firinn

Master Esarian hadn't moved for days. Firinn rose at his back, and around him spread a sea of tents and the beleaguered armies of every race cloaking the land as far as the eye could see. There were no open spaces, no room to breathe, as all wanted to be as close to refuge as possible. None could quite get close enough to escape the *Darkness*. Firinn's thread of power was nearly wasted. Too much time had passed since the god had rested his feet upon the footstool of Truth. Too much *Darkness* set itself against the final breaths of Guardian Flame. Too many lives had been lost to a war that they could not win alone. The inklings of this knowledge made the other Summoners restless, disturbed even more by his silence—more so than by the silence of the *Darkness* laying siege around them. The Summoners paced like animals trapped in a cage, round and round a large circuitous route around Firinn. He doubted whether they truly understood their own danger. Their restlessness didn't touch him. He knew whatever was coming would come whether he wanted it to or not—and truly it had to come—because there was no hope for them here if something did not change, and whether for good or ill this change would be the breaking point for them all. The Darkening War had finally reached its head: to fall or arise were the only options left.

A terrible blackness came with the silence, crumbling in upon Firinn gradually as the *Darkness* followed the retreat of the Resistance from every direction. They were trapped, their backs to Firinn, their eyes toward the Dark One . . . Esarian sighed . . . and no savior in sight.

"Esarian, look!" D'Faihven exclaimed, interrupting his silent meditations, motioning frantically at something he couldn't see. Being a young giant, his friend often forgot that others were not as tall as she nor could they see so far.

From her tone, Esarian gathered that she was quite disturbed by what she saw, so much so that she would break the silence loudly enough for all to hear. He unfolded himself painfully from his long-held position, grimacing slightly at the stiff aching in his legs as they rebelled against him. He braced himself momentarily against Firinn to keep from sprawling on useless legs onto his face.

"What is it? What do you see?" Orlok growled abruptly, turning from his pacing to join her.

Nulet climbed her limbs like a tree to perch upon her head. "Where?" he asked as he balanced.

"There!" D'Faihven said impatiently. She thrust her arm out in the direction she wanted them to look.

"I cannot see it," Orlok said. "But I can hear it." The hairs dangling from his supersensitive dwarf ears bristled.

"What? What is it?" Nulet whined, stamping his foot in aggravation, forgetting he was on D'Faihven's head. "Tell me. You know I can't see like a Giant or hear like a Dwarf!"

Esarian gazed openmouthed where D'Faihven pointed; having found the strength to move his legs, he drifted forward to join his friends. The other Summoners gathered in mute horror behind him. "It is the arising," he said softly in answer to Nulet's question.

"The arising? Of what?"

Darkness, already so thick that it felt impossible to even breathe now, pressed in so that they could not be separated. The Resistance cowered in its midst. The fear, the rage, the hatred were growing more violent in their possession. *Thud. Thud. Thud.* From somewhere behind him, footsteps resounded in the abyss. Phantom breaths filled the dark, falling hotly over them. Voices rang out all around them so faintly that they barely seemed whispers. They came from within and from without, spreading confusion in their wake.

Esarian shook his head. "Only time will tell, my friend, but I fear not all of us will survive it."

"Where is Trin?" Nulet whispered. "Where is this hope he spoke of?"

"We're out of time," Orlok said sharply.

"We need more," D'Faihven said just as sharply. "Esarian, what do we do?"

He trembled. "The One Whose Name is not Spoken comes," he whispered in terror. "I have a plan, but it's dangerous."

"Tell us."

The Summoners all gathered close around him. Esarian spoke in a low breath. "You rally our forces while I distract the Dark One."

"Are you mad?" D'Faihven asked suddenly. "You can't face him alone!"

"This is my choice, D'Faihven. He would have us all face him alone," Esarian said gently. "I am stronger now. I can feel the power of the Firebrand within. Perhaps it was given for such a time as this, but if not, better one die than all. Do as I say. I will buy you what time I can. Do not waste it! We are stronger together! Unite them quickly!"

"Do not die," D'Faihven whispered, touching his shoulder softly before turning to make her way toward where the Giants camped.

One by one, the other Summoners bid him wordless farewells. Likely, before this day was passed, he would lie in the earth with his ancestors.

Darkness.

*   *   *

I laughed at the mountains of death, at the rivers of blood, at the wails of terror and despair that rang out before me.

"Look, Master," my pitiful, twisted creature whispered in my unformed ear. Gnoll pawed at my *dark* visage affectionately. "Look how they flee from you." A wicked smile spread across his face.

"Watch," I said quietly. "Witness my power." I thrust my anger before me and raised the foot of despair, a streak in the dark, and plunged it into the earth. Blackness spread out, poisoning the natural veins of the earth in every direction, driving my power into the heart of Firinn. Rocks shattered as the earth collapsed in upon itself and the blackness rushed after the fleeing inhabitants of the world.

Gnoll threw his head back and laughed. I laughed too, wheezing out a black breath to poison the air. Day and Night fled before my breath, descending to hang precariously by their sky cloak from Firinn's pinnacle. The Mother and Father of Guardians trembled in their untouchable places high above the earth. Blackened stars fell from the sky.

I climbed to my feet. Fury burned in my eyes. Gnoll clapped his grotesque hands as I drew a deep breath and slowly exhaled, waiting for the violence and chaos to ensue.

Screams returned to fill the blackness, but this time they were quite real.

"*Arr-ahh!*" I cried as I thrust *my* hand forward, casting *darkness* out before me.

Holes opened in the earth to swallow my frantic prey, but up out of this glorious chaos climbed an unexpected challenge. Gnoll hissed, suddenly petrified. I kicked him aside with disgust as I appraised this bold, foolish being—this child—who gazed back at me without fear.

"I am Esarian," the boy said.

His voice trembled, making me question my assumption that he was not afraid, yet if he was afraid, why was he here casting himself into the full brunt of my wrath.

"The Firebrand of the Highest," Esarian said, speaking an ancient Guardian name for the god who rested his feet upon Firinn in the beginning.

Another hiss rose. This one came from the *Darkness* all around me. Gnoll fled back toward the pit of my power where Lorshin gave himself mindlessly to Death.

"High Commander of the Resistance," Esarian said, smiling slightly, despite his fear, at the Dark One's discomfort. "Master Summoner." He displayed the Styarfyre orb shard around his neck.

"Am I supposed to be afraid, boy?" my black breath whispered around him.

"I command you to stop," Esarian said. He shivered as fingers of *Darkness* ran down his cheek.

"So brave," I said. "So foolish." My hands smashed hard into his chest, knocking him to the ground.

Esarian rolled before the *dark* could crush him, springing lithely back to his feet unscathed, simultaneously drawing a dagger from his belt.

I smiled. "You don't want to fight me, child," I whispered. "Surrender is so much easier."

"And far more foolish," Esarian answered coolly.

My laughter flowed around him mockingly. *Come then.* I whispered to his mind. *Come face my Darkness and you will taste my wrath, for I am all that you fear and more.*

"I fear no one—only he who gave life—I do not fear you!" Esarian's shouted words sounded far bolder than he felt as he charged headlong toward his demise.

I laughed, letting my visage drift back into unformed *Darkness* surrounding him in the depths. "Now, child, I will teach you that Hope is in vain!" My illusion reformed, holding the boy off the ground in a stranglehold. "And then, perhaps, I will let you taste Death, which is the only hope you have left!" I laughed again. "Or perhaps not. Perhaps I will let you suffer. Perhaps I will break you to my will. Perhaps."

Esarian stared with a mocking smile on his boyish face. "Those who stand together for the hope of Hope are stronger," he said hoarsely.

I cocked my head to the side, appraising this child. "Still so brave?"

"Not brave," Esarian said. "Branded." Suddenly he thrust his dagger into the midst of *Darkness.*

I snarled out of anger not pain; he couldn't hurt me, yet the rash defiance of a child already beaten startled me. I dropped him as I staggered back and ripped the blade from my belly. "You will pay for that, boy."

Esarian smiled. "Perhaps, but not today, I think." He spun suddenly out of my reach, and as I stalked after him, he shouted, "Now Summoners, arise!"

My laughter was cut short as the whistling of ten thousands of arrows filled the air. More a nuisance than any real danger to me, the attack was hardly worth my attention; still, if they wanted a fight, I would give them one. I turned slowly to face the army at my back. At my will, the illusion billowed apart, arraying the *Darkness* around my prey. An issue of black breath broke through the front lines, flinging the Resistance armies' bravest and best into oblivion before their screams had drifted into silence. Chaos scattered their ranks as the arrows descended toward the *dark.* With little effort, I turned them in a horrible tide back upon their masters.

Brazen shouts rose from Firinn's shadow. The Summoners charged, unexpectedly arousing the courage of the Resistance.

"To Esarian! For Hope!"

The armies of every race reformed behind them, charging with insane shouts into the blackness where they hacked and sliced at incorporeal *Darkness* to no avail. Esarian joined the fight.

It was hard not to admire the effort, idiotic though it was, and for one moment, I considered their fate. Such insanity could be useful in the long days ahead before the void reached completion. There was no reason why I should annihilate all of my future subjects, not if I could break them. Vile laughter rang through the *Darkness* as I pulled back into its illusive frame. As *my* fingers came together in a fist, drawn abruptly to *my* own chest, their weapons were torn from their hands by *my* power. I broke the weapons with a thought, twisting the metal in upon itself before casting the useless relics aside.

"When are you going to realize that you are powerless against me?" I asked in a quiet menacing voice. "Do you think I *like* doing these things to you?" As I spoke, I let my gaze sweep across the Resistance. One by one, they dropped before me, choking on their own lungs. "Do you think I *want* to destroy you?" Last of all, I looked upon Master Esarian. He gazed back untouched. I snickered low under my breath, so he really was branded by a power still greater than I. Him I would just have to annihilate. I looked away abruptly, refusing to acknowledge him any further. He could wait. There was nowhere to run. "We could be friends," I said seductively to the retching forces bowed before me. "I can give you all that you desire."

"Liar!" Esarian shouted.

I growled, suddenly furious, and yanked the child from the ranks. "I have no more use for you, boy!" I raised him high, preparing to dash him upon the rocks of Firinn, when suddenly I felt a tingle of power graze across *my* back. *Darkness* trembled all around me, clothing itself with fear.

"Let the child go." The voice was firm, authoritative—a voice, I imagined, that would belong to a king.

I turned slowly, shoving Esarian aside—no longer interested in his immediate demise. "Who dares to command me?" I stopped as I faced them. *Humans.* A smile of mocking welcome crossed *my* lips. "Here I expect a real challenge and I find humans." The black-clad army dropped beneath the force of my power, but the one who had spoken stood as Esarian had stood, untouchable. "Who are you?"

The man hesitated, uncertain it seemed; he glanced down at his cowering guide—a Fairy I had previously overlooked, nothing real impressive about him to warrant any concern, yet at the Fairy's nod of encouragement, the man raised his pale hands to his golden helm. "See for yourself, Dark One." With trembling hands, he withdrew the helm and cast it aside. "Behold the Mark of Caladrius!"

Gasps rose from the bowing armies of the Resistance as I staggered back from the sight. The Mark that plagued the recesses of my mind burst into view—*a waxing crescent around which a young Guardian draped.* "No!"

I backed away. *Darkness* beckoned with safety to *my* retreating form.

A cheer rose from the Resistance as I fled, yet one thought consumed me: destroy the Mark!

Darkness.

Master Esarian crawled to his feet and brushed the dirt, as best he could, from his horribly stained white robe. His shaggy blond hair hung in disarray around his boyish face caked with the dirt and grime of the battle, yet he didn't notice. His eyes were fixed in wonder upon the Mark and its bearer. With cautious steps, he approached the man upon the white horse and his reassembling army.

Trin rushed forward the meet him. "Master Esarian," the Fairy said excitedly, "I have brought Armahad Caladrius, the An Taoseach of Isear." He indicated the man on the white horse.

Armahad dismounted and strode out to join them. His Mydrian shadowed his move, but a raised hand kept them a few feet back. "Master Esarian," the king said, "I have heard much about you."

"And I, you," Esarian said quietly. "I have seen the wonders of your land."

"Yet you refused my offer of help to test me in the *dark* land?"

Esarian glanced at Trin.

Trin shrugged helplessly. "I tried."

"I see you survived," Esarian answered the An Taoseach as if this was everything that mattered. "You withstood the evil."

"And nearly died," Armahad said sternly.

"But you didn't," Esarian said with equal firmness. He sighed, "I had to know if all that Trin told me, if all that had been whispered about you, could possibly be true. As you can see, I led many and I could not risk their lives for a rumor."

"An entire nation depends upon me, Esarian. What if I had failed your test? What would have become of them? You risked too much."

Esarian shook his head slowly. "No, great king, I did not, because there is not just one nation that needs you but an entire world!"

"Is it as I thought, Master Esarian?" Trin asked in hushed excitement.

Esarian nodded. "You were right to hope, Trin. I am sorry I did not believe." He met Armahad's gaze and held it. "I can see what Trin could not honestly tell me before. A Guardian made that Mark, but it is the Mark of the Promised—the Mark of Prophecy. Your kingdom, your throne, your line has been chosen and I—" He dropped to his knees in obeisance. "We all—" the hosts of the Resistance bowing now—"pledge allegiance to His Mark. Let the Light shine forth and awaken hope! Let Mhorag arise! Let the Promised come!" The Summoner leaned forward and kissed the An Taoseach's feet.

* * *

Darkness.

Let them relish their newfound dream. Let them think they have won, but their new stronghold bore all the weaknesses of humanity underneath that hideous Mark! There had to be a way to have him, to stop the Prophecy in its tracks! For now I would take my anger out upon those who couldn't escape. Someone would bow to me this day—my day—my Time! A sigh drifted through the blackness. And when I had spent my wrath, I would find a way.

"There will be no Hope!" I screamed to the black.

Outside the churning *dark*, no one listened. No one cared. I turned inward, escaping the sting of failure that was still too bitter and fresh. Anger drenched my heart, the Heart of Evil. I sensed it beginning. Throughout the world, hearts were no longer so conveniently vacant. Rumors of Guardians and their dormant Prophecy had been awoken, spreading like wild fire, igniting forgotten dreams. *Hope.* The word twisted mockingly in my troubled thoughts.

Darkness.

Loriath, Kingdom of the Elves of Light:

Elvin warriors crept soundlessly through the Red Wood that had grown too silent around them. A heavy fog was seeping down through the leaves of the ancient giants into the deep valley. Other trees, fighting for survival beneath the canopy were shedding their leaves out of season to paint the soft brown earth with vibrant colors. A gentle river carved its way down through the valley from its distant mountainous source, making tiny white falls over fallen, mossy logs and exposed green-clad rocks jutting smoothly from the earth.

The trees seemed to shutter uneasily, sensing the danger the fog masked. *Darkness* stained the bronzed armor of Elvin elite who moved with unrelenting swiftness toward the safety of Loriath's invisible walls. Their mission weighed heavily upon them, and they sensed yet again the horrible toll this news would have upon their people. The forest rushed past them, virtually invisible in their haste, as they sought to outrun the threat they could feel but not see.

Cadclucan gazed across the valley from the height of a gold and amber bridge hovering between the conical crowns of two massive redwoods, draped in the slightly drooping branches of each. His unnatural, flaming blue eyes saw beyond the magical walls cloaking Loriath, beyond the fog creeping into the forest, beyond even the howling fury of *Darkness* riding hot upon its back. His powerful breath came slow and steady even as he sensed the coiling blackness encroaching upon him. The Stone of Existence glowed defiantly around his neck, catching the Light of his eyes, his breath, and the artificial light of elfin halls. This sanctuary would not contain his secret much longer. He knew in his heart the day was coming when the magic of the Elves failed, when *Darkness* would sense one of the objects of its desire and seek it relentlessly, when he would be forced to flee alone—horribly alone—with a burden too strong for him to bear, and yet he was its Guardian—it was his burden.

"Baculus." The reverent name the Elves had given him shattered the silence growing like its own fog within his mind, yanking him back from the brink of *Darkness* just before either of the coiled powers could fully comprehend the presence of the other.

He whirled around to face the unexpected intruder—not quite in control of the power burning out of him—sighing softly when he saw Maizie standing mere inches away, watching the uneasy play of emotions upon his face. The fear in her eyes banished his own, arousing him from the vision that pulled wildly at his senses. "My lady," he said softly, inclining his head to her.

His gaze captured the trembling of her hand as she raised it to caress his rugged, unshaven, yet glorious face.

"You haven't slept for many nights," Maizie said quietly.

Cadclucan caught her hand in his and drew it to his lips.

The elfin queen blushed deeply. "I know you will not tell me what plagues your mind, Baculus," she began in a whisper, struggling to form a single coherent thought out of the chaos he read easily enough in her mind, "but I-I am afraid. I am afraid for you. I—"

"Stop." Cadclucan placed a finger on her lips. "Please just stop. I can't—" he sighed and turned away to hide from the hurt in her downcast eyes. "You can't . . ." He fell silent, leaving unsaid the turbulent thoughts that slithered through the shadows of his mind in time with the rapid beat of her heart. The longing of her heart matched his own. Her troubled thoughts seemed a reflection of his, but time was against them.

"We are both trapped," Maizie whispered.

A horn sounded deep within the valley.

Maizie brushed the tears from her eyes. "The warriors have returned."

Cadclucan nodded once. "I know."

"What do you know, Baculus? What do you sense?"

The Guardian didn't answer as he turned around to face her once more. "Danger," he finally said in a whisper as they walked side by side down through the streets of Loriath. "The Dark One is close . . . very close."

"Open the gate!" the warriors yelled, flinging themselves toward the invisible walls of Loriath. In their panic, they were flung back again and again by the barrier cutting through the heart of the Red Wood. *Darkness* broke over the trees rushing down to devour them.

Cadclucan could see them plainly, though he knew they could not see him. "Get them inside, quickly!" he ordered, drawing away from Maizie's side. "Now!" he nearly growled.

"What is it? What do you see?" Maizie asked, hurriedly rushing forward to catch his hand.

The Guardian swung around to face her. Blood dripped like tears from his flaming eyes.

"Talk to me, Baculus!" the queen shrieked. The sight of his blood made her legs weak. She sagged forward; his strong hands held her up.

The warriors' horrified screams pierced the silence.

Equally panicked, Elves within the walls scrambled to rescue their friends outside. Warriors mounted the walls, readying their bows while the ancient tomes containing all the magic of the Elves were opened. In the midst of the sudden chaos, their keepers performed a powerful and complex ceremony to open the gate. Their voices were hushed into whispered chants. Their bodies convulsed with the great strength of the spell until one by one they collapsed beneath the exertion. Weakened too greatly to stand, their bodies lined the base of the invisible walls, which slowly—like the trickling of a gentle stream—shimmered into view.

A single narrow doorway opened out upon the forest. The warriors tumbled through, their screams dying on their lips as they looked up into the eyes of the Guardian. They crawled toward him, each grasped a hold of him, clutching tightly to his midnight robe, to his ankles to his hands. "Great One!" they whispered. "My Queen." They breathed when they looked to her.

"You are safe," Cadclucan said gently.

"Great One! The Walls!" one of the elfin warriors cried from his post on the wall.

The keepers had not yet risen. The pages of the ancient tomes whipped wildly in the first waves of the Dark One's black breath. *Darkness* crept soundlessly into view. Grass charred beneath their feet in a wide berth around the Guardian. Flowers shriveled. Even the giant trees seemed darker.

"Take her," Cadclucan ordered, pushing Maizie gently into the arms of the warriors clinging to him. He freed himself easily and efficiently from their grasp, defying gravity though still maintaining his human form; his movement was so quick that he was there and gone in a second.

Their frantic eyes sought and found him by the ancient tomes of the keepers.

"What is he doing?" one of the warriors breathed.

"Saving us," Maizie answered.

"He will betray himself to the Dark One!" one of the warriors cried.

"No," Maizie said. "He can still hide himself. The Dark One's power is growing, but it is not strong enough yet to seek him out! Look!"

Cadclucan placed one hand upon the tome and one hand upon the closest keeper. The keeper stretched to grasp the hand of the next on and on until all the keepers were linked through the one before to the Guardian. The keepers chanted softly—too softly to hear—repeating the incantation the Guardian breathed into their minds, stronger than any breathed before it. The wall vanished; the door banged closed; the tendril of blackness trapped inside burst into Flame. Its ashes drifted away on the wind, washing the *Darkness* from the earth of Loriath.

As the last of these ashes vanished before the eyes of the awestruck Elves, Cadclucan stepped away from the keepers and their tomes. Blood streamed from his eyes, dropping off his face onto the earth, reviving what *Darkness* had scarred. The earth trembled mightily before erupting with life once more, but this Guardian power was contained, safe within the walls of Loriath momentarily beyond the Dark One's probing gaze. His breathing was hard—rasping inhumanly in his chest—when Maizie rushed into his arms.

His gaze became startled when she rose up to kiss his lips. He deepened the kiss with tenderness and longing before he set her aside.

Maizie looked at him questioningly.

He smiled with gentle reassurance before nodding once toward the warriors they had just rescued. *Duty first.* His voice touched her mind. The queen nodded, turning toward her warriors while staying close to the Guardian's side.

"What did you find?" Maizie asked them.

The warriors shook their heads.

"Nothing?" Maizie whispered.

Cadclucan frowned, seeing it all in their minds.

"We tried to reach the Resistance as you instructed. It had been so long since we heard of them," one of the warriors said quietly, "but we made for Firinn only to find we couldn't make it through! We are surrounded, my queen."

"Any sign of the Resistance?"

"No," the warrior answered. "We saw only ruin and death."

Maizie glanced from her warriors to the Guardian. "What do you see, Baculus?"

"*Darkness*," he whispered. Fresh blood dripped from his eyes.

*   *   *

Hope. Neither word, nor dream, nor confident expectation . . . Hope was a threat. I brooded, oblivious to the world around me. The passing of time was beyond my comprehension, until, quite unexpectedly, a weak light broke into my *Darkness.*

With a piercing wail, I unleashed my black breath upon my newly chosen prey. They would taste the throes of woe and then so would the vessels of Hope . . . whatever the Light harbored against me . . . I smiled to myself, suddenly focused in my purpose. This was my Time, and it would not fall!

Chapter Thirty-Three

RETURNING KING

Nithrodine Castle, Isear

A parade of figures dressed in elaborate costumes of brilliant colors, which flashed like the first rays of dawn on the cobbled streets of the city, their faces hidden by masks, leaped and danced to the music of a thousand instruments. Over the music, their voices sang, "The An Taoseach draws nigh! The An Taoseach is returning! Arise! Arise!" Other dancers bedecked like the great *bird* of legend, the Caladrius, crying loudly, "He comes! The Caladrius comes! Arise!" joined the masked figures.

Stilt walkers rapped on the shuttered windows of sleeping peasants. Acrobats made full use of the streets for their tricks while the shimmering white fabric wings of the Caladrius fanned the flames of the celebration.

From the first plaintive note of the pipes to the very last echo of the drum, the parade proceeded toward the very doors of the palace itself high within Nithrodine. Conjuring a magical world full of mythical beasts, madcap fools and dancing masked figures, the parade grew in size as peasants emerged from their homes to join them. "The An Taoseach draws nigh! The Caladrius comes! Arise! Arise!"

Their cries drifted up to the impressive height of the palatial mountain that gave all of Nithrodine its name and sheltered the Royal House of Caladrius. The voices whispered faintly through the open window of Queen Keliah's chamber, arousing her from a fitful sleep, but she didn't rise from her bed. She imagined Armahad's return so often she had given up responding to the false hope. Keliah turned her face into her silken pillow to muffle her scream. Sleep after sleep, the same dream woke her from her rest, and still Armahad did not return though the weeks dragged painfully into months and the months crept relentlessly toward a year. Her only comfort had been those precious orphans—Kinjour, Cait, and Goldya—who, in her heart, she now claimed as her own. Their laughter eased the long hours of light, leaving only the night hours to plague her mind and heart. *Darkness* loomed with bitter mockery on the distant horizons in every direction while rumors of death and ruin whispered through the streets of Nithrodine's lower courts carried in by travelers from the far reaches of Isear. Though no one would speak them in her presence, Keliah was not immune to these whispers and the fear that kept her from rest.

The dream was stronger this time, holding on to her mind, though sleep slowly fell away. Music continued to ring faintly in her ears, all but drowning out the whispery cries, speaking the only words she longed to hear. "The An Taoseach draws nigh! The Caladrius comes! Arise! Arise! Your true and rightful king approaches! Arise! Arise!"

Keliah lifted her head, listening.

"Arise! Arise! The An Taoseach draws nigh!"

Quickly, suddenly possessed by the certainty that this was not a dream, she threw off the regal sheets and jumped from the bed. "Guard!" she cried as she pulled on her a silken robe.

One of the Mydrian appeared a moment later and bowed deeply. "Majesty?"

"Do you hear it?" she asked.

Just then the trumpets blasted from the highest tower, vanquishing any doubt. Keliah didn't wait for the Mydrian's answer now as she ran from the chamber. Her bodyguards converged around her in silence as she rushed through the dim halls of Nithrodine, making her way down through the labyrinth to the lowest court where her beloved would return. A buzz of activity erupted in the palace all around her, another indication that this was not a dream.

The music and the cries grew louder as she descended through the palace, beckoning her toward her one desire. "The An Taoseach draws nigh! The Caladrius comes! Arise! Arise!"

His face, shining as sunlight at midnight, Armahad rode through the awed throngs of his people. Their hands stretched through the lines of his bodyguard to touch his boot, the hem of his robe—anything—just to touch him. Their songs of exaltation died on their lips as they actually beheld him, returning to them upon the back of a white horse, the Caladrius flying on a thousand banners above his crowned head.

The streets of Nithrodine were packed with acrobats, fire breathers, dancers, and people from every region of Isear slowing their progress. All around him the Mydrian maintained a vast, loose but watchful barrier. Extending for countless miles behind him came a procession of pilgrims—strangers from every land and every race—seeking refuge within this strange land of Light. Most of them were far from human.

"Make way! Make way!" his herald shouted. "Make way for the An Taoseach of Isear!"

The crowd heaved around them, contractions that mounted slowly and painfully, carrying Armahad toward the height of Nithrodine and home.

Keliah waited upon the wall, gazing out from a throng of soldiers over the outermost gate. Her eyes strained against the dark to see the approach of her beloved. Tense minutes extended into torturous hours of anticipation as Nithrodine fell silent inch by horrible inch, beginning in its lowest bowels and creeping upward. Night drifted into day, the Light growing brighter rising up before her eyes as the herald's cry finally reached her ears.

"Make way! Make way!" the herald shouted. "Make way for the An Taoseach of Isear!"

Keliah flung herself down the narrow stairway that descended the interior of the wall. "Open the gate!" she cried breathlessly. Her heart pounded excitedly in her chest.

The gate was heavy, impressively thick and strong, and opened very slowly. Heavy chains ground around a massive wheel worked by brawny, sweat-covered slaves. Keliah rushed through the narrowest opening she could to the excitement of the peasants at the gate. Mydrian shadowed her in a protective arch. She rose on her tiptoes to see through the throngs of people for the first glimpse of the royal banners, preceded by the hush of the crowds. There he was.

Keliah ran through the narrow opening caused by the contraction of the crowd. "Armahad!"

The An Taoseach dismounted and ran toward her through the other end of the narrow opening as the Mydrian shouted in objection, joining the herald in his demand to make way for the king!

"Armahad!"

"Keliah!"

The An Taoseach opened his arms, and his queen ran full force into his embrace. He hoisted her into his arms and kissed her to the cheers of his people.

*   *   *

Armahad placed another log in the fireplace of the quiet chamber, thankful for the solitude after so many months on the road. Keliah's arms circled his waist when he rose; though he smiled in response it did not touch his eyes. His gaze remained far away as he pondered the changes taking place around him. The weight of a nation already rested upon his shoulders, and after tonight's grand feast, the weight of a world would be added to it.

"Come back to me," Keliah whispered as her lips pressed his bared chest in a soft kiss.

His face cleared slightly as his arms closed around her. "I am here."

"Not completely." Keliah rose up on her toes to kiss his lips. "Maybe this will help." Her lips brushed against his.

Armahad sighed, coming awake it seemed, as he pulled her closer, lengthening the kiss. Without breaking apart, they staggered away from the fireplace toward the waiting bed.

Far below, the palace was busy with near-frantic preparations for the feast; but, for the moment, Armahad was free of the duty that plagued his mind—no different than any man in the embrace of a woman he truly loved.

Chapter Thirty-Four

EMPIRE OF LIGHT

The Grand Feast of Unity, Year 1092 of the Darkening War—in the Tenth Year of His Majesty Armahad Caladrius, the An Taoseach of Isear:

A brooding of *Darkness* and Light served as the backdrop to peace—neither one quite tranquil or silent, yet all assembled, keeping their backs warily to the *dark* and their faces to the Light as much as was possible. The waxing crescent moon hung low upon Night's crown made nearer by the wide-open space in the center of the palace. Except for the moon hanging low, it was easy to overlook the height of this place caught as they were in a wide, oddly shaped bowl nestled between a ring of mountain peaks each interlaced by the grand architecture of Nithrodine palace. The secret of its construction was closely guarded, like all things pertaining to the Royal House of Caladrius, by the Mydrian and dated back to the days of Nudhug himself.

In the exact center of this bowl stood a lump of stone. Visibly rough in texture, the stone looked to be made of unique pebbles all plastered together within a mass of gray, cracked and weathered with age. In another place, the stone could have been mistaken for a foundation stone, but here it rose for several solitary inches out of the fertile bowl. A round hole in its crown, lipped like an open mouth was the only remarkable thing about it, yet its legend lived in the hearts of all who called themselves Isearians! Even the strangers, who did not know the tales, sensed its importance by the ring of Mydrian who stood guard around it, looking every bit as menacing as if the stone was their king himself. A reverential silence marred only by the brooding of two supernatural forces settled over the assemblage until it was abruptly shattered by an eerie cry, almost an echo that seemingly came from the earth itself centered beneath the stone.

The Light of the strange star and the silver hue of the moon came together at that moment upon the surface of the stone. Three silver crescents, their meaning long clouded in myth, appeared and the whispery cry rose into a powerful, subterranean shrieking. The sound should have inspired fear, but as it rose in exultation from the earth, an insane cloud of joy cloaked the land—unexplained, yet irresistible. Trumpets sounded over the din of the earth's cry. A ripple passed through the innumerable host packed so closely that they moved as one organism, and a narrow aisle formed to the cry of, "Make way! Make way for the An Taoseach of Isear!"

Trumpeters leading a thousand banners bearing the royal emblem, preceded by the dancers with their fabric Caladrius, came into view followed by two long ranks of Mydrian, four thousand strong at least, on either side of the famed ruler and his queen, both dressed in shimmering white samite clothes, contrasting sharply with their black-clad protectors.

The An Taoseach's face caught the Light, his royal Mark reflecting it so that his features were all but obscured. Even his queen gasped in awe at the sight. In addition to the Mark that always shone upon his face, there appeared two other crescents formed by moonlight and starlight as it did upon the stone.

"Hope!" Esarian shouted from the edge of the assembled crowd.

A frenzied cheer rose, beginning in the ranks of strangers come from the *dark* lands spreading to fill the bowl, the invisible hallways of the palace, the bowels of Nithrodine, out into all this empire framed in Light, sweeping beyond the burning shadows into *Darkness* where all the earth whispered in response. *Let the Light shine forth and awaken hope. Let Mhorag arise. Let the Promised come.* Abruptly, silence returned as Armahad's hand passed over the stone. He ceremoniously bowed once to the rock, which, for him above all others, held the legend of his birthright in its mysterious possession—a story little believed, the truth uncertain and diminishing with each telling but still inspiring the traditional reverence of his ancestors—and turned regally to face his kingdom.

"Noble Isearians," he said in a loud and commanding voice, "friends from distant lands, tonight we become one nation, an Empire of Light, united against *Darkness!*"

Another cheer rose longer than the one before.

Esarian rushed forward, falling on his face before the An Taoseach before the guards could thrust him back. "Great king!" the boy shouted, clutching to Armahad's ankle. "I come in the name of the Resistance."

"Rise and speak, friend," Armahad said.

The Firebrand obeyed. "I offer this gift." Esarian held in his hands a magnificent sword, the sword of a king. "Its master died for Hope. May it be wielded to victory by one who bears the Mark of Prophecy! The Resistance is now—"

"Aros![6]" The interrupting shout came from an invisible point within the crowd. Murmurs spread at the shout—disorienting by its diversion from the common language—and some looked around sharply for one who would dare to speak unbidden by the great king.

"Show yourself," Armahad commanded without any trace of anger on his princely face.

Startled exclamations preceded the eruption of a host of flying figures—straight and sure as arrows—falling now in a hail of fire.

Shouts of warning set the Mydrian on edge, but Armahad raised his hand signaling them back. "Wait."

The figures contorted in upon themselves, rolling into flaming orange balls before landing with extraordinary grace upon the balls of their feet. Fire spread minutely as they straightened, snapping out almost instantaneously except for their hair which continued to burn and smoke like lava.

Queen Keliah drew back behind her husband suddenly wary.

"Peace, good lady," their leader said with a smile that was too menacing to be comforting, though it was meant to be. The twisted mouth was a mass of very deadly teeth.

"What are you doing?" Esarian whispered uncertainly, only to be ignored.

"I am Wirtbam, King of the Poeth."

Armahad inclined his head once in acknowledgment.

"I will speak," Wirtbam continued to the disapproval of the Isearian court—and the Summoners at Esarian's back—a number of laws were being broken, but none dared to chide him, however, silenced by the silence of the An Taoseach.

"I will hear," Armahad answered after once tense moment.

"Then you may well be worthy," Wirtbam answered, looking up sharply to meet the An Taoseach's gaze. Up was the only way to look. Raised to his full height, the King of the Poeth stood only as tall as the length of a human pointer finger (a variable measurement to be sure), and he still stood a head and shoulders above the rest of his race. His pitch-black eyes held a lethal, violent flair.

---

[6] Welsh word meaning, "Stop!"

All Poeth followed their leader's example. Despite their size—or perhaps because of it—the Poeth managed to make even the bravest of men uncomfortable. Their dwindled numbers and the fact that every single one of them—woman and children included—were walking masses of scars, not to mention their berserker type rage lurking just beneath the surface, attested to the years they had spent on the frontlines of battle, springing from the core of the earth itself. Had the *Darkness* feared them? Or was their easy anger the undoing of many, leaving them only hundreds in number rather than thousands?

Armahad waited in silence for Wirtbam to continue. His regal aura remained calm, revealing nothing to the masses. Queen Keliah gripped his arm but stood her ground, while Mydrian, subtly closer than before, stood in tense alertness all around them, waiting.

Wirtbam smiled again and flung his arms wide to indicate the hosts around him. "Many have come to pay homage to you, great king," he began. "I too have come, for the *dark* lands offer no refuge, yet unlike the noble humans, who were my allies just hours ago and now stand already integrated among your own people so completely they have lost their distinct identities, I will not be bound until I am satisfied."

"No one seeks to bind you, King Wirtbam," Armahad said quietly.

"Don't they?" Wirtbam asked fiercely. His eyes shifted to Esarian and the Summoners. "Not all embrace this thing called Hope so blindly," he said through clenched teeth.

Armahad followed Wirtbam's gaze with his own eyes to the uncertain grouping of white-robed Summoners and the serene, peaceful face of Esarian. "Are they not your leaders?"

Wirtbam glanced at Armahad. "They have led the Resistance true. When Summoners speak, I hear. Their counsel is sure. I have trusted them in battle. I trust them now, but as Esarian—their leader—can tell you, his power is none and all Races stand free!"

A cheer rose from every non-human member of the assemblage.

"Esarian is good and brave, but you are no Guardian and he no king. If my people are to be bound to yours, then you must acknowledge me and I you. Great, you may be, hope, you may offer, but answer my question and answer true."

"What is your question, King Wirtbam?" Armahad asked. "Speak it, and I will answer if I may."

"Where were you when Light failed?"

Armahad was silent for a long moment, framing his answer carefully in his mind before speaking. "Light did not fail, not for those whose hearts remained true. You survived the *Darkness*, and Light beckons to you once more. Will you be bound by it?"

"By you?" Wirtbam nearly snarled, trying to hide the effect Armahad's words had upon him.

"By Light," Armahad sighed. "I am human, prone to weakness and failure like all Men, but I am also the figurehead of something greater— something Esarian—and the Summoners understand far better than I. What I know is that Light is still stronger with promise than all the vastness of *Darkness*." Wonder filled his own voice at these words. He remembered vividly how the Dark One had fled from the Light shining from the Mark upon his face, and he couldn't comprehend it.

"Am I to be a slave or free?" Wirtbam asked.

"A subject of Light, King Wirtbam, is always free," Armahad answered. "I have no desire to make slaves out of nobility that has stood against *Darkness* for thousands of years. You, I think, will be far more equipped to lead me, as I am sure the Dark One will seek to retaliate for his failure, yet there is but one throne prepared for the One who is marked."

"Remember the Prophecy," Esarian interjected. His voice belied his age for the authority it contained. "Our ancestors well remembered its words and have handed the promise down to us. We hold to our fear, because it is what we have always known, but for now *Darkness* is behind us!" The Summoner looked upon the assemblage with earnest expectation. "There was only ever one *Hope*, my friends, and it is laid out before us—for some reason known only to the *god* who once rested his feet upon Firinn—our *salvation* rests upon this human and his lineage. One throne. One promise. One Source! Hear me, friends! Lay down your vestiges of power. Lay down yourselves! Leave no foothold for the *Darkness*! Embrace the Promise!" He offered the sword to Armahad. "Come see *hope* for yourselves. Touch the Mark! Breathe the free glow of the Light!"

Armahad took the sword in his hands with a slight bow of acknowledgment while Wirtbam and his people drew back to observe, with hard, critical eyes, the reactions of their allies—loosely allied at that, out of necessity in the *Darkness*; here in this place of Light those allegiances were already slipping but still strong enough to sway judgment in the human's favor.

Esarian's words inspired others to emerge from the host. White-robed Summoners silently flanking their leader bowed low before the An Taoseach and his queen. They did not speak or lift their heads to meet his gaze, yet the eerie red glow of the Styarfyre orb shards was a statement of authority even now. Whispers drifted through the assemblage, moving in distinct factions according to race—hosts that combined rivaled the numbers of the Mydrian (tens of thousands, innumerable). Esarian encouraged them with his shining eyes while the kingdom of Men waited in stunned silence for the An Taoseach's response.

Clop. Clop. Clop. The hooves of horses fell slow, cautious yet deliberate, whispering through the grass bowl.

"Come," Armahad said to the sound of the first hesitant footsteps.

Throngs parted as two Centaurs walked majestically forward— one slightly behind and to the right of the other. Human knowledge of the Centaur was available in the oldest of manuscripts but hardly trustworthy—bearing no reference to their genteel grace and wild beauty. Queen Keliah crept forward ever so slightly.

The Centaur moved just as hesitantly. The female matched Keliah's wondering gaze with her own, a small, shy smile touching her pale lips. "I am Hempress," she said softly, "Queen of the Centaur." She was diminutive (her size starkly contrasted by her hulking escort who looked every bit the fierce protector, muscle-bound from head to flank) with soft brown eyes—the kind that spoke volumes for the purity and goodness of their possessor. Upon her head was a crowning headdress made of leaves, nutshells, and dried pine needles. Little black-and-white speckled birds, singing happily, nested within it. Long black hair tumbled down from beneath it and draped around her soft, horse like ears in shiny, thick cords (solid and straight in appearance like the branches of a tree), curling ever so slightly at the ends to weave lightly in the breeze. Dew hung in glittering beads upon her long eyelashes—extra-long by human standards—and upon the healthy brown coat of her equestrian parts. Her belly was big with child, much bigger than seemed possible for her small frame, and there was a frailness about her that went beyond mere shyness. Her deep honey complexion was unblemished. She wore a sleeveless surcoat, open at the sides, to make room of the child in her belly that descended sharply over her pleasing, human frame in gauzy, saffron silk, ending in abrupt Vs at the waist in the front, cutting off higher in the back, so as not to become entangled elsewhere. Dirt covered her hooves and up her horse like legs; her human hands were stained brightly with berry juices. Her tail was flying freely in dark crinkles. Curiosity was overcoming her fear as she came closer, but her companion never relaxed his protective stance beside her.

He took in everything with his quick eyes, measuring it, judging it much as the Mydrian were doing all around them.

"She's so young," Keliah whispered to her husband.

Armahad nodded. "They very nearly all are," he whispered back. He stepped forward slowly so as not to alarm the Centaur queen or her escort. "You are welcome here, Hempress. Do not fear."

The Centaurs whinnied and pranced nervously at their queen's separation from the herd as Hempress stopped before the An Taoseach and his queen. Her escort bared his teeth in a none-too—friendly greeting and a sound, some weird combination between a whinny and a growl, emanated from deep in his big chest.

Armahad stood perfectly still, letting the Centaur queen make the first move before the curious eyes of the assemblage.

Hempress smiled tentatively up at him, relaxing more when he smiled in returned. Her stained hand rose, trembling, to touch his face; the smell of an orchard in summer wafted off her skin as her delicate fingers lightly traced the Mark shining there. "It is true," she said mostly to herself, awe coating her voice, "I can feel power growing here." Her gentle eyes met his. "I have never seen your like before, but—" Her hand fell away as her voice drifted off uncertainly.

"Or I you, my lady," Armahad said in a hushed voice, still seeking not to alarm her.

Hempress laughed, a melodic sound that suddenly shattered the tense atmosphere. "Then we are both mysterious." Her smile slowly faded. "We, Centaur, have long memories. We keep the old ways, but what say you, my Giant friends who discern what others cannot?" She turned to face the assembly filling the vast tranquil bowl. "This power I feel, is it truly divining the promise? Dare we have hope, as the Summoners declare, or is hope in vain?"

All followed her gaze with their own, expecting to see the Giants standing like towering trees above the plain, but they were nowhere to be seen. The crowd shifted as they strained to see whom the Centaur queen was gazing at so intently in the rear of the assembly where it looked like huge gray boulders rose from the plain.

The gray-clad Giants crouched in the shadows where nature began to give way to the palace once more—hiding low upon the ground as much as was possible with their massive frames hunched down into tight knots. Drenched in sweat and gawking in disbelief as they realized they were discovered, the Giants looked frantically from one to another. Huge they were. Brave they were not—least of all the Races assembled, yet the Centaur were old friends, and when one called, no Giant would refuse to answer.

"King Dubber, come speak with me," Hempress encouraged, beckoning to one of the Giants.

A single Giant rose, leaving a gap in the "boulders" and doddered forward. The crowd shifted even more out of the line of his huge, thick feet which he thrust out before him in such a way that made his upper half always seem to lag behind and truthfully left everyone in fear that he would fall and crush them all. His skin was weather-beaten and his complexion disfigured, to say the least, by countless scars, healed and rescarred into thick, raised mounds of red, angry-looking flesh. Three eyes bulged from the matted tangle of his face, two shifting restlessly in their sockets—wide and owlish—taking in the nervous skittering of the assembly (as small as rodents) while the central eye remained fixed straight ahead. This gift of Guardians saw what other eyes could not, peering over his gourd-like nose, which was strictly too large even for his huge face, and studied the An Taoseach's face intently. Frazzled blue-gray hair framed his face coming down into a long, rat's nest beard, which he compulsively stroked with one beefy hand, over his pendulous jowls. Under this ghoulish visage, however, there was an air of nobility to his gigantic sculpted frame. Nothing about his appearance screamed royalty. His clothes were ragged scraps. His feet were bare and caked in mud. He bore no ornaments of authority, and yet a king he was.

The Giant king made his way through the crowd and stopped at Hempress's side. He looked down at her with his right eye, rolled oddly in its socket, and smiled half a smile. "Queen Hempress," he acknowledged her with a rough voice. All his eyes shifted abruptly to Armahad's face. "I, King Dubber, greet you," he said.

"And I you," Armahad answered, leaning way back to meet the Giant king's gaze.

"King Dubber, what do you see?" Hempress asked quietly.

King Dubber leaned down over Armahad so that his huge face was nearly mashed against Armahad's. The putrid blast of his nostrils on the An Taoseach's flesh was hot and uncomfortable, yet Armahad resisted the urge to shrink from the Giant's appraisal. Queen Hempress moved in closer to observe and so too did Queen Keliah—the curiosity of these strangers overcoming her unease of this night's events. "This one's human, nothing special about him," The Giant said after a long moment.

"Hah!" Wirtbam declared, suddenly rushing forward.

King Dubber frowned, ignoring his tiny interrupter and continued, "But there is promise here. Master Esarian sensed the work of a Guardian, you, Queen Hempress felt power, and I see both upon the flesh of this human. I see that they go deeper into the very core of his soul, but the power is not his and the work is not done." His words silenced Wirtbam's objections before he could speak them. Satisfied with his assessment, King Dubber straightened, letting Armahad straighten as well, and turned to glance at the assembly. "If Summoners say hope, I think we must obey; yet—" he hesitated, stroking his beard, "there may be some who can discern these signs better than I."

"Better? How can it be, friend?" Hempress objected.

"Ach," King Dubber sighed, "*Darkness* has weakened my eyes, but do not lose heart, fair lady!" He patted her hand affectionately. "Elves have always borne special knowledge of Guardian work. Let us ask them."

"The Elves of Light are not here, good friend," Hempress answered sadly.

"Yes," King Dubber agreed, frowning—the stress of these words weighed heavily on the faces of all, "but the Faedran are."

"Dark Elves!" Hempress exclaimed.

"*D-Dark* Elves?" Queen Keliah repeated in a whisper, not liking the sound of those words. Her husband's tale of the *dark* lands still plagued her mind. She curled her hand into Armahad's and pressed herself slightly behind him.

The Giant king looked down at her with one great eye. "Not dark as in servants of *Darkness*," he explained. "Dark as in mysterious, mystifying, dangerously powerful, but I assure you, your Majesties, the Faedran are true friends of the Resistance and all who love the Light."

"Dark Elves," Hempress said again, in awe. "Here? And you've seen them? Truly?"

Dubber nodded his huge head with a smile. "Rare it is for the Faedran to ascend from their solitary land, but here they are. Come forth, my friends! Give us your wise counsel!" His voice boomed through the deathly quiet gathering.

At first there was no sign of movement, no indication that the Faedran had even heard the Giant king's call or felt any inclination of appearing. Indeed, it seemed likely that they were, in fact, not in attendance this night, for no one, visible at least, came forward, yet the Giant king smiled confidently into the masses waiting.

Esarian stepped away from the Summoners to join the motley throng of royals. "The Faedran never bother with the affairs of this world," he whispered. "If they are here . . . now . . . the Prophecy must surely be at hand."

"Do not confuse us with Guardians, Firebrand." The voice echoed from the night. Lightning streaked from the barren sky, breaking into three bluish spears that made the air sizzle and left gray vapors curling away from it like smoke from a furnace. In the second it took the startled masses to look up, the lightning hissed violently down to earth, and there from its fracture, as if through a door, three apparitions unexpectedly took shape. "We are but mere echoes of the glorious being, power and responsibility given them."

Three Faedran flashed into view. They possessed the renowned grace of the Elves and all of the mystery King Dubber had promised, yet to label them "Elves," even dark ones, was a sorely insufficient description being not quite solidly in the present, almost spectral images, it seemed, yet not quite translucent either, filled with an aura of omniscience that made everyone else feel small.

All three were endowed with pitch-black growths, textured like the slimy segments of a worm's body, only thicker and harder, gradually rising from the smooth flesh of their forearms upward, branching smoothly around the shoulders, thinning to outline their collarbones and streak down, unite from either side of their bodies toward the heart; rising further over the arm itself into thick, semi-solid, black appendages that reached up to frame the head with wide spidery fingers. The tips caught the light just perfectly to imply movement, wavering greedily in the breeze. Droplets of an unknown, scentless substance burned in the air, sending wide wisps of black vapor rising into the night. Too undeveloped for wings, too armored for mere ornamentation, these appendages had no obvious purpose beyond the shadowy menace of their possessors, though they appeared, in this light, to be straining back behind the Faedran, keeping the fissures from completely closing so that a thin scar of white hovered in the dark halos, casting them in a distorted smoky, gray light from which the Faedran seemed to draw their substance and vitality—like parasites. Over their hearts, each bore a pale dagger-shaped scar, sheathed by the same black of their appendages. The scars glowed a soft silver-white, much as the An Taoseach's own Mark did, only theirs shone dimly in comparison. Their eyes were a striking shade of purple, even rimmed as they were in black. Beneath them, angry-looking shadows, growing more defined and painful in appearance with each second, discolored the perfect flesh—angry and red like blood blisters trapped beneath the smooth surface of their skin—spreading inch by inch down their other worldly faces, with no more provocation than the gentle flow of the evening breeze, leaving the impression that this world in time would cause their bodies to split open and hemorrhage, leaving their dried husks to burn away into dust. Here, however is where the similarities ceased. Each was, in truth, a unique creature.

"I am Hakan," the first ethereal Faedran said as he stepped forward, "Supreme Blood." He motioned regally to his left and then his right. "May I present Kateirah Forever Sorrow and Ethany Long Breath? My sisters and I govern the Faedran."

Hakan Supreme Blood was tall and lean, with long, silken black hair and smooth russet skin. His features were distinctly human but heightened with majesty that was distinctly inhuman—Elf-like perhaps; his frame was solid and strong, with a ferocity that no weapon known to man could stop once unleashed. His chest was bare and finely toned, visible down to the breechclout and thigh-length leggings (tied at the sides and tattered at the bottom) and decorated with elaborate, painted symbols that swirled and knotted upon themselves with precision. His feet were bare. Kateirah was about the same size, only darker. Her black hair was short and frazzled in appearance, while her skin was a deep chocolate. Her features were softer, more rounded in places, and her eyes betrayed some horror that could never be spoken, though it was sapping life from her in ill-defined ways. Her beauty was not quantifiable by her features alone but was held deeper, a mystery to be discovered and treasured. Forever Sorrow seemed a befitting surname. Ethany Long Breath was paler than her companions. Her hair was far longer than Hakan's yet just as black and straight. Her skin was alabaster, and her eyes veiled as if she saw a world different than others. She was willowy in frame, appearing as frail as Hakan appeared strong. Kateirah and Ethany wore semi-tattered black gowns held on by fraying threads at the shoulders.

Queen Hempress immediately dipped forward into a bow as the Faedran came forward. King Dubber laughed, clapping his hands once with thunderous delight. Queen Keliah gazed wide-eyed at the Faedran, whose beauty could not be defined by mere words, as Armahad slowly stepped forward to meet them despite the ill ease of his bodyguard.

Hakan studied Armahad with hard, supernatural eyes.

"What do you see, friends?" King Dubber asked. "Is it as we have been told? Is it Hope?"

"It is said the Faedran commune directly with the *god* who rests his feet upon Firinn," Queen Hempress said quietly. "Tell us, please."

"Again, you confuse Faedran for Guardians," Hakan answered slowly. "Our realm is in danger of collapse, just as yours is if the Dark One's power continues to grow."

"We are here because we too are seeking," Kateirah said.

"The Hope that must come and will come," Ethany concluded.

LettheLightshineforthandawakenhope.LetMhoragarise.Letthe Promised come.

"Yet within us are *eyes* that *see* as no other here assembled can *see*," Hakan said after a moment. He glanced at his sisters. They nodded once, and all three simultaneously raised one hand, palm up, to the spot over their hearts. Their eyes fixed upon Armahad.

Armahad shifted uncomfortably beneath their scrutiny, sensing an unseen presence gazing through them as if they were indeed the earthbound eyes of a *god*. Gazing back through their purple eyes, the An Taoseach felt strangely asleep, the atmosphere taking on a dreamlike quality, but something was awake.

"From blood of Guardians wept forth in *Darkness*," Hakan said quietly.

"From Sorrow risen when the Old Ways fell," Kateirah said sadly.

"From powerful Breath breathed forth against *Darkness*," Ethany said firmly.

"Our symbiosis comes," all three said together.

The heels of the Faedrans' hands touched the dagger-shaped scar as the seconds dragged. A Light opened out of them onto their palms.

"Do you have knowledge of the Guardians?" Hakan asked.

Armahad nodded slowly, though his meager knowledge had been gleaned only from stories.

"Then you know that Guardians shed life the way you exhale breath—constantly, essential to their very identity and survival—immortal though they are—inseparable from the Flame blazing in their hearts," Ethany said. "Flame given by the *god* who rests his feet upon Firinn."

"Power and life flows out of them, yet it binds not to the Flame within them, but to the Source," Kateirah added. "As all Flame is bound to the Source."

"From the byproducts of their shedding, more life comes."

Armahad could almost *see* through them to such a time and place. Was it a dream? Or was it somehow their memory planted in his subconscious mind? Either way, it felt real, momentarily creating its own reality . . .

Blue, flaming eyes gazed from the supernatural face. Blood dripped in crimson streams down the glorious face, dropping silently to the earth. The earth trembled violently with power as the bloody tears sank into the soil.

A strange, intoxicating nectar flooded Armahad's senses as a beautiful, delicate blossom lifted its head in that spot before his eyes, a mere whisper of life, but then he looked closer . . .

The dream or memory faded. Armahad realized that in those unconscious seconds, he had drifted to within an inch of the Faedran. Upon their open palms were similar beautiful and delicate blossoms encrusted by an odd glow. Hakan's was crimson. Kateirah's was a stormy blue, while Ethany's was opaque. The glow of each swelled like the buds of flowers in the sun, and to the An Taoseach's wondering eyes the secret was revealed. The blossoms were not flowers at all, not really, but tiny free-moving creatures. They were extremely fragile in appearance, oddly horse-shaped with a slightly elongated, reptilian maw, with legs ending in vaguely doglike paws and wings as delicate as dragonfly wings. Feathery ears streaked back from their gentle faces, and a long mane ran from head to tail, curling around to form the shape of the blossom. The coloring was unique for each, varying within the color spectrum of the outer crust. Their eyes were wide and golden. Their breathing was shallow and strained. The Faedran sagged behind them, looking almost too weak to stand.

"Ask them what you will," Hakan instructed.

"Ask quickly and true," Ethany added.

"They cannot survive long outside our bodies. Nor we outside their power," Kateirah concluded. "Yet they from Guardian blood, breath and sorrow are sprung. If truth you seek, their answer receive." She glanced once at Esarian. "Though the word of the Firebrand should have sufficed."

"What is hope?" Armahad asked.

No beginning. No ending. Hope is One long promised whose heart is one and lives are two. The little creatures answered cryptically. Their whispery voices floated on the breeze. *Whose treasured seed the Faces of the Moon unite.*

Queen Hempress came closer. "Is this human," she indicated Armahad, "the One long promised?"

Promised, yes, but not for himself. His seed is greater still, shining with a Light all his own and reflecting no other. The time is shadowed from our eyes. They suspired a continuous breath that mysteriously rang like words in the minds and hearts of all.

Behold the signs here set forth by which all shall know the meaning of the two faces of the Guardian Moon, but lest despair take hold upon your souls here are foretold they whom our hope shall restore.

In the beginning, Sanctus brought forth from the void of His creation Nine grains of power, hence planted in the Light and the Stone of Existence plucked from his crown to give unbelievable might.

Father and Mother set on high, the diadems of Day and Night. Grains of Power there remain, but sacred stone concealed away. No Guardian shall harness their hidden might till Bynthroenine again has a king.

Before that time is come, the mighty Guardians shall cling in unity to the Chosen One from a Colorless sprung.

The heavens will bleed. The Chosen One veiled in weakness shall be taken when the Heart of Evil is revealed. *Darkness* secretes through all that lies within its reach. Song of Guardians, fire and blood, Dark gift of power, Shadow and *Darkness* now combined seek power of a greater kind. A curse upon the Forbidden Kiss and the bestower's race.

The greed of Men will cause alliances to end. Sea of Sorrows, the portals shall be sealed. From ancient gift by Guardians given, song of haunting beauty takes flight, giving Evil might. The day of its creation shall be cursed when the secret of the Gemshorn is unleashed on the earth.

Crowned Head among the race of Men, who does not know his worth, within resides the hidden power that mortals ne'er possess. A battle rages for your unproven soul. Bitter, sorrowful, and in touch with Death, you must reach the end, where dwells the One naught of Humankind hath seen and bring Hope to the races once again. In the Guardian's seed no weakness shall prevail, but heed your mortal father's fate; traitors lie within your gate. This test you must endure in the frailty of Human form, but when it is past, your crown will last; and you will be weak no more.

Great Guardians, of this beware, danger lurks beyond your lair and will seek to bring great harm. A journey into stone awaits this One held dearest to your hearts. It shall be when *Darkness* covers all the earth, but do not fear, for Mhorag shall appear and silence the Gemshorn with his mighty roar.

A babe rests unknown in the womb of stone. Mhorag's seed none shall behold till the stronghold of Death is shattered from above. The One and her sleeping Guardians at once awake. Throughout all distance, the Guardian voices shall be raised in answer to Mhorag's call, and all shall fear the Guardians might. Summoning stones shall be reforged as all creation for the Guardians call.

The catalyst of war must be reclaimed the Evil Heart to break. Grains of Power will revive to test the purity of all hearts once more, for soon Mhorag's armies shall converge behind the Nine; but take this warning, Heed only the sign of the Guardian Moon set in the flesh by Sanctus formed, for *Darkness* is closing in on you.

Nine thrones of Light and Gold, Mhorag's seed and the Circle of Power that you need to find the Treasure of *Darkness* born.

He of black and tortured soul calls forth the wraiths by *Darkness* sown, and when through Mhorag's fire he safely passes, Two Faces of the Moon unite. Then by the Stone of Existence unleash the power to bring *Darkness* into subjection to the Light and seal it by the might of Nine.

The words of the ancient Prophecy, never before spoken in the land of the Isearians, had more effect upon the gathered Races than all the words spoken thus far this night. They looked upon Armahad with new wonder, their fears forgotten in the course of a moment.

"I am the Firebrand, Master of Summoners, long your friend and commander! You have heard with your ears! You have seen with your eyes! Hope stands before you!" Esarian shouted. "Now! Will you not bow?"

Thewayisdarkened.Thedeepestfoundationseeks.LettheLightshine forthandawakenhope.LetMhoragarise.LetthePromisedcome.Thetiny creatures faded back into the bodies of the Faedran, letting the silence return. The Faedran shuddered slightly as the power, made stronger by being confined within them, radiated through their bodies, restoring the broken connection. They sagged against the appendages, darkly holding them to their realm, looking weak and drained as if they had expended a great amount of energy in those brief moments and the connection had been restored just in time.

In the moment of silence following, two others disengaged themselves from the ranks of the assemblage and waddled and flopped forward. Some of the humans responded with unease—emitting almost terrified cries or low whispering objections as this former ally, a convenient relationship nothing more, came past.

"May I present, Eek-ash and Uleya the Suzerainty of the Kot who rule the salt seas," Esarian said to Armahad.

Even with their awkward movements, it was impossible not to sense the proud feline grace of the Kot. Eek-ash carried himself like a lion, only he looked softer than the mighty king of cats, a mushiness that had nothing to do with excess fat. Uleya was smaller than Eek-ash in overall size, but also bigger in other ways. In all the ways, he was mush; she was full and hard. His golden eyes said, "I'm the boss," while hers said, "I think I could take you," yet both had an air about them that was too bonded to imply rivalry—soul mates—but also too comical to imply anything other than the happy-go-lucky nature of friendship or maybe the closeness of siblings. There was a slight family resemblance, but it was difficult to judge as there was nothing "human" about the Kot who had the face and forelimbs of a cat put on the hind parts of a dolphin. Their faces were gentle and catlike (not wild cat, despite their regal heirs, but those long kept for companionship) down to the profusions of whiskers—white for her, black for him, leaving Armahad to question the reactions of some of his people. Both were covered with a thin sheen of fur. Eek-ash was dark, a black-and-brown tiger striped, while Uleya was paler, a brown to white (especially under her chin and around her mouth), with just a smattering of black (especially down the spine) in a subtle tiger-stripe pattern. His golden eyes were fixed with longing upon the birds in Hempress' headdress. Uleya licked her lips.

Their faces were gentle and expressive—his features demonstrated an innate tendency toward the dramatic, while hers tried to imply dignity and seriousness but failed miserably, leaving her with an altogether ornery appearance. Their forelimbs were webbed, suitable for their watery home. Eek-ash's limbs were striped on top, but pitch-black on the bottom. His feet seemed strictly too large to match the rest of his body—adding to the comical air—but were also sharply clawed. Uleya's feet were smaller and paler, yet still clawed. Their dolphin-like tails were strong and well-toned, virtually useless on land, but well suited to their watery homes.

"Welcome," Armahad said with a nod in their direction.

"Careful, sire," one of the humans called from the crowd. "They lure Men to doom! I have seen them devour humans trapped upon the coastal rocks."

"Men infected by *Darkness*," Eek-ash said.

"Murder," one of the humans retorted.

Uleya turned on the man with a whiny growl, flashing two rows of sharp feline teeth. "You say! But what have you *humans* done to us!" For half a second, she looked as fierce as any tigress defending her cubs and just as deadly.

Eek-ash placed one of his paws on her side. "Uleya," he said softly, and his voice was magical—all cat, yet as clear and understandable as any humans. "Do not mind them. They are fools." He moved on without a backward glance toward the angry murmurs of the humans.

Armahad stared sternly toward the unruly humans. "All assembled here are equal and friends. I will not tolerate prejudices among my subjects toward those who seek my protection!"

Uleya stuck her pink tongue out with a smile so big that her other facial features were obscured as the humans fell silent, and then with true feline grace she turned to rejoin Eek-ash, waddle and flopping her way—with remarkable speed—back to his side where with amazing agility she tackled him. Still all smile, and to his utter annoyance, she rubbed her scent glands all over him in a big feline kiss. Eek-ash shook her off, annoyance turning to amusement, and swatted at her with his large paw—claws out. She snickered a laugh, dodging away just inches from where his paw landed with a soft thud.

Esarian cleared his throat, and instantly the Kot straightened out of their playful crouches, shaking their heads as if to ruffle their nonexistent manes and started toward the An Taoseach once more. Armahad waited, uncertain whether he should go meet them or let them come to him. Their features said much about them. They were, by his estimation, highly changeable, complicated, sentient beings, to which he felt fairly certain he could dedicate his entire life learning to understand them, and when at last he came to his grave, his knowledge of their Race would barely scratch the surface. Eek-ash and Uleya's features only revealed curiosity as they drew alongside him.

"Hmmrr," Uleya purred. "This one *is* special. Can you feel it, Eek-ash?" she said, her whiskers nearly vibrating as she tested the air around Armahad.

"As we have heard," Eek-ash agreed in his own purring voice.

"Chosen, indeed," Uleya continued. She rose up, cautioning the An Taoseach with her golden eyes before she placed her paws upon his shoulders and rubbed her soft furry face—cool nose, tickly whiskers, and scent glands—upon his Mark. "Hmmrr," she purred softly.

Eek-ash crept closer. Uleya dropped down beside him, touching her whiskers to his. Both purred as if they were communicating one with another in a language no one else could understand—except perhaps the Summoners. Esarian seemed especially pleased with how this all was playing out.

Quite suddenly Eek-ash broke away from Uleya, turning upon Armahad. "The Kot need to hear no more," he said firmly. "Our choice is made. A Guardian's work and a Prophecy cannot be ignored." He threw back his head then, releasing a great bellowing roar that was instantly joined by all the united Prides of the Kot. When the roar faded, the Suzerainty drifted back into the masses, leaving others to ponder the path awaiting their feet.

"What do you say, General? Where will your Dwarves stand? With this rabble?" King Wirtbam shouted.

"Rabble?" Queen Hempress demanded. "Your words betray your heart, I think, Wirtbam."

Wirtbam bared his teeth at the Centaur queen. Cyrock rushed forward to put his queen behind him while King Dubber whirled furiously, straightening to his full height, upon the Poeth with a deafening shout.

"Calm, friends!" Esarian exclaimed.

The Dwarf general ambled forward and nodded once toward Esarian and the An Taoseach, waiting to be properly introduced.

"General Ickluck Lorndop," Esarian presented him, his face uncertain. The reclusive Dwarves' commitment to the Resistance alliances had been failing for some time, and now, finally, it was to be put to the test. He glanced at the Summoners, all of whom—even Orlok—looked stressed, sensing as he did the importance of this moment and the price of the general's words, one way or another.

General Lorndop stood sharp and erect—short, stout, and bundled like a bear ready for a long winter's nap. The standard "wild, tied to nature" mold Armahad had come to expect from the refugee Races was instantly shattered. Here was a being that was ready and willing to wipe everyone else off the map—if the right catalyst emerged. Ickluck Lorndop carried himself with arrogance and order—everything in its proper place from his hat, which resembled a pancake with an orange pom-pom in the center, to his toothbrush mustache, to the thick lines of his gray woolen coat and pants, to the insignia and medallions affixed to his breast, to the polished stick slapping ominously against his open palm.

Armahad opened his mouth to speak, but the general smiled—ignoring him completely—taking Keliah's hand and kissing it before anyone could object. Keliah blushed.

"Welcome, General Lorndop," she said quietly.

Ickluck nodded sharply and turned with a click of his heels to address the King of the Poeth. "Wirtbam," he said just as sharply, "your nature burns too hot and works against you in this matter. Almost anything is better than *Darkness*!" The general looked sharply at Armahad. "I say we stay, extend this alliance, and we see the heart of this king displayed by actions not words," he paused, looking back at King Wirtbam ominously, "and if he proves unworthy of our allegiance," he said, shrugging and smiling at the thought, "we take him out."

The Mydrian bristled at those words. Armahad raised his hand to keep them from taking down General Lorndop in that same instant. "Wait," he said in a hushed voice.

Esarian grimaced, though the reactions of many were less pronounced, many heeding the general's rash words more than all the rest. "General Lorndop, King Wirtbam, we have a chance at peace—the first in our lifetimes!"

"I'm just saying there are options available to us should the need arise, options that were not feasible against the Dark One," General Lorndop said with a condescending smile.

Esarian narrowed his eyes suspiciously. "No one is forcing you to stay."

General Ickluck Lorndop nodded. "I would be a fool to leave."

"Then control yourself," Master Esarian commanded with all the authority he possessed in his boyish frame.

A wheezy chuckle disrupted the murmurs of indecision that followed. "I am old. My wisdom is sound. Receive it if you will."

The eyes of the assemblage looked toward the sound of that thin, cracking voice. Up out of the bowl she flew, her bow-spined body carried upon frail, bronze wings, which were too large, as if she had shrunken. Her fleshy wattle face was horribly contorted as if pain ceaselessly shot through every recess of her body, yet she managed a toothless pucker of a smile that was barely visible beneath her long, bronze, beak-like nose. A pair of octagonal glasses sat upon the beak, pushed up to her sunken blue eyes. A thinning sheath of fine silver-white hair hung down over her drooping shoulders, past her withered breasts. Loose folds of cyanotic skin covered her frame down to her two thighs, merging into one leg ending in the foot that would, when she had made her cocoon, break off completing the course of her life while giving birth to another. A thin crack was already visible along the swollen ankle.

"Majesties," Esarian said, "may I present Subara, Mother Superior of the Shee."

"Speak, Mother," Armahad said as Subara battled forward through the wind.

"I've seen too much war, but there's some fight left in these old bones, and I think, my friends, we have too quickly forgotten the horrors we left behind in the *dark* land." She drew a wheezy breath and continued, "How we held to every whisper for the sheer possibility of the dream of hope." She took another breath and said, "Now here in this lighted hour when we find ourselves awaking, we resist the *dream*—we deny it—we choose the very horror we sought to escape! Shame on us!" Subara hovered low in the air before Armahad's face, leaning close. "And shame on you," she said softly for his ears alone. "Shame on you for doubting. Oh, I see it plain enough, great King. You wish a hole would open up in the earth and swallow you." She chuckled again without humor. More loudly she said, "We didn't need to *hear* or *see*! Who are we to judge the work of a Guardian? By seeking not to be deceived in this, we deceive ourselves, blinding ourselves to that which has already been revealed by burdening ourselves with that which has not! This is my wisdom—for what it's worth."

"It is worth much, Mother," Esarian said.

Subara straightened as best she could with a laugh. "You flatter me, child."

"Our noble friends have spoken true," King Dubber said after a long moment. "What are we waiting for, a sign? Did we not already receive it upon the field of battle when this one," he said, indicating the An Taoseach with his big hand, "drove the Dark One from before him?" The Giant king turned to Armahad and dropped down onto his knees. The ground trembled with the weight of his vast frame. All the Giants followed his example in silent obedience.

Esarian strode past him with determined steps. "Friends in Resistance, we who have known only *Darkness* may now choose to risk much for this Light and a Hope not yet fully revealed or we can return to *Darkness*!" he shouted for all to hear. "We stood in *Darkness*. Will we not now stand in the Light?"

"It has been so long since we dared to hope," Queen Hempress said softly.

"I don't know what I am, my lady, or what I may be." The An Taoseach floundered for the right words. "I don't know my purpose, and I am as afraid and uncertain as you about what the future may hold, but we will stand together, my lady," Armahad said gently. "Together we will embrace Hope and discover its mysteries."

Queen Hempress inclined her head. "So be it, great King. Cyrock?" she said, speaking to her escort for the first time.

"My queen?" Cyrock answered, bowing deeply.

"Give me the token."

Cyrock looked less than pleased as he obediently removed a single nutshell from his queen's headdress and placed it wordlessly in her hand.

Hempress offered it to Armahad who received it in silence. "This shell came from the first nut that was ever harvested from our ancient homeland. It is the symbol of all we are, and it is now yours, great King. The Centaur embrace the Light, this night, may it never go out!" At her words, her people fell silent, and she bowed regally before Armahad to the accolades of humans and Summoners alike.

To see her bow before the An Taoseach made an impact upon the assembled hosts of every Race. The non-human refugees came in timid procession to present themselves before him. Most held back from approaching, sending one or two—their leaders in title or deed—to speak for them all. Esarian heralded each.

Armahad and his queen waited to receive them, though the night air grew cool and the feast waited. These were the birth pangs of a new empire, a process that could not be rushed or ignored to some later time. Its delivery must come in its own course without interruption so that they could withstand the *Darkness* of the morrow as one.

In the end, an elaborately adorned document was presented, signed, and sealed by the signets of twenty rulers, one Summoner and three witnesses.

Document of Unification

We, the heads of the Resistance Races by our own free will, do hereby pledge ourselves, our people, and our offspring to this Empire of Light. We place full authority, for the sake of peace and unification, upon the One who bears the Mark in all generations hereafter, henceforth bound and forever sealed to the day of the Promised upon pain of death.

Signed in the Darkening Age:

Hempress, Queen of the Centaur
Dubber, King of Giants
General Ickluck Lorndop, Dwarf leader
Subara, Mother Superior of the Shee
Akule, King of the Merar
Zoan, King of the Astoni
Eek-ash and Uleya, the Suzerainty of the Kot
Tuernok, Seneschal of the Faun
Hakan, Kateirah and Ethany, Rulers of the Faedran
Porig, King of Trolls
Astraya, Queen of the Sylph
Fugwort, Gnome Commander
Sariel, Jantot, Occolia, and Hoomroosh the Ambassadors for Umber III,
King of Fairies.
Wirtbam, King of the Poeth
Esarian, Master Summoner, Resistance Commander, Firebrand

I bind myself and my kingdom to the service of all kingdoms and Races under my charge. I pledge myself, my substance, my life, and that of my offspring to preserving the identities of all Races and their homelands, to reclaiming what *Darkness* has unrightfully taken, and the furtherance of Hope for all living things. I bind myself to the Prophecy and to the Cure it foretells. I promise to aid those afflicted by *Darkness*, to provide refuge for all driven from their lands by tyranny and oppression. I promise to rule with honor and justice.

Armahad Caladrius, the An Taoseach of Isear
Before these witnesses:
Kinjour, the orphan prince, for all Humans
Cyrock, Centaur, for all Free Races
Dlynam, a Mydrian High Captain, for service of Mark,
Throne and Crown.

Chapter Thirty-Five

DISRUPTION

C rouched in *Darkness* where hours passed unmarked, Isentara
struck the flint stones together, trying to ignite a spark, hoping
for a flame to warm her too cold limbs. The seasons did as they pleased,
and it was always by extremes, always shifting, and always there was
Darkness. She couldn't tell how long she had journeyed in its depths.
Years could have been passing before her very eyes and she wouldn't
have known it. The *dark* land had become a wasteland. Only one thing
was certain—the one thing that stood all around her—Death, and there
was no escape—Death and *Darkness* . . . fear, brokenness, despair, and
finally doom. Death was the *dream* in this place. *Life* was the curse.

The sparks ignited her kindling. Isentara fed its meager flame, trying
not to focus upon the bitter possibilities arrayed before her people—her
twin. All the *hope* of all the Ages was laid in ashes around her, yet . . .
Isentara sighed softly, her hand closing around the Guardian rune amulet
at her throat, clinging to its ancient promises, though she would not let
herself think the words. Left in the shadows of her mind she could almost
believe them—almost—but only in the shadows. For all her whispered
pleadings, there had only been silence, so how could *hope* really exist
in the void? How could promises endure when their keepers were as
unfeeling as Death?

The growing light of the fire startled her. She had almost forgotten
Light and its painful but glorious revelations. She wiped her eyes,
roughly dislodging the tears. It would be so easy, so natural, to give up,
but to do that would be to surrender to the *Darkness*; evil would have
triumphed and the end would be worse than the beginning. Her fire
crackled weakly, struggling to maintain its life, a valiant battle; suddenly
she wanted the fire to win. She wanted its flame to burn bright and strong

against oblivion. No, it was not this flame she wanted but another greater *Flame*!

In the same second this realization struck her mind, the silence was shattered by an angry snarl. Her eyes widened in terror as she discarded the flint stones and jumped to her feet. Isentara tensed herself for whatever was drawing closer through the *dark*, jumping when the snarls turned to shrieks all around her and finally to an eerie silence broken only by the steady breathing (bombarding her flame) of an unseen presence. Her eyes wildly scanned the *Darkness*. A cold wave of power—the scent of honey, Flame, and corruption, a scent she knew too well—washed over her with unsettling familiarity.

"Father," she whispered, knowing in the back of her mind that it could not really be him, though her heart rebelled for the longing it contained.

Darkness.

Her tiny fire against so much *Darkness* would not hold illusion at bay. She backed away as a darkly glowing black fog poured through the greater blackness. She shouted, ripping her dagger from its sheath, though the weapon would do her no good in this fight. The fog shifted and grew into a ring of black dogs, formed of streaming *dark*, as big as oxen, with flaming emerald-black eyes, long protruding teeth, and equally threatening claws. Her fangs ached; hunger stirring, as the unnatural scent of corrupted Flame filled her little camp.

Isentara eased back, her fingers flexing around the hilt of her blade. *Darkness* drew ever closer.

Isentara.

Her twin's voice filled her mind in that instant, but it wasn't real. A note of falseness betrayed the illusion and gave her a sudden, irrational surge of hope. If she could see through the illusion, then her brother had not fallen beyond rescue. She looked up into the weird eyes of the *dark* and screamed. Her hands raised defensively before her. The illusion clawed at her, but the power of the amulet protected her. The claws of the beast made the invisible shield ripple as they bounced off. Isentara lashed out, piercing the *dark* with her dagger. A surge of power hurled her away, tearing the blade from her hand. She landed on her feet a short distance away as the *dark* visions circled.

Claws ripped across her abdomen. She screamed in pain. Her hand groped for the amulet that had fallen from her neck. Her blood dripped from the claws of the beast.

Isentara.

Her twin's voice was stronger now, real and defiant. "Isentara."

"Lorshin," she whispered his name. Their minds touched. *Darkness* moved to strike again.

"No! Stop! Please!"

At Lorshin's shouted plea, the *dark* froze above her. Their father's mangled voice filled the distance between them. All Arawn's children heard the Dark One speak.

You know the price . . . son.

Release her. Take me instead. I am cursed already.

Isentara shook her head. What was happening? What was Lorshin agreeing to? Surely, he knew it was not really their father talking to him! At once the illusion withdrew into the black fog from which it had formed and receded toward the East. "Lorshin?"

His sad voice grazed her mind in answer. *Forgive me, Isen.*

She stretched out her hand. For the briefest moment, she sensed Lorshin reaching for her, and then he was lost in the *dark*. Isentara fisted the amulet. There was no understanding what had happened. She could not even make sense of it. Her mind rebelled against every possible explanation. *Darkness* never surrendered its prey without a fight, but maybe the battle had not really been for her. She inhaled sharply. Her glowing eyes flashed toward the East. "Lorshin! What did you do?"

Darkness.

Lorshin covered his face with his hands. He sensed eyes watching him from every nook and cranny of *Darkness*, but it was Death's knowing—almost pitying—gaze that made him tremble inside. Those eyes were worse than the uncertain gazes of his people, worse even than the greedy, possessive gaze of the Dark One because those eyes *knew* him. Those eyes saw his failure and *loved* him—at least in some twisted way. The only eyes that could have brought more suffering were Isentara's, and he didn't need to see her to know her disappointment. *Wise Ones.* His thoughts choked around the silent plea. *Please, hear me.*

Sithbhan's arms wrapped around his waist. "Lorshin, my love," she said.

He groaned, trying to twist away from her.

She held him tighter. "At last, you understand."

A pitiful moan escaped his lips.

Darkness laughed.

*   *   *

Spent fury gave focus to my wrath. Mankind had long been a race divided against itself. Wars, prejudice, and greed, all creations of the *dark*, had helped to corrupt them in the past. Humans were so easily swayed by my power that it was barely even fun to watch, yet in all the Ages past, the humans had failed to destroy themselves or anyone else.

"Vile dragons, Guardians of refuse!" I spewed the bitter words.

No one would save them from my wrath! They would know what it was to face the *Darkness*, to wither, to despair, to surrender or die beneath my stare! I would find a way.

Darkness—that living blackness foaming out its own shame, that hated thing breathing forth its mindless despair coiled for the strike as I measured the choices before me. This marked human was a disruption to my plans, a distraction, nothing more. Still a puzzlement to me, however, was this revelation. A *human*. I snorted with disgust. Why choose a *human*? Why attack me with weakness? Why link *Hope* to the one being as prone to failure, as susceptible to temptation, as hungry for power as myself? Humans were nothing but flawed masses of flesh, waiting for their defects to be exploited, to give themselves empty excuses for empty deeds, which they pinned squarely back upon my shoulders!

Was there some *deeper foundation*, hidden from my sight that gave strength to the Mark and its vessel—a strength greater than all the power of all the Guardians combined? Could this disruption herald the Source coming to bring balance to a world in upheaval? Could such a thing be so concealed? All these things built layer upon layer in my mind, always circling back to the same point—the utter humanity of my prey. Fear of the unknown, fear of disruption, had to be playing tricks on my mind! To flee from a human—Mark or no mark—seemed ridiculous to me now. He should flee from me! I was the one with power! I was the one who had beheld the Source! This was my Time! And what *human* was strong enough to withstand me? All Light could drain from their wounded souls in an instant. All that was needed was a catalyst—a vulnerability—for my capable, formless hands to manipulate.

I would deal with this human and then with the Prophecy off-balance, I would find the Gemshorn and the Stone of Existence, I would strike the Guardians before they could emerge from their secret realm and then rise to claim the Source before Sanctus could unleash its power against me. With everything under my control, I would end the Prophecy of Hope once and for all!

Darkness.

Chapter Thirty-Six

IN THE BITTER WATCHES

Isear, Nine Months Later

The floorboards of the long, drafty hall creaked beneath the An Taoseach's polished boots as he paced from one end to the other and back again. His haunted eyes were ringed with a dark mask of worry and flashed, every few seconds, to fix upon a distant doorway. In the bitter watches of the night, Keliah had awoken with screaming. A sickening wave of terror welled up from the pit of his stomach as another of her screams reached his ears. His regal features were haggard and unkempt.

Armahad. The wind from the open windows whispered his name.

"Armahad, drink!"

The raspy voice broke into his thoughts. Armahad glanced at his father-in-law who nodded toward the far wall. The An Taoseach silently accepted the golden chalice from his adopted son. Numbly, he raised it to his lips and grimaced as the liquid burned a course down his throat. With a sigh, he threw the chalice away. It crashed noisily against the stone hearth of the fireplace. A servant scrambled to clean the mess as Armahad turned away. Kinjour caught his father's hand. Armahad squeezed it once and pulled away to resume pacing.

"My thanks, Kinjour," Armahad said hoarsely, but not even that powerful concoction could drown his unrest.

"Keliah is strong, Armahad. Do not be afraid," his father-in-law said.

The young king's gaze shifted back to the distant door. A dry laugh escaped his lips. "Stronger than she have died in childbirth." He did not meet the old man's gaze or speak of the children they had already lost nor of Keliah's frailty.

"Keliah will live. Your child will live. You will see, lad."

Armahad smiled woodenly and resumed his agitated pacing. His sweaty hands wiped absentmindedly upon the handsomely brocaded and gold trimmed blue coat that extended almost to the heel of his tall black boots. His mind reeled with one horrible thought after another. *What could be taking so long?*

Just then a terrible scream shattered the quiet. Armahad raced across the hall and crashed through the thick door that barred his way. A tangle of emotions welled within him as the stench of blood and sweat filled his nostrils.

"You should not be in here, my lord!" the midwife shouted.

"Armahad," Keliah breathlessly cried, lifting a frail hand toward him.

"Wait outside," the midwife shouted again. She barred his path with her portly frame, but Armahad quickly and effortlessly moved her aside. She did not resist, possibly because of the Mydrian all around him, shadowing his every move with their protective force.

"Armahad." Keliah's pale hand caught his as another terrible scream erupted from her even paler lips.

"What is wrong with her? What's happening?" he shouted to the midwife. The king grimaced. Her nails dug into his flesh. A knot of fear hardened around Armahad's heart. With his free hand, he gently brushed her long blonde tresses back from her eyes. Streams of perspiration flowed down her regal face. A cloud of pain darkened her beautiful eyes, and she moaned softly as she fell back upon the mound of silken pillows. Keliah's grip eased with the pain.

"Armahad," she whispered deliriously.

"I am here, Keliah," he said with a gentle squeeze of her hand.

"What if I die?"

A spasm of doubt masked Armahad's face. "You will not die, my love," he whispered as her long fingers curled affectionately into his hair. His lips caressed her wrist. His denial raised a feeble smile upon her lips. Tenderly, Armahad leaned over her, careful to let her feel none of his weight. The salty taste of sweat passed his lips as they kissed.

Keliah melted against him as the kiss deepened with passion. Abruptly, she broke away with an anguished cry. Her delicate body arched violently against his rock-hard frame.

"Keliah! What can I do?" he nearly shouted at her. He did shout at the midwife. "Do something!"

"Stay with me," Keliah moaned.

"Forever," Armahad promised gently.

"Sire, you must leave now!" the midwife shouted.

Armahad watched as the large woman drew a thin, gleaming blade from the fire and moved toward them. He could tell by the scowl of her heavy-jowled face that she disliked his stubborn persistence. The midwife was used to having her orders obeyed. He started to draw away, but Keliah clung to him as another surge of pain raked her body. Her cry rang forebodingly in his ears.

"Do what you must, but I will not leave," he said with all the authority of his rank.

"Hold her then," the midwife barked.

Armahad swallowed at the lump in his throat and nodded. He clenched his eyes tightly shut as the blade sliced into his wife's belly. He felt her stiffen and then go limp. Moments, that felt like an eternity, later he heard the first sweet cries of his baby's life.

Armahad.

*   *   *

Remnants of Rowlyrag

Sithbhan strummed her long, dark nails loudly on the arms of her throne. Her dark eyes were fixed on the *Darkness* and her unseen master. They communed in silence, having no need to speak out loud.

Ihavesomethingtoshowyou,Death,andIexpectyouwillknowwhat to do. Gnoll, tell her where you have been and what you have found.

"Sithbhan." She glanced down at Gnoll, her master's *pet*, with disgust. Her displeasure at the interruption was evident on her face and in her voice. "Where have you been?"

"Seeking treasures," he replied with a mischievous grin. "Look! Look!" Gnoll withdrew a silver box from his humped back and placed it on her knee.

The box was small and encrusted with jewels on all sides. A crystal dragon leaped from the lid's center. Gnoll pawed at her darkly draped legs. He smiled at her expectantly. Sithbhan lifted the box. Her features softened, and a hint of curiosity glittered in her eyes. The box was inlaid with rich, green fabric. On it lay a worn parchment and a white stone pendant carved with tiny floral designs painted with silver. Sithbhan set the lid aside and lifted the parchment from the box. She unrolled the scroll. In a bold and unwavering script were these words:

> *My dearest love,*
> *Long have we awaited this day and come what may I will*
> *always love you.*
>
> *Armahad Caladrius.*

As Sithbhan read the words aloud, a wicked smile crossed her dark lips. Beneath the signature at the bottom was an exact replica of the Mark. "A true treasure," she breathed.

Gnoll pawed at her bosom gleefully. The treasure was more wondrous than he had expected. It contained words of love that mirrored his affection for his dark mistress.

"What have you awaited, Marked One?" she said softly to herself. "What is your weakness?"

"You like words of love, Death?"

"No, they are hideous."

Gnoll shrank from her, back into the deeper blackness to his master's feet.

"Still they will be useful to ensnare *my* prey. Tell me, Gnoll, where did you find this treasure?"

"In the land of Light. It was tricky, but so am I."

"Ah, yes." Sithbhan smiled into *Darkness*. Death rose from her throne. Lorshin watched in silence from his throne as she stepped through the gossamer veil of the *dark*. She extended her hand to him. "Come, I will show you the pleasure of being Death's consort."

"What pleasure, Sithbhan?" he asked hollowly.

"A mortal's fear." She smiled.

"Fear of death?"

"No, my love. The fear of loss is far stronger than the fear of death."

Lorshin hesitated. He understood the fear of loss and the lengths to which it could drive men, whether mortal or immortal. Had not his father's fear led to their curse? Had not his own driven him to give the forbidden kiss? Even now, did it not tempt him to cave to the *Darkness* in which he was so tangled he couldn't break the surface? If he were driven to such lengths by fear, a mere mortal would be consumed by it.

Sithbhan studied him silently. Her face revealed nothing, while his was a riot of emotions. She smiled. "Come."

The chains of shadow appeared at his wrists and drew him into her arms. For the briefest moment, a familiar rage gripped him then he looked into her bottomless, black eyes. He caged his emotions as quickly as they had surfaced. This was a game—his game. He grasped her hand with far more enthusiasm than he had meant to reveal, yet it seemed to please Death. She caressed his cheek. He swallowed dryly, suddenly and horribly aware that he reveled in her touch. *Darkness* flashed around him. His blistered heart held him paralyzed there. Even his nagging fear of *darkness* was all but silenced.

Together they descended to the portals. One glowed with emerald-black Flame. Sithbhan held him close. He could not hide the strange excitement that had come over him. For years, he had harbored a dream that one day he would see beyond this dreary existence. The dream occupied his every waking moment. A taste of freedom to strengthen his failing resolve in this battle was exactly what he needed. Here was his chance. He melted with her into the *Darkness*. They passed through it into the Kingdom of the Isearians, one of Death's many playgrounds.

"Take me to Armahad Caladrius," Death said as they entered.

A second later everything fell away except *Darkness*.

Nithrodine Castle, Isear

Armahad's hand fell away from Keliah's as his head lulled in sleep, sitting on the side of the bed. The infant was nestled safely in the basket cradled between them. How many hours had passed since the birth? Did Night still rule or had Day emerged? Time was blurred so that the minutes were inseparable from each other. The midwife had tried to send him away to rest, promising to inform him immediately if there was any change, but he refused to leave Keliah's side. Sleep had escaped him till the sheer force of his body's weariness painfully overtook him. All he knew in these blurred hours was Keliah's feverish suffering and his own powerlessness to help her.

An agonized moan escaped her lips, jolting him from his slumber.

Armahad.

"Hush, beloved, I am here," he whispered as he stroked Keliah's hand. Even as he spoke those words of comfort, an uneasiness washed over him. Armahad shuddered. His gaze strayed from Keliah's furrowed brow to his infant daughter sleeping peacefully and finally to the small narrow windows that allowed a little air to enter the birthing chamber.

A strange wind blew outside. Giving into the sudden impulse of fear, though he couldn't explain it, he jumped to his feet.

"No!" he screamed, simultaneously drawing his sword as a shadow passed through the narrow opening into the room. Was he sleeping?

Malicious laughter met his cry. The shadow shifted to an upright position beside Keliah's bed.

Armahad. You are not sleeping, human.

"Sire!" Mydrian appeared instantly.

Armahad shook his head. Whatever he had seen was now gone and with it the conviction that he had seen anything. "I—" He frowned. "It's nothing."

The Mydrian High Captain on duty nodded once, his eyes quickly scanning the chamber to satisfy himself, and then he ordered the Mydrian back to their posts, leaving with a bow.

Armahad laid his sword aside and sank back onto the bed beside his wife, still trying to clear his muddled thoughts.

Armahad.

He glanced up, seeing nothing. Surely this was a dream.

No dreams survive the dark, Armahad.

Armahad squeezed his eyes closed. Rest. He needed to rest, that's all this was.

No one noticed as a youth stepped out of the insubstantial shadow. His eyes were a pale and luminous shade of blue. His lips were parted to reveal his gleaming white fangs. The hunger was a visible agony on his face as his nostrils filled, unwillingly, with the scent of Flame hidden in deep traces within the humans that resided here.

"Painful?" Death asked with soft mockery.

Lorshin glanced behind him in time to see Sithbhan appear. Her emotionless black eyes stared with a seemingly lifeless glare on the world. In her hand she cradled a hunter's knife, sharper than any fashioned with mortal hands, to plunge into the heart of her prey and draw forth the soul. Fear momentarily overwhelmed Lorshin. She looked more like Death now than she ever had before. Sithbhan did not notice his scrutiny as she turned toward the bed upon which a frail-looking human woman lay.

"Who is she?" Lorshin whispered.

Death's knife glinted in the firelight. She passed over the woman. "No one of importance." She raised the knife over the sleeping infant in the basket.

Lorshin gasped as the reality of the situation dawned on him. "No!" he shouted. Moving so fast, he all but disappeared; he seized the human's discarded sword and threw himself between Death and her prey. The powerful clash of their blades pierced the eerie silence all around them, and he half expected the humans to sense their presence once more.

"Out of my way, my love," Sithbhan said. Her voice did little to conceal the true menace behind her words.

To Lorshin, it seemed that time slowed. Thousands of tiny shards hung in the air where his sword had shattered.

"Not the baby," he said quietly.

She smiled at him slyly. "How will you stop me?" she mocked him. "Will you kill me?"

Lorshin sighed. Killing Death was not something he could do, at least not now. He didn't know if it could even be done. "You cannot do this!" he shouted at her anyway even as the miserable knowledge of his own powerlessness dragged him to his knees before her. "You cannot. If you must take one, why must it be the child?"

"I am Death," she said simply. Sithbhan turned from Lorshin, simultaneously releasing time to its normal pace. The shattered sword fell around him.

Before he could react, Death's blade pricked the infant's flesh. "I did not come to take her life, Lorshin," Sithbhan said softly, "merely to break him." She motioned toward the human man. "Fear of loss, as I said, is greater than the fear of Death."

The infant awoke with a cry. Her father gently lifted her from the basket, oblivious to their presence or the magical wound on his daughter's body.

Lorshin turned away. The trace scent of Flame was more than he could bear. "Please," he managed to say. "Please." Was he really begging Death to free them?

Sithbhan faced him. She let Gnoll's treasure drop a little from her hand. "What happens to this child is up to her father, Lorshin. For the right price, I will gladly set her free."

Lorshin snatched the pendant from her hand. "What price?" he asked fiercely.

"I will make the child whole when the Mark of the Promised is no more."

Lorshin flinched. *Darkness* pressed enticingly into his mind, luring him to accept his place at her side. *Think of Isentara.* The corrupted voice whispered to him. *Would you honestly risk losing her for the sake of this human? The child will live. Her father will save her, but who will save Isentara?* Lorshin closed his eyes. His fists clenched at his sides.

"Come, my love. Our work is done here for now."

Sithbhan passed noiselessly from the Kingdom of the Isearians into the ruined mountain. She released Lorshin from her embrace. He walked away without a word.

Gnoll waited until the train of Lorshin's dark robe had disappeared, before slinking out of the shadows. He pounced on Death. His webbed feet pawed at her affectionately. "Mistress, I missed you."

Sithbhan kicked him aside and walked toward her throne. "It is done," she said into the *Darkness*.

"What is, mistress?" Gnoll asked as he crawled sheepishly after her.

"The marked human will soon come seeking us."

"When?" Gnoll asked.

Sithbhan smiled. "When his child begins to die." Her maniacal laughter resounded through the lair, echoed by *Darkness*.

Gnoll squealed with delight and leaped on her. His large lips pressed against her cold face with a kiss.

Sithbhan roared with disgust and sprang from her throne. *Darkness* threw Gnoll to the ground. He cowered as she walked seductively past him. He watched as she descended the stairs of fire and stone into the pit. He knew her precious Prince of the Samhail was down there. She would go to him.

Darkness grew around her, obscuring everything from his view. Gnoll hissed at the dark. He hit it with his hands, yet it closed around him. *Gnoll.* The Dark One called sharply. Reluctantly, he went to attend his master.

* * *

The mighty resonance of the bell came purling through the quiet, signaling the changing of the guard. Its melodic voice surpassed even the wind's piercing wail. Keliah sighed softly in response. Armahad breathed his own sigh of relief. The hours she had lain there unmoving had been unbearable! He had spent them perched on the bed with her head resting on his lap and his infant daughter swaddled in his arms. Love and relief glowed in his smoldering eyes. His wife was alive. His child was strong and healthy. Their gentle breathing surrounded him. An involuntary smile adorned his face.

Armahad. He ignored the voice whispering in his mind.

The fire burned low in the hearth. Shadows danced across the floor as the first dim rays of sunlight fought their way through the dark. Keliah stirred restlessly. Her moan of pain hung between them. Armahad tenderly smoothed back her hair with one hand.

"Shh," he soothed her lovingly. "Lie still. Rest, my love."

She groped for his hand weakly. "Armahad."

His strong hand meshed with her smaller one and gently drew it to his lips.

"Our baby?" she whispered as he kissed her.

The king released her hand and lowered the sleeping infant to her breast. "Keliah, meet our daughter."

"Oh," Keliah breathed. "She is beautiful."

"Like her mother," Armahad replied.

Keliah smiled. "And strong like her father."

"Yes," he said, distracted. Laughter filled his mind. *Armahad.*

Keliah reached up to touch his face. "Is something wrong?"

"No," Armahad said quickly. "It's nothing."

Keliah nodded, not convinced, but unwilling to invade his private thoughts. "Does our daughter have a name?"

Armahad smiled. "Yelizaveta Caladrius."
Armahad.

* * *

Lorshin knew Death was coming after him before she was there. He didn't want to think of her as Sithbhan—the woman who, despite everything, he was uneasily bonded to. He wanted to hate her!

"Tell me what will happen to that child!" he demanded, seething with anger. The blisters in his heart swelled dangerously, throbbing with horrible warning. His fists clenched at his side. "Don't lie to me!"

Death reached for him. He shook off her embrace.

"No!" He couldn't bear her touch; it would weaken him, dampen his anger, make him remember she was nothing but a slave just as he was, and he did not want to *feel* what he knew he would feel. Lorshin whirled around to face her, baring his fangs in fury. "Don't touch me!"

The hurt on Sithbhan's face lingered for only a fraction of a second before it was masked, but it was enough to silence his fury. He forced his fists to unclench as he waited for her answer.

"Is it so awfully important?"

Lorshin breathed deeply in and out to maintain a tenuous hold over himself. "I was there. I *let* you—"

"You fought me," Sithbhan interrupted, not unkindly.

"I didn't stop you."

Sithbhan and Lorshin faced each other—huntress and hunter— enemies and lovers drawn together by *Darkness*. Lorshin broke away first, his gaze dropping with shame.

"Tell me," he whispered.

"She will grow old before her time. She will suffer greatly, but others will suffer more."

"Precisely as the Dark One wishes?"

Sithbhan nodded. "The child's sickness will mar the peace, weaken the Empire of Light, and divide the Races." She smiled. "An empire is only as strong as its ruler, after all."

Lorshin groaned.

"Why take the burden of my crime when the guilt is not yours?" Sithbhan asked softly.

"Because I am not beyond *feeling* it," he answered, an edge of bitterness in his voice.

She touched his face with understanding. "You could be, Lorshin."

He grimaced, yet he leaned into her touch. *Wise Ones, please.* Those desperate words were all he could muster these days. *Please. Please!*

Chapter Thirty-Seven

WITH BATED BREATH

*D*arkness.
No sight, no sound, no stirring breath broke the suffocating black. The orange flame of the torch curled back in upon itself toward his unprotected hand, illuminating nothing. He gasped. Disembodied laughter rang sinisterly on every side, snuffing out the fire as the torch fell from his grasp.

Armahad. His name was a whispered breath in his mind.

Darkness.

He couldn't see his hand held up before his face, yet he knew even in the silent black that he was not alone.

Abruptly, Armahad awoke from the recurring dream, drenched in sweat. On the bed beside him, Keliah slept peacefully. She pulled the silken sheet over her and their fourth unborn child. Keliah had survived Yelizaveta's birth and returned to him strong. Since then, they had been blessed with three more children: his daughters, Talashe and Racille and soon another. He hoped for a son—one who bore the Mark and would one day inherit his throne, yet as blessed as he had been, he was also cursed.

Armahad slipped from the bed, careful not to disturb his wife and, taking the candle from the bedside stand, left the chamber. The Mydrian followed him as silent as shadows, sensing that he needed time with his brooding thoughts. He wasn't paying attention to where he was going until suddenly he was standing in the doorway of his daughter's room.

"Daddy," the inflectionless little voice called from the darkened interior.

He rushed into the room. His hand tightened around the gilt candlestick, and anguish darkened his weary eyes as he looked upon the fragile child lying upon the huge feather bed.

"Daddy's here, Yelizaveta," he said, struggling to control the quavering of his voice. Not even the passage and decay of time had hardened him to his daughter's ravaged image. It had started shortly after Yelizaveta's birth, a mere seven years ago; the unknown disease had laid its claim on her.

Only a few thin strands of silver hair lingered on the child's large, veiny head. The thin, wrinkled and spotted skin of an old woman was draped over her small, frail bones. She never left this room—high in the palace—its four walls protected her from prying eyes.

A brave smile lightened Yelizaveta's pinched face but did not reach her sunken eyes. Armahad returned the smile as he walked toward her. "You are supposed to be asleep," he said gently. "You need your rest." He stroked her clammy brow.

Yelizaveta caught his fingers and weakly pulled them down. She admired the sparkle of the royal ring as it gleamed with purple in the candlelight. "I can't sleep, Daddy," she said quietly, still playing with the ring on his finger.

"What can I do?" Armahad sat on the bed beside her, and she snuggled close to his side against a backdrop of gold, velvet pillows.

"Tell me a story."

"It's late, Yelizaveta."

"Please, Daddy."

He smiled, she was so much like her mother, and brushed a kiss across her cheek. "What kind of story?"

"One about a little princess on a great adventure."

Her father smiled wearily. "All right. Are you ready?"

Yelizaveta nodded weakly.

"Once there was a beautiful princess who lived in a kingdom surrounded by four towering stone walls."

"She hadn't ever seen outside the walls, had she, Daddy?" Yelizaveta snuggled closer.

"No, sweetheart, she hadn't." His voice cracked, but he pressed on. "The beautiful princess wanted to see the world outside, but the walls were strong and tall and offered no way out. There was no door and not even a window."

"Because they were magical, right, Daddy?"

"Yes," he said. "But the beautiful princess refused to give up."

"Because she didn't want to die," Yelizaveta said softly.

Armahad hesitated.

"She would too, Daddy. She would." Yelizaveta's voice was momentarily stronger.

He swallowed the lump in his throat and glanced down at his daughter's distorted face. "Why would the princess die?"

"Because a monster trapped the princess in there so it can eat her up. It will get her, Daddy. You won't let the princess die, will you, Daddy?"

Armahad closed his eyes and shook his head. "The beautiful princess tried everything she could think of to escape. First she built a huge ladder."

"But the monster chopped it down."

"Next she made herself a pair of wings," Armahad said.

"But the monster burned them up."

"The beautiful princess tried to climb the wall."

"But the monster had covered it with oil," Yelizaveta said weakly.

"By now the beautiful princess was very tired and the monster was very hungry."

A breath shuddered from Yelizaveta's mouth. A tinge of blue painted her lips. Armahad winked at her.

"Just then the beautiful princess was saved as a handsome prince sprang from a hole he had dug beneath the wall and slew the monster with his gleaming sword. The monster's magic was broken. The princess lived and spent the rest of her days exploring the wide, wonderful world with her handsome prince. The End."

Yelizaveta clapped her frail hands.

"Time for you to go to sleep." Her father brushed another kiss across her cheek and rose from the bed. "Goodnight."

"Goodnight, Daddy."

Armahad tucked her in snugly. "Sweet dreams."

Yelizaveta watched her father carry the candle across the room to the door she had never seen beyond. "Daddy."

He stopped and turned back.

"You won't let me die, either, will you, Daddy?"

Silence filled the shadows looming between them. The best physicians could not save her. How could he?

"Daddy?"

"No, sweetheart," he said quietly. "I will not let you die." He turned abruptly and hurried out of sight down the long hallway. Shadows broke in the faint light cast by the flame of his candle, gradually illuminating a sweeping marble stairway. His robe trailed behind him as he glided numbly down the tower stairs. A whispered voice echoed eerily around him.

Armahad. Armahad. I can give you all that you desire, Armahad Caladrius, An Taoseach of Isear.

The candle flame went out.

I am waiting. Your child cannot!

Armahad broke into a run.

"Majesty, no!" one of the Mydrian shouted, but it was too late.

*   *   *

Darkness.

No sight, no sound, no stirring breath broke the suffocating black. The orange flame of the torch curled back in upon itself toward his unprotected hand, illuminating nothing, exactly as in his dream. Armahad cried out in pain, the torch fell from his throbbing hand toward the invisible ground. Disembodied laughter ran sinisterly on every side, snuffing out the fire.

Darkness.

Armahad couldn't see his hand to ascertain the extent of the injury or, more importantly, to find out the presence he knew was lurking close by in the silent black.

"I'm here," he shouted. A chill ran down his spine.

I know. The black breath whispered around him. *I know what you desire, Armahad Caladrius.*

"You know me. Who are you?"

No time for the supernatural, eh?

"I said, who are you?" Armahad asked, his words tempered by the sheer force of his desperation alone.

Cackling laughter filled the black. "I have many names, but do you really want to waste the last precious moments of your daughter's life on that?"

"In truth I know you, S . . . S . . ." he choked on the unspeakable name.

Laughter resounded. *Sgarrwrath?*

Armahad flinched at the name. He drew his sword from its sheath with an ominous scrape. The black breath circled him. Armahad froze as Yelizaveta's frail voice echoed mockingly through the black.

You won't let me die either, will you, Daddy?

"Yelizaveta?"

Darkness laughed again.

"You did this!" Armahad screamed. His sword sliced through the black, finding nowhere to lodge. He cursed. "She's just a child!"

"Yes. Fight me, but it is you who will let her die. You've been watching her die for seven years and are powerless to prevent it."

"No!"

Yes.

"Why?" Armahad screamed, swinging violently at the black.

"This is all because of you, Armahad Caladrius. You and your royal house, you and your kingdom of Light—you who are marked to stand against *me!*" the Dark One ranted, his voice rising in wild tirade. "Too long has your kingdom stood a bastion against the Void! Too long have your kind resisted *me!*"

"What does any of this have to do with my daughter?" Armahad's sword sliced through the black to no avail.

"Nothing. Sweet little Yelizaveta is a means to an end. Nothing more. Her life means nothing to me."

"But everything to me," Armahad said softly, understanding.

I have you now. The black breath whispered. *Can't you see? One way or another, I win.*

Armahad lowered his sword a fraction. "What do you want?"

To know if you are as noble as your ancestors? Will you suffer or will you choose another way? The black breath sighed around Armahad. "This is the choice before you: Yelizaveta dies, you live out all your days and sire many children, your kingdom prospers and my plans are thwarted, but you are broken because you know that one word—just one—could have saved your precious daughter." *Darkness* laughed. "The noble way." More laughter. "Or Yelizaveta lives, you live out all your days and sire many children, you prosper and your heirs after you. You let me in, and *I* will *give* might to your swords, gold to your coffers, and glory to the names of your heirs—all that you desire will be yours." *Power. Wealth. Yelizaveta.* The voice faded lower than a whisper, tempting Armahad toward the fall.

"At what price?" Armahad spat.

"What lies beyond your grave is not meant for you to know, Armahad Caladrius."

"Am I to have an early grave then?" he asked bitterly.

Silence.

Armahad sighed and sheathed his sword. "And what of Yelizaveta's life? She deserves better than a grave."

"Do you know what you are asking?"

"All my desire, remember?"

Darkness laughed. "She will live on when your bones and the bones of your heirs are returned to dust. She will live on when the stones of your palace are laid in ash. She will live on beyond her time. So, what is your answer?"

"Yes."

Of course, I have a price.

Armahad stiffened. "What price?"

"Nothing too painful. Nothing you will miss. I just *need* you to do something for me."

"What must I do?"

"To seal your choice, you must take your sword from its sheath and scar the Mark upon your face."

Armahad hesitated.

"What's more important to you, Armahad Caladrius? Upholding your ancient, noble myths or Yelizaveta?"

"Why do you even need to ask?" Armahad said with bitter desperation. He raked the blade of his sword across his face, disfiguring the Mark. "Do it!"

From far away Yelizaveta screamed.

Armahad whirled toward the sound; the sword clattered noisily from his hand.

Darkness.

"What is happening? What have you done?"

"Your sword is the only weapon that can kill your daughter now."

"Then I will destroy it!"

Darkness laughed. "You cannot. To destroy the sword, you must destroy the bond between us that she now embodies."

"Speak plainly!"

"You gave yourself to me, Armahad Caladrius! To free yourself and your noble line, Yelizaveta must die!"

"Never!"

I thought so. The Dark One's laughter grew fainter until Armahad felt the full weight of his deed this night, and an emptiness he had never felt before came over him. He turned away from the *dark*, yet he felt it still.

*   *   *

Sprawling trees heaved into sight and then melted back into the brackish fog that crept through the burning shadows to cloak the night. Boisterous, howling wind echoed with the rhythmic and unbroken succession of hoof beats on the frozen earth. Armahad astride his snow-white stallion emerged from the *dark* and raced toward the palace looming in the distance. Its blackened turrets were lost in the night. Its proud stone frame was overcast by the brackish mist through which glowed a haze of firelight.

"Whoa, boy," Armahad said as he tugged lightly on the reigns.

The brackish mist expelled a single occupant. She was small, the size of a young child, but she looked nearly as old as the trees though not so well kept. Her wrinkled skin sagged over her bony frame like wax from a burning candle. With a gnarled hand, she raised her lantern and fixed her eyes upon him.

"You did it, Daddy!" she exclaimed.

Armahad gazed at her dumbfounded. "Yelizaveta?"

"Don't you recognize me, Daddy? Look at me! I'm strong! I can walk! And run! I can do anything!"

Armahad swung down from his saddle. "But your face—" His fingers traced the wrinkles and veins.

"I can play with other children now, can't I, Daddy?"

"No!" Armahad shouted in horror.

Yelizaveta recoiled. "What's wrong, Daddy?"

"No one can see you this way! No one can see that face! Not now. Not ever!" Armahad shouted, grabbing her by the arms and shaking her roughly. "Do you hear me, girl? Not ever!"

"Daddy, you're hurting me," Yelizaveta wailed.

Armahad sighed and pulled her close. "Shh. I'm sorry. Please don't cry, Yelizaveta. Daddy's here. Daddy loves you."

Yelizaveta sobbed against his chest until she had no more tears. As she heaved in soothing breaths, she felt the change in him. "Daddy, what happened?" she asked. Her fingers traced the bloody scar on her father's face; the Light streaming from above failed to make the Mark glow; the light seemed dimmer than ever before.

"The price for your life," Armahad said softly as he scooped her up into his arms. "But from this moment on, no one must know you still live."

Darkness.

Chapter Thirty-Eight

OPPRESSION

N ithrodine's great hall, open to the sky above by panes of finely crafted glass, was filled with Light. The golden floors burned, and the white walls glowed whiter. Summoners and Resistance leaders were assembled amidst the throngs of noble-born humans and the profusion of royal banners all bearing the same seal: the waxing crescent moon around which the form of a Guardian draped. In this gilded hall, there were only servants awaiting the great Caladrius, the white *bird* of Isearian mythology, and today the Emperor of Light who bore the seal upon his own face.

Excitement was in the air, in the thrill of hushed voices, in laughter, and in the anticipation of the arrival of the An Taoseach himself. Master Esarian couldn't shake the uneasiness that had been oppressing his mind since the royal summons had arrived at his door. He still couldn't get over the fact that he had a door! And not just a door, but a house in the lower city, a roof over his head, and a dog to fill the long peaceful hours of his life now. Eight formative years spent in war were bound to leave their evidence, if not in scars then in spirit; still he had no complaints; others bore more of both kinds of scars than he did. None of these things oppressed him. Seven additional years of peace had eased their burden, though nothing could erase them entirely. The oppression went deeper than the largely superficial issues and concerns of humanity, deeper than the flesh, deeper than the spirit piercing straight to the soul. As the Firebrand, he *knew* things he did not consciously know—things that were before and beyond his time, things that no other mortal could possibly know or fathom. This secret knowledge had been burned into his soul. He wondered, silently, if the oppression he felt now in any way reflected the oppression the great Guardians had felt when the Races fell at the end of the Guardian War or, further back, did it rival what the Guardians had felt when one of their own surrendered his heart to the *Dark* and his Flame went black. Could the oppression possibly mirror what Arawn had felt as that *Darkness* he had embraced began to devour him? The Master Summoner frowned, absentmindedly stroking the Styarfyre orb shard hanging at his neck. Truth be told, he could name no singular cause for his skin to crawl and his stomach to twist with nauseous foreboding. He had observed no shifting within the Light, felt no disquiet in the night that would make him fear the coming of *Darkness*. The oppression had come upon him like a black fog as he had moved step by step with those also here assembled to await the emperor. As the moments passed, the oppression grew till he staggered beneath the weight of it.

D'Faihven and Orlok caught him before he fell and held him upright. Nulet eyed him uncertainly and stepped out of the line of his potential fall.

"Are you ill?" Orlok demanded.

"Please do not throw up in here," Nulet whispered.

D'Faihven silenced them with a scowl. "What is wrong, Firebrand?" she asked lowly.

Esarian shook his head, having recovered some and pulled away from them, still a little unsteady. "I don't know. I was overcome by this . . . *feeling* . . ." His voice trailed off; the youth shrugged.

"What feeling?" Orlok whispered.

Esarian glanced helplessly at each of his friends and fellow Summoners. His answer was overpowered by trumpets blasting from the balcony above, from every side of the vast chamber and finally from the guarded corridor that was for royal use alone.

A voice cried out, "All hail the Royal House of Caladrius!" The procession began as the herald's cry silenced the din. "Prince Kinjour, Champion of the Realm!" the herald continued to shout. "Princess Goldya! Princess Cait! Her Royal Highness Princess Talashe. Her Royal Highness Princess Racille! Her Royal Majesty Queen Keliah! All hail the exalted and noble An Taoseach of Isear, your true and rightful king, Armahad Caladrius! All hail the heir apparent His Most Supreme Majesty Prince Liacin!"

Esarian watched as each member of the royal house took their place upon the dais—from the orphan-turned-hero to the newborn heir swaddled in his mother's arms. His gaze came to rest upon the An Taoseach as all bowed themselves to the emperor. His eyes instantly narrowed. His skin crawled as if some invisible insect was making its home in his flesh, burrowing painfully in through his pores to nest between the sinew and the bone. Esarian immediately identified the change that had spawned this reaction, and he understood the foreboding he had experienced just moments before.

"Look at his face," the master Summoner said in hushed fury.

"What?" D'Faihven whispered, turning her face slightly toward him without lifting up from her bowed position. The giantess had grown so tall in seven years that when completely bent over her head was exactly on his level.

"The An Taoseach," Esarian said with fierce impatience, "look at his face, D'Faihven!"

D'Faihven looked up from beneath her lashes and gasped, jerking upright so abruptly the Summoners around her automatically looked up as well. Their faces showed varying degrees of horror as soon as they did.

"What is the meaning of this?" Orlok whispered, not taking his gaze from the offending object of his glare.

"Esarian?" Nulet asked, his tiny fists clenched at his sides, his head smoldering and his teeth bared.

Other Summoners glanced Esarian's way with eyes full of unspoken questions.

The An Taoseach seated himself upon his high throne, signaling all to rise.

The response of the assemblage was quick in coming. Hushed voices and wary glances passed between the Resistance leaders and even among the humans, throwing the hall into muted confusion as all beheld the ruined face of the An Taoseach for themselves. Gone was the glorious reflection of Light that had once consumed the regal face. The Mark stood in stark contrast to the Light, visibly deformed by a *dark* angry wound; reeking and pussy, the wound seemed to scream in defiance, permeating the very air with its corruption. Armahad sat proudly upon his throne, and the Light poured emptily around him; it was not the Light that was truly empty.

Esarian pushed his way forward through the crowd. The Summoners followed him in silence. Impulsively ignoring the laws of protocol, the master Summoner shouted, "You seem different, my lord!" He said this just mere seconds after the An Taoseach had seated himself.

The An Taoseach raised his ring-laden hand, wordlessly restraining his Mydrian guard. "If you have something to say, Master Summoner, by all means—" he said, motioning nonchalantly, "speak on."

"I fear you have forgotten your promise," Esarian said. His voice was steady with just a hint of his former authority; he sounded worthy of it now, though its burden had been his even in the earliest years of his young life—a burden usually only placed upon princes, yet he, a peasant, carried it well.

"What promise would this be, Master Summoner?" the An Taoseach asked, his voice defensive now.

Esarian took two steps forward so that he was standing just below the short flight of steps leading to the throne and reached into his long white coat, which swept the ground as he walked, and withdrew a parchment scroll, aged by constant touching and use. He carried it always near his heart. "Have you forgotten the Document of Unification, my lord?" he asked as he produced his copy of the agreement between the An Taoseach and the Resistance.

Armahad rose from his throne. "Have you?" His voice contained no drop of kindness now, only anger. His hand dropped, and the nearest Mydrian left their posts to surround the Summoners and level their swords upon them. "I am master here!"

"Armahad," Keliah said softly, placing her pale hand on his arm. Her beautiful face barely contained the fear that lurked in the shadows of her eyes as she met her husband's gaze.

"Father!" Kinjour objected at the same instant. He rose from his seat to stand at Keliah's side, looking every bit the knight of legend he was whispered to be. Goldya and Cait rose to stand with him, ready for a fight, while Talashe and Racille peeked from behind their mother's skirt too frightened to even cry out.

Esarian didn't back down from the sword at his chest. He was no longer the boy broken by *Darkness*; youth had brought health, strength, and tempered will, filling out the once wasted frame so that he rivaled, in size, the Champion of the Realm. The body of a warrior, finely toned for battle, with the blond mane fit for a lion, belonged to him—the Firebrand—and he used it now, pressing forward against the sword, ignoring the sting as its tip pushed through the fabric of his clothes into his flesh just over the heart. He ignored the hot trickle of blood that oozed from the tiny wound and stained his white garments. "No!" he shouted boldly to the An Taoseach. "Hope is master here!" He flung the scroll at the emperor's feet where it unrolled before the eyes of all. "If I must bleed for its sake, then I will bleed!"

"Father, stop this madness!" Kinjour shouted as the truth of Esarian's words became ominously clear by the growing red spot upon his white coat.

"Armahad, please. You are scaring me," Keliah pleaded in a soft voice that was overshadowed by the cries of others from the assembly that seemed to swirl wildly through the Light in a distorted haze around them all. Time seemed to have slowed. The Summoner's Styarfyre orb shards glowed, casting shadows like pools of blood upon the golden floor.

"Sire?" the Mydrian cried, seeking direction as the Summoners, taking no thought for their lives, almost as if they couldn't stop themselves, pressed forward against the swords, simultaneously forcing the Mydrian to drop back to keep from killing them outright.

Armahad glared at Esarian with black eyes, and the youth stared back. The brands on the Master Summoner's smooth forehead glowed dimly in the Light; the An Taoseach snarled inhumanly.

Kinjour gripped Armahad by the shoulders and shook him roughly. "Father!" he screamed. "Father! Enough!"

Armahad moaned pitifully and sagged back into his throne; he raised his hand to his face, which had taken on a grayish tint, and in the moment he broke his gaze away from Esarian's, time released back to its normal pace. Tension fractured into chaos as everyone shouted at once—no one voice discernible over the others. Mydrian, determined in their duty though desperate for orders from the captain or king, drifted— swords dripping with traces of Summoners' blood—back, up the stairs of the dais toward the throne; the Summoners impaling themselves by fractions upon the sharp blades, not far enough to endanger their own lives, drove the An Taoseach's bodyguards, who could have struck them down if not for the law stating that the lives of all—even enemies— belonged to the An Taoseach, to within a foot of the throne itself where Armahad cowered.

"Stop," Armahad said; the command came out as a moan.

"Sire?" the Mydrian cried desperately.

"Stop." His voice was stronger when he spoke. Mydrian lowered their swords but did not sheath them. Summoners froze where they stood. "Release them." Armahad rose unsteadily to his feet and staggered toward one of the private corridors.

"This matter is not yet settled, my lord," Esarian called after him. "What you have started here will not stop merely because you command it to."

The An Taoseach hesitated for an instant, his back remaining to the Summoners even when he answered. "You forget whose court this is, Summoner. You are no king. Remember into whose hands you placed your life. The next time you challenge me, it will be your last." He walked away as his ill-omened words threw the assembly into despondency.

Keliah hurried after her husband with only a glance toward the assembly, her brief gaze filled with fear and pity. Kinjour followed after her in silence, his brow furrowed by distress. In a matter of moments, the Royal House of Caladrius departed the great hall as did all but a handful of the Mydrian Guard.

"Are you hurt?" Queen Hempress asked rushing forward.

Esarian rubbed his hand over the bloody spot and shrugged. "I'll survive."

"Is this it, then?" Hempress whispered. "Has hope failed?"

Esarian shook his head. "Hope stands."

"But what may we do?" King Dubber asked.

"We signed the document, Master Summoner," Eek-ash agreed.

"We pledged ourselves to this empire," Uleya murmured.

"And placed full authority over ourselves and our people into his hands and those of his heirs," Subara added in her frail voice.

"Upon pain of death," General Ickluck Lorndop concluded bitterly.

"What may we do?" a chorus of voices cried out.

"We must have hope," D'Faihven said softly. "The Firebrand will lead us."

Esarian smiled slightly. "The Light will lead us, D'Faihven. We must trust in the promise and power of the One it foretells."

*   *   *

"Armahad!" Keliah called as she hurried after him. "Please wait. Tell me what's wrong."

"Leave me alone!" he shouted, whirling around. His hand caught her around the throat, shoving her hard against the wall.

"Armahad," Keliah cried softly. Prince Liacin wailed in her arms.

"Father!" Kinjour shouted, rushing forward to free her.

The An Taoseach shoved his adopted son back with unnatural force. "Stay out of this!" he snarled. A black force crushed down on him, making him sag abnormally beneath it.

Kinjour hit his head against the opposite wall to the screams of Cait and Goldya.

"Armahad, stop!" Keliah cried, trying to break free to reach Kinjour's side.

The An Taoseach shoved her back against the wall. "You can go when I say you can go," he said menacingly. "Or have you also forgotten that I am master here?"

Keliah winced but resisted. "You are no master of mine, Armahad, and no king can truly be a master if he cannot first be a servant to his people! I thought you knew that."

Armahad's face contorted violently. For one second, he faltered as if trying to hold something back and failing miserably. Keliah's eyes widened in alarm; his hand flew out at her face, a murderous glaze dominating his sight. The queen shrieked. Mydrian were already upon him, desperately trying to haul him away from her.

306

"Stop, Majesty!" the captain screamed, grabbing his queen and the heir apparent, pulling them to safety a second before Armahad landed his second blow.

Five Mydrian wrested the An Taoseach to the floor, holding him down as he continued to scream and thrash madly beneath them.

"What happened to you?" Keliah cried through her tears. "What happened?"

Darkness.

*　　*　　*

Red Wood

Isentara stumbled through the maze of giant trees, blundering in the *dark*, as her heavy feet dragged over roots and stones and knobs of earth. Her vision blurred by fever; she could not tell where she was or how serious her injuries had become. Her nostrils flared with the scent of Flame, tucked away in her flesh as in all flesh, aggravating her hunger, driving her to a fevered delirium that was worse than the pain tearing at her joints.

Darkness hounded her every step—real or imagined—she was beyond knowing, but her senses wildly cast their demented accusations through her mind. *Footsteps.* A twig snapped. *Lantern oil. A thread of fire and smoke.* She gagged involuntarily in response to the smell, though it was not strong enough to suffocate. The instinct for survival took over, forcing her to flee the danger of a forest fire where there was none. *Footsteps.* She couldn't tell how many or where from, yet she was being chased!

Isentara ran falteringly. Cold water splashed over her feet, pricking like a thousand needles. She slipped on the submerged rocks, falling hard. Her cry was stifled as her lungs filled with water. She clawed her way to the shore, squelching up through the muddy bank, regaining her feet with effort. The footsteps were closer now. "Stay away from me!" she shrieked.

"No! Wait!"

Isentara flung herself toward the shadowy opening between two trees. The earth suddenly dropped away beneath her feet, and she plummeted into a black pit. She clawed wildly for some purchase. Her fingers slipped from wet leaves. Her body glanced off protruding rocks, but she couldn't tell the pain of these new injuries from the rest. At last she landed hard with a sickening crack of bones in the rocky base of the pit.

She could hear her pursuers glissading down the ridge after her, yet she couldn't move. Her legs, it seemed, were gone. Not just her legs she realized, her entire body was numb except for her head, which screamed with agony and fear at the unfeeling *Darkness*.

The faces of her pursuers appeared over her moments later. Their faces were pale, ghostly, draped in dismal gray hoods. "Do not be afraid," one of them said with a gentle smile and equally gentle voice as he crouched over her. The other held back, his sharp eyes warily scanning the wood around them.

She didn't understand what they wanted. Why didn't they just kill her and get it over with? Perhaps the Dark One wouldn't let them. Perhaps she would not be given the mercy of seeing Death's face. The stranger kneeling over her reached out slowly.

"No. Don't try to move," he soothed her, sensing the panic that was quick in seizing her. "You have broken bones."

Isentara whimpered as his hands came closer.

"Shh," he comforted.

"We must be going," his companion said uneasily.

"Yes," the one closest to her said. "There is nothing I can do for her here, but moving her is—"

"The Great One will know what to do," his friend said. "Here." He shed his gray cloak and handed it to his kneeling friend. "Wrap her in it." His flesh took on a bewitching pale glow.

Isentara cried out softly.

"You must trust me," the kneeling stranger said softly as his hands deftly lifted her and wrapped her tightly in the woolen expanse of his friend's cloak. "We mean you no harm."

His words were far away to her ears.

"We are Elves of Light, Isentara," he said, "your friends of old."

Her name from his lips surprised her even in this semi-disembodied state, but she felt no relief, only panic heightened by the numbing oppression of her bound limbs. *Lorshin!*

The stranger lifted her effortlessly, and he and his companion sprinted off into the wood.

Lorshin. Lorshin. Lorshin.

"I fear she is out of her mind."

"The Great One will know what to do. He will help her."

Darkness.

* * *

Nithrodine

Esarian's house was snug and warm, nestled in the heart of the lower town, between two domineering structures protruding widely from the outermost walls of Nithrodine. His house sat slightly askew on its small plot—an afterthought of some forgotten peasant craftsman. Its original purpose was a mystery far older than he dared to guess, but its cramped corners, short doorway on which he was forever bumping his head, and squat fireplace was home. The single room was organized, if it was assumed that he had his own system unobserved in the clutter. Everything was absolutely essential from the maps and scattered genealogies—a Summoner's work—to the fiddle at which he had become quite proficient in seven peaceful years, to the innumerable vials and potions and herbs that provided the main components of his occupation these days. A healer—the Resistance Races did not trust the human doctors and their "science," which in truth had little knowledge of his non-human patrons, some of whom had as little in common with a human as humans had with a flea. Though human himself, he was also a Summoner and therefore free of such distinctions. A Summoner was a friend of all people, a people unto themselves and yet part of all others. In short, a Summoner was whatever circumstance and need demanded. Question was, in this dismal oppressive hour, what was demanded of them—of him, the Firebrand?

He reached down absently to stroke Bear's black, velvet soft ears. The dog pressed hard against him, looking up with aware, soft brown eyes before rubbing his head against Esarian's leg. Bear was not big, but he was woolly, with a mane thick enough to fend off the attack of a wolf and a loyalty that went beyond mere attachment. His paws were caked with dirt and his hair with dust, natural enough, as he was forever digging holes—treasure hunting. Esarian kept a chest full of Bear's treasures that included: arrowheads, broken pottery, and expensive dishes and the porcelain figure of a naked lady from some long-forgotten artisan's wares. In his spare time, Esarian was secretly convinced that Bear ventured high into Nithrodine's bounty, hunting his treasures and enjoying a nice dip in the river to cool off during a run, followed by rolls in the mud with the farmers' pigs. The Summoner handed his plate down to Bear, smiling as the dog's eyes lit up and he started to wiggle excitedly—scattering dirt everywhere—at the sight of the bone. Bear snatched the meaty bone and settled down with it before the fire.

Esarian was still deep in thought when a knock sounded on the door. Bear's jaws froze around the bone. Another knock. Bear lifted his head, looked at his master cocking his head to one side when Esarian made no move. A third knock failed to rouse the Summoner. Bear barked at the same instant a familiar voice called out from the opposite side of the door.

"Ho there!" A brief pause followed. The doorknob rattled.

Bear barked fiercely, launching himself between the door and his master.

"Esarian!"

The Master Summoner looked up, his trance broken. "Bear," he said. The black dog instantly and happily returned to his bone as Esarian made his way to the door. "I'm surprised one measly door stopped you, Orlok," he called to the dwarf. "Some blacksmith you are."

Orlok laughed. "I'm not a blacksmith tonight." He lumbered through the open door. His sharp eyes swept the room critically. "Just as you are no healer." He waited while Esarian closed the door against the night. The town outside was still very much awake, and prying ears could not be allowed to hear what passed between them this night.

Chapter Thirty-Nine

TRANSFORMATION

E sarian closed and barred the door to his little house and turned to face his friend.

"I'm here because of this," Orlok said with a growl. He tossed the thick rectangle of folded parchment to his friend. "Fresh off the press. Tomorrow's edition. D'Faihven smuggled it out of the guild, told me to get it to you as soon as possible." He grinned. "Well, she didn't quite say it like that, but you get the idea."

Esarian grinned too and unfolded the parchment—*Isearian Herald*—was written in large black letters across the top alongside the seal of the An Taoseach. His smile instantly faded as his attention turned to reading.

TOURNAMENT BEGINS AT DAWN!

The bans have been published by royal decree. Visitors from across the kingdom are flocking into Nithrodine and the outlying villages for the weeklong festivities. The tourney begins with a formal procession through the streets of Nithrodine at dawn, led by the An Taoseach himself! Knights will take part in numerous events including: sword, club, and the much-anticipated Joust. Prince Kinjour is to compete and is the Tournament favorite.

"Not that one," Orlok interrupted. His thick finger tapped the front page lower down. "This one."

An Taoseach revokes Document of Unification

By royal decree, the Document of Unification is repealed and nullified. His Majesty is to be the only authority from henceforth. Any who speak against him will be imprisoned. Any who oppose his dominion will be guilty of treason most foul for which there is but one punishment: Death. Be it known throughout the land, those strangers among us who wish to stay, unoppressed, must cast off allegiance to the Summoners and pledge themselves to His Majesty. All Summoners are to be arrested on sight, to be presented before the Judgment Seat for crimes against the Empire! Any found harboring these menaces of society will share their punishment.

His Most Supreme Majesty, Armahad Caladrius, An Taoseach of Isear

The royal seal appeared below the name. Esarian frowned. One glance toward Orlok told him that he had read the decree as well. The Master Summoner threw the paper onto a cluttered table. "The tyrant!" he said with a snarl.

"Who? The An Taoseach?" Orlok asked grumpily. "Some would call his actions those of a king!"

Esarian snarled in disgust. "Not him," he said after a moment. "These actions have the stink of *Darkness*, Orlok. You were there today. You saw the change in the An Taoseach with your own eyes."

"Yes," Orlok sighed deeply. "But others did not and in truth, I myself, do not want to believe it."

"Nor I, Orlok, but I think our desire has very little to do with it," Esarian said wearily. "What we want and what is are two very different things now. Our empire is failing. The One Whose Name is not Spoken is seeking to spread his *Darkness* through the burning shadows into this land of Light, leaving no sanctuary for the oppressed."

"What do we do?"

Esarian pulled an old scrap of a map from the contents of his table. "Do you recognize this?" he asked.

Orlok nodded once.

"Then gather the Summoners, hide here. You will not be easily found."

"What about you?"

Esarian met his friend's gaze; his eyes glinted fiercely in the firelight. "At dawn, I go to the tournament. Instead of pleasure, all will see the corruption of the An Taoseach's soul!"

"It's too dangerous!"

"I am the Firebrand, Orlok. Whatever power has been burned into me is for this purpose. I can feel it!"

Orlok couldn't argue. The brands burned red hot; he could feel it too—how completely the last seven years had transformed his friend. If he hadn't known Esarian since both were children, he would be afraid of him now. There was something inhuman about his friend, something . . . mystical . . . maybe even prophetic.

*   *   *

Loriath, Kingdom of the Elves of Light

A cool cloth pressed lightly to Isentara's feverish brow. She shivered as its icy moistness broke through the searing heat. An unfamiliar voice whispered in her ear.

"Rest easy, Isentara. The Great One has been summoned."

Her mind rebelled against these words. What hope could be found in this *dark* place? A moan escaped her lips.

"The Great One saw you. That is why we came looking for you. He told us where you would be. He will help you now."

Isentara tried to shake her head, tried to tell the stranger not to lie to her—not to make her promises that were impossible to keep. Hope would kill her where her injuries had failed, but the words wouldn't come. She couldn't feel her lips.

"You must hold on."

Lorshin. Lorshin.

The door opened then. A glimmering illusion drifted regally through the drafty curtain of air. Midnight robe swirled ethereally around the body of the illusion, and flaming blue eyes lit the shadows.

Lorshin. Lorshin. Isentara moaned deliriously.

Slowly, the figure drifted closer. The face, framed by a midnight hood, blurred in and out of her vision, beckoning with familiarity and hope, yet she couldn't identify it. She wasn't even convinced it was real. Her eyelids felt heavy. She struggled to see around their dropping sheath. Real or not, her fevered mind was drawn to him. Why? Why now? How?

Strong fingers wove between hers. "Isentara."

This voice she knew. It touched a locked corner of her memory. Forbidden memories exploded at the sound of his voice.

Lorshin. Lorshin.

"She keeps saying that, Baculus," the stranger whispered.

Was she really saying her brother's name out loud? Isentara couldn't find her lips to stop.

Isentara. The powerful voice of the Guardian curled into her mind. *Rest*.

She couldn't resist the subtle command, growing quiet before the Guardian fell silent.

"Will she live?"

She felt the light pressure of the Guardian's hands—felt by the tingling sensation of his probing power and not by any other means.

"The wounds are infected. Her spine is broken," the Guardian said quietly. "One of her lungs is punctured. She has lost a lot of blood. Her mind is another matter altogether. I am surprised she did not turn on you, my friends. She is beyond reason. You would not have escaped with your lives. *Darkness* has taken a strong hold." He sounded repulsed.

"Will she survive, Great One? Can you heal her?"

"Leave me alone with her."

Isentara struggled to find the surface. She could no longer frame a coherent thought. She wasn't sure what was real and what was imagined. *Lorshin. Lorshin.*

"Isentara." The powerful voice of the Guardian delved beyond the delirium. *You must not resist me.* He instructed softly in her mind. *You must trust me as you once did.*

She wanted to question him, to beg him not to hurt her, but she couldn't, and then suddenly she knew she was dying. The numbness vanished in an instant; her screams broke free into the silence.

"Lorshin!"

Glass exploded somewhere nearby. Bones cracked sickeningly.

"Lorshin!"

Darkness.

Secret torture darkened Lorshin's eyes. The air was transformed by the scent of Flame—dark, corrupted, mocking imperfections of glory, but Flame nonetheless. His mouth hung open as he panted beneath the pull of temptation so great his screams of torment rent the silence of oblivion.

"How long has it been, *son*?" His father's ruined voice whispered from the abyss. "You must be strong. You must feed."

"No!" Lorshin half-cried, half-moaned.

A low growl came from the *Darkness*. "You are no good to *me* starved and cowering!" The black voice shouted, all illusion gone for one terrible second.

Lorshin recoiled, expecting to see the beast emerge as it had all those years ago when his father had vanished into these depths. Anger passed quickly however. The illusion returned.

"Feed, *son*." The black parted. Out of the shadows stepped a human male.

The human was huge, with the strength of ten. His body was all muscle and scars, a champion of many battles. The skulls of victory hung from his garments, grotesque trophies claimed with the swing of his axe. Though he held his weapon aloft, the fight had left his eyes.

Come. The black breath commanded.

The human walked obediently forward. Lorshin backed away on all fours like a frightened animal. He could smell the Flame hidden in the flesh and blood before him. He could hear it bursting through famished veins. He could see it rising with the rhythm of the frail human heart. His fangs ached. Wild hunger awoke with a horrible shrieking moan and the flash of his deadly teeth. Lust or need, he was beyond discerning, stopped his retreat. The sound mingled with the smell tempted him toward the man till the raised axe was all that separated them.

"What did you do to him, *father?*"

"Nothing. He chose." *Darkness* laughed. "Come, take him. He will not resist you. He will give you the satisfaction you crave." To the human, the black breath said, "Lower your weapon."

The axe landed with a dull thud on the parched earth. He tilted his bullnecked head. Lorshin could almost taste the trace of Flame lurking there, yet he hesitated. In the beginning, the Samhail had killed because the curse demanded the nourishment of Flame; for centuries more they had preserved life, taking only what they needed, never enough to kill, but prey had awoken, cursed with their unnatural hunger—changed forever—so for centuries more they had suffered in seclusion. *Darkness* and Death had taken even that small dignity away from them.

"Take him, *son.* I need you strong. He will make you strong." Illusion drifted into threat. *Or shall I return for Isentara?*

Lorshin took the step to close the distance between himself and the human with a low growl. His prey never moved—never even flinched—till his fangs had pierced deep into the flesh. He promised himself he would only take enough to mask his hunger, not quench it. He would not kill.

For the briefest moment, the man resisted and then became the docile prey that had stepped from the *Darkness.* Lorshin fed, and as the *life* flowed between them, so too did their memories. The memories of his prey stretched further back in history than Lorshin had anticipated. His prey's name was Frag, and he had once been the Champion of Ischyrion, a land so far distant Lorshin had never heard its name, yet Frag's memories painted an idyllic emerald isle rising on steep cliffs from a sapphire sea. Ischyrion was a land as beautiful and fierce as the people who inhabited it—a people Lorshin immediately admired, for they had given their blood, drenching the earth of their homeland for the right to live and be free, to hold onto their unique culture against the oppression of a neighboring land.

Frag had left it all behind for the song that came to him on the wings of the *dark*, riding to Ischyrion's distant shore upon a great storm that beat upon the borders of that island as no storm ever had before. He was not alone in hearing the song. Hundreds more were drawn with him onto the highest of the island cliffs, all out of their minds. The cliffs rose sharply from the sea. The enchanted stood on the very edge of the dangerous brink. Frag faced the wind's bitter wrath; the incessant violence of the waves sprayed over him even at this height. The song raged, and then suddenly it was silent. The enchanted flung themselves from the cliff into the rocky cauldron of water—a silent, certain death, and yet here Frag stood.

Lorshin trembled. He recognized the voice of the Gemshorn as soon as he heard its song in Frag's memories, yet it still surprised him when he heard how it changed itself to mirror the desires within Frag's heart, even now, carrying promises of peace and kingdoms without war.

Frag surrendered to the dream of living a full life: one where his family could be sure that he would return home each night; one where his wife and daughters would not have to fear losing everything when Death finally claimed him; one where his sons would not know the life he had now. He surrendered, hoping to find a place where there was no need of warriors and he could at last know peace, never once considering that the promise of the song was all a lie!

That the human did not sense his own danger enraged Lorshin. This man knew love. He knew freedom. He had fought to keep it, yet he had followed the Gemshorn's song into the arms of a beast! Without thought, without question, Frag had left the woman he loved, the children he adored, and the land for which he had bled to become the mindless prey of *Darkness*! The Gemshorn's song was long silenced, lost in the final battle of the ancient Guardian War, but its spell remained over Frag. Lorshin pulled back. The memories—the blood and Flame that coursed with them—could not lie, not to him. The human did not deserve love, freedom, or even life, not if he would waste them all for an empty promise! Lorshin suddenly hated Frag as he hated himself. A feral growl erupted from the Prince of the Samhail. *Darkness* sparked in his eyes. He ripped the man's throat without thought of preserving life, pouring his wrath, pain, bitterness, and longing back into Frag with his own memories, without pity for the horror he was creating.

In the recesses of his mind, Lorshin sensed that something was wrong. His insides burned, the pain rapidly increasing and snatching his breath away. Lorshin growled, his fangs flashed, as the pain dragged him to his knees. Frag fell lifeless beneath him. His enslaved people watched in horror as smoke rose from his body. His mind raced. Only sunlight had ever done this to a Samhail. There was no sunlight here!

Lorshin crawled toward the Heart of Evil, beside Death's throne, where *Darkness* was at its most impenetrable. *"Father!"* he screamed to the *Darkness*. His thoughts had slipped unconsciously beyond the boundaries of memory, and now he couldn't stop them. White hot Light seared through his consciousness before dissolving enough to make out a shape on the horizon. The distance between them was rapidly closed so that he had no doubt about the identity of his assailant. Intense rays of blue-white Light formed wings around his sister. Her long, dark hair loosely bound in leather sheaths starting just below each shoulder had been woven in thick locks with tufts of fox fur, and all of it was matted with blood—her blood. His nostrils flared with the scent of it. *Sister?*

Isentara's eyes had lost their glow, nearly invisible now through the close frame of her hair. Her full lips mouthed his name. Though her voice did not reach his ears, he sensed she was screaming for him. *Lorshin!* She was clothed in dark cloth broken by deeply bruised flesh. Her bones protruded at odd angles, some even bursting free of her skin. Another's hands worked over her, and it was from those hands that the burning Light came—pure and glorious as sunlight.

The Light had no effect on her, yet he burned with its power. Lorshin gasped her name. "Isentara."

Darkness turned to him, at once, encircling him with its power and protection. Breathing heavily, Lorshin reached for his twin and the supernatural dawn. The beauty and meaning of this Light were not lost to his clouded mind. *Sister?*

Isentara was the other half of himself, his twin—their bond was both a blessing and a curse. His soul was the price, but as sure as she was his twin, she was also his link to the Light. Where there was Light, *Darkness* could never reign supreme. The part inside him that knew Light sparked again.

Wise Ones, please help me!

A moment later, his link with Isentara was broken by the quickening descent of the black fog. *Darkness* growled.

"Lorshin," Sithbhan appeared above him.

He looked up into his lover's eyes uncertainly as she lifted him in her cold, deadly embrace. His thoughts scattered in a million directions without even one forming into something coherent before her lips found his and her sickly sweet breath banished thoughts into oblivion—still inside, in secret, he felt stronger . . . transformed.

Darkness.

* * *

Nithrodine, Isear

Queen Keliah gazed out across Nithrodine through the night, letting the tears fall at will. As she stood there, the lights of the outer villages of Isear and Nithrodine's lower tiers pricked out one by one. *Dark* climbed over the smoking embers of dying fires to envelope the shadows in total blackness. At least that was how it seemed to her. Though the Light continued to pour from the heavens, it found no place to rest, as it once had, and as it found no rest, she found none, for both had been forsaken. Light poured down, drifting away into nothing. Her tears came until she had no more; pain slowly transformed to a hollow space carved into the pit of her being, growing numb except for the frayed edges around her heart. The dark of Night grew *darker* and the queen trembled.

"Are you cold?"

Keliah stiffened apprehensively at the sound of her husband's voice. Her hands curled tensely on the stone of the balcony wall. She hadn't heard him come in, and now that he was there, she couldn't bear to face him—to let him see the wounds he had inflicted upon her, wounds that went so much deeper than the physical—or how desperately she craved to feel his strong arms holding her safe against the fear as they once had, or even how, in her twisted mind, the fear for which she sought the relief of his arms was of his own making.

"No, my lord," she said quietly.

Silence hung between them for several long moments. Keliah didn't hear when he moved to stand behind her; her heart was beating too loud, but his arms constricted around her waist, pulling her hard against his body. She didn't mean to flinch when she felt his hands hotly through her thin chemise, but she couldn't stop it.

"Keliah."

She bit her lip to keep from crying out as he turned her roughly around to face him, wrenching her hands free of their perch too forcefully.

Armahad's hand abruptly cupped her chin, guiding her head up. Keliah shook with unshed tears; she resisted crying out in terror. Gently, Armahad brushed the blonde hair back from her delicate face.

"Look at me, Keliah," he commanded.

Keliah raised her eyes to meet his. She used to know his face so well; now she couldn't read the look she saw there. To see him so transformed beyond her recognition frightened her, yet the scent of his skin, the feel of his body were the same . . . safe. She shuddered despite herself, wanting to recoil from him.

Armahad's sharp eyes read the panic on her face; his hand tightened like a vice. "Don't be like that, my love," he said too harshly to soothe.

She was sure he could see the terror in her eyes, but he ignored it; his hand eased from her chin, gliding down to intertwine lovingly with her trembling raw hand. Keliah swallowed at the lump in her throat, offering him a small, shy smile to appease him. Armahad's other hand stroked her hair—adoringly, soothingly, familiar—and around her face. His fingers gently brushed over her darkly, bruised cheek. She grimaced.

"Why did you make me do this, Keliah?" Armahad asked softly. "I didn't want to hurt you."

As much as she wanted to scream at him for his words, Keliah couldn't doubt the sincerity of them. "I-I-" she stammered, unsure of how to answer him.

Armahad drew her back into his arms, too roughly, too possessively, but his lips smothered her cry of pain. His fist knotted into her long, soft hair, again too aggressively; pain seared through her head. His mouth tore away from hers, moving gradually downward, and still too possessive began searching, seeking to know every part of her.

Keliah had known his love many times before, never this. She gasped, trying to catch her breath.

"You know I love you," Armahad said, his voice husky. His words came out sounding like a question.

Not trusting her voice, Keliah said nothing. Armahad didn't seem to notice.

"You know I would never want to hurt you," he said; again it sounded like a question, as he lifted her into his strong arms.

Again, she said nothing and lowered her head to his shoulder. This was what she wanted—what she had been crying for! She wanted Armahad to hold her, to love her. Didn't she? Her mind raged so wildly she couldn't find the strength to resist him, and then it was too late. Armahad had her pinned beneath him, the silken sheets and feather mattress and gossamer veils of their marriage bed transformed into a prison.

"Please," Keliah managed to whisper. "I can't."

Armahad silenced her with his lips.

Her eyes fluttered closed; her soft pitiful gasp hung between them, ignored, in the *darkness*.

Tourney, First day, Dawn Parade

A perceptible thrill was in the early morning air as Esarian emerged from his little house well before Night began to consider lifting the massive sky cloak to reveal his beloved Day. The streets of Nithrodine were mostly deserted still except for a black mother cat that screeched as he and Bear passed. Five pairs of eyes peeked around her, curious, but wary. A rooster crowed, heedless of the dawning Sun's absence. Horses nickered in the stables; pigs grunted in dark pens; and above the slowly, waking town, soldiers patrolled the walls of Nithrodine, tier upon tier rising up into the clouds, yet behind every vacant window, within every sentry's footsteps, the Master Summoner felt the exultation of a festival day erupting to life.

Already the gates of the impregnable Nithrodine were groaning open to admit the first wayfarers who would soon be jockeying for prime positions to cheer on their chosen champion who would at dawn parade in full regalia through the streets. Esarian ducked around a corner into the shadows of one of Nithrodine's many cramped and seldom used back alleys as one of the An Taoseach's knights rode past, headed for the summit palace where the parade was to form behind the banner of the An Taoseach. With the order of their arrest in place, it was best not to be identified as a Summoner by one already intent upon winning his emperor's favor, at least not before his purpose was fulfilled this day. Somewhere far beneath his feet, the deepest foundation of this kingdom waited to be rediscovered. All the decadence blinding this land would be laid waste—only from the ashes of its ruins could Hope rise anew for all peoples. Whether or not Armahad Caladrius was in that number was entirely dependent on how deep the infection extended.

Esarian let his hands trail along the damp walls framing the dark alley. Black mold crept in their wake, transforming the strength of Nithrodine into a reeking sore. The stench rushed ahead of him, making the air rank as the An Taoseach's wound stank in his memory, rising to darken the splendor of Isear as the An Taoseach's Mark had been darkened. As the pathway before this nation had been woven with such power that not even he was immune, so too did all the stones of Nithrodine taste the putrid vapors of exposed corruption—all but one, the Shrieking Stone, point of secrets, its myth remained, but few eyes would see it. He only knew because of the dream that had consumed his mind in the last moment of sleep, a dream made not by his imagining, but by the finger of Light pouring in through the window of his house. He had *seen* the Source, though his mind rebelled against the supernatural even as he knew he had become a part of it. High above space, beyond Time, he had *seen* the spiral of golden blood in the mysterious flesh; he had *seen* those eyes of flaming amber that broiled down through the universe, searing *Darkness* into burning shadows. He had seen *power*. He had felt it inflaming the brands on his forehead, giving knowledge back beyond the beginning—before even Firinn stood in the cavity of the universe, back when existence, the first and only mark on the compass of the Kingdom, had belonged to Sanctus and the Source alone, Father and Son . . . back when the Source had been a bearable weight, contained as he was within the Orb of Power, back to that paradise of Flame and Breath and Life. There had been no beginning for them, and there was no ending that Esarian could see, just existence, growing, expanding, consuming . . .

Esarian shivered, letting the *dream* fade from his mind. It was said, and rightly so, that Flame was the most mysterious and powerful substance in the universe, but he would say more. He would say, the Source was *alive* and that this Source was the true prize—the desire of all—and the best kept secret of the Ages. Light hadn't changed. *Darkness* hadn't really changed either. Though it would be nice to blame the One Whose Name is Not Spoken, he couldn't. The Dark One's desires had been the same since the *beginning*. All of this—all of history—came down to choice . . . the choice of a kingdom . . . the choice of a man.

If the An Taoseach chose to give his life over to the pestilence, well then, his kingdom could wallow in it. The rankness of the An Taoseach's soul would fill the nostrils of this kingdom before the Sun reached its apex this day! Trust was a fragile, painful thing, almost as consuming as fear; it could pierce like a double-edged sword to the very recesses of the soul and inspire great valor, or it could strike to the quick and drive a kingdom to its knees. A king's hold over his subjects, even a king as high and lofty as the An Taoseach, was only as strong as the trust he inspired, and that hold must weaken or else *Darkness* must come—this was the choice—and it would shape everything that was to come for all of them.

Colorful streamers hung over the streets, little fabric bridges upon which birds perched, between the walls and houses of Nithrodine. Each color represented a knight to take part in the tournament. Esarian watched the reeking mold climb out of the deep shadows around him out into the main streets, creeping up through the swirl of color up toward the summit. The sky was lightening; if he strained, he could just make out the ethereal visage of Poulderon, Lord of Darkness, Night, as he lifted the lowest edges of the sky cloak, illuminated by the faded glow of his beloved Day, Diastrilis, Lady of Light—both friends of the Resistance, allies against the *Darkness*. They would be his allies once again.

Esarian's gaze lowered. Trumpets sounded from the palace, wafting down on the air currents into Nithrodine's lowest tier. The clamor of peasants filled the main street. Children ran to and fro, trying to catch the first glimpse of the An Taoseach and the knights. They waved colorful banners for their chosen champions and shouted with delight. The Master Summoner waited, holding back into the deep shadows of the alley. Reeking mold continued its relentless climb, its stench permeating the air so thickly the peasants' shouts of delight soon diminished to choking gasps.

The parade reached the lowest tier of Nithrodine in total chaos. Horses reared. Knights shouted as they tried to hang on to their startled animals. The An Taoseach covered his nose and mouth with his regal hand. Esarian stepped from the shadows.

"My lord," he said with a low bow.

"You!" Armahad gasped. "What is the meaning of this?"

Esarian smiled. "How do you like the smell, An Taoseach?"

"You did this?" Armahad shouted.

"No, my lord, you did this," Esarian answered, each word forcefully delivered.

"Me? I am no sorcerer!"

"Nor I," Esarian answered. "But you did indeed bring this stench upon your kingdom."

"Get rid of it!" Armahad ordered.

"I cannot. Only you can free this land from the treachery you have brought upon it!"

"You dare to defy me!"

Esarian inclined his head once. "Prove yourself worthy, my lord, and your kingdom will be made whole. Fail and the pestilence of your soul will spread. I will return."

"Seize him!" Armahad shouted.

Bear flung himself into the gap, baring his teeth in a warning growl.

The knights' horses bolted in wild disarray, though they had been trained for battle. Peasants ran screaming, and in the chaos, Esarian and Bear vanished without a trace.

Chapter Forty

FOR GLORY OR DESPAIR?

P rince Kinjour drew a deep breath, feeling his stomach reel with
nausea as he inhaled the reeking air that covered Nithrodine.
The weight of the chain mail pulled on his weary limbs as he raised
his arms for his squire to pull the surcoat over the whole of his armor.
He wore the surcoat of the An Taoseach, emblazoned with the mythical
white *bird* of Isear, the Caladrius, whose wings were spread wide and a
plume of Flame issued from its mouth. The rich colors and seal all bore
a great honor for the wearer—flaunting distinction—suddenly Kinjour
wasn't sure he wanted to wear them. His deeds would bring glory to the
An Taoseach, his father and master, but would this glory produce only
despair? Two days ago, he would have embraced the glory. Today he
wasn't as sure as he looked down into the pale, sickly face of his squire.
The boy offered him no assurances, not that there were any he would
have believed.

"Am I disturbing you?"

Kinjour looked up. "Cait," he said quietly, acknowledging his sister.
"Leave us," he added to the squire.

The boy bowed and retreated.

"He doesn't look well," Cait said softly as she watched the boy leave.

Kinjour shrugged. "He's said nothing, but it's the smell. I'm sure."
He smiled slightly and held out his hands to his sister.

Cait smiled in return and came forward to grasp them. "I know I'm
not supposed to be here, but I had to see you."

"About what?"

"I wanted to wish you luck." She pulled a strip of silken fabric from
the jeweled pouch at her hip and tied it around his arm.

His sharp eyes narrowed and his smile faded. "There's something more."

Cait lowered her eyes. There was no point trying to deny it. Kinjour would know she was lying.

"What is it?"

Trumpets sounded outside.

"That's your signal," Cait said, hopefully.

Kinjour grunted but made no move to leave. "Tell me."

"I will. Later. But right now you need to go. How would it look if the An Taoseach's own Champion held up the tourney?" She gave him a light push toward the tent flap. "I'm serious. Don't laugh!"

Kinjour did laugh as he grabbed his helmet. "Fine, but afterward we are going to talk."

"Be careful," Cait hurriedly called after him.

* * *

Esarian emerged from the maze of colorful pavilions and strode toward the open field of combat. He watched in silence, with Bear at his side. Neither stood out in the chanting crowd.

"Caladrius! Caladrius! Caladrius!"

Before a grandstand of nobility and throngs of screaming peasants, all bearing a sickly pallor, two knights prepared to face off against each other. On the left was a knight upon a white charger. The horse wore a caparison, finely brocaded in the An Taoseach's colors. The knight was equally adorned, and upon his surcoat was emblazoned the image of the Caladrius. He was easily identifiable by these tokens as Prince Kinjour.

Kinjour raised his lance in acknowledgment to their cheers. His charger pranced restlessly against the gilt bridle in the squire's restraining hand, already anticipating the great charge across the field. The prince's gaze never left his opponent.

On the right was a knight upon a brown horse. Both horse and rider wore yellow, bearing a crest of black and red with two-crossed bird's talons.

A trumpet sounded. The knights charged. The hooves of their horses tore up the field as they raced toward one another. Their lances lowered for the impact as Esarian stepped out between them.

A shout rose from the horrified onlookers. The horses reared, instinctively shying away from the Summoner, sending both knights crashing backward in their saddles. The lances splintered overhead, both knights landing near-perfect blows before being thrown to the ground. Squires ran to help their fallen masters as the An Taoseach rose from his seat.

"What is the meaning of this?"

Esarian raised his head. "Your people are getting sick, my lord. I came to offer you relief on their behalf."

"You brought this upon my people!"

"We already had this conversation," Esarian said firmly. "You and you alone are to blame."

"Can you take the smell away?" the An Taoseach demanded.

"The answer depends entirely upon you, my lord. Are you ready to admit your crime?" Esarian asked with equal authority.

The An Taoseach scowled from his raised seat.

"Then it seems you have your answer," Esarian said after a long moment. "More of your people will die, and this Tournament will be remembered not for the glory of its knights and their king, but for the despair of your people! And all will come to curse your name, Armahad Caladrius, An Taoseach of Isear!"

"You will pay for this treason!"

Esarian shook his head slowly. "Not I, but you. The cries of your people will fill this land. Your fruitfulness is no more."

"Seize him!" the An Taoseach shouted.

Esarian vanished from their sight.

"Sire, look!" someone shouted.

"Impossible!" the An Taoseach screamed as he looked out across the field. The grass was dry and withered. As far as the eye could see every plant, every fruit-bearing tree, every field of crop lay desiccated in the Summoner's wake.

Kinjour approached, supported by his squire. "Father, please," he whispered. "You must intercede for your people."

Armahad glanced down at his adopted son with a deadly stare. "Must I?" he asked bitterly. "What right do you have to demand this of me?"

"Father, I know you are a proud man, but obviously you are up against a power you have no means to combat! People are sick, dying! Now the rest are to starve? The father I know would not stand by and allow this to happen if it was in his power to prevent it."

"Kinjour!" Cait shouted as she ran across the field.

Kinjour glanced back at her, knowing immediately that she had seen his fall and knew he was hurt, but he ignored the pain and the blood to lean closer to his father. "Father?"

Armahad had sunk back into his chair. His hand covered his eyes, and he moaned softly.

"Kinjour!" Cait was closer now. The panic in her voice told him that she could see the blood, gushing from the cut on his head plainly enough.

"Father? Talk to me."

Armahad sprang forward, whipping his dagger from its sheath. He pressed the blade to Kinjour's throat, his eyes erupting with blackness. "Who are you to address me? I am no more your father than you are my son!"

"Kinjour!" Cait screamed from just behind him.

"Armahad!" Queen Keliah screamed from the An Taoseach's side. She placed her hand on her husband's. He shook her off.

Kinjour motioned them back without taking his eyes off his father. "Father, please, remember who you are."

"You are an orphan. Lower than a peasant. Lower than dirt!" Armahad screamed the words, spitting in Kinjour's face.

"It is true I do not possess your blood, but I am your son, sire. Kinjour Caladrius, Champion of Isear. You knighted me, called me son, and gave me the title of prince and your own last name. I am your son. You are not well just as your kingdom is not well."

Armahad moaned, falling back into his chair. The dagger clattered from his hand.

"Take the An Taoseach to his chambers," Queen Keliah ordered the Mydrian standing close.

"Let me see," Cait said anxiously as she rushed forward.

Kinjour wiped blood from his face. "It's nothing serious."

"You need a physician," Cait said to her brother. "Come with me."

They hobbled back toward the pavilion.

"I hate him," Cait snapped after a moment.

"No," Kinjour said quietly.

"I hate him, Kinjour, I swear I do!"

"Is this what you wanted to talk to me about?"

Cait nodded.

Kinjour spoke quietly to his squire. "I want you to leave me with my sister and go. Now!"

The squire nodded and left.

"Why did you do that?" Cait asked, scrambling to maintain her hold on him.

"Because what you said and what I have to say are not for the ears of a servant." He winced slightly.

Cait pouted feeling his disapproval, though he hadn't voiced it. "I do hate him," she mumbled.

"What will that prove? Your hate won't change what happened, and it won't change him, Cait. It will only change you."

"But he could have killed you! Twice now!" Her voice rose into a shriek.

"You don't hate him, Cait. You're upset. That is understandable, but no matter what he has done, the An Taoseach is still our father."

Cait shook her head. "He is no father of mine."

"Cait." Kinjour touched his sister's cheek just below her brooding eyes. "He is. He rescued us when we had no one. If for no other reason than that, he deserves our forgiveness."

"I'm worried, Kinjour." Cait met her brother's gaze. "We are all in danger. This kingdom is in danger! I can feel it!"

Kinjour sighed.

"I know you don't want to see the change in the An Taoseach—I know how much you look up to him—" she rushed, "but—"

"Cait." Kinjour stepped away from his sister with a grimace. "I know him."

"You *knew* him," Cait corrected. "Would the man you *knew* have done this?" She touched the nick caused by the dagger.

"Regardless." Kinjour pushed her hand away. "I swore an oath to him. As his Champion, I owe him my loyalty for as long as he and I both draw breath."

"I am serious, Kinjour!"

"So am I!" Kinjour snapped. He turned and limped away.

"Kinjour!" Cait called after him, but he didn't respond.

*   *   *

A horrible silence settled over the palace summit of Nithrodine. The kind of silence that made the skin crawl as some part of the mind sensed disembodied eyes watching, waiting. The lower tiers were more restless full of pitiful moaning that rose through all the hours. Dead lay in the streets. The stench of rotting flesh rose in visible vapors over the land. Rats scuttled among the ripe corpses carrying disease into every household. Hunger drove them all toward madness, yet in their secret sanctuary the Summoners found rest.

"They put a price on your head yet?" Orlok asked as Esarian and his dog ducked into the cramped quarters. The dwarf took a big bite of sausage. It was a mystery to him how their stores had survived the plague, but he wasn't about to complain.

"Orlok!" D'Faihven punched him in the arm.

"What!" Orlok demanded, around the mouthful of meat.

Esarian laughed. "The An Taoseach is beyond that. He just wants my head on a spike." The Master Summoner sank onto the damp floor and broke his sausage in half. One half he gave to Bear. The other he ate himself.

"Is the food truly gone out there?" Nulet asked quietly.

Esarian nodded. "The peasants have started dying, and there is nothing the An Taoseach can do to staunch the tide of death. Even the grain stores have rotted."

"Could we?" D'Faihven nodded toward their food stores. "Could we help the peasants?"

The Master Summoner shook his head slowly. "The food would rot instantly outside this sanctuary, and were they to come here, the plague would follow. No, only the An Taoseach can help his people, but I am afraid he is too stubborn to admit his wrongs against them."

"What can we do?"

"Hope," Esarian said quietly after a long moment. "Hope for the arrival of a new time, one of true glory and not despair."

The Summoners sat in silence for a time, listening to the howls of the kingdom drift down from miles above their heads.

"Will you return to the An Taoseach?" D'Faihven asked unwillingly.

Esarian nodded once in the near darkness. "Tomorrow."

Chapter Forty-One

THIRST

Loriath, Kingdom of the Elves of Light

All trace of pain had been erased from her body. Isentara shifted on the bed and felt gentle hands holding her. Without opening her eyes, she grappled with her memory, trying to remember where she was, whom she was with, and how she had come to be there, but everything was a blur.

"You're safe." The voice instantly calmed her, yet the pain did not stay gone. A different kind of pain shot through her heart, piercing her soul.

"Uncle Cadclucan," she said softly.

The arms tightened around her comfortingly as if their owner sensed the effect his presence had on her. "Hello, child," Cadclucan said gently.

Isentara let herself melt back into his embrace, though she could not stop herself from asking the one question that now consumed her entire being. "All those times—" she hesitated and started again. "Couldn't you hear me? Couldn't you see me? All those times I called, why didn't you answer?"

Cadclucan didn't answer, and she sensed that he wouldn't. There was no power she possessed that could make him answer.

Isentara sighed, "I guess I already know why."

"Yes, I suppose you do," the Guardian said softly after a moment.

She let her memories drift back to another day, the end of another Age . . .

For two days and two nights, the earth shook and the Guardians' did not breath.

When at last they stirred, the Guardians' breath lasted days without sun and nights without moon. It was impossible to tell the passage of time. How many days had been lost to their thinly veiled sorrow? How many nights had harbored their silent pain? How many raindrops had concealed their bitter tears? When at last the Sun showed his face, the Guardians thawed from their ridged stance. The birds burst forth with singing. The trees danced in the wind. The earth slowly exhaled, and the various scents of life sprang forth once more, but *Darkness* had spread a thread of corruption. Innocence was gone.

Cadclucan slowly turned. "We knew this moment would come," he said. His voice carried softly across the world. "All that Sanctus revealed in his Prophecy of Hope must be fulfilled, even this Sea of Sorrows! Though it breaks our hearts, the coming *Darkness* cannot be prevented. The One Whose Name is not Spoken will arise in many hearts to trouble the whole earth, and in that endless blackness, the races will call out to the Light once more!" He was quiet for a long moment before he spoke again with his mind, *Let the Light shine forth and awaken hope. Let Mhorag arise. Let the Promised come.*

Lorshin and Isentara crouched in the shadow of the Guardian. Their blue eyes burned dimly in the shadows . . . a single trace of Flame . . . a hint of the heritage that was both a blessing and a curse. They could not claim the perfection of the Guardian bloodline, no Samhail could—that had been denied them long before their birth. There was just enough Flame in them to light their eyes and that was all. Still, their ravaged hearts, beating slow and steady in their chests, felt heavier than they should have. They had borne many weights in their lifetime. Lorshin had seen his mother die. He had seen his father become the Heart of Evil, and through him Isentara had seen it too. They had endured this curse from birth because of their father's choice, but this time the weight felt too big, or perhaps they were just now acknowledging their own weakness.

"Must you go?" Lorshin asked softly.

Cadclucan glanced down at him. "To every season there is an added sorrow. Consider, nephew, the beautiful flowers of spring that wither in the heat of the summer sun, the trees that bring forth bud only to have those garments fall and rot upon the ground, the ground that freezes in winter locking up its bounty, but to every sorrow, there is a purpose. There is always the promise. There is always hope," he answered cryptically.

Lorshin shook his head. "I don't . . . I don't understand this. How can you think of leaving? We need you here to lead us!"

"This world has had us to lead them from the beginning," Cadclucan answered quietly. "Look around you, Lorshin, *Darkness* is everywhere, and yet can anyone see it? They fight, but the One Whose Name is Not Spoken comes in many forms and they resist only in the ways that please them." He shook his head. "No, this world has blinded itself, and now they must face their choice."

"Not all have forgotten!" Lorshin cried.

Cadclucan sighed and the other Guardians with him. "I know."

"Will you leave those who still desire only Light?"

Cadclucan held out his hand to Lorshin. "Will you come out of the *Darkness*?"

Lorshin hesitated. He glanced toward his sister.

"In good times the world grows and prospers, but it is in the *darkest* of times that all living things find what is really inside themselves," Cadclucan said.

Lorshin looked up into his uncle's piercing eyes. "I know what is inside me."

. . . Isentara wiped away a bitter tear and the memory with it.

"So what is inside of you, Isentara?" Cadclucan asked.

It did not surprise her that her uncle knew where her thoughts had drifted, yet she shuddered.

"All those years ago, you chose to follow Lorshin. Now I must ask you, Isentara, will you come out of the *Darkness*?" Her uncle's voice fell into a whisper. "I see what is inside of you. I can see the thirst for Light and freedom. I see the need for Hope that drives you, but I also see the fear that keeps you always on the verge of *Darkness*."

"I feel so lost," Isentara whispered.

"You are not alone," Cadclucan answered gently.

Isentara tried to twist around in his arms, trying to see his flaming eyes. Somehow she sensed that his words were about himself and implied something more than his physical presence. This, of course, seemed absolutely ridiculous. He was a Guardian—not prone to the weaknesses and insecurities of lesser beings!

His arms held her tightly so that she couldn't turn, and again she was not surprised that he knew her thoughts. "You might be surprised," he said in a whisper.

"No." Isentara shook her head stubbornly. "*Darkness* has no power over you."

Cadclucan laughed once without humor. "Yet I bleed in its presence."

Isentara squirmed against the prison of his arms to no avail. She wanted to see because she couldn't be sure otherwise, but she would have sworn, in that fleeting moment, that he trembled.

* * *

Nithrodine, Isear:

Prince Liacin squawked testily in his mother's arms.

"Make him stop," Armahad groaned to Keliah. He rolled over on the bed.

"He's hungry, Armahad," Keliah said gently.

"So feed him," he snapped.

"I cannot." Keliah patted Liacin's back, humming soothingly as she paced the length of their bedchamber.

Armahad scowled, propping himself up on one arm. "Why not?"

"Because apparently my milk is considered fruitfulness," Keliah said, stopping long enough to look pointedly at her husband.

"Are you trying to make me angry?" Armahad asked, fixing her with a withering stare.

"No," Keliah answered softly.

"Then call for a wet nurse!" he shouted.

"It won't do any good, Armahad."

"Excuse me?" the An Taoseach reared out of bed in a fury.

Keliah took an involuntary step back, shielding Liacin from whatever came next. "I said it would not do any good," she repeated softly, but firmly.

"Why not?" Armahad demanded as he stalked toward her.

The queen swallowed at the lump in her throat. "We've all run dry," she whispered and then purposefully met his gaze. "Your fruitfulness is undone," she quoted the Master Summoner. "How long will you stand by and do nothing?"

Armahad growled. Keliah cradled Liacin closer and inched toward the beckoning light of Mydrian watch fires in the antechamber, but she gave up quickly, knowing she was trapped. There was no escape without having to go through him. She opened her mouth to scream for the guards, but the cry died on her lips as his hand circled her throat, cutting off the flow of precious air.

Keliah struggled. He held her fast, seeming to take pleasure in her wild panic-stricken stare.

"Haven't I been good to you? Haven't I loved you and cared for you? Didn't I keep you when your womb was empty and useless?" Armahad seethed.

Keliah sobbed hoarsely. "Armahad, please."

"I love you! All I ask for in return is a little respect!" he shouted.

"Can't you see yourself?" Keliah cried almost soundlessly.

Armahad groaned as Light poured through the open window. The Light came and went these days, almost as a child's face might appear and disappear in a game of peekaboo, but when it came, the Light was stronger than ever before—a blinding, blood-curdling force. He released his wife, staggering back as it flowed toward him. Keliah drew back into the Light, gasping for breath.

"Respect is earned," she said between gasps. "I do not know you anymore, Armahad."

The ashen mask of his features lightened, and from beneath the near-permanent shadows etched on his face, she could see her husband gazing back at her. "I have not changed, my love," Armahad said wearily as he raised a shaking hand to shield his eyes.

"Yes, you have." Keliah raised a trembling hand to her throat. "And the fact that you cannot see it—" She shook her head and didn't finish her thought. The queen hurried toward the antechamber, cradling Liacin closer as his screams intensified. Her footsteps were quick and quiet at one with the fluttering of her heart.

"Keliah. Don't—" Armahad stretched a hand toward her.

Keliah hesitated at the door. "I love you, Armahad Caladrius," she said without turning back, "but I-I can't do this anymore."

Armahad caught her hand before she could leave. "No, please. I promise. I won't hurt you again!"

Keliah looked at their joined hands, letting her tears fall. She did not dare to meet her husband's gaze, for fear it would weaken her resolve. "Please let me go," she said in a whisper.

"What might I say to change your mind?"

Keliah could hear the desperation in his voice. Her heart clenched in her chest, a mirror to his suffering. Her eyes squeezed shut. She sighed, resisting the urge to melt into his arms and tell him all was forgiven. "Nothing." Her voice trembled. She pulled her hand away from his and hurriedly left. "I love you," she whispered just before she disappeared from his sight.

Armahad's fist punched a hole in the wall.

"Sire?" a Mydrian appeared beside him.

"Leave me!" he seethed, black fury pressing down upon him once more.

*　　*　　*

Tourney, Fourth day

The mood of the Tournament had grown *darker* over the last few days. Hungry knights once assembled by a peaceful series of games now feuded amongst themselves. The games turned to death matches. Blood drenched the parched earth, but the thirst for it did not slacken though the smoke of fires fueled by the dead hung thick and black—an unnatural night—over the land.

No crowds assembled to cheer on their champions. The peasants were sick or starving, dropping one after another, too weak to rise. Some were even choosing to cast themselves into the fires while they still lived because there was no one to carry them out once they died. Through all of this, the An Taoseach abandoned his people to their fate.

Esarian, with Bear whining at his side, walked this maze of death. His mind did not want to comprehend the carnage before his eyes. Could any hope arise from these ashes of its former glory? Could *Darkness* so great ever be defeated? The Styarfyre orb shard around his neck felt heavier than it had in years, maybe because of the *Darkness* increasing its presence in this empire of Light, maybe because as the Firebrand he was more susceptible to feeling its desperate strength and malignant force, maybe because the end was near. These thoughts consumed his every waking moment and dripped down into his restless dreams. He had no answers, only purpose driven by the Light that burned in every black shadow, through every reeking vapor hanging in thick tapestries between the walls of Nithrodine. His eyes full of despair looked up to the palace summit barely visible in the black. The An Taoseach had much to answer for.

Armahad paced the length of his deserted throne room. Blackness whispered around him, mingling with his own muttered ranting—the ranting of a mad man. His boots made a sharp click on the floor as he walked.

Is there any sign of the Summoner?

"No. Not yet," Armahad muttered. "Where? Where could he be? It has been three days!"

Hewillcome,andwhenhedoes,youmusttakehim.Makeanexample of him!

Armahad nodded his head up and down, smiling happily at the thought.

Whatever happens, you must stop him. Do you understand?

Armahad nodded. "Whatever happens," he muttered. "Yes, I understand," he whispered quietly to himself. "Whatever happens."

This Summoner will ruin everything. Destroy him at any cost!

"Whatever happens," Armahad muttered.

The doors panged open with a gust of unnatural wind. Armahad whirled, shielding his eyes against the sudden Light that preceded the white-robed figure. When the Light cleared, the Master Summoner stood defiantly before him. The brands on his forehead shone fiercely against the *dark*.

"Guards!" Armahad shrieked. "Seize him!"

Mydrian appeared from every recess of the chamber and its numerous antechambers.

Esarian raised his hand. The guards flew back and were pinned to the ornate walls. "I am the Firebrand, and I come on behalf of the Light."

Darkness shrieked all around the An Taoseach. Throughout the room, shadows were tumbling down in a red, fiery haze.

"Speak then and be gone," Armahad shouted.

Esarian lowered his hand. The Mydrian dropped to the floor. "This land has smelled your corruption. Your people wallow in it, my lord. It infests your very house and ravages the fruit of your loins. Will you persist in this course of despair or will you set this land free from the *Darkness* you have brought upon it?"

"You thirst for *my* power!" Armahad ranted madly.

Esarian laughed. "I thirst for the power of One and One alone—the Promised who will bring Cure and Hope in his wake!"

"Who is this Promised that I should bow to him?" Armahad shouted.

Esarian raised the Styarfyre orb shard. "So that you may know the power of the Promised, this land shall know thirst."

Armahad reached for his javelin and thrust it at the Summoner.

Bear growled an instant before he and Esarian vanished. Only a gust of wind was evidence of their passing. The javelin struck the wall.

Two unnatural days without water had left a deep scar upon the land. Riverbeds stood dry and barren. Waterfalls turned to dust. Wells gave forth nothing. In the An Taoseach's rash effort to overcome the plague, countless slaves died digging for water in a land that had never known lack. The funeral fires finally died, their keepers no longer strong enough to sustain them. Bodies lay to rot in the very streets of Nithrodine, yet Armahad's heart was harder.

To hide his hunger and thirst, he planned. Nithrodine would be a reflection of his glory and power when the work was done. The dead lost everything to his coffers. The living suffered beneath the crushing weight of his plan, taxes claiming what little they had, but he didn't care. He was the An Taoseach, the true and rightful king, and everyone would know it when he was done. He would have a golden statue built in his image that was plainly visible to all, and then he would see what became of this *hope*.

Armahad spread the plans in front of the forced laborers—some so sick the soldiers sent to find them had been forced to drag them from their beds.

"This is your priority," he said in a parched voice.

When he looked up, Esarian stood before him.

"You!" he growled.

"Your plans change nothing," the Summoner said.

Armahad spit at Esarian's feet. "Be gone from my sight, Firebrand!"

A peasant licked the morsel of water from the floor.

Esarian lifted the Styarfyre orb shard. "So that you may know the power of the Promised and the Hope of his Cure, deadly serpents shall cover this land." He vanished as soon as these words were spoken.

The tournament's end came with more chaos and death. Knights driven mad by hunger, thirst, and fear fled Nithrodine, swords flying, to carve a path through the latest plague. Peasants, many too weak with hunger and thirst to defend themselves, fell where they were bitten—an instantaneous end to their week of suffering.

Even high in Nithrodine's palace summit, the An Taoseach was not immune. Armahad stood on his throne. Deep black rings surrounded his eyes. He hadn't slept. His days and nights were consumed with the constant slash of his sword. Anger gave purpose to his exhausted limbs as he raised his sword again to slash at the mass of serpents entangling his royal seat.

"Esarian!" he screamed. "Esarian! Show yourself, Firebrand!"

For hours . . . perhaps days . . . he had called, and for all his screaming, there had been no answer. How many of his people had been bitten? How many were dead? The reports had stopped coming. Was Keliah alive? Was Liacin? Kinjour? His daughters? "Esarian!"

The tapestries rustled in the wind.

"I'm here, my lord," Esarian said quietly.

"Take the serpents away!"

"The Promised commands them."

"You are his prophet!"

Esarian spread his hands and raised his face skyward.

As the Light returned, the serpents died in great heaps, in every house and village across the land. The stink of death spread in its wake barely noticeable in the gory cesspool Nithrodine had become as the bodies decayed before their eyes, dissolved into dust, and blew away with the breath of the Source.

Armahad stepped down from his throne. "What took you so long, Firebrand? I've been screaming for you for—for—how long has it been?"

Esarian smiled. "Yes, I know," he said, ignoring both questions. "Once a *true* word is spoken, it cannot be taken back." The Master Summoner delivered the words like a threat. "Now I ask you again how long will you persist in your defiance? This land has smelled your corruption. Your people wallow in it, my lord. It infests your very house and ravages the fruit of your loins. Will you persist in this course of despair or will you set this land free from the *Darkness* you have brought upon it? Will you restore Hope to your people?"

"Never! I am ruler here!" *Darkness* drifted back into the Light.

Esarian shook his head sadly. "How long will you make your people suffer? How long will you forbid them Hope?"

"You cause them to suffer!" Armahad shouted. "The stink, starvation, dehydration, disease, snake bites! These are all of your making! Not mine!"

"I have done nothing outwardly that is not already manifest inwardly, great king. In you! The stink of your wound cannot be washed away. The hunger you feel cannot be appeased with mortal food. The thirst you feel cannot be quenched by water. Disease cannot be nullified by medicine or the snake bites sucked free of their poison. No, my lord, all of this rests squarely upon your head, and there is but one Cure! One Hope!"

"Hope?" Armahad sneered the word. "What is hope? A word? A dream? An all-consuming agony?" His scowl deepened as he echoed the ancient words spoken by Arawn long ago—words he had never heard before but now whispered in the black. "Be gone from me!"

Esarian lifted the Styarfyre orb shard. "This too is of your making," he said.

Armahad looked up as hail ruptured the sky, crashing down like falling stones upon Nithrodine. "No!"

"Prove yourself worthy, my lord, and your kingdom will be made whole. Fail and the pestilence of your soul will spread. I will return."

Fire ran along the ground and walls of the palace as would torrents of rain. In the same second, Esarian was gone.

Chapter Forty-Two

AGONY OF HOPE

Kingdom

The Source dropped back into the bowels of his sanctuary. He couldn't sink far enough into its recesses to escape the screams of the universe. Thousands of voices were cut off in the black; thousands more rang in mindless despair when Light shot through. Light and *Darkness* beat upon his senses, tearing him first one way and then the other. His eyes squeezed tightly closed against the chaos below. He didn't want to gaze down into the universe—to watch the void encroaching hard upon the burning shadows, yet he couldn't resist an occasional peek. Not knowing was too hard. Turbulent, battered Light greeted his eyes as he looked. *Darkness* as he looked away; both violent in their strength, drawing their *life* from ill-defined points, a dizzying conflagration of opposing power. Each force sought to dominate the other, waxing and waning in tides of hope and despair—neither stable enough to overwhelm the other or withstand the other, but *Darkness* seemed so great before his eyes that he could almost feel the black breath beating upon the borders of the Kingdom. Try as he might, he couldn't help remembering when once it had been close enough to possess him. He remembered Sgarrwrath. He had seen within that formless *Darkness* as no other ever had, no, not even Sanctus in the beginning when he cast Sgarrwrath down, nor Arawn in his years of oblivion; but once back when existence had belonged to him and Sanctus alone—back when Time was nothing more than a god's immaterial dream—long, long before the beginning . . . he had seen . . . he remembered when *Darkness* took a mirror of life all its own from one drop of golden blood . . .

Darkness.

Yet the Source could still see. Past, present and future mingled before his sight. Screams rose from that distant place beyond the Light, where *Darkness* breathed forth its mindless despair. The blackness loomed so high it seemed to have no end just like the Light embroiled against it, precisely as he had seen it so long ago; yet high above the Sun and Moon, high above Light and *Darkness*, far beyond the weightlessness of space the fountainhead of all Flame heaved forth from the zenith of the universe and all these things fell away beneath his feet. What were they by comparison to his glory? From his unfathomable height, the Source watched with eyes, once amber, now inflamed with the same liquid gold of his blood, its raging tempest tamed within his flesh once more. His eyes had seen too much yet he couldn't look away. The universe revolved around his feet. From the Kingdom's dust, Existence was born and scattered throughout the galaxies. All Light; all baring his reflection.

Mhorag tried again to press through the barriers surrounding him. His efforts only made Flame shine brighter from every inch of his body; no matter how hard or long he struggled to escape he could not break free and time was endless. It was not measured in the Kingdom was measured in the universe below his feet. Existence was the first and only mark on the compass of the Kingdom and his existence was the heart of all existence. With his hands he braced himself against unbreakable walls. The Flame grew cold around him. Its violent heat banished to memory. He shivered and the tongues of colored fire with him.

Time flew by. Days, weeks, years—a blur of moments too indistinguishable to truly mark, yet he lingered on alone and unchanged, shackled by Flame and breath. He bowed his snow-white head against the orb. *Darkness* crept across the universe sending bitter wails of death and despair rising up into the perfect stillness all around him. He watched the passage of present and future Time, listening, watching, waiting as wars played out and *Darkness* arose; its turbulence swelled upon him with a knot of power collapsing under its own gravity, sucking all things toward its black void. The universe turned beneath his feet. The Seasons of earth slowly decayed. Flowers once colored in vibrant and chaotic hues faded, withered, and died. Leaves paled upon the branch and the wind drove them to the ground in shades of yellow, red and brown. There they rotted as the trees soared above clawing the sky with naked limbs. Evergreens shed needles and cones like unwanted ornaments to earthen beds. Birds flew in great sky blackening droves as deadly frost covered the earth. Slowly, *Darkness* triumphed over Light and overwhelmed the world. As for him, nothing ever changed except in his dreams.

Mhorag dropped back into the bowels of his sanctuary as time stretched on. He couldn't sink far enough into its recesses to escape the screams. Thousands of voices were cut off in the black; thousands more rang in mindless despair when Light shot through. Light and *Darkness* beat upon his senses, tearing him first one way and then the other. His eyes squeezed tightly closed against the chaos. He didn't want to gaze down into the universe—to watch the void encroaching hard upon the burning shadows, yet he couldn't resist an occasional peak. Not knowing was too hard. Turbulent, battered Light greeted his eyes as he looked. *Darkness* as he looked away; both violent in their strength, drawing their *life* from ill-defined points, a dizzying conflagration of opposing power. Each force sought to dominate the other, waxing and waning in tides of hope and despair—neither stable enough to overwhelm the other or withstand the other, but *Darkness* seemed so great before his eyes that he could almost feel the black breath beating upon the borders of the Kingdom itself. Try as he might, he couldn't escape this moment—a moment he *remembered* though it was only now coming to pass, a moment when once this *Darkness* was close enough to possess him. Yes, he *remembered* Sgarrwrath. He had *seen* within that formless *Darkness* as no other ever had—no, not even in this moment. Mhorag shuddered, trying to awaken from the memory of the dream that was past, present and future all at the same time! Gone was the light of the Flame. Gone was the comfort of its constant, burning presence.

Sgarrwrath rose up, changing size and shape at will, till his face was mere inches away. The Dark One's heated breath sent intense, body-jarring shivers running down Mhorag's spine so that his teeth chattered and his bones creaked in his frame. A twisted smile spread across Sgarrwrath's blackened lips, pushing up the hollowed illusion of cheekbones to shadow the deeply set, violent ruby eyes of an insubstantial face. Born of an errant thought, Sgarrwrath had no form, no life, as the Source did, only the vague aura of them visible in the stolen eyes of Dullahan, and in time, the stolen heart of Arawn and the stolen Flame within it. Existing in a formless *Darkness*, Sgarrwrath was the incarnation of the void . . . all hate and greed and lust and illusion wrapped in the semitransparent guise of humanity, smeared together by the black streaming out of him. Sgarrwrath was not quite whole but he reeked of danger!

Mhorag shivered violently as the cold intensified. Why was he so cold? He could feel the ice forming on his lips, on his eyes, on his fingertips. The cold crept through his extremities dousing the Flame inch by painful inch. He let out a strangled cry that slowly degenerated to a childish whimper as his teeth shook violently against one another and the icy dagger penetrated his chest, snatching his breath away. The memory pressed in around him, faltering, as the cold dragged him down toward its numbing embrace. Sgarrwrath loomed out of the collapsing tunnel bringing a wave of black fury with him.

His breath gusted from the orb futilely scattering their ashes in every direction. *Darkness* rose higher, stronger, upon them. This was not part of the memory! Even numb, Mhorag grasped the horrible reality. Something was wrong. His dreams were vivid, his visions too, but this . . . this was something else and he was too cold to panic, too numb to fight it! In the distance he heard muffled footsteps, whispered voices. He tried to call out for help. His voice froze in his throat as Sgarrwrath's large, black hands erupted through Time and Space to grip his shoulders.

"I know what you are!" Sgarrwrath said with an echoing roar. "I know where you are! You will be mine!"

"Mhorag." Sanctus' voice shattered the silent panic of his being.

His eyes flew open. Light burst across the black. The horrors of memory and vision evaporated. He knew well that moment of existence when *Darkness* and Light were birthed forth into the formless universe. He *remembered. He had been there.* He was there now. His power flowed to extend life to Sanctus' creation. They had no power over him! He had always known this day would come and if he concentrated hard enough, he could almost envision the answer to those horrible foreknown screams. A mark appeared behind his eyes, glowing with a faint golden light. It curved like a waxing crescent moon only tipped with a head and trailing a gleaming tail. Beneath this mark a face began to appear: snow-white skin, unnaturally flaming amber eyes, a lion's mane of snow-white hair, a beating crystal heart. That face gazed back at him reflected upon the walls of his breath!

All around this vision, Flame flowed. The furthest reaching points were the tops of huge wings. A beautiful horse-shaped head crowned with a single iridescent horn appeared as the presence rose up with a noble cry. The glittering mane tumbled down the long neck. From the top of the head to the end of the long, thick tail, the massive body was made of Light divided into a covering of tiny, close knit scale-like flames. He stood at the center of this Light shadow—a mixture of lion and youth and Guardian. The noble head tossed upward. A great cry rang out. Golden blood rose to the surface, kindled with the rapid beat of his heart.

Mhorag shook his head trying to clear it. This was nothing more than a shadow around a fixed point. He focused on that point with all his might. It was his reflection. Suddenly, the Flame threw him back into silhouette and the vision was gone, yet it still frightened him because in this dream he was the prey! "I *remember*." He breathed. Golden blood swirled freely through the Source's body from the beating crystal heart where Time found its course.

A star went black.

Darkness . . .

*　*　*

Nithrodine

The An Taoseach was seated on his throne, scowling down at the rabble before him. The work on his image had ceased. Prince Kinjour and an assembly of nobles stood before him airing their grievances and those of the people. It was as endless as the flaming hail that fell from the sky. These had been the longest days of his life, and the complaints of his nobles were wearing on his nerves.

"Enough!" he shouted at last.

The nobles looked to Prince Kinjour and he to his adopted father.

"Father, please," Kinjour said again. "The crops are dead. The water is dried up. The villages are burning. Your people are hungry. They have suffered thirst and infestation and now—"

"I said, enough!" Armahad shouted. His hand lashed out across his son's face.

Kinjour didn't back down. "Even your palace is burning, Father, and still you won't listen!"

"Be quiet," Armahad said, rising menacingly.

"I will not." Kinjour looked his father squarely in the eye. "Caladrius means Cure—is Cure—and you no longer embody the goodness of that promise!"

Armahad snorted, "Since when do you believe in children's bedtime stories, Kinjour?"

"Is that all Caladrius was when your ancestor, Nudhug, received his Mark?" Kinjour stared at his father, searching those features he barely recognized. "Deep down, you know the stories are true."

"You should listen to your people," Esarian said, appearing before them.

"What do you want, Firebrand?" The king growled as he sank back into his throne.

"I said I would return," Esarian answered simply.

"Take the flaming hail away."

"It is done."

"Now get out!" the An Taoseach shouted.

Esarian stood his ground. "What's it to be, great king, surrender or more suffering?"

Armahad cracked a smile. "You don't want to do this."

Esarian waited.

The An Taoseach's ringed hand, which had been stroking absently over the scarred Mark, dropped to his side. "Well, perhaps you do, but you forget. I knew you would return." A net dropped over the Master Summoner and was pulled tight by four Mydrian who kept their eyes downcast with shame. "I gave you a chance. You persist in defiance, so now I prefer to choose my own course of action, Summoner."

"And what's that?" Esarian asked as the Mydrian bound him tightly with ropes.

"Your head on a spike."

"Father!" Kinjour shouted in objection.

"Or something along those lines," Armahad sneered. "First though you will regret the day you were born. The suffering will be your own, Summoner."

Esarian laughed. "You think too highly of yourself, great king."

"Take him away. Tomorrow he dies!"

"Father, please!"

Armahad leaped from his throne. "Get out!" he screamed. "All of you! Go!"

"May the worm on the inside be visible on the out," Esarian said softly as he was led away. "May all who look upon you cry in terror. May your glory be laid in ashes!"

Prince Kinjour was the last to leave the An Taoseach's presence. He looked back at his father one last time. The Mark was splitting open at the scar. Maggots tumbled down from the angry wound. "Father, you can end this. Please."

Armahad slammed the door to the throne room shut in his face.

*   *   *

Kingdom

Sanctus came to kneel beside the Orb of Power. Arawn stood close to his side.

"Mhorag," Sanctus called softly.

The Source crawled forward. His hands, shining with the mysterious swirl of golden blood pressed against the walls of breath just beneath where Sanctus's hands had come to rest. He whimpered. Tears of fear and dread dripped from his eyes, through the walls of breath into Sanctus's glowing hands.

"Do not be afraid," Sanctus said softly. He stroked the walls of breath. His touch tingled through the barrier, penetrating deep into the Source. "You are safe."

"The Dark One wants him," Arawn said softly.

"Sgarrwrath cannot reach so high. Not yet," Sanctus said.

The Source whimpered. Flame trembled as he trembled.

"Be at peace," Sanctus said. "There is still Hope. The dark time is not over yet. There will be more suffering. It is the price of the choice, but one day Mhorag will break free and Hope will arise to fight for all living things. As I am, so is he. Flesh of my flesh, living Flame."

Arawn sighed, turning away.

Darkness. Always *Darkness* . . . that living blackness foaming out its own shame; that hated thing breathing forth its mindless despair was coiled and ready to strike. It never faded. Hours and days passed. Years had flown by: one, two . . . a hundred . . . a thousand . . . an Age. His brothers had carved out his heart with their Flame to free him, and yet for Arawn, it still felt like a trap. Each moment in the Kingdom was endless—a breath of thought—a glorious, waking dream. Time had all but lost its meaning. Existence was far beyond the frail confines of life that he had known before.

He breathed no air, for he had no need of it. He ate no food, for he never craved it. He took no sleep, for he never grew weary. He had no heart, for it had been taken long ago. The hole carved out by the Light had never healed, and it never would. He was kept by Sanctus's hand, and all his desire was fixed there, forsaking all else and the world below.

On one hand, his existence was fathomless peace and on the other the secret agony of the past. Arawn trod the ever-lengthening miles of eternity by his Maker's side, but nothing could blot out the stain he had left behind. He suffered alone from a consuming sadness.

The *Darkness* was always there, lurking below, mocking his peace as it threatened the world Sanctus so greatly loved. His heart was down there in that black void. He would always know its vile beat and the boundless dread it awoke in him. *Thud. Thud. Thud. Thud.* Its beat filled his ears, growing louder day by day, bringing pain into his joy. *Darkness* haunted him, silent and unstirring; yet he knew how restless and alive it really was. He bore it in silence, ashamed to admit its hold over his mind, afraid of its power.

"The One Whose Name is not Spoken will never surrender," Arawn said softly.

"I know," Sanctus said.

"I gave him such power," Arawn said. He couldn't meet Sanctus's loving gaze. He couldn't bear to see the Source gazing from the Orb with eyes that saw everything!

"If you had not, Sgarrwrath would have lured another and possessed them just as he once possessed you. Only they may not have been strong enough to escape in the end."

Arawn stiffened at the name that all but Sanctus feared to speak.

Sanctus smiled gently. "Dullahan gave life to Sgarrwrath, and it destroyed him. You gave Sgarrwrath power, and I showed him mercy."

"You could end this now!" Arawn said. "Weigh out the justice that has been so long deferred! You could put out the Flame and put all things to rest! You could make Hope more than a word!"

"Hope already is more than a word," Sanctus said quietly.

Both gazed down at the Source. He shrank back into his sanctuary.

"Yes, but—" Arawn began.

Sanctus shook his head. "I have the power to end this now, Arawn, but I will not use it to destroy Sgarrwrath. He serves a purpose you cannot yet understand."

"But he means to cover the world in *Darkness*! He means to destroy the Light and the races, the Guardians . . . my brothers and sisters . . . you . . . Mhorag!"

"Yes," Sanctus said, smiling, "but you cannot burn away the past, Arawn. You cannot eradicate the future. You cannot deny others their choice or the agony of Hope." Sanctus said gently, "Nor will I."

Thud. Thud. Thud. Thud. Arawn's face contorted grotesquely. His eyes widened as he beheld the *Darkness*. "Did you know?" he whispered. "Did you know what he would become? Did you know what I would become?" He could barely frame the words. He couldn't meet Sanctus's all-seeing gaze.

Sanctus sighed softly. This was unexpected, and Arawn looked upon his Maker in wonder. Those eyes were touched with pain and sorrow from some deep wound he could not understand.

"Sanctus?" Arawn whispered.

The Source whimpered.

Sanctus gazed past Arawn, down into the depths of *Darkness*. "Before the beginning, Mhorag dreamed, and from his dreams, I conceived every possible choice and the price of each one, and I knew which one would be chosen."

"You knew what Dullahan would become, and yet you still gave him life?"

"Yes."

"Why?" Arawn asked.

"Because I had Hope. Because the life I put in Dullahan was more than enough to guide him to me, but I would not take away his choice! And because you cannot begin to imagine what it is to have no beginning and no ending and to exist in nothingness forever alone, you cannot fully understand the joy of the agony of that Hope."

"When he betrayed you, why did you make us?"

"I poured life into the Guardians and let it burn in their veins to be a guiding Light even in *Darkness*. I made the Races for the same reason I made Dullahan in the beginning, and I have left them with the same choice, so you see these things must come to pass. I still have Hope, and I have given it to all my creation in the Guardians, in the Prophecy of Hope, in the choice." Sanctus's voice trailed off. He looked back to Arawn, and his eyes softened.

"I don't understand."

"Remember how your brothers loved you? They showed mercy, denying you what you deserved—eternal *Darkness*—and freely giving what you did not. They loved you even in *Darkness* with a love so unyielding that it carved out your heart . . . your Flame . . . life itself from your chest to free you from *Darkness* and carried you to me!" Sanctus searched Arawn's face.

Arawn nodded without meeting his gaze.

"Guardians are the closest to me—to him—" he said, motioning toward the Source, "of all living things. It is life, Flame that is within them. If you can understand your brothers' love, then you can begin to understand mine."

"I cannot," Arawn whispered. "*Darkness* haunts my every moment!"

"Do not fear the *Darkness*, Arawn. It will not come near you."

"So long as hope remains," Arawn said quietly as he buried his face in the Light of Sanctus's embrace.

"Still you doubt though you have seen he lives?"

The Source whimpered at Sanctus's words. They reminded him too much of his dream—the endless knot—where only a thin line separated Light and *Darkness*, weaving Time into a trap around him.

Sanctus's gentle laugh echoed through the kingdom. "Oh, Arawn, you will see in time. The time of the Promised will soon be at hand, and the agony of Hope will give way to Light."

Darkness growled, "I am Sgarrwrath, the One Whose Name is not Spoken. I am the Heart of Evil and the Plague spot from which all that is vile is sprung. I am the residue of Dullahan and the corrupted Flame of Arawn. I am *Darkness*."

Light whispered back. *Let the Light shine forth and awaken hope. Let Mhorag arise. Let the Promised come.*

Corrupted laughter rang boldly in the dark.

"So long as hope remains, I will fight you! I will not bow! Do you hear me, Sanctus? I will not bow!" *The time is at hand when I will arise and Death will go before me to bow all the world to my command. I will have the Gemshorn and the Stone of Existence hidden somewhere in the world. I will have the Source!* The *Darkness* churned as it brooded in the bowels of the universe, aware of all that happened above so great was the lust for power!

* * *

Nithrodine

Esarian stared blankly at the stark, damp walls of his tiny prison cell. The stench of human filth and death was all around him, suffocating every breath with its foulness. Rats scurried all around him in the dark, but Esarian refused to cower. What judgment awaited him? A traitor's death? If death was to be his fate, then he would face it with the courage of a Summoner. He would die with dignity and honor, unflinching in the face of his enemies. He would die for Hope. He would die for the promise. He would not fear. Instead he sang. He sang an ancient song of the Summoners, learned from the Guardians themselves in Ages past. He sang the Prophecy in the ancient tongue, but the words held meaning in any tongue. If tomorrow he died, he would die with Hope on his lips and freedom in his heart!

Chapter Forty-Three

SECRETS

Esarian heard the key in the lock. He struggled to his feet as the heavy door swung open. Solemn-faced guards took hold of him and roughly led him from the cell. The An Taoseach's own guards had come for him, and they looked afraid. Loyal men to a disloyal king, he held them blameless. The Summoner forced all doubts from his mind as the soldiers led him to stand upon the scaffold in the courtyard. Every member of the House Caladrius stood upon the balcony. Their expression fixed in varying degrees of horror except for the An Taoseach who wore a malicious grin.

"Esarian, Master Summoner," the An Taoseach said authoritatively, "you stand accused of treason. Do you have anything to say in defense?"

The Summoner glanced heavenward toward the Light, struggling to burn through the *dark*. This last stronghold against the void was crumbling. Day was *dark* with unnatural night, and there was no end in sight, but he would be free. He would not live to see this *darkness* much longer.

The executioner reached for the lever that would send him plummeting to his death.

Esarian looked toward the balcony. "I have no words that you desire to hear, An Taoseach," he began, "but I will speak anyway for those who are seeking a better way than this." He scanned the faces of the royal family. "What I say here matters little. My guilt has already been decided, and no words will stay the executioner's hand, yet you, my lord," he said, fixing his gaze upon Armahad, "were born for a higher purpose—one that even now is within reach! If not within your reach, it is within the reach of your heir, and I say let his time come!"

"Kill him," Armahad said.

"May the sentence be upon your own head!" Esarian shouted.

The executioner reached for the lever once more.

"Look to the deepest foundations!" Esarian shouted at the same instant. Time seemed to slow.

Esarian.

The wind whispered around him.

Esarian.

The voice was more pronounced though still a whisper. He looked over his shoulder. No one. The lever creaked. The trap door dropped from beneath his feet. He fell, and as he fell, his quick gaze caught the image of a mysterious girl emerging from the castle wall. She was not the one who had been calling his name.

"Daddy!" she screamed. Her gaze fixed upon the balcony as he fell toward his death. "Let the Summoner go!"

Water sloshed around the toes of the mysterious girl's thigh-length boots. It had stopped raining, and a cold misty fog replaced the smoke from the fires to hang like white tapestries in the black. She moved swiftly and quietly through the deserted courtyard. The voluptuous hood of her cloak fell back in the wind. Horrified gasps rang from above as the mangled face of the young girl appeared.

"Yelizaveta," Queen Keliah whispered. She turned on Armahad. "You told me she was dead!"

In the chaos, Esarian realized the rope never snapped. The final deadly jerking of the knot never came.

Esarian.

A hand gripped his shoulder. "Esarian." The voice was firm. The hand was solid. Out of the corner of his eyes, he saw a flash of blue-white Flame reflected off a stormy sky. Esarian turned and found that he was upon the scaffold no longer. He was upon a shining mountain.

The Summoner instantly dropped to his knees.

A Guardian stood before him in human form. "I am Ylochllion, a Guardian of Prophecy."

Esarian hid his face. He was afraid to look for fear this was all a dream. "Why did you leave us?"

"We have only been silent, Summoner," Ylochllion said.

"For so long?" Esarian asked. His voice cracked.

"Yes."

For the briefest moment, Esarian felt the sadness contained in that simple affirmation. "Then why?" he said in a voice that was barely loud enough to be a whisper.

"A choice was made long before your birth, Esarian, and long before mine. The time of restoration has not yet come, but we Guardians have seen the affliction of all Races. We have heard your cries and your songs. We know your sorrows, and I have come to deliver you for your faithfulness."

Esarian shook his head and pounded his chest with his hand. "Who am I that you should rescue me?"

Ylochllion smiled gently. "The path of your life was chosen by One greater than I. You are the Firebrand, and your work is not finished. One day you will go before the Promised to prepare the way, and for that purpose your life cannot end here."

The Guardian transformed before his eyes, soaring high into the pure Light of Bynthroenine. Wind beat down upon Esarian from the Guardian's massive wings.

"Rest now." The wind seemed to sigh, and then it was gone and the Guardian with it.

*   *   *

The executioner cowered before the An Taoseach.

"What do you mean the prisoner escaped?" Armahad shouted.

"You saw it the same as me, sire." The executioner nearly shrieked in fear. "The Summoner was there one second and gone the next!"

Armahad growled. "You let him escape!"

"No, sire! He just vanished!"

"We shall see," Armahad said. He signaled two of his servants. "Make him talk."

"No! No!" the executioner screamed as they seized him from either side. "I swear I speak the truth!" He fought as they dragged him from the king's presence. His screams had not faded when Prince Kinjour came to his father's side.

"You did see it, Father," Kinjour said quietly. "We all did."

Armahad glared murderously at his son. "Do you wish to join him?"

"Armahad," Queen Keliah said. "Haven't there been enough lies?"

The An Taoseach looked at his wife.

Just then the doors banged open. Yelizaveta swept regally into the room. "Hello, Daddy," she said with a twisted smile. "Did you think I would just stay hidden forever?" Were it not for the ring on her finger, her features that were so much like those of the queen, the rich fabrics that all bore the crest of the Royal House of Caladrius and clothed her, it would have been easy to deny her. She was so mangled. Her flesh hung from her frame like melted wax still clinging to a candlestick.

Keliah shook her head, trying to grasp what was taking place. Her child should be dead; the physicians had said she would die—the queen had grieved as if she were because she had been told the child was dead! It was all too much. She staggered back into Kinjour's arms, needing the support. "You were hidden?" she asked slowly, measuring each word into its own numbing sentence. Her gaze shot to her husband's. She barely recognized him anymore.

"Yes, Mommy," Yelizaveta said firmly. "Daddy let you cry yourself to sleep night after night. He let you grieve by an empty grave. He let you suffer!"

"No," Armahad gasped.

"And he didn't care!" Yelizaveta shouted over him.

"No!" he said again more forcefully.

"Because his secret was safe!"

"Stop this!" Armahad snarled at his daughter.

"What secret?" Keliah whispered.

"Can't you guess, Mommy?" Yelizaveta asked. "Look at the Mark!"

Armahad grabbed his daughter. "Enough!" he shouted, shaking her hard.

"Daddy! You're hurting me!"

"Stop!" Keliah shrieked. She surged forward from Kinjour's arms and shoved her husband with all her strength.

Kinjour shouted, reaching for her. Mydrian rushed forward. Yelizaveta fell backward. Keliah watched as Armahad fell beneath the full force of her blow. His head glanced off the throne and crashed dully to the floor.

"I trusted you!" she wailed.

Armahad groaned.

"Why? Why?"

"For you," Armahad moaned. "All of it was for you, but then—" he said, shaking his head, "her face—I couldn't—I had no choice."

"I loved you!" Keliah wailed, sinking down to her knees beside her husband.

"I still love you." He reached a bloody hand toward her.

"No." Keliah shook her head, cringing away from his touch. "You are not the man I married. He was good, gentle, just. You are none of those things. Too much blood is on your hands! Too much suffering! Too many lies."

Armahad cupped her chin in his hand, holding tightly when she tried to pull away. His eyes gazed back into hers, darkening as he read the sincerity of her words. His face twisted in agony and then into hatred. "Go then!" he snarled. "And come into my presence no more!" He shoved her aside as he crawled to his feet. *Darkness* descended. "All of you! Leave!" he screamed. "Leave me!"

An aura of decay hung heavily over Nithrodine's melancholy stones. The royal fortress soared forlorn and decrepit through the dark abyss cloaking the night. Its palatial towers ascended like spikes lit internally by a mighty light. The *darkness* was alive with timeless whispers that surpassed even the wind's piercing wail. A chorus of bells purled through the gloom, signaling the changing of the guard, stirring sadness in earth and stone. The sound of weeping resounded in Nithrodine's streets, dripping like rain from the blackened heights.

This weeping bled with ancient sorrow. All Nithrodine screamed with the awakening of memory far older than itself, shaking the kingdom of Men to its deepest foundation before spreading out into the world. The earth trembled. Time slowed, and all creation waited in deathlike silence for whatever would come next.

* * *

Redwood

"Did you feel that, Baculus?"

Cadclucan smiled slightly at his Elvin name. It had grown on him, or perhaps it was just a response to the one who spoke it. Queen Maizie came to stand beside him. Her fingers brushed lightly against his. The Guardian twined their hands together wordlessly. His flaming blue eyes never left the wood upon which he had been gazing so long.

"Baculus?" Maizie asked again softly.

He could hear the smile in her voice but also the worry. "Yes, I felt it," he said with a sigh as he squeezed her hand comfortingly.

Maizie smiled weakly. He was always so warm, and his voice could soothe a raging storm, yet the peace exuding from him did not quite penetrate her fear. "What was it?" she whispered.

Cadclucan looked away. "The season is changing," he said, avoiding her question—avoiding her!

Maizie hesitated. She sensed the shift in his mood—friend to protector . . . man to Guardian. Invisible barriers rose between their hearts. "You do not need to protect me from who you are and what you know." Her hand tightened around his. With all her strength, she held them together. Could he even tell? The closer to him she let herself become, the closer to him she wanted to be and the further out of reach he seemed. Their love was unplanned, and she knew he was not free—not his own—no Guardian ever truly was, but his burden weighed on him always—always drawing him away to secret places she could not follow.

Cadclucan didn't answer. He stood as still as a statue, with his face angled away from her.

Her heart clenched in her chest. "Baculus? Please talk to me."

"You know I cannot."

"I hate this," Maizie whispered, lowering her head against him.

Cadclucan leaned his head against the top of hers.

They stayed that way in silence for several long moments, neither one sure how to move beyond the barriers between them.

The earth trembled. Lightning pierced the *dark* from East to West, shedding Light from the blackness all around. Through the crack, whispers came. *Let the Light shine forth and awaken hope. Let Mhorag arise. Let the Promised come.* Other whispers came too, some so low and sinister they made Maizie's skin crawl, some echoing the fear in her heart. Cadclucan's arm wrapped around her waist in silent acknowledgment of her secret thoughts—she should have known he knew them. If only she could read his thoughts so easily! She tried to meet his gaze, but he had turned his face further away from her, covering it with his other hand and holding her so firmly against his side she couldn't reposition herself.

"Baculus! My queen! Come quick!"

"What is it, Laeginlast?" Maizie asked only half listening to her guard's response. The Guardian was too still at her side.

"There is something you and the Great One must see, my queen!" Laeginlast exclaimed. The tone of his voice told them this was no trivial matter.

"What is it?" Maizie asked, her focus shifting in response to his uneasiness.

"The heavens burn! The earth screams! It is the end!" Laeginlast shrieked.

Cadclucan sighed. "No," he said, thawing at last, "it is only the beginning."

Both Elves looked at him in shock as he turned to face them. Blood streamed dark and red from his flaming blue eyes.

"Please, Baculus, speak plainly," Maizie said softly in plea.

The Guardian's gaze dropped to hers. His fingers brushed lightly across her panic-stricken face. His eyes bore through her, piercing beyond flesh to capture the secrets of her soul.

Maizie felt him searching—felt him scouring the *dark* places inside of her. She watched his eyes close against the fear inside her; his features twisted with the depth of it. When his eyes opened, his gaze had gentled.

"You are right to fear," he said softly. "The Darkening is complete, but the Prophecy still stands against the void. A new war is beginning and its end—" he hesitated, shaking his head, "its end not even I can see. Blood has defiled this land and will defile it again. The universe cannot be cleansed except by the blood of him that shed it or by that of One pure of heart and older than Time."

"You speak of—" Maizie floundered for the right words.

Cadclucan smiled slightly. "I speak of dreams," he sighed. A memory of the future echoed in his mind.

"Will the Guardians return?" Laeginlast asked, trying to hide his hope and steel himself for disappointment. "It is the dream of many," he added when the Guardian did not immediately answer. "Baculus?"

Cadclucan sighed again, "The Colorless come. They feel the call of the Mother." He motioned toward the bloody, waning crescent rising over the trees. "It is the first time in many years that the portals will be open. Does this give you Hope, my friend?" He kept to himself the *Darkness* that would follow. They could not bear such knowledge. "Come, your peoples' fear is great. They need you."

"They need us," Maizie said quietly as she took his arm.

*   *   *

Nithrodine

"Esarian should have returned by now," D'Faihven said softly. The giantess struck a match to light the single remaining candle.

The Summoners exchanged a wary glance over the tiny flame.

"Something's happened to him," Orlok said sourly.

"The An Taoseach," Nulet muttered. "The traitor!"

Their voices whispered through the cramped hideout. For days they had seldom spoken for fear of discovery. They had scarcely taken a breath of fresh air or glimpsed outside the four earthen walls. Esarian brought the only news of the outside world, and that news had stopped coming.

"What do we do now?"

D'Faihven looked at each of the Summoners. "We act like Summoners."

"That power is broken," one of the Summoners said bitterly.

"That doesn't mean we have to be," D'Faihven snapped. "Esarian showed us that. I say we gather the Races and show this An Taoseach who he is messing with!"

"Are you mad?"

D'Faihven smiled. "Maybe, but who's with me?"

Chapter Forty-Four

DESCENT

"Find *me* the Gemshorn!" Death's final words rang still in Zrene's ears.

The last of the Calianith had every intention of finding the Gemshorn, but for her own purposes not Death's. She passed from the East into the wider world in a plume of emerald-black Flame, spewing, churning, and growing with the screams of all who beheld the burning heavens. The ancient weapon crafted from the talon of a Colorless was the greatest weapon she had ever held in her green hands. It would be the instrument of her revenge, and she could feel it waiting out there somewhere for her skillful touch. Zrene gave herself over to the hunt, guided by an inner sense gained when first she had touched Arawn's dark gift. Its power pulled her in a straight course toward its hiding place.

Hiding it had been an effective course of action, for it bound itself only to one who had mastered its song, and all the Calianith were believed dead, killed by the Colorless—the unproven seed of Guardians—in the last great battle of the Guardian War so long ago. It almost worked. Zrene had believed herself dead. The memory of her last mortal day replayed in her mind.

Black Forest, End of the Guardian War

In the dark of night, behind the thick curtain of black wood, Zrene's green fingers groped along the earthen and stone wall of the den. Only a thin sliver of the moon lent light to the earth below. Still, her fingers were accustomed to the task at hand, and soon they rested upon the object they sought. A soft click whispered in the wood. A circular portion of wall rolled aside.

Within was *darkness*. It caressed her and beckoned to her. On staggering, booted feet, she entered. Her green hand trailed along the cold, damp stones. A streak of blood followed in its wake. The stone rolled back into place behind her. She shuffled over the dirt floor. Her body was bowed with exhaustion as she made her way through the dark, narrow passage. Her hands glided across the stone on either side to steady herself; their powerful claws left deep cuts where they dragged over its face.

The passage was much shorter than it seemed. It opened upon a large chamber by way of a single arched entrance of hewn stone. Light came from the circular chamber. Torches rested in stone sconces upon the round walls that were lined with layer upon layer of tombs solemnized with great effigies of the dead. There were thousands of dead contained within this single room stacked from ceiling to floor with scarcely a gap in between. The floor was made of bricks revolving around the iron bed in which the Gemshorn had once rested. This floor had been carved with the history of her people, but many of the bricks were still bare. The circle of their history was incomplete.

Zrene. Calianith. The black breath whispered in her mind. She forced it aside. Her labored breaths pounded hard from her weakened body. She fell upon the ground near the bare bricks. Into her shaking hands, she took the chisel and hammer. With the skill of a craftsman, she scarred the floor. The rhythmic beat droned sorrowfully around her and mingled with her tears. Uncertain periods of time passed, days, perhaps weeks, she worked to record the history. Beneath the noise of her work rose these words: War is a time when friends and enemies reveal themselves. Long have we been at war. Long have we suffered. It was to our enemies that the Races came, making the war their own. The Dragons came and with them came warriors of every Race against this great army, and we stood alone. We stood ten thousand strong behind Matwyn, who was an enemy by birth but now stood as one with *Darkness*. The land was filled with our blood, the blood of the Calianith, but one survived. I, Zrene, daughter of Caruk a Mistress of the Gemshorn.

Zrene.

The sounds of battle faded. Day's light was embraced by Night before I rose from the earth. The ashes of the Calianith poured from my body and were scattered to the wind, and with them all our hope was stolen. I will reclaim the Gemshorn. I will pour all the evil malice and wrath of my people into the Gemshorn's song once more. My hand will avenge you, my people.

Zrene. Zrene.

356

Some foul voice enters my mind. Death haunts me. Its dark visage lingers at every turn, in every shadow . . .

Death had claimed her, but not all. Zrene clenched her fists at her side. Soon Death would pay for the years she had imprisoned her!

A rush of wind crossed her path. Zrene hovered as she watched it cut through the forefront of the emerald-black Flame. At first the wind seemed harmless enough, but then its strange glow intensified, sweeping out into lacy wings trillions of miles across, flaming blue-white where it intersected the *dark*. Voices—powerful, irresistible voices—raised in an ancient song echoed out of it.

Ageless Mother shine down on us. Guide through darkness till the Light of hope is reclaimed. Great Ones, bleed while fires burn. Remember the blood from which you came.

The song continued wordlessly, rising upon the beautiful voices. She knew enough of Guardian ways to know that they were remembering. The deeds of the past were never spoken where enemies might hear. Zrene waited—too mesmerized to move, though nothing pleasant would come from lingering.

The emerald-black Flame shifted. Zrene was not surprised to see the first small Guardian emerge from the wind. It was visible only by the blackness roaring up and over its little, colorless body to clash with the lacy wings of Light. Its head was similar in appearance to that of a horse, in shape only, with intensely glowing blue Flame eyes that pierced through the veil of greenish fire to see her. Its nostrils flared tiny shards of glowing crystal and smoke with every breath, and its small wings sliced the air with every beat.

She sneered, "Dragon!" Her luminous red eyes locked with those of the Colorless.

"Dragon? Only the Dark One and his servants would dare to call a Guardian that word," the Colorless said. "Why are you in this place?"

"To finish what I left undone and so much more."

The Light faded. The Colorless nearly vanished against the black except for those flaming eyes. Zrene's red eyes wavered from the little Guardian's intense gaze for the briefest moment. The change in them came without warning. *Darkness* flashed through Zrene's eyes; at the same moment, a whip of emerald-black fire tore at the Colorless's wing. The little dragon roared in pain as another whip of fire made a tether around her neck. Zrene vanished into the fire and the fire into *Darkness* as it dragged the writhing Guardian through the sky.

The Colorless pulled against her, releasing her own power with such force that the fire tore itself free. She floundered, exhausted as the dark

Flame recoiled, cutting deeply into her belly and piercing beneath the plates that protected it. She screamed. Light sprang from her mouth and cast Zrene, shrieking, away from her. Blood spewed from the wound. She fell toward the ground. She struggled to flap her small wings, but one hung useless at her side. The Colorless wailed horribly as she plummeted toward the ground.

Neither Zrene nor the *Darkness* behind her, of which she was unaware, gloated at the victory. The little dragon was not dead. Even now, they had no real power of life or death over Sanctus's prize beasts. *Darkness* could not enslave or kill them, not without the Gemshorn and the Stone of Existence.

Remember the blood from which you came. Let the Light shine forth and awaken hope. Let Mhorag arise. Let the Promised come.

Bynthroenine

Through the door that let the Colorless out one by one, the faint echo of a whisper flowed in.

"Wise Ones, hear me and be merciful! I am in desperate need of your guidance. If I am consumed by this *Darkness*, so be it. Justice will be served, if such is my fate, but my people suffer when the sin that bound us was mine alone. I, who am undesirable and least worthy, beseech you, not for myself, but for my people. Hear me, I entreat you. Come to us once more! We languish in this dismal place. Let us find favor in your presence. Wise Ones, hear me! Do not leave us to drown in this *Darkness!* Hear me and be merciful!"

Even when the portals of Bynthroenine were long ago sealed, the Guardians had kept their silent vigil. Few were wise enough to still seek the wisdom of the Guardians. Fewer still were found worthy to enter this secret realm. Guardians no longer moved visibly among the Races. They were the silent, virtually invisible and forgotten protectors of all that lived. When called, however, they would answer. The voice that called to them was faint. It was a voice no louder than a whisper out of the *darkness* from one who was seeking the Light.

Darkness. Light. The opposing forces recoiled from one another. Power rose in the hearts of the Guardians, pumping out through their veins with blue-white Flame, hovering just beneath the surface of their human masks, yet they were not deaf to the desperate cry rising from the blackness. The voice that called stirred the very soul of Bynthroenine before it fell silent.

Light whispered around them, filling the silence. *Let the Light shine forth and awaken hope. Let Mhorag arise. Let the Promised come.*

Nithrodine

The bloody crescent moon cast its strange light across the stone walls, giving an eerie feel to the shadowy streets. The Summoners remained huddled close together, keeping to the shadows as much as possible. Soldiers patrolled the lower town. Their shadowy forms were visible in the light of the moon and in the light of the torches they carried.

"Are you sure this is a good idea?" Nulet whispered.

"Quiet," Orlok snapped in a whisper of his own.

D'Faihven cast her friends a withering glance, and both fell silent. She motioned all the Summoners forward. The tight grouping began to weave through the most shadowed streets—the ones seldom used and therefore seldom patrolled. As these streets narrowed sharply between thick walls, their group gradually straightened into a line. They did not heed the large, emerald-black Flame clawing, like huge fingers, across the sky, nor the chill wind laced with a putrid stench that blew around them. On the wind's back rode faint and ancient whispers. *Let the Light shineforthandawakenhope. LetMhoragarise. LetthePromisedcome.* A horrible scream pierced from sky to earth as a streak of blue fire cascaded across their path.

The Summoners stifled cries of fear behind their hands. The soldiers' shouts were drawing close. They had seen the fire too! Thunder crashed. A wail drifted from above. The eyes of all turned toward the sky.

The greenish veil churned violently as a small, thrashing object fell from the sky. The wail came from it.

"Quickly!" D'Faihven said, darting out of the way further into the shadows.

The Summoners followed as the soldiers screamed in terror, running from beneath the object's shadow. The earth shook with its impact; the creature lay silently upon the cobbled street. Blood rushed from open wounds into the earth. Tremors of power radiated from beneath the little beast, and dark, richly fragrant blossoms formed a bed around it.

The green veil passed, leaving the stench of death and decay in its wake. Silence settled over the lower town. Soldiers crept toward the fallen beast, visible by the blood drenching its small, horse like head and torn underside. One of its wings was crushed beneath it. The other was bent and broken; blood dripped from a slowly, closing wound.

"It's a Guardian!" Nulet whispered. "A young one."

"We should do something," Orlok whispered. "What if the soldiers try to kill it?"

"Shh," D'Faihven warned.

The creature lay completely still; only tiny shards of glowing crystal from its nostrils hinted of life. These were few in number, with spaces of time in between.

"Caladrius," the soldiers whispered. First the word was uttered in astonishment and then with great joy.

The great **bird** of mythology had returned to them at last! The soldiers bowed their faces to earth before lifting the unconscious creature in reverent hands.

"Are we just going to stand here and let them take the Colorless?" Orlok whispered.

"We could use the young Guardian, D'Faihven," Nulet agreed.

"You don't *use* a Guardian, you fools," D'Faihven whispered back.

"You know what I mean," Nulet snapped.

"We will get the Guardian back," D'Faihven said softly. "But we need help, or do you really want to take on all those soldiers without a single weapon and only these broken Styarfyre orb shards at our disposal? Besides maybe one glimpse of a Guardian will turn the An Taoseach back to our side. You saw how his soldiers responded. Maybe he will bow too."

"Maybe," Nulet whispered.

"Doubtful," Orlok grumbled.

The other Summoners exchanged whispers uncertainly.

"Enough of this," D'Faihven snapped in a hushed voice, taking charge again. "We need to stick together and to our original plan. We cannot rely upon the Humans or even trust them, I fear. We need to find the other Races. They will not be here in Nithrodine—it is too big, too penned in. They will be out there!" She motioned broadly toward the gate. "We need their weapons, their armies, and their allegiance. Or we have lost before we have begun!"

* * *

Armahad stalked his throne room like a caged animal. His crimson robe swept the floor in a constant swooshing sound accentuated by the strike of his boots as he paced and roared. All of his wonderful plans were descended into ruins—laid in the ashes of his former glory. The Firebrand's curses were one by one coming true. Those closest to him had betrayed him. His people thought him mad. He heard their whispers behind his back. At least, he thought he did.

Whispers dredged his land, scarcely discernible one from another. **Darkness** was everywhere and in everything. He did not feel mortal hungers anymore. The pangs of his empty belly did not dominate his thoughts; nor did the dryness of his lips; nor the stench that filled his nostrils. By some unnatural magic, he withstood this suffering, and by this same magic, his infant son and heir still lived, though there was no milk to nourish him; Yelizaveta lived also—the constant reminder of his guilt. He couldn't feel his guilt, but he could see it—in her, he could see it.

"What have you done to me?" he roared to the blackness always hanging over his head.

What have I done? the black breath whispered around him. *All that you have desired.*

"All that I have desired!" Armahad shouted. "I never desired this! I never wanted to lose Keliah! I never wanted to hurt my family! I never—"

The Dark One's laughter cut him off. *Desire is a tricky thing, Armahad. Given the right circumstance—the right catalyst—your desires and mine blur into one. You are the puppet. I am the master, or have you forgotten how at my bidding you turned your own sword upon yourself and scarred the Mark?*

"I had no choice!" Armahad shrieked. "My child was—"

Yes, poor sweet Yelizaveta was dying, but of course you had a choice. Temptation works that way, Armahad. I teased your fragile mind, but it was you who decided to turn that into action. You let me into your measly, human heart, and for what it's worth, I'm enjoying myself. No one suffers as beautifully as humans. The Dark One laughed again. *I can almost see why Sanctus crafted you in the first place. Almost.*

"Be quiet," Armahad snapped.

Or you'll do what? Make me leave? Kill me? Please. I am here to stay. There is only one of us in this room who can—

The main doors to the throne room burst open. Armahad whirled to face the intruders. The Dark One grew quiet mid-threat.

Soldiers, not his Mydrian but lower Isearian soldiers responsible for defending Nithrodine, approached without a word. Between them, they carried a creature. *Darkness* snarled quietly, feeling the unconscious power within the small body.

"What is the meaning of this?" Armahad asked.

"Sire. We found—" the soldier said, shaking his head, "you must see it for yourself, sire." The soldiers lowered the creature to the An Taoseach's feet. "A Caladrius. We were patrolling the lower town when it fell out of the heavens in a flash of blue-white fire. The legends are true, majesty!"

Armahad gazed down at the creature with mute horror. *Darkness* snarled in his mind. "Leave me!" he seethed to the soldiers. The soldiers scattered as the An Taoseach dropped to his knees beside the creature's blood-outlined body. His hands wonderingly felt the hard smoothness of the translucent scales. He felt the shallow rise and fall of the *bird's* noble chest. He saw the wispy threads of smoke and crystal dropping with each tiny breath from the nostrils. "The stories are true," he whispered. "Caladrius existed. And his seed has returned!"

Yes, so it seems.

"You knew," Armahad said. "You knew the stories were true. You knew and you—you let—"

Here we go again, An Taoseach. The Dark One said with not so subtle hostility. *You blame me for your own actions. Well, let me tell you something. Yes, your ancient stories are true. Yes, Caladrius exists. Yes, this is his seed, but where does that leave you?*

"Me? What do you mean?"

Your ancient stories, what do they tell you about Caladrius and his seed?

"The stories say that one day the seed of the great *bird* will return to claim the loyalty sworn to Caladrius by my forefather, Nudhug."

So you, An Taoseach, will lose your throne. Liacin will lose his throne. Your line will end.

"How do you know?" Armahad looked to the blackness. "Is this a trick? Are you trying to twist my mind again?"

I am trying to warn you. I promised you a long line of heirs, but if you would rather this little one be allowed to steal the hearts and minds of your subjects away from you and your seed by all means ignore me, but do not say I did not warn you. All will rise against you because of this little one! And here she is having fallen into our hands . . . The Dark One's voice trailed off temptingly in Armahad's mind.

"What can we do?" Armahad asked quietly.

Bind her.

The An Taoseach looked back to the little creature. His heart clenched. The Caladrius was so small, so fragile looking—so young. "Is there no other way?"

Not for you both. One free. One enslaved. There is no other way.

The creature stirred, moaning softly. Armahad cradled the little scaled body in his hands.

"Daddy?"

The word startled him. "You can speak, little Caladrius!" His voice roused the creature who raised a fearful eye to appraise his face.

"Do you have a name, little one?" Armahad said quietly.

"Sian Seela, daughter of the Guardians Fyrdung and Teile," the little Caladrius said, her beautiful eyes fluttering closed.

Darkness snarled. So it was as suspected.

She sensed it. Her eyes flashed open. "You!" she nearly screamed, though she was too weak to do more than lift her head. "Stay back! Stay away from me!" The room trembled as she trembled.

Armahad glanced over his shoulder to the *dark*, sensing the power within his hands.

Bind her now before it is too late! Before she destroys you!

"I want her. Alive. Her power—"

Then bind her, and we will find a way to break her!

"Yes," Armahad said quietly, descending headlong into the abyss of his mind. "Show me the way, and I will follow."

Chapter Forty-Five

MOUNTAINS OF DIFFICULTY

The nameless forest

*D*arkness, inescapable and without measure, loomed around him. Ylochllion's nostrils flared as he took in the land's scent—death and rot. Its fetid stench tormented and appalled his senses. Burning deep in his soul, like a raging fire, was an unquenchable yearning for Light. He missed the splendor of Bynthroenine and the pure ecstasy of unabated Light.

Here there was only unending darkness, vaster and more enduring than Night. Neither Day nor Night held any sway in this forsaken place. Lambent waves of heat crowned the suffocating abyss in threatening welcome. *Is it possible for life to exist in such a place as this?* he questioned within himself.

His mighty wings sliced the dark, and from them great gusts of wind tore into the unknown. *Darkness* pealed back at his approach and bowed from his presence. Through the retreating canvas rose an ancient forest like phantoms from another time. These charred giants had long ago been lost in the dark and by it unnaturally preserved. Parched earth trembled beneath the wind's force. Dust and thorn parted before him. From the depths of a black mountain, the roar of thousands of beating hearts reached his ears in a cacophony of joy; yet not all welcomed him. A darkness laced the joy spewing its vile malevolence at him. *Fear, longing, hatred* he sensed from the mountain. *Death.* Indeed, Death lurked below, but the more sinister breath of the One whose Name is not Spoken overshadowed her presence. He felt it in his soul. *Secrets the Dark One wishes to keep!*

The ground shook as his mighty bronze talons pressed upon the dry surface. Shards of glowing crystal grew from his nostrils as he slowly exhaled a mammoth breath. *What was it that lurked beneath the Darkness, and why did it call to him as if it knew him?* He considered this a long moment. *The ruined heart of Arawn. The Heart of Evil.*

"I will not face monsters in the dark!" Ylochllion said in a thunderous voice that rang with all the haunting melody and power of a proven Guardian. With his mind, he probed the hearts. *Those of the Samhail beat as one. Theirs is the joy. No malice comes from them, only pain.* "You will come into the Light, Death!"

Sithbhan howled defiantly as she was summoned from her lair. She rose through fire, *darkness*, and illusion, though it was against her will. The Guardian could not be disobeyed. His power was still greater than the *dark*. But not for long, she thought.

Lorshin followed her more slowly. Fear mingled with the joyful pain of his heart's cry. The Guardian's voice echoed in his mind.

You called to the Wise Ones, and I have come. Now I call you, and you must come. You must stand before me in the Light.

Ylochllion let his mind drift deeper into the dark beyond the hearts of the Samhail, beyond Death. *Someone seeks revenge*, he thought as his mind touched upon a hidden heart. One word came to his mind. *Calianith!* It seemed impossible, yet he could not shake the image that had formed from the heartbeat. Had the Dark One's power grown so strong that he could hide life?

Sithbhan circled the Guardian. Disgust was evident in every movement of her body. "Prince of Dragons," she said mockingly, "reduced to an errand boy! Why are you here?"

"Do not challenge me, Death. I have already proven myself!" The power of the Guardian's voice drove her to her knees. "I am Ylochllion, a Guardian of the Prophecy, and I did not come here alone." At his words, the Light opened to reveal eight more Guardians hovering within.

Lorshin lingered in *darkness*. Sunlight blazed on the scales of the Guardian. *Darkness* bowed beneath the massive frame, leaving no barrier to protect the Samhail from the deadly rays of the Sun the Guardian had let through.

Prince of the Samhail, you must not doubt the promise of a Guardian. I have come through Darkness and shadow to you. Do not fear the Sun, and do not fear me. The powerful voice brushed his mind. *Come to me, Lorshin. All will be as it was before your fall. I will protect you.* The Guardian's power extended to cover him. Though the sunlight still poured like gold fire over the land, it did not hurt him as he walked into its blaze.

All at once, Ylochllion sensed it. A surge of power rose from the *dark* and clashed momentarily with his own. The heartbeat of evil joined that of the Prince of the Samhail for one instant and then faded. The power disturbed him. He grimaced. *You choose to play a dangerous game, Prince of the Samhail,* he said with his mind.

Lorshin bowed before him. Their minds touched. *Great One, Sithbhan must not know of what we speak.* A scaled paw lifted the Prince of the Samhail until his eyes met those of the Guardian.

Ylochllion nodded minutely. *She will not.*

The Dark One seeks the Stone of Existence and the Gemshorn.

I am aware, the Guardian answered.

I have given myself in the hopes of defeating Darkness and Death. Lorshin trembled beneath the Guardian's hard gaze. "It's all my fault," he said softly. *I brought this upon my people. If I am consumed in this game so be it, but my people suffer when they committed no treason!*

Ylochllion nodded. *As it was prophesied.*

True, my lord.

Ylochllion frowned. *But you risk too much. Freedom is one thing. Your soul is another. Do not fool yourself, Lorshin. I can see what is inside of you.*

Lorshin hung his head.

Sithbhan watched as Lorshin communed with the Guardian. What passed between them, she couldn't tell. A wave of jealousy rose in her soul. Lorshin belongs to me! This Guardian would fall whether proven or not. He was still young, and her power was old!

Ylochllion turned on her with a growl.

She staggered back beneath the breath of his nostrils.

Without shifting his gaze from hers, he broke the link between himself and Lorshin. *I will speak to the Chosen One.* He now carried with him more than just suspicions. Another war was drawing near, and he could only hope that these dark omens did indeed precede the coming of Mhorag whose rising was prophesied long ago.

Lorshin bowed his head.

"Death," the Guardian said.

"My lord?"

"The Guardians will be watching."

Sithbhan bowed dramatically. "My lord."

Ylochllion did not linger to hear her answer. He spread his wings and leaped into the air. *Darkness* rose after him, obliterating the sunlight. Lorshin felt the sorrow of the Guardian's leaving even as Sithbhan drew him back into her possessive embrace.

Her cold kiss caressed his neck. His eyes closed as weary acceptance caused him to relax in her arms. They descended without another thought.

* * *

Isear, Kingdom of Men:

The emerald-black fire moved through the night, blotting out the moon as it hovered over Nithrodine and the outlying regions.

"Where is it?" Zrene whispered to herself. She could feel it close. The Gemshorn's evil called to her from someplace quite deep, she was sure, but where?

Whip-like tentacles of fire lashed out from all sides as she scoured the land with her sharp eyes. Trees withered to dust at the touch. Only those who dwelt in the heart of the land heard their cries of agony. Drums beat wildly in the deep places beneath the forest. One by one, winged warriors rose from their cavernous lair. They hovered in the air, forming a canopy above their beloved forest. They clutched their spears in their hands, waiting for the perfect moment to strike.

Zrene glanced at them curiously, but curiosity quickly turned to annoyance. They had not been near the Gemshorn. They smelled of earth and dampness, nothing more. "Who dares to defy me?"

"I am Subara, Mother Superior of the Shee." The frail leader drifted forward. "You have defiled this land. Be gone from this place, or the same fate that was brought upon these trees shall be yours." Subara raised her spear, but not alone. Another held up her wasted arm.

Zrene let out a bone-chilling laugh.

"So be it," Subara said in a hoarse whisper, but she may as well have screamed it. A shrill whoop rose from the warrior at her side, and together they reared back. The spear was loosed by their combined strength, and all the Shee warriors responded in kind.

Spears hurled through the air all around the putrid, greenish fire. The weapons, from their shafts to their iron blades, were consumed before they even penetrated the outer ring of vapor that surrounded Zrene.

Whips of corrupted Flame cracked through the air and ripped with force across Subara's emaciated body. She reeled back in pain and another slammed into her body, throwing her across the sky and out of sight. The Shee hovered in stunned horror that quickly turned to screams. "Mother!"

Zrene smiled. "Your turn."

Dart-like projections of fire streaked at them. The Shee scattered; their cries pierced the night. They disappeared into the earth, leaving the emerald-black fire to its own purpose. Silence as still as death filled the *dark*.

Redwood

The redwood was dark and still. Lebuaile River raged white and rough over the rocks, making small waterfalls surrounded by moss-covered rocks. Frogs sang in the moonlight along the shores while deer drank in quiet watchfulness. All around rose the quiet, peaceful giants for which the wood was named. Moving soundlessly along the shores of the great river were two riders cloaked in long, gray robes. They rode upon huge horses. The silken, fiery red coats of the animals gleamed even in the dark. Each had three horns upon its head. One horn pointed toward the sky from each side of the horse's head, and the third curved downward from the center to a sharp point. Around their hooves were sharp spikes. The fierce-looking horses plodded gently along the trail. They moved so softly that the timid creatures of the ancient wood did not fear their presence.

Suddenly, a low wheezy moan broke the stillness. The deer ran into the shadows, and even the frogs silenced their chorus. The riders turned their horses toward the sound.

"I have never heard such a noise in this forest," the first rider said. "Have you, Nothaniel?"

The Elf scout shook his head. "No, Isentara, I have not. Khartang, Gyceal, can you take us across the river?"

"With great ease," both of the red horses said with a snort.

Isentara clung to Gyceal's large, red neck and squeezed her eyes tightly closed.

Nothaniel laughed at her as his own horse, Khartang, stepped into the raging water. "They are Enechelbrah, Isentara," he shouted above the noise of the river. "Ancient allies of the Elves! They are most sure-footed and swiftest of all horses. You needn't be afraid!"

Isentara laughed uneasily. "You forget, Nothaniel, I was at the last battle of the Guardian War. The Enechelbrah are also fierce warriors, who hate bridles and reigns as much as they hate strangers! You offer me little comfort!"

"As you are a friend of the Elves and of the Great One's own lineage, I will not let you fall, Mistress Isentara!" Gyceal called as he stepped with great mastery across the slippery, submerged rocks. "Now please stop pulling my hair!"

Isentara did not loosen her hold.

"You know, you've ridden on Gyceal before," Nothaniel said matter-of-factly. "Of course, you won't remember. It was when I rescued you in the wood."

Another moan pierced the calm as they reached the other side of the river. Nothaniel dismounted and walked toward the sound. Isentara followed, clutching the Guardian amulet around her neck. Elf and Samhail followed the sound through the undergrowth. Her heightened senses proved valuable in this section of the wood where sounds echoed through unsuspected ravines. The grass crunched softly beneath their feet. Another moan, this one louder, reached their ears. The source was close.

Isentara led Nothaniel beyond the shadowy line of trees into a small clearing hanging precariously over one such ravine. A white form lay unmoving on the ground.

"What is it?" Nothaniel asked.

Isentara shrugged. "Not even my eyes can tell from this distance."

They moved silently forward. Their footsteps were softened by the pine needles that blanketed the region around the clearing. Isentara cautiously approached the form. Nothaniel came behind her, his hand upon his bow, ready, should the need arise.

Isentara knelt in the grass. The gentle moonlight revealed to her the creature that lay there. "It is a woman, Nothaniel!" she exclaimed.

"Elf?" Nothaniel asked uneasily. His eyes warily scanned the dark.

"No," Isentara said. "Look closely."

The Elf removed his cloak. The soft light that emanated from his body made the woman's appearance visible. True to Isentara's words, the woman was not an Elf. In many ways, she appeared human, but there were striking differences. Nothaniel had never seen a creature like her before. "What is she?" he whispered.

"Shee," Isentara said. "The Shee were once my allies. They live beneath many forests, yet I do not know why she is here. The Shee left the Red Wood to the Elves long ago."

"Yes," Nothaniel breathed. "The story is recorded in the Trovengiln. No Shee have been seen in these borders since that day. I am familiar with the history though I have never seen one." He glanced down at the gaunt creature. "So why is she here?"

Isentara shook her head. "Her injuries look severe. The Shee probably believe her dead."

Nothaniel placed his cloak over her before meeting his friend's gaze. "We must take her to Loriath. The Great One will help her." He rose, lifting the Shee in his arms. She was so frail, he scarcely felt the burden. She groaned. He whispered softly in her ear words that Isentara did not understand, and the Shee made no further noise. The Elf carried her back to where the Enechelbrah waited by the Lebuaile River. He laid the Shee across Khartang's solid back and mounted effortlessly behind her before Isentara even reached Gyceal.

"Khartang, Gyceal, we must make haste to Loriath. There is no time to waste!"

Isentara took her time mounting Gyceal, but once on his back, she had no time to grab hold of the red horses' mane before Gyceal sprang forward across the river to the far shore. She wailed her objections. Gyceal raced on unheedingly.

As he laughed with Nothaniel, Khartang reared up on his hind legs, pawing the sky with his front legs and neighing loudly. He then sprang into the river and easily reached the shore beyond. Despite his added cargo, Khartang quickly overtook Gyceal. "Can you not keep up?" he called as he rushed past.

Gyceal charged forward laughing wildly.

"Slow down!" Isentara cried, but she was ignored by all until Nothaniel sensed the line of invisible magic that sealed the entrance to Loriath.

*   *   *

A Mountain of Difficulty

Far away in a secret place, a barren black mountain rose from the earth. It stood devoid of life, surrounded only by barren wilderness and hot sulfur springs whose eruptions veiled the land with thick, yellowish steam that smelled of rotten eggs. A single path led through the springs into the mountain. It was rugged and little traveled. On this night and indeed on many nights, Gnoll wandered the path alone. As morning encroached on the world, he would scurry beyond the yellow veil and into the mountain.

He bounded up the mountainside, leaping agilely from ledge to ledge until he entered a narrow crevice midway up. His webbed limbs clung to the slippery stone walls like those of a lizard. He crept noiselessly through the *darkness* down, down, deep into the heart of the mountain where a vast sea of emerald-black Flame illuminated his world. The corrupted Flame scorched even the fragments of stone that fell from above, yet, thanks to his master, it had no effect on him.

Gnoll dove, squealing into its depths. He swam through the flames as if it were water. The undulations of his deformed body mimicked the movements of a giant frog in water. He was careful to keep his hump above the surface as he swam to the great rock that arched above the sea.

From the center of the rock extended a stairway of stone and swirling flame. As he leaped from the sea to the stairs, emerald-black Flame spewed from his body.

He crept up the stairs, through the **Darkness** that connected all things to his master. The stairway ended at the great thrones of stone and thorn. Flame and blackness swirled beneath the Heart of Evil perched between them and encircled the feet of his beloved Death and her lover.

Sithbhan smiled at him. He crept toward her.

"Gnoll, you have returned," she said with pleasure. "What news do you bring?"

He smiled and withdrew a black sack from beneath the cloak that covered his hump. Its absence lessened the size of his deformity. His greedy fingers fumbled foolishly with the laces that held the sack closed. "No, mistress," he hissed. "Treasure first then news."

Sithbhan drummed her nails impatiently on her throne.

Gnoll groped at the bag until the knot was undone. A proud grin spread across his face as he withdrew a small trap from it. The trap of woven bark closed by knotted twine contained a small gray bird, still bearing the down of a baby. The baby screeched helplessly, futilely flapping its wings and hopping about. His eyes sparked as he gazed at the small, helpless creature. "A treasure for you, mistress," he said, holding the cage out to her.

He watched with anticipation as Sithbhan took the cage. She looked at the little bird in silence.

"What is it?" she asked.

"A bird from the kingdom of Men. I caught it while visiting the master, and I brought it to you, mistress," he panted.

"I know, Gnoll," she said irritably. "But why? What use do I have for this bird, as you call it?"

"Its song will lift your spirits, mistress!"

Gnoll watched. His eyes searched for a hint of pleasure on her face, but he saw nothing. Sithbhan sliced the twine with her nail and opened the small gate. Her pale hand moved into the cage. The bird screeched loudly as her hand closed around it and drew it from the cage. Gnoll screamed in protest. Sithbhan drew the bird to her mouth, which arched upward with wicked pleasure. A moment later, the little bird was silent. Gnoll groaned with remorse before his mistress as she ran her dark tongue over her lips.

"I like birds. You must bring me some more, Gnoll."

He wailed loudly, "You should not have eaten it!"

371

She howled angrily. "Just tell me, what news you bring, or your fate shall be worse than that of your precious treasure!" Death rose from her throne and extended her hand.

From the pit rose her double-bladed scythe of fire. She raised the weapon into the air, ready to slash his body and set it ablaze. Gnoll cowered before her and moaned wildly.

"Speak!" she cried.

"Zrene moves with corrupted Flame. She leaves blood, death, and fear in her wake."

"The Gemshorn, Gnoll, does she have the Gemshorn?"

Lorshin grimaced at the word. Both Sithbhan and Gnoll ignored him.

"I cannot say for certain, mistress," Gnoll wailed.

"Wretched creature!" Sithbhan howled. The weapon sliced through the air at him. Streaks of emerald-black fire poured from it.

"Mistress, no!" Gnoll wailed, rolling onto his back and raising his webbed limbs as defense.

The blade stopped short of his head. Sparks of Flame stung his skin. Sithbhan threw the weapon aside. "I will seek the answer for myself." She glanced toward Lorshin. "Come, beloved," she said as she pulled him by chains of shadow into the *Darkness* around her and vanished like a black mist from the lair.

* * *

Loriath, Kingdom of the Elves

A drop of dew, sparkling in the Light, slipped from the tender leaf and fell with a whispered plop to the earth. The sound, completely missed by weaker senses, filtered down into the Guardian's dreams, forming an image in his mind. The dewdrop darkened into a deep red and dropped audibly onto a gilded floor.

A shuddering breath rumbled through the Guardian's sleeping body as he felt the power in the droplet of blood. Even asleep, it told him everything about its owner. Another drop of blood. Another of power rocked the whole perspective of the dream that was not a dream at all—not really.

The gilded room swirled with people—living beings from every Race and every nation. Upon the throne, raised above the swirl, sat a king, his face an open mass of wormy sores. *Darkness* hovered above his head, and at his side, a Colorless Guardian crouched. Blood dripped from the small body of the Colorless from wounds that did not heal. The Colorless raised its small head, staring back at him with eyes of frozen Flame flecked with gold, exactly like her father's. "Uncle Cadclucan," she screamed.

"Sian Seela," he whispered.

Instantly, the dream deepened, changed. He saw a vision he had seen before. He moved swiftly through the Light. This was the safest place. *Darkness* could not sense him here, and no one could be lured by the power of the Stone of Existence. He was alone—neither in the world nor the secret realm, but somewhere between the two.

The Stone of Existence hung heavily around his neck. It was a weight only he could bear. He was its Guardian until Mhorag the Promised King came. The Light made the stone heavier, stronger. He let the power flow as he hurtled forward through Light and silence toward Sanctus's will.

Suddenly, the silence turned to chaos. That which was passing outside the Light came into his mind. He saw the faces of his brothers. Fyrdung and Azolat stood side by side, wielding the Light. Arawn faced them. *Darkness* clothed him. His breath was black and his eyes dark. It was a fleeting memory, however, that was soon displaced by something stronger. A storm was gathering all around him, and at its eye was the cry of innocent blood rising from the heart of the earth. This blood was yet unshed, but the time of its shedding was rapidly approaching.

The earth was shaken apart by the black breath, and a fathomless *Darkness* opened before his eyes. Mountains fell and new rose in their place. These new mountains were black, binding all the universe to the One Whose Name is not Spoken, framed from the carcasses of the dead of every race and all manner of living things. Screaming trees were swallowed in the blackness. Water stopped flowing. The seas dried, and all that lived within lay suffocating beneath the boiling sun.

Father, Cadclucan thought as he gazed upon the sun. It ruptured into a thousand flaming balls before falling into *Darkness.*

Mother, he nearly cried out as the moon turned to blood and poured into nothingness.

Cadclucan fell to his knees as the vision brought him into *Darkness.* He spilled from the Light onto a bed of pine needles and leaf mold. Massive redwoods and pines rose up around him. He heard their soft singing and the creaking of their boughs as they greeted him. Sunlight found its way through their canopy in brilliant columns that broke the vision's hold over him. He remained frozen on the ground, breathing heavily, for hours. His bloody tears soaked into the earth. The Red Wood trembled with his power.

Light flowed to him from the far reaches of the earth—from open portals and Guardian voices. *Darkness* watched and waited. Between the two gathering storms, a boy with eyes of amber Flame arose.

The universe spun rapidly around him, mimicking the swirl of the golden blood shining unnaturally in his flesh. This boy walked into the blackness, shining brighter than the Sun ever had—casting the blackness into burning shadows. Flame crackled all around him, inside him, burning out through his eyes.

Cadclucan bowed to the forest floor beneath the weight too great for him to carry alone. He bore a power that only one could wield.

The Light whispered around him, "Let the Light shine forth and awaken hope. Let Mhorag arise. Let the Promised come."

Darkness wielded the Gemshorn. Everything fell into ashes.

"No!" he screamed as he saw the Colorless rise, wielding the Flame that had grown dark. Last of all, the little boy fell, leaving nothing but the void . . .

Cadclucan threw his head back and roared. It began as the shout of a dreamer and grew into the cry of a Guardian. The vision could not contain him, so great was the depth of his sorrow. His emerald and gold scaled, horse-shaped head lifted heavenward. He roared, awakening. His scream shook all of Loriath so fiercely that none could stand until he was silent—even the trees trembled.

The vision released him slowly, never quite fading from his mind. His great talons plowed the earth. His huge wings fanned the air into a windstorm. His tail pounded the earth, sending tremors deep into the land. Blood dripped from his eyes as he roared. When at last his screams stopped, his breaths continued to hammer roughly in his chest. Smoke poured from his flaring nostrils, and all around him he felt fear. Slowly, so as not to frighten his friends further, he rose from his bed, lowering his wings. One final exhale of power and he transformed into the guise of humanity before striding out of his den.

Elves gave him a wide berth as he passed, dipping into deep reverential bows.

"Uncle!" Isentara shouted, coming through the magical gates at the same instant, shattering the tense silence. "We need you!" She turned to help Nothaniel lift a body from the back of one of the Enechelbrah.

Cadclucan was beside them in a flurry of midnight robe and a gust of wind. He crouched beside the still form.

"Can you help her, Baculus?" Nothaniel asked.

"She is fading fast. Her injuries are severe," he said, frowning, "made by the Dark One's corrupted Flame, but they are not what is killing her." His breath fell on the face of the Shee, rousing her slightly. His hands held her lightly. "Don't move," he said. "You are safe."

The Shee gazed up at him uncomprehendingly. Her weak eyes fixed upon his flaming ones, and she gasped. "I never thought I'd see eyes of Flame," she said weakly.

"Sanctus blesses those who love the Light," Cadclucan answered quietly, "and I see that you, Subara, have loved Light."

Subara strained to focus on him. "I must—I must tell you," she managed to say with gasping breaths. "A Calianith lives clothed with corrupted Flame. She seeks the Gemshorn."

"I know," Cadclucan said.

"My people—"

"Your people will endure."

Subara nodded taking comfort from his words. "Then I can die in peace now," she said in a whisper.

"And peace will endure forever," Cadclucan said.

"Help me build my cocoon."

Cadclucan lifted her in his arms.

Darkness.

*   *   *

Isear

Trin ran, raising a cloud of silver dust across the land. It felt good to run for a cause again—far better than sitting around waiting for the *Darkness* to come. He kept his eyes level, safely away from the greenish fire overhead and the blackness all around. A thrill of excitement and fear drove him faster in flight than he had been able to achieve during those brief years of peace. His feet had wings again. He was a Resistance scout once more! He let out a laugh of pure exultation and hurtled faster through the *dark*. The Summoners were waiting!

Chapter Forty-Six

LAID IN ASHES

Nithrodine, Isear:

A rmahad sat upon his throne, arrayed in all the glorious excesses of his position, yet his face was an open mass of wormy sores. His ringed hands gripped the arms of his heavy chair. The candles of every candelabrum had dissolved into pools of wax, leaving the throne room covered in deep shadows. Dozens of ancient manuscripts were strewn around him, forgotten. He had scoured every source for some clue to the riddle's answer. How did one bind a living, breathing Caladrius?

The noble hall had taken on a sinister air. Sculpted figures protruded from the walls like angry beasts. Open-mouthed Caladrius leaped from the darkest recesses threateningly even in stone. His mind wandered from the riddle to the room and back again. The room was filling with a colorful swirl of people—his subjects from every Race. They were restless in their waiting, the *Darkness* too as it brooded hungrily overhead, but Armahad ignored them. He had read of the Gemshorn, the one instrument that could lull a Caladrius into submission or paralyze an entire army, precisely as the Dark One had whispered. The histories of his adopted subjects had told him of the song that had claimed hundreds for the Dark One and left thousands more dead in its wake. No one seemed to know what had actually happened to the Gemshorn only that it had disappeared long ago in the last great battle of the Guardian War. Legend said that the Elves of Light had crafted a magical box to conceal the Gemshorn's evil power and that the box was then hidden away in the *deepest foundations*. There the stories had even ceased to speak of it. Armahad closed his eyes. Lack of sleep pulled at his body. He resisted the need, forcing his mind to refocus on the riddle.

The deepest foundations. Master Esarian had used those same words. Of course this was a useless memory . . . or was it? Armahad considered the memory carefully in light of all that he had read. Not only had he read the legends of other Races, he had read those of his own people, and he had studied the histories of his forefathers as far back as Nudhug. The first reference to the Gemshorn's song had been in Nudhug's time. At once, the An Taoseach's eyes jerked open. "Of course," he said to himself. "Nudhug, the deepest foundation of my own royal house." His voice was low for his own ears. If legend was right, the Gemshorn lay with Nudhug in the *deepest foundation* of Nithrodine. *Darkness* seethed above him, continuing to brood even as the doors of the throne room were thrown open and the Summoners walked in.

"An Taoseach!" D'Faihven shouted, leading the motley group.

Armahad smiled wickedly. "Summoners!" he said in mock welcome, rising from his throne. "Have you forgotten there is a price on your heads?"

The Mydrian eased into view. Armahad raised his hand, restraining them.

His quick eyes flashed over them and around to the assemblage. "Ah, I see you have been busy," he said. The An Taoseach pointed one by one to each of the Resistance leaders. "Hempress, Queen of the Centaur; Dubber, King of Giants; General Ickluck Lorndop, Dwarf Leader; Akule, King of the Merar; Eek-ash and Uleya, the Suzerainty of the Kot; Hakan, Kateirah, and Ethany, Rulers of the Faedran; Astraya, Queen of the Sylph; Sariel, Jantot, Occolia and Hoomroosh, Ambassadors of Umber III, King of Fairies; Zoan, King of the Astoni; Tuernok, Seneschal of the Faun; Porig, King of Trolls; Fugwort, Gnome Commander; Wirtbam, King of the Poeth."

As Armahad picked them from the assembly, each noble ruler stepped forward, casting off the hoods meant to conceal them.

"There seems to be one missing," Armahad said. "Dissention in the ranks, perhaps?"

"Subara, Mother Superior of the Shee is dead," D'Faihven answered. "But I suppose you knew that."

Armahad leaned back into his throne with a laugh. "And I suppose you've come to punish me. Do you really think you can?" *Darkness* moved menacingly lower. "You know this is treason, don't you?" he asked. "Rising up against the ruler to whom you have all sworn your allegiance!"

Hempress stepped forward, her hooves clopping lightly with each step. "A good ruler will sacrifice himself for his people, not the other way around. You, great king, have committed the treason, not we."

Armahad scowled, "I will have your tongue!"

"I'd like to see you try," General Ickluck Lorndop shouted, coming to stand at the Centaur queen's side.

"Enough games," D'Faihven snapped. "We stand united against you, An Taoseach, but we have not come to fight!"

"Then by all means," Armahad said with a wave of his hand, "tell me. To what do I owe the pleasure of your company?"

"I think you know the answer, my lord," D'Faihven answered.

"Where is Esarian?" Orlok demanded, rushing forward.

"And the Colorless!" Nulet shouted.

Armahad laughed, but it was not really his laughter. It came from the *Darkness*. "So now we come to it. You know about the Caladrius," he snarled. "Well, let me show you your precious little hope!"

An iron cage descended from the ceiling. Inside, bound to a velvet pillow by three strong, crossed chains lay the Colorless. Dried blood made her visible to them all.

"No!" Hempress screamed, drawing King Dubber's huge sword.

Eek-ash and Uleya leaped forward with fierce bellowing roars.

King Dubber grabbed Hempress's hand. "There are too many!"

The Resistance leaders tensed for war as the uneasy Mydrian emerged even more and *Darkness* drifted slowly downward.

The small Guardian didn't raise her colorless head. She looked at them with frozen eyes of Flame flecked with gold; her breaths came shallow and uneven.

Armahad rose. "Choose wisely," he said. "Your lives or her freedom." *Darkness* opened around him, and Death descended with the Samhail at her back.

"Villain!" Queen Astraya shouted.

"We are outnumbered," General Ickluck Lorndop said, the voice of reason. "We need to fall back. We cannot fight the Samhail! We have no weapons that can touch them! They are of the Guardians' own lineage!"

Akule agreed. "Under the *Darkness* not even Sun's light can quell them!"

The Samhail stalked forward.

"Back!" Hempress screamed.

The Summoners watched their allies back away, knowing there was no other way. D'Faihven rushed forward to the cage. In the chaos, she ripped the Styarfyre orb shard from around her neck and thrust it onto the pillow beside the Colorless whose tiny talon closed over it. Only up close could the Summoner see how alert and focused those flaming eyes really were. Orlok grabbed D'Faihven and yanked her aside out of one of the Samhail's reach.

"We would have followed you to the end, but now you will never rise from these ashes of your glory!" D'Faihven shouted to the king.

"Let's go!" Orlok growled.

"Run!" Nulet shouted.

Armahad watched with satisfaction as the throne room cleared. "Let them be," he said softly. "They are of little importance now." Soon— very soon—he would have the legendary power of the Caladrius at his disposal and a weapon that would devour all his enemies once and for all!

*   *   *

Black tides filled the dark. Samhail slaves carried the Colorless in her iron cage, under the cloak of their master, in solemn procession behind the An Taoseach. To the bowl of land where the Empire of Light had been fashioned, they now returned to tear it all down—this thing called Hope.

Armahad smiled to himself. If he was right, the Gemshorn lay within reach and the Dark One's promise would be complete. His wicked pleasure grew with each footstep until the great cry of the Shrieking Stone shattered the silence. In the exact center of this bowl stood that lump of legendary stone. The An Taoseach stopped beside it. "The deepest foundation," he said quietly.

The Light of the strange star and the bloody hue of the moon came together at that moment upon the surface of the stone. Three bleeding crescents, their meaning long clouded in myth, appeared, and the whispery cry rose into a powerful, subterranean shrieking as if the earth itself shouted. He ignored the fact that he could no longer feel the tingle of power on the surface of his flesh. Legend said that this stone lent voice to the ashes of Nudhug to herald the true and rightful An Taoseach of Isear and no other. Mark or no, he was still the An Taoseach. Armahad felt around the lip of the stone, searching for its secret. There had to be a way inside!

The shrieking rose up, piercing through the horrible deathlike silence of the land. Zrene shifted toward its sound. A single stone had escaped her gaze until that moment. Visibly rough in texture, the stone looked to be made of unique pebbles all plastered together within a mass of gray, cracked and weathered with age. In another place, the stone could have been mistaken for a foundation stone, but here it rose for several solitary inches out of the fertile bowl. A round hole in its crown, lipped like an open mouth was the only remarkable thing about it, yet as she inhaled a breath, she knew she had found the Gemshorn at last.

The Calianith rushed downward with an animalistic cry. Tendrils of emerald-black Flame seeped through the first cracks of an opening ahead of the Dark One himself.

A concealed wheel and pulley system shifted the Shrieking Stone and its earthen bed, revealing a narrow passage of treacherous earthen steps, knotted with roots and earthworms, dropping down uncomfortably into a dark hole—made darker by *Darkness*. Worms squished loudly beneath Armahad's feet as he led the procession down into the dark, unmapped recesses of his kingdom's foundation. The trailing greenish light of the corrupted Flame illuminated the blackest regions enough to pass safely downward. From below the Shrieking Stone's cry took on an ominous sound as it totally encompassed them. The walls seemed to close in around them—suffocating—like there wasn't enough air.

Armahad drew in a ragged breath.

"You should turn back now," Sian Seela said softly.

The An Taoseach smiled. "So our little Caladrius has decided to grace us with her presence again," he said mockingly. He glanced back at the little creature contained in the cage borne behind him.

The Caladrius lifted her head slightly. A dark mane cascaded silkily down her long neck from the top of her small, horse-shaped head. "You should turn back," she said again in an alluring voice. "This place is blessed."

Armahad laughed and moved on. "*I* am blessed."

"You were," Sian Seela said weakly, lowering her head onto the pillow, "before you let that One in." Her eyes flashed toward the *Darkness*. "But this place . . ." she said, her gaze shifting to the earthen walls surrounding them, "this place is still blessed. No amount of evil can scar it."

Darkness growled.

Don't listen to her! the Dark One whispered, swatting angrily at the cage.

Sian Seela bared her teeth and let her smoky breath hiss menacingly between them.

Armahad hesitated, "What do you mean?"

"When your kingdom lies in utter ruin, when your bones and those of your heirs return to dust, when the stones of your palace lie in ash upon you, this place will remain and Hope will stand supreme upon you!" Sian Seela answered, her voice rising slightly with each word.

Darkness growled again.

Armahad flung himself against the cage. He gripped the iron bars with ghostly white hands that shook with rage. "There will be no ruin!

There will be no ash!" he screamed. "There will be no Hope!" He snarled the last word at one with the *Darkness* around him.

Sian Seela's eyes flashed with Flame—two, endless, spinning wheels of blue fire flecked with gold that pierced straight through his soul as they fixed upon him. "For you," she said simply. "But the Prophecy will stand and Hope will endure." She paused and let her gaze shift back to the *Darkness*, "Forever!"

The Dark One howled with rage and all his slaves with him. Quite suddenly, however, the howl of despair turned to insane laughter.

"Now you will bow to me," Armahad whispered.

Sian Seela lifted her head to gaze fearfully into the *dark*. Her talon tightened around the Styarfyre orb shard.

"At last!" Zrene shouted. Her green hands reverently lifted the magical box from the pile of treasure deep within the secret bowels of Nithrodine. There was no doubt in her mind. All of her senses were screaming. Within this box was the Gemshorn!

Her worshipful touch passed over every detail of the box as she sought its opening. Its craftsmanship was unfamiliar to her—a perfect cube with no line or opening visible to the naked eye. Strange symbols surrounded its outer shell, and as her fingers traced over them uncertainly, a flash of blinding white Light shot out of it into the gloom.

Zrene shrieked, dropping the box back into the mountain of long-concealed treasure as she backed away. The sting of power filled the deepest, *darkest* corners. She cowered away from it, though *Darkness* crashed in with greater force than the magic here. She would not touch that box again. She would not feel the sting that reminded her too much of the paralyzing sting of a Colorless' barbed tail. She would wait. Let another creature of *darkness* feel the wrath, and she would steal the Gemshorn for herself when it was done!

The Samhail lowered the cage to the floor of the treasure room and stepped aside. Armahad lifted the magical box in his hands. Its wood vibrated between his hands.

"It's real," Armahad said softly, wonderingly.

You can open it, the Dark One whispered.

Armahad shook his head. "Not me alone," he said softly. "I read about this kind of magic in the most ancient manuscripts of my people." He smiled. "The Elves had its secrets omitted from their histories, but thankfully, my people felt no need for such measures."

But you know the way. the Dark One encouraged.

"Yes. I am only one piece of the puzzle." He touched a single symbol upon the side of the box. The rune began to glow. "Now you, my sweet." He crossed to the cage.

Sian Seela surged to her feet and shrank back as far as the cage and chains would allow. She growled fiercely. A swipe of her paw rent the bars of one cage wall asunder, and she leaped free on three good legs, shredding the chains asunder. One leg and one wing hung useless. She backed further away. Her eyes flashed wildly from enemy to enemy as they all converged around her, penning her in.

"Be calm, my pretty," Armahad said in a voice that was meant to be soothing. "I only need your breath."

Sian Seela smiled. "If its breath you want . . ." she said, letting her voice trail off mysteriously. She raised her talon and cast the Styarfyre orb shard on the ground. "Then breath you shall get!"

No! the Dark One screamed too late.

Sian Seela's smile broadened. Her small chest heaved as she breathed. The whole of Nithrodine shook with power. White smoke billowed from her nostrils, slowly pouring out to fill the chamber. She would not be tamed this night!

Too young to control the full force of her innate power, she relied upon the broken shard to give it focus.

Stop her! the Dark One shrieked, flinging Armahad aside.

The second rune was already aglow.

The Samhail surged upon the Colorless.

Sian Seela's enchanted laughter filled the blanket of thick, white smoke, which suddenly burst into blue-white Flame.

The Samhail screamed, fleeing back from the Light. *Darkness* clashed against the Light. In the midst, where the bed of shards lay, the breath of the Colorless awakened and stretched into a sword of Light. Sian Seela seized it in her talons and with one quick flick sent it flying. The Dark One roared, shrinking back from her. The Colorless threw back her head and laughed, flinging evil away with an overwhelming surge of Light. The unnatural sound shook Nithrodine from top to bottom; the earth shifted to her command, crashing down upon the line of Styarfyre orb shards, trapping her beyond their reach.

"No!" Armahad screamed, his eyes bulging with horror as the dust cleared. He threw the box away from him and scrambled on all fours to the spot where the Colorless had disappeared. His hands clawed frantically into the earth. "I want her! You promised," he screamed to the black silence around him.

The box bounced once and fell into a shaft of Light. Light poured down from the heavens, erupting the blackness into burning shadows.

Yes, the Dark One breathed. The third rune began to glow and the magical box cracked apart.

Zrene flew forward. Her greedy hands snatched the Gemshorn from its bed before the dust of the box settled upon the ground. Her exultant cry surged with her in a blaze of emerald-black Flame up into the heavens. She raised the Gemshorn to her lips, sending the melody soaring out through the *Darkness.*

Deep in the earth, Sian Seela heard and trembled. The embers of her breath slowly turned to ash, leaving her alone, momentarily forgotten, in the *dark.*

Chapter Forty-Seven

MADNESS AND POWER

Armahad threw himself into the dirt. His hands clawed through the earth in desperate frenzy, seeking the lost prize of power. A Caladrius was worth more than all the treasures of the earth, more than all the promises of the Dark One. Such promises were empty if a Caladrius roamed this earth free! His throne would fall. His line would end! A Caladrius would reign supreme!

"You promised me!" he shouted to the blackness. "You said the power of the Caladrius would be mine!" Dirt flung in great heaps around him. "Where are you?"

The blackness didn't answer.

"Sire!" The Mydrian descended upon him. Their swords were drawn. Their faces panicked. "Sire!"

Armahad dug deeper into the earth.

"Sire, please!" the Mydrian Captain shouted. "You are not safe here! The Races have come in force!"

The clash of steel rang around them. The screams of war filled the *dark*.

Armahad shook his bodyguard off. "Leave me!" he screamed.

Yelizaveta emerged from the black. Her hand lightly trailed along the line of her father's shoulders. "Let me speak with him," she said to his guards.

The Mydrian Captain nodded once and moved a short distance away.

"Daddy."

Armahad ignored her. Dirt hit her legs.

"Daddy," Yelizaveta said unpleasantly. She yanked him around to face her. "I have a gift for you." Simultaneously, she plunged a little dagger up under his ribs.

Armahad gasped, his eyes widening in disbelief. "Why?"

Yelizaveta laughed bitterly. "As if you don't know," she said. Her skin sagged over her bones in loose wrinkles like wax from a burning candle. "Madness and power." She pushed him away from her into the hole he had dug. "You dug your own grave. You changed me! You changed yourself! You changed everything!"

A shout rose from the Mydrian as the An Taoseach fell.

Armahad's hand was stretched toward her. "No!" he screamed as a Mydrian blade pierced her from behind.

She smiled. "Don't you think I already tried to end this?" she said. She drew the blade free and watched the wound close. "He did this to me!"

"Yelizaveta must never die," Armahad said softly. "Never." His last words came softly and faded quickly as the Mydrian tackled his daughter. As he breathed his last in *Darkness*, the earth began to tremble. All of Nithrodine shook as the An Taoseach's soul was eaten away by Death and the decay of his Mark spread into the land.

*   *   *

The Gemshorn's melody flowed out through the *Darkness*. All living things fled before it until at last it grew silent.

Zrene's path of destruction was easy enough to follow. In the *darkness* of a new dawn, Sithbhan and Lorshin passed unnoticed to the stagnant black water of the Bocain River. The Hill of Nerald, where the Dark One had claimed Matwyn to lead his army in the great Guardian War, stood beyond it, concealed in mist, indicating the Borderland. In the mist, Sithbhan saw the eyeless spirits bound to wander the desolate land. All were victims of the Calianith and the Gemshorn.

Sithbhan scanned the river, and despite the black, muddy water, she quickly spotted what she sought. A sly smile crossed her face as she plunged her hand into the river. Sludge oozed around her hand and squished between her fingers. She grabbed a small leather pouch and pulled it from its hiding place. Sithbhan shook her hand free. The sludge fell with a splash into the river and sank out of sight. "Know your enemy," she said softly to Lorshin. "Know their weaknesses."

Lorshin stiffened apprehensively and said nothing.

Her long nails sliced into the pouch and pierced the contents. She withdrew her finger from the pouch. A rotting eyeball was skewered by her nail. With a smile, she turned to face the Hill of Nerald. *Darkness* smoldered around them angrily.

"Zrene, come forth!" Sithbhan howled. Her voice gave evidence to her rage.

The mist parted. Churning, emerald-black fire passed from the hill toward her. The spirits pawed at the fire, wailing loudly, but none could touch her. "The Gemshorn is mine!" Zrene cried, leaping upon Sithbhan.

Corrupted Flame surrounded them both. *Darkness* like a shield thrust the Calianith to the ground. At its touch, the greenish fire was extinguished. Zrene lay before Death with her limp, green tail tucked between her legs and her hands stretched in surrender above her head. Her luminous red eyes were fixed on the *dark*.

"I have something that belongs to you," Sithbhan said, holding up her finger.

"Give them to me," Zrene purred.

Sithbhan stared venomously down at Zrene as she moved in a slow circle around her prey. "First tell me where you put the Gemshorn."

Zrene shook her head.

"Answer me!" Death howled. She flung the pouch and the eye from her finger in her rage.

Lorshin shrank back from her.

The Calianith's grisly treasure fell to the ground and rolled a short distance before lying still in a pool of mud. Zrene rolled over and pounced forward with her hands. She pulled the eyes beneath her and curled her hands over the top, under her chin. Her back end stretched up. Her tail sprang high and wagged happily.

"Mine," she purred over them.

"Where is the Gemshorn?" Sithbhan asked again, cold and threatening.

Zrene was silent. She rose from the mud and gathered her treasure. Death glared at her while she placed each one into the pouch at her hip. The Calianith continued away from them into her lair. Her booted feet left no evidence of her presence in the muddy earth.

Sithbhan seized Zrene's course, knotted, cord-like hair. The Calianith screamed as she was pulled back.

"I have not dismissed you," Death said, at one with the *dark*. "Where is the Gemshorn?"

"In there. In there," Zrene whined.

"Show me."

Glad to be released, the Calianith smiled. "Come. I will wield it for you." She said. She took Sithbhan's icy hand and pulled her into the haunted mists that encircled the Hill of Nerald. Lorshin followed hesitantly.

Sithbhan allowed herself to be led beyond the mist to the solid stone wall built around the hill. As she waited, Zrene placed her green hand into a crevice in the rock. There was a soft click and a circle of gray stone rolled away.

"This way," Zrene said softly before stepping into the *dark*.

Sithbhan and Lorshin followed. The stone rolled back into place behind them. They walked down a narrow tunnel. The path turned moist beneath their feet. The air grew stale and hung heavily with the stench of rotten flesh. Zrene's lips twisted up in a wicked smile as she proudly led them through a small circular door at the end of the tunnel.

The walls were lined with opened crypts exhibiting the cracked effigies of the Calianith. The stone floor was a swirl of engravings. Skulls hung from the ceiling and the eyes of numerous dead peaked from small nooks in the stone walls that writhed with maggots and creatures which fed on filth. Zrene paused in front of one unremarkable crypt. From its shadowy interior she drew the forbidden gift. The Calianith turned, raising the curved instrument to her lips and played.

The Gemshorn's melody, ripe with power, faded. Only Lorshin and the Shades of Reality remained. He saw Isentara. He heard her scream, but he could not reach her. Then it was over. The blisters on his heart burst, shooting their black poison through his veins. No price was too great to pay for freedom.

Lorshin opened his eyes. Their gentle, blue glow dissolved into bottomless black pools. His dark robe billowed around him as he rose. Renewed power filled him. He felt the *dark* pouring in, consuming the Light. *Darkness* laughed.

Yes. Yes, my son. Surrender.

His eyes fixed on the Gemshorn. Ages of fear diminished in that moment. The power that came from it rivaled only one thing he had ever known before—a Guardian's voice. Strange that he had not recognized that before, but it was as if everything was new to him. Even his *father's* voice—something he had thought an illusion—was different. The corruption in it was gone. The voice was as beautiful as the one he remembered from his childhood.

Take the Gemshorn. I know you want it. Flesh of my flesh, the blood of a Guardian flows in your veins, though you cannot take that form or wield that power. Only you are worthy to play the instrument. Only you can awaken its full power and make it a weapon more worthy.

Lorshin couldn't resist the urge that came over him. Part of him wanted to. He remembered the evil the Gemshorn had brought in the days of the Guardian War. He remembered the horrors of war and the lives that had been lost. He remembered the glory of the Light, but that part of him was drowning in the dark. His hand extended toward Zrene and her prize.

Zrene recoiled from him. "The Gemshorn is mine! I am its mistress!"

Death appeared behind her. "Your usefulness is wearing thin."

The Gemshorn is mine. The Dark One said.

"I will avenge my people!" Zrene shouted, clutching the Gemshorn to her breast. "Revenge is my right! My people were slaughtered!"

And I was stripped of my identity so that none dare to speak my name and I was banished to this place. The Dark One answered with equal fierceness. *I was a fool to think that your people were ever worthy of wielding the power of the Gemshorn!*

Lorshin advanced. Death prodded Zrene forward. The Samhail converged behind their prince and the Shades of Reality rose dark and sinister on either side. Zrene tried to escape, her eyes wide with fear. Death's cold hands held her firmly until Zrene's screams were stifled beneath Lorshin's hands. His fangs flashed before everything went black.

Darkness.

"My love," Sithbhan said. "I have a present for you." She circled around to face him. The Gemshorn was held out to him.

Dark desire drove away his opposition. He rose, dropping the Calianith's lifeless husk. He drew Death into his arms. *Together,* he whispered to her mind.

Sithbhan smiled and pressed the instrument into his hands. Blackness flashed in her eyes. "Together," she said, whether for the Dark One or for herself it was impossible to tell.

And I will teach you, the secret of the Gemshorn and together we will destroy the Light. Once we have the Stone of Existence. Soon. Very soon.

Darkness.

* * *

Solais, Kingdom of the Faedran

Solais, a kingdom of pathways—Light ways—as dazzling to the eye as a diamond in sunlight was etched into creation's very design by Sanctus so long ago; once uninhabited now it was the home of all Faedran and in turn the Faedran's bodies were home to the Echoes of Guardian power. Solais and its inhabitants were mysterious and seldom seen, yet Solais remained an inner reality within and unseen to the outside world but very real and supremely vital. If the Light ways collapsed, all Faedran would die and so too would the outside world—a slow, painful imploding. The void would eradicate the foundations of the *beginning* and Hope would certainly fail. The Light ways, once incomprehensively vast, were weak and crumbling. No Guardian had wielded the Light to renew them since the Great Exodus. The Sun, the Guardian Father, had subtly nourished them for a time, but with the *Darkness* growing his power was weakening. Already the Dark One exerted his power from a distance where a world in utter chaos thought of nothing but itself never dreaming that their *darkness* would lead to greater *Darkness* still. Solais had become a forgotten front in a futile war, yet fight they would for the hope of Hope until the last Faedran fell. Within the Light ways, the Blood Band led by Hakan Supreme Blood and the Breath Band led by Ethany Long Breath were right now marching toward war.

Kateirah Forever Sorrow remained on the central throne in the heart of Solais where it was said no *Darkness* would ever fall so long as sorrow remained—a dream perhaps, yet it was the only hope left to them if the Guardians did not return soon. The thrones on either side of her stood empty and foreboding. She had already bid her brother and sister a final farewell, knowing they may never be reunited in life.

The portals were open, yet *Darkness* was too great; its infection too pervasive and Hope possessed the fragility of a mere word. It would be so easy to give in to despair yet Kateirah would not. She could not! She had already embraced Hope—its promise, its cure. There was no turning back now; there was no easy way out; there was only the agony.

Darkness.

Chapter Forty-Eight

AN EVIL THAT DEVOURETH

Darkness, yet a new day slowly dawned. With a growl, I turned from the carcasses of the dead. The time had come to subdue the Light invading these long hours.

I am not a keeper of Time and Seasons. Their order stands against the void, yet there is some use in the terminology. As these days of peace end, a *season* is come. A *season* I alone longed for. A *time* of **Darkness**. Time stood frozen against me with Sun and Moon hanging as equals upon the heavens—Light and **Darkness** arrayed against each other around them. I scowled at the Guardian Father's flaming orb and the Mother's bloody-hued, waning crescent, and their interruption of the Darkening. When the void was complete there would be no place for them, until then I had to endure their remnants of glory invading my black domain, thankful for their weakened state which could not penetrate the deepest depths of **Darkness** where I lurked. Slowly, as I watched their opposition, Urgilis, the Sun dimmed. A fierce wind blew in descending oddly from a high westerly point, rushing into the black from open portals. Upon it rode the disembodied voices of Guardians raised in song—the paragon of perfection, ripened by Time and Bynthroenine's unending Light.

I resisted the urge to scream, refusing to give the **dragons** the satisfaction of my pain. Their immaculate voices writhed about the great black shoulders of my **darkness**. I blocked out their words, focusing instead on how distant the sound was, even in its strength. My enemies remained in their secret realm of Light untouchable despite my power, but I also knew the meaning of the First Face of the Guardian Moon and whom it left at my **mercy**.

From where the wind blew brilliant white balls of Flame appeared in quick succession approaching the Guardian Father. I cringed at the Light searing my naked eyes but I refused to turn away and hide. The balls of Flame ceased their flight hovering before the Sun—a sight at first more painful but then the balls seemed to darken before my wide eyes. Staring at the Sun could no longer make one blind, its Flame lessened by the Darkening, though still too strong and bright to appease me, its effects did manage to lesson my pain as I watched. Minutes dragged into hours before the balls of Flame resumed their flight, picking up speed as they swept forth in a near straight line. Some disappeared in the distance; some fell down where they had previously hovered. Some rose toward the blackness. They made no sound as they came upon the air in their interlocking lines. One by one they separated; each ball becoming more defined with a tail of a fathom long or more, wider at the base where it adhered to their burning bodies and gradually decreasing to terminate at fine points.

I could make out no other features yet I knew what they were. Colorless—the young, unproven seed of the Guardians who sang mournfully to the Waning Mother. The balls of Flame disappeared by degrees until they were lost from view entirely. They came for higher purposes than I cared to imagine. One Colorless had been threat enough.

Anger stirred deep inside me.

My gaze silently turned to the withered, black heart—once Arawn's. I had not forgotten how other Guardians such as these had defeated my army in the days of the Guardian War nor had I forgotten my threat to take them for my own. I wanted them more now than ever before—their bodies, their form, their Flames, their breath—and other things that had been denied me by Sanctus who stripped Arawn of his identity among the Light wielders; things that could give strength to the *Darkness*, to hold Light at bay, to give shape to my amorphous substance, a shape more defined and enduring than the illusionary body currently at my disposal.

Hollow footsteps resounded in the abyss as I brooded back and forth. An ancient whisper, so faint it barely seemed a whisper echoed through the *Darkness* mocking me. *Let the Light shine forth and awaken hope. Let Mhorag arise. Let the Promised come.* The Heart of Evil clenched painfully. I must confess that the heart, in which I reside, once burned with Sanctus' Light. I speak of Arawn who was once ranked among the powerful Light wielding *dragons*, but who young and untested fell prey to black desire. That precious Flame, that link to the Source of ultimate power burned black in his heart . . . my beautiful, withered heart. His proven, Light wielding brothers had been forced to carve it from his chest in the name of *love, forgiveness, hope* and it still bore the scars; it still trembled at the sound of Light so perfect and beautiful mere words cannot describe it.

Such whispers will guide any who seek truth to the invisible doorway concealed within the mist. *Bynthroenine*, the secret realm of Guardians long sealed was beckoning once more! Thousands of Guardian voices rang in otherworldly melody to the world beyond, shining needles of Light pricking apart the void as the air shivered with the translucent edges thickening to a milky white center of an opening portal. Their flaming eyes divided between *Darkness* and Light, fixing upon the thin sliver of the Moon's waning crescent. By Night's reemergence tomorrow, the Moon's face would be hidden. They sang the ancient song, their voices resounding—ancient and powerful—full of secrets while another drove of unproven Guardians swept into view.

"Ageless Mother, shine down on us. Guide through *Darkness* till the Light of hope is reclaimed. Great Ones bleed while fires burn. Each crescent bares a tale that must end. Remember the blood from which you came."

A single ball of Flame burning down into a scarcely perceptible cobweb of glittery power landed gracefully at my feet. The lingering threads of visible light rapidly vanished before my eyes and blended perfectly into the black. Flame could not hide from Flame however and though dim I could still see that small heart Flame hovering low over the earth, countering the dark Flame stolen from Arawn with its lighter one.

I scowled down at the Colorless seed of my enemy knowing that if I took one step out of the greater *Darkness*, my illusion would hold for only a few moments before it lost its effectiveness in the young one's sight.

The Colorless whimpered softly.

The Time of the Waning Crescent was cruel, hard, and lonely—a trial through and through—yet it would leave the one who endured to the end with a pure heart, the strongest weapon of the Light: a Guardian proven, incorruptible, immortal . . . a thorn to my void! This feeling of perpetual black terror seized upon the Heart of Evil driving my foot forward. A thousand lesser illusions extended with me out of the dark toward other heart Flames.

The Colorless looked up with eyes of blue fire fixing squarely upon my illusionary perfection. Those eyes danced above the ground within an invisible head that was lifted, it seemed, to test the scent of the air. The Colorless cried out with a small, windy roar and scrambled back. The invisible talons left deep furrows in the earth.

I forced a smile across my features and slowly extended a hand, hoping to appease the terrified creature at least for the moment.

Eyes of blue Flame studied the offered hand for a long moment. All my strength was focused on keeping the illusion intact just a little bit longer. Hesitantly, the Colorless crept forward: invisible paws stirring the grass, unnatural eyes gazing in curiosity at my face, breath coming quick but steady from its young lungs.

I wiggled my fingers invitingly.

The Colorless arched its back, curling into the touch of my hand. I felt the slick impenetrable scales and stroked greedily higher to the back of the neck as the Colorless made a contented rumbling sound in its throat. My smile shifted from friendly to sinister in a second's time. My fingers closed upon the unseen neck, a vice grip, and I yanked the head back just enough to make the Colorless scream. My illusion dissolved as rapidly as it had formed. The young one's screams throbbed with wild bursts of Light and power as it fought to free itself from my grasp—as useless an effort as a young kitten trying to resist being carried by its mother—not that my intentions were so noble as protecting my young!

All across the blackness more screams arose. *Darkness* wrapped around their throats contracting till their screams cut off with horrified squeaks as I laughed insanely before their frightened eyes.

Guardian voices bathed in Light flowed free upon the land; the words and melody coming from deep inside them. "In the still of the night, great warriors arise! Chains must be broken; hope restored. Carved into stone; sealed with ancient blood. Never bow beneath the tormentor's claw, 'til stars fall to leave a naked sky. Remember and be free. Remember and be free. Dreams gilded with heroes blood. Ancient beacon of starlight calls. Clouded hope forged the past. Fated choice has sealed its ending—crushed beneath another's curse! Blood cries from the earth. Fight! Fight! 'Til our souls rest beyond the Sun, Flame returned unto Flame!"

Sun and Moon sagged impotent upon the heavens. *Darkness* slithered over their faces, blotting out their Light inch by inch. Time resumed its courses when the Guardian song broke into abrupt silence.

Darkness sighed. "Oh, brothers," I whispered with *Arawn's* ruined voice. "I told you I would take your children."

Out of the silence came a roar, a many layered thing that made the earth quake violently beneath its power. Bursts of blue-white Flame erupted across the black expanse, devouring the last vestiges of illusion. The Colorless bucked against the dark shackles trying to breach the surface of my *Darkness*, to reach the proven host arraying themselves upon my borders.

Darkness held them fast, strengthened by my twisted Flame. My illusion gathered once more to the Heart of Evil, rapidly joining by vile power to frame a visage of incorporeal *Darkness*. The Heart of Evil masked itself within Arawn's guise—an illusion stronger than all the rest—and I turned toward the proven Guardians, rising with all my corruption between them and their wailing seed. Not a single living creature stirred to answer their call. No one dared—not now, despite the desperation, all sensed that an evil that devours stalked through the blackness.

Whispers of Light, sizzling down into the black bowed *Darkness* into bitter folds around the Heart of Evil. For the death of a prophecy, I let myself be pulled toward the sound of Light rushing free. Emerging like magic from the living blackness, I walked with head bowed through the mist to the door beyond. I knew the way, guided by the Heart of Evil that had once been counted among the Guardians, stopping at the door. I had no magic words by which to open the door, no key, no summoning stone—only the corrupted Flame flowing in my veins, but no right. Already I could feel Light coiling against me holding me at bay. Instinctively, I held back from its touch, sure that *my* heart would die if ever Light intersected its dwelling place again.

Light and *Darkness* oriented themselves around each other. If one moved, so must the other. The Flame was one as the Source was one. It all burned back to the same point, tied to the same power. Weren't they therefore the very nature of equality? Merely Flame twisted out of shape . . . given a value . . . a pole? Didn't this make the Flame stronger than its original, neutral form? So could there really be Light without *Darkness*, hope without despair, desire without lust, life without Death? I slowly looked up.

A huge mass of restlessly undulating *dragons* was submerged within the portal, ill-defined except by their thrashing movements around each other. They sensed my presence as I sensed theirs. Their blue flaming eyes bursting open at the same instant I emitted a sinister laugh. Ear shattering roars drowned out the whispers of the Light and in an instant the mass of *dragons* multiplied in the milky—white, a roiling sea of Flame and sinew, crashing in vehement tides against the door. I raised my shadowy hand. *Darkness* flowed at my command. As I could not enter their realm, they would not enter *mine*!

"Dark One!" They screamed in their painfully beautiful voices.

A tremor ran through the black. Real horror was as close as a desire. Desire could cause you to give everything for hope and leave your heart broken and wasted . . . a desolation. The Source was as much a problem as he was a desire. *Darkness*. Desire. Was there really any difference? They were as close as Flame, mysterious and powerful in all its promise and predominance, contained in the vulnerable heart of a wretched hope. The secret was in the Prophecy. The secret was in the heart and with the Stone of Existence I could make the Source my weapon—indestructible and eternal! I thrilled at the thought of this magnificent new future

I had envisioned. The Heart of Evil thumped erratically, mirroring my joy. *Thud-thud. Thud-thud. Thud-thud. Darkness* with desire. The Source would be mine but not if the wretched Light wielders disrupted the void now, not if Hope was restored! My black gaze flashed.

"You started this," I hissed. "Your kind altered this story long ago with a journey into the past to save Arawn, but no more! I will not let you interfere again!"

"The will of Sanctus cannot be stopped by the likes of you." They answered, their voices as enchanting and fierce as lightning and thunder in a storm.

"I am stronger."

"What has been spoken shall come to pass." They said.

"There will be no hope!" I roared. "The Prophecy will fall! My Void will rise! I will reign supreme!"

Thousands of Guardian voices rose in laughter.

"You will fall! All of you!" I screamed. "The Source will be mine!"

Their laughter stopped abruptly. "You could not claim the Source in the beginning. You will not claim the Source now." They paused; their flaming glances darted back and forth among themselves—guarded, secretive, knowing . . . even desperate. Before I could process this change, they said, "We will not let you!"

I smiled, a dark lecherous smile. "And how will you stop me? I am here. I have the Gemshorn. I have your precious marked humans crushed under my foot; your chosen ones will feed the fires while mine sit on the throne! I have your prophecy on the verge of collapse. I have the world running mad. I know Cadclucan is in this world and I know the Stone of Existence is with him. Soon I will find it, and you—" I laughed—"you are not here to keep me from it." *Darkness* sighed. "Nor will you be." I smiled to myself. With time and the right lure, the Source would be easy prey precisely as the Colorless in my grasp.

The Light wielders stared at me with unfathomable eyes of blue Flame. A glimmer of horror fixed deep within each as they guessed the intricate depths of my plans, yet their power shook the portal, ripping into the void as their talons and breath attacked the lingering barrier between their realm and *mine*. Their talons furrowed through the milky white, digging, destroying—penetrating. Their breath leaked free.

I took an involuntary step back from the portal. A few seconds and my plans would collapse beneath righteous fury before I could even finish plotting them. "In your long silence have you forgotten that I am Sgarrwrath, the One Whose Name is not Spoken? I am the residue of Dullahan and the Heart of Evil from which all that is vile is sprung. I am the corrupted Flame of Arawn." I raised my head and breathed corrupted Flame. Slowly, the blackened Flame clotted through the Light in mockery of the power that had once disrupted my plans. The earth and the blackness shook violently with the power that erupted darkly from my body. My voice penetrated their minds.

Cruelty. I said as the first clot of emerald-black fire punched its way into the cavity between the realms.

Immorality. I said as a second clot swelled over the first.

Dishonesty and Faithlessness. I said as the third clot caused Light to shriek eerily against the

Dark.

Chaos and Wars. The fourth clot seemed to swallow the one before and together they strangled those that had preceded them.

Arrogance.

The Guardians cried out. Light lashed out angrily at the clots of *Darkness* where their bloody tears, tremulous with power, dripped free.

Self-indulgence.

Sorrow and Fear.

Guilt.

Hate.

The clots of *Darkness* sealed over the portal of Light. Black breath swirled over and around it blotting it out. Guardian tears slipped through, dropping soundlessly into the earth. The earth shook violently throwing me momentarily off balance as the void faltered in the shock wave of life's exultation at Hope's revival, yet the power was short lived without its wielders roaming free. Through my laughter I breathed one last breath of blackened Flame.

Despair.

"I remember the beginning," I whispered. "I was there, born of lust for the Source. I am the Evil that Devoureth, and I will invade every soul." Light cried into silence and my *Darkness* wiped the void clean. Beneath the surface of this *perfection*, I could still see the brooding spot where the portal had been, but the danger was passed—for now. I exerted my lordship and watched the united army of the Resistance races break before me, their weapons falling like refuse to the ground as they realized the Guardians could not save them this time! Hope faltered beyond repair.

Darkness was alive with timeless whispers that surpassed even the wind's piercing wail, stirring sadness in earth and stone. The sound of weeping resounded, dripping like rain from the blackened heights.

This weeping bled with ancient sorrow. All creation screamed with the awakening of memory far older than itself, shaking the kingdoms of earth to their deepest foundations. The earth trembled. Time slowed and all creation waited in deathlike silence for whatever would come next as Casara, Mother of all Guardians hid her face in the natural dark of the heavens as the unnatural *dark* came upon her children and their time of testing began.

*   *   *

Bynthroenine:

Esarian watched in horror as the milky portal was blacked out before his eyes. The scar remained but the blackness was leeched away by the unending light. Evil still had no power within these secret borders, yet it seemed the land of his childhood was devoured, sucked dry of any innocence it may have once possessed. All around him Guardians surrendered their true forms for the guise of humanity even so there was nothing tame about them. The horror in his human eyes was magnified in their inhuman ones, eclipsing his own in eternal Flame. Without thinking, his pale, white hand moved to the Styarfyre orb shard on the cord around his neck; his fingers froze around the cool remnant of a Summoner's power as his racing mind slowed to embrace the tortured silence of his companions. He took in their unmoving stances, their fathomless eyes, their tremulous power concealed behind unreadable masks of perfection. Not a single Guardian moved or even breathed while his heart hammered obscenely in his chest. A question died on his lips. Firebrand he was, yet his power could not approach that of a single, proven Guardian and he was surrounded by tens of thousands.

Esarian let his hand fall back to his side. If they could not penetrate the barrier, there was no use for him to even try. His heart clenched in his chest. A spasm of pain rippled down through his body. Was this how hope would die?

Chapter Forty-Nine

Darkness Arising

Lorshin trembled. Sithbhan pressed the Gemshorn more firmly into his unresponsive hand. The talon given by Arawn had grown calloused and grotesque—nothing like the blades of a Colorless' paw which it had once been. Its former splendor was marred beyond recognition. Lorshin's body quaked from head to toe as the weight of the talon radiated into him, adhering to his bones.

"I can't." He whispered as he tried to recoil from the instrument and from her.

Sithbhan held him fast. Her black nails dug into the flesh of his hand drawing blood. "To wield the Gemshorn is you birthright, Prince of the Samhail, Consort of Death, son of Arawn." She spoke each word deliberately, allowing their sting to take effect.

"No." Lorshin groaned between clenched teeth. His heart hammered in his chest in rhythm with the heartbeat of evil—a heart that had once loved his mother and Light. Together they were opposing truths but truth nonetheless. His life was not so different—not in this desperate game he played with the *Dark*.

Darkness loomed before Lorshin. Deep down, he knew he should run the other way. He should seek to destroy this weapon whose song mirrored the voice of a Guardian. He intended to do just that but his legs suddenly felt too heavy to lift, and deep down he knew it was already too late to turn back. He was aware of his movement but far from in control. His tortured thoughts ran through every spectrum of possibility as his fingers wrapped, unbidden, over the instrument. It seemed he had no real choice. For him there would always and only be one outcome in this life—the insanity striving to dominate him.

The voice of his *father* whispered from the blackness. "Lorshin, my son." Drawing upon the Shades of Reality, *Darkness* took on flesh once more. It was all illusion. *Arawn* stood face-to-face with Lorshin. His eyes were no longer black and soulless but radiant beams of blue light caught in the eerie glow of the moon.

Lorshin's desire to run faded in the presence of his *father*. New desire emerged unbidden from the intentions of his heart. He raised the Gemshorn till the curved instrument was level with the eyes of both. He spoke with his mind. *Father, teach me the secret of the Gemshorn.*

The illusion studied him. It was so complete that the memories of Arawn's life—all the way from the beginning—filtered through its mind. *Arawn* knew his own descent into madness. He knew of lost love, dying hope and unending pain. He knew Lorshin, his sin, his sorrow, his despair, and his curse. He knew the grief of losing mother and father to the beast. He knew the raging hunger and the feverish lust that came with it. He knew the shame of having innocent blood on his hands. He even knew the sacrifice of surrender and the lingering thread of Light that constantly fought to remain in Lorshin's soul yet found its strength in his twin, Isentara.

Darkness growled lowly. The time was rapidly approaching when Isentara must either die or pass into the dark. Her influence and bond with Lorshin could not be allowed to continue. It was too dangerous but Lorshin, the willing vessel, must never know. Shades of Reality arise!

At last the illusion spoke. "You know the Prophecy."

"I do," Lorshin said

Darkness waited, enduring the recitation of the Prophecy. There would be no hope. Finally, the illusion spoke pleasantly. "Then in time, my son, I will tell you the Gemshorn's secret. When you are truly the master of it."

"Father, I—"

Arawn raised a hand to silence his son. "Lorshin, first you must be strong. You must feed."

Out of the black an offering came. "Take them. All of them!"

Lorshin's eyes widened in horror as he recognized the prey. *Hempress, Queen of the Centaur, Dubber, King of Giants, Eek-ash and Uleya, the Suzerainty of the Kot, General Ickluck Lorndop the Dwarf Leader, Hakan Supreme Blood and Ethany Long Breath of the mysterious Faedran*...on and on they came—the noble enemies of the Dark One—from every race who stood for the Light! He saw it in their eyes—the great wilderness spreading out raw and terrible before them all, yet they couldn't *feel* what he knew they should. All will, all strength, all *feeling* had been drained away by the Gemshorn's song and they stood empty, exposed and numb before the overwhelming tide of **Darkness**, awaiting their end. He could see that in their eyes too and he cried out on their behalf. The Gemshorn fell heavily to the ground yet its weight did not leave him. His hands flew to the sides of his head as he screamed—trying to silence the whispers of the Dark One—trying to control the hunger stirring in his gut as his nostrils filled with the alluring fingerprint of Flame hidden deep within their flesh.

The Samhail wailed with him, mad with their hunger.

"Take them. All of them!" the illusion commanded.

"Please," Hempress said quietly holding out her hands to Lorshin, begging him to end her life.

"No." He screamed.

The Centaur queen moved majestically forward. "Please," she said again.

Lorshin backed away, running into a wall of black. "Stop!" he shrieked. "You don't know what you're saying!"

His words may as well have fallen on deaf ears. Hempress didn't stop; she didn't snap out of the Gemshorn's grip though Zrene had fallen and the weapon lay silent at his feet; she didn't *feel* the fear! And quite suddenly, neither did he. With a cry of insane need, he fell upon her. Legions of Samhail broke out of the black upon the mindless leaders of the Resistance and their frantic armies.

Where illusion walked, chaos ruled as the Dark One watched the Empire of Light come crashing to its knees and the void breach the confines of its ancient prison, flowing out in tides of black breath, dragging the Colorless in its wake.

Darkness.

* * *

Bynthroenine:

In an instant the tortured silence of the Guardians was shattered. The Guardians of the Portals—each the unique fingerprint of a doorway to the outside world—crumbled to their knees before Esarian's eyes, wailing eerily their milky-white heads jerking lower than their sagging shoulders. More Guardians swooped down from the mountain peaks and knocked their tormented comrades away from the portal's scarred remains.

"What is it?" Esarian shouted. "What's happening?"

"Firebrand."

Esarian whirled to the sound that flowed with quiet power straight into his heart silencing the panic. Even the air seemed lighter and yet full of unseen power, more power than had been there just moments before. His ears filled with the rush of wings. He looked up into eyes of blue flame, shining mysteriously out of a cool, glowing, white mist that descended rapidly from the highest peak of the Shining Mountain.

A spasm of hope seized his heart as he watched the glow become stronger and more defined. The ghostly silhouette of nine trees broke into view and out of that glittering haze a figure emerged, hooded and cloaked in a midnight robe that left only those eyes of blue flame visible. Time had not hardened Esarian to the glory of the supernatural and he hoped it never would. His hand stretched out toward the vision.

The Guardian spoke as he wove sinuously from the mist, out through the hosts of his kind. "They are bound to the portal, my friend. They suffer its hurts." Light shone brighter as the Guardian pulled the hood of his cloak back to reveal his short cropped, slightly spiked buckskin hair and that ageless, perfect and impossibly human face. On either side of his neck he bore the images of the Guardian Moon. On one side was the waning crescent moon and on the other was the waxing crescent moon—one a symbol of agony, the other a symbol of hope, both symbols of the Prophecy. As he spoke, eight more Guardians, hooded and cloaked emerged behind him. It was not often that all nine Guardians of the Prophecy came down off the mountain. These were not like other Guardians. They were wilder, fiercer and seemed far less human than others of their kind even in the veil of humanity.

Spoken of only in whispers, even in Bynthroenine, they were only slightly more frequently seen than the Chosen One. They communed always with Sanctus upon the Shining Mountain, it was said, who had tied them to each other, to the Prophecy and to its mysteries in ways only Sanctus could comprehend, yet all knew and revered them, giving way before them like a receding tide. Through the pathways of their emergence, the Guardians of the Portals were carried back into the heart of Bynthroenine's Light where the tormented wails diminished into shallow moans.

Ylochllion moved past Esarian. His sharp eyes appraised the scar. "This should have healed," he said softly. His face revealed nothing, yet his eyes smoldered with some unrest. He glanced back over his shoulder. "Tlachtga."

His mate glided forward, shedding her midnight robe. Egrontallas, a Colorless in human form, clung to her hip. Though younger than those who had gone through the portals, his eyes carried knowledge of Time before himself.

Ylochllion smiled at her and their seed, his eyes full of adoration as they passed him.

All waited in a tense silence as Tlachtga raised her hand, covered in runes, to the milky scar on the otherwise perfect border of Bynthroenine. A breath hitched in her throat as the runes began to glow. Her eyes fluttered closed.

"What do you see?" Esarian whispered. He looked around at the Guardians of Prophecy who had now encircled him. The crescents on their throats glowed as the runes on Tlachtga glowed. He measured their silence with the beats of this own heart, *Thud. Thud-thud. Thud. Thud-thud. Thud. Thud-thud. Thud*, wondering if they were counting them too. Blood dripped from their eyes, falling with power to the earth. "What is become of your young ones?"

"*Darkness*." Tlachtga whispered. "Powerful, binding *Darkness*."

"The *Darkness* of souls," Ylochllion said as he draped himself protectively over his mate and their son. "So the time has come at last."

Esarian felt the weight of those ominous words deep within the brands on his forehead though he did not understand them, though he could not *see* what these Keepers of the Prophecy saw, deep in his being he knew that everything was about to change. From the protective circle of his parents' arms, Egrontallas looked at him and smiled.

Chapter Fifty

DARKNESS OF SOULS

D rip. Drip. Drip. The sound of blood falling off his hands onto the stony earth punctuated the silence calling Lorshin, Prince of the Samhail forth from the depths of insanity. Hunger and madness momentarily sated with Flame, he gradually reclaimed his senses. His first, clearest thought was of the stillness and he couldn't remember how he had come to this moment. A body fell from his hands a second before his conscious mind registered its lifeless weight; of what Race the victim had been was now indiscernible in the mangled mass of entrails and broken bones. Revulsion instantly overtook him. The body hit the ground with an ominous thud. His heartbeat pounded in his head—a painful pulsing of shameful pleasure, satisfaction and inescapable guilt. His fangs ached for more of the Flame but the dripping of blood haunted his mind. He cried out, desperately trying to shake the blood off his hands. These crimson hands were his, he knew that as he gazed at their long, lean lines yet his mind rebelled against the crimes he knew he must have committed. He was a demon who lived among Men and passed as human but in the *dark* he was the thing that made them hide in their houses till the Sun returned, and even then they were not safe. Not anymore because even the Light was growing *Dark*. He allowed his senses to cautiously probe the surrounding territory before he permitted himself to draw a breath. He could not allow himself to lose control again! At first he heard only the pounding of his own heart and the dripping of blood; he saw riven flesh left to rot, and he felt the relentless torture of Time.

Time went on and on, tearing its victims apart piece by piece till the pain was so severe its victim just wanted it to stop for one tiny moment of blessed relief. He snickered bitterly to himself. Humans had a saying, "Time heals all wounds," but what did they know of Time? They didn't know what it was to be immortal. Death was coming for them as she had come for these pitiful remnants of beings arrayed in a wide bed of carnage before him. Truth be told, he envied them. An end or just the possibility of one was all he wanted! He knew the irony of these thoughts. He had once feared an end of this immortality and the Sun that could bring it. What he feared now was losing himself into the nearly ever-present *Darkness* and always finding blood on his hands.

His gaze fixed upon the amorphous collection of black matter as it slowly gathered into the vague shape of a man.

No illusion tricked his eyes this time. "Sgarrwrath." Lorshin whispered, hating the name, hating its bearer, hating himself as he breathed it.

The essence of the *Darkness* was known by actions, and reactions, the effects caused by his power and his being. The Dark One extended an unstructured hand. His voice slipped fluidly into Lorshin's mind layered beneath the familiar sound of *Arawn's* voice.

Lorshin whimpered as his *father's* voice filled every synapse in his brain.

Do not be afraid, my son. I am here. You have done well. You are strong. You will be strong. Truly a weapon more worthy. Come.

He raised his hands. Blood glimmered upon them still, refusing to be cleansed. "What have I done?" He screamed at the *Darkness*. "What did you make me do?" His mind was clouded with blackness so that no single coherent memory explained the carnage before him and within him, yet he could not escape it! The tiny thread of Flame within him would not lie to his sight! Lorshin screamed, clawing at his eyes, gouging deep into their fragile beds, wanting to rip them out as his body rocked forward onto the earth. Death's hands ran lovingly down his spine while the earth muffled his gut-wrenching sobs. In that instant, when he longed only for the silence of oblivion, he heard the sound of brooding forces warring against one another. Light and *Darkness* thundered in defiance against each other. The very elements were rent with their violence. Rain fell in driving nails yet the blood refused to wash away and the whispers of *Darkness* grew louder.

Lorshin. Come.

No!" Lorshin screamed. "Leave me be!"

Lorshin.

"Get out of my head!"

Instantly, stillness erupted with throes of fury.

No wind stirred the trees around them. They thrashed of their own freewill; their wild rustling screams filled the bloodied plain, yet as Lorshin crouched in their circled passion he sensed that their screams did not touch the pain that was within them. At the same time, he knew he could never outrun them all. If they chose to strike, he would let them! He deserved no less than to be crushed beneath their roots and fed upon for all eternity, but even as they screamed, they towered over him, slowly growing too still. Their roots delved into the earth deeper than they ever had before and at last they were silent.

Darkness sighed, an unpleasant sound in the intense silence.

*　　*　　*

Solais, Kingdom of the Faedran:

The *Darkness* was too great; its infection too pervasive and Hope possessed the fragility of a mere word. It would be so easy to give in to despair yet Kateirah would not. She could not! She had already embraced hope—its promise, its cure. She had embraced its agony.

The agony came upon the roots of trees. Their deep screams sliding down through long columned throats echoed with despair in the pathways of old. More screams followed.

Kateirah Forever Sorrow launched off her throne and ran through the shining paths. The frayed train of her blood-red gown flew out behind her. Her bare brown feet hit the ground as lightly as a breath of air floating over the surface of a tranquil pool and the skittering ripples they caused were scarcely visible to the naked eye. Her black hair hung in course frazzles, a neglected beauty in a maze of neglected beauty. Behind her marched the Sorrow Band, Faedran warriors, willing to sacrifice themselves to the last for the survival of the Light ways.

Even now the *Darkness* was pressing, snapping the foundation of all the universe apart inch by inch. The sheer nakedness of the encroaching void loomed before her violet eyes. Fear's icy hand crept the length of her spine. She shuddered as that blackness dripped from the delving roots down the lighted fastness of Solais, resounding into her very soul as the trees tried to nourish themselves. She skidded to a halt as the kingdom shivered.

"They will be the death of us!" Faedran were gathering, screaming.

Kateirah shook her head. "This is no time to think of ourselves! They are just trying to survive! So are we!" She cried as she drew her sword.

The warriors broke around her, running into battle with wild, barbaric screams. Having blinded themselves in order to withstand the illusions of the *Dark*, they saw only through the symbiotic union of the little dragons living within—creatures born of Guardian blood, and breath, and sorrow—creatures who saw no lies and felt no fear! They charged madly ahead, like lightning bolts streaking through the gloom of a gathering storm. Brief sparks of light that scattered the blackness into more defined illusion—at least to her eyes. Kateirah was not blind. She did not see with internal eyes that could not lie or fear though she felt them within her giving her the boldness to raise the blade in her hand. She saw with natural eyes as the blackness spread its spidery legs and the first of its illusions cast its great shadow over her. Her people scattered behind the warriors and their queen.

Kateirah held her sword high as the beastly illusion reared back spitting poisonous black goop toward her face. The blade took the force of the blow, dissolving to its hilt in her hands. The metal and goop dripped together over her hands burning her flesh. Her screams echoed through Solais as she dove for cover. The illusion reared again. Its red eye catching her movement and another stream of goop narrowly missed her. The Sorrow Band flashed into its line, shielding her at the last second with their bodies. Her life was too precious. If she died, all three thrones of Solais would stand empty.

Their flesh was dissolving. Blood and black goop gushed through its cracks. Smoke rose where the wounds burned.

"Fall back!" Kateirah screamed, leaving a trail of blood and goop as she crawled to her feet. "Live to fight! It is too strong!"

"Do not trust your eyes! What you see is not real, my lady!" One of the band shouted. The Sorrow band pushed ahead. They let their swords drop from their hands as they pressed in a great circle upon the illusion.

The heels of their empty hands pressed to the pale dagger blade scars over their hearts. "From Sorrow risen when the Old Ways fell." They screamed. A light opened out of them onto their palms.

"What are you doing?" Kateirah screamed.

The Sorrow Band charged.

The Illusion shrieked, rearing violently.

"Run, my lady, and remember do not trust your eyes! It is the heart that matters! Look for Hope. Serve *Him*. Die for *Him* as we die for you!" The Sorrow Band said as one as they flew toward their prey with one final cry of miserable glory. *"No beginning. No ending. Hope is One long promised whose heart is one and lives are two."* Words she remembered well.

Kateirah ran as the Light way began to shake, tearing itself apart on top of its prey.

Darkness.

* * *

Bynthroenine:

Master Esarian, the Firebrand, gazed mutely at his powerful allies. Guardians proven and Colorless alike raised their majestic heads and wailed. A sound so haunting, so powerful, terrifying and compelling that he remained frozen where he stood for unfathomable hours, just listening, transfixed by the intricate melody of inhuman voices. So many subtle changes were lost to his human ears but he heard enough to sense the shifting of power within their song as they embraced with sorrow and longing the change that gripped his heart with fear. He couldn't stop the tears that welled in his eyes as he listened. "What does this mean?" He whispered.

Ylochllion motioned to his friend with a pale hand. "Come." His midnight robe brushed softly upon the ground as he led the way. "There is something you should see."

Esarian followed him in silence to the pinnacle of the Shining Mountain.

More Guardians came, hooded and cloaked in their midnight robes, silhouettes against the glory of the Light. Their blue flaming eyes burned with the Light, shining out beneath their hoods with subtle power. Beneath the flame of their eyes what was hidden just moments before emerged through an apparent fracture of root and brilliance that was nothing more than a trick of the unified Light. The Guardians spoke softly, reverently. Their hushed, yet powerful voices flowed as one upon the Light. "Let the Light shine forth and awaken hope. Let Mhorag arise. Let the Promised come."

The words of prophecy burned with Flame before their sight, a reminder of the Source they all served, felt distantly even in the most fragile and insignificant of all living things under their protection, searing in the power beating from their own hearts. Unbound by time, this ineradicable core of existence had long been beheld as if through a darkened glass—a whisper of Hope, a word, a dream, a hidden promise. The prophecy had thrust the Source into the realm of an incurable need, but in the silence and *Darkness* this need dissolved into pain. In the outside world, some surrendered into bitterness, some clung desperately to unseen hope, yet the Flame still burned . . . beckoning, calling to a universe that had all but forgotten the Source for the oblivion and unfeeling destruction of The One Whose Name is not Spoken. Blind to the offering of life.

Esarian gasped, clutching at the shard of the Styarfyre orb hanging around his neck as he looked closer. The Prophecy was interrupted, distorted by strange markings he had never seen before!

Behold the signs here set forth by which all shall know the meaning of the two faces of the Guardian Moon, but lest despair take hold upon your souls here are foretold They whom our hope shall restore.

In the beginning, Sanctus brought forth from the void of His creation Nine grains of power, hence planted in the Light and the Stone of Existence plucked from His crown to give unbelievable might.

Father and Mother set on high, the diadems of Day and Night. Grains of Power there remain, but sacred stone concealed away. No Guardian shall harness their hidden might till Bynthroenine again has a king. Before that time is come, the mighty Guardians shall cling in unity to the Chosen One from a Colorless sprung.

The heavens will bleed. The Chosen One veiled in weakness shall be taken when the Heart of Evil is revealed. *Darkness* secretes through all that lies within its reach. Song of Guardians, fire and blood, Dark gift of power, Shadow and *Darkness* now combined seek power of a greater kind. A curse upon the Forbidden Kiss and the bestower's race.

The greed of Men will cause alliances to end. Sea of Sorrows, the portals shall be sealed. From ancient gift by Guardians given, song of haunting beauty takes flight, giving Evil might. The day of its creation shall be cursed when the secret of the Gemshorn is unleashed on the earth.

Darkness.
"I cannot see beyond it." Tlachtga said.
"How can that be?" Esarian demanded. "You are a Guardian of Prophecy."
"The Dark One's strength is increasing." Ylochllion answered for her. "He feeds upon the *Darkness* of souls. Every heart that falls increases his might. She cannot see because not all choices have been made. We are not omniscient, Firebrand, and as you can see," he said with subtle authority, "we are all trapped here."
Esarian shook his head trying to clear it. His eyes refused to focus as the strange markings gleamed with white fire, dancing with *Darkness*, upon Time itself! "What is it?" He cried, his horror leaking out.
"We do not know." Ylochllion said softly. "It has always been there, but we cannot read it. The markings were distant, but now they grow stronger day by day as the *Darkness* grows stronger."

408

Esarian frowned. The Guardians of Prophecy were as frightened as he yet they hid it well. As Firebrand, perhaps he could distinguish some meaning here. He stepped hesitantly forward. It hurt his eyes to focus on the markings and let all else fade. Silence hung tensely among the gathering for a long moment as Esarian struggled to focus. At last, he broke away with a cry of pain. "I cannot see past the *Darkness*."

Ylochllion nodded with understanding. "No one has ever been able to. Not even we, the Guardians of the Prophecy nor Azolat, the One to whom the Prophecy was first given. But as you can see, though the prophecy is distorted and interrupted it still stands."

Crowned Head among the race of Men, who does not know his worth, within resides the hidden power that mortals ne'er possess. A battle rages for your unproven soul. Bitter, sorrowful and in touch with Death, you must reach the end, where dwells the One naught of Human kind hath seen and bring Hope to the races once again. In the Guardian's seed no weakness shall prevail, but heed your mortal father's fate; traitors lie within your gate. This test you must endure in the frailty of Human form, but when it is past your crown will last; and you will be weak no more.

Great Guardians of this beware, danger lurks beyond your lair and will seek to bring great harm. A journey into stone awaits this One held dearest to your hearts. It shall be when *Darkness* covers all the earth, but do not fear for Mhorag shall appear and silence the Gemshorn with his mighty roar.

A babe rests unknown in the womb of stone. Mhorag's seed none shall behold till the stronghold of Death is shattered from above. The One and her sleeping Guardians at once awake. Throughout all distance, the Guardian voices shall be raised in answer to Mhorag's call, and all shall fear the Guardians might. Summoning stones shall be reforged as all creation for the Guardians call.

The catalyst of war must be reclaimed the Evil Heart to break. Grains of Power will revive to test the purity of all hearts once more, for soon Mhorag's armies shall converge behind the Nine; but take this warning, Heed only the sign of the Guardian Moon set in the flesh by Sanctus formed, for *Darkness* is closing in on you.

Nine thrones of Light and Gold, Mhorag's seed and the Circle of Power that you need to find the Treasure of *Darkness* born.

He of black and tortured soul calls forth the wraiths by *Darkness* sown, and when through Mhorag's fire he safely passes, Two Faces of the Moon unite. Then by the Stone of Existence unleash the power to bring *Darkness* into subjection to the Light, and seal it by the might of Nine.

Chapter Fifty-One

CIRCLE OF AGONY

In the Dark:

A pale polydactyl paw, visible only for the blue, heart Flame that blazed in contrast through the Colorless' body, breached the surface of the *Darkness*. The thrumming of the burning organ in the young one's chest beat faster, shining more fiercely, as he raised his small finely scaled head. His eyes slid open lazily, a crack of bluish Light leaked through the slits as he battled the heavy lids that kept trying to close. *Darkness* hung in great living cords, which stuck to him like mire refusing to be shaken off. His paw weakly parted the black breath only to have it spring back against his body. With a grimace, he collapsed to the earth. A whoosh of breath faintly illuminated the space just in front of his face. Eyes of blue Flame gazed nervously back at him. "Valon," he breathed.

"Aceldune." Valon whispered back as the *Darkness* flowed thickly in between them.

The Dark One's laughter drowned out their voices filling and echoing through the abyss but it did not enter their minds. Their hearts pounded harder, faster, saturating their Colorless bodies with impenetrable Flame.

Valon, Aceldune whispered to his friend's mind. *Where are we?*

"I don't know." Valon answered softly. "The *dark*—"

"Shh." Aceldune warned. His eyes flashed through heavy slits to measure the *dark*. Faint footsteps echoed around them. Light of Flame and breath and eye combined could not penetrate that abysm for more than a few feet. "Show yourself, villain."

The Dark One laughed. "Not enough power resides within your reach yet, my friend, to force me to obey."

"Friend? I am no friend of yours." Aceldune snarled.

"Nor am I." Valon said, rising slightly against his bonds.

"Not yet but perhaps one day soon."

"Never!" Aceldune and Valon screamed. Their noble voices reverberated trapped in the *dark*. The sound served only to map their prison, whirling in a wide circle as their cry bounced from monoliths of solid stone somewhere just beyond sight. The Colorless could *see* the stone circle in their minds: massive rocks tattooed with entrails of focused power gutted the desolate plain protruding up through the black prison fashioned from these fractured bones of the earth. The stones bled white with their horror and grief at being forced to stand against the seed of Guardians, and the earth between sagged in upon itself in despair. Upon this tortured bed, chained by *Darkness*, Aceldune and Valon lay. Their talons curled into the soil bracing them against the sudden onslaught of nature's wails answering their own. For one brief moment the Mother of Guardians breached the unnatural *dark* with her waning blood-red face. Her light went nowhere except to ignite the roiling black that suddenly thundered with thousands of heartbeats. Seven more pairs of blue Flame eyes opened within the circle to capture the last moments of the Mother's face before *Darkness* swallowed her into its depths.

The One whose Name is not Spoken stepped by illusion into view. "You nine have been chosen."

Nine? Aceldune whispered to Valon's mind. *But there are ten stones? I am chained to one. You to another . . .* his thoughts trailed off uncertainly.

"You will be my experiment. I can sense your highborn rank and parentage. If I can break you I can break the others."

"You know nothing!" Valon exclaimed.

"I know you are a son of Azolat, twin brother of Arawn whose heart still beats here in my *dark*, both being sons of Urgilis by direct descent."

Valon gazed at the Dark One, openmouthed, and mute with horror.

The One whose Name is not Spoken smiled menacingly. "And you," he said turning to Aceldune, "are even more highly born: the youngest of all Firstborns, still a speck in Casara's womb when the Scarrow's storm came and Casara and Urgilis were set on high to light the earth; I know you were framed and developed these years in Sanctus' kingdom; and have now returned as ageless and new as the day of your birth in preparation for the Promised King's appearance having known only the perfection of the Kingdom and the secret realm. Shall I go on?"

Aceldune cried out in agony as the bound up corruption brushed over him when the Dark One turned to stroll the borders of the stone circle. "How could you know such things?"

Darkness sighed amongst the stones. Thud. Thud. Thud. The Heart of Evil beat its ominous answer from some black corner and the Dark One continued on oblivious to the other six Colorless thronging together against the pull of their chains.

Closing ranks helped the Colorless breathe easier. Aceldune took stock of his companions. *Nine?* He thought. *But ten stones?* He looked around their tight circle. *All of us chosen for our highborn rank and parentage.* One by one he considered them. *Valon, third son of the Guardian Azolat, third son of the Mother and Father; Fembra, daughter and firstborn of the Guardian Celacmar, firstborn of Fyrdung, second of the Mother and Father; Xillion and Xaxell, twin sons, firstborn of Scrymgeour and Eithne Guardians of the Prophecy, firstborn in their own right he from Daracha, the first daughter of the Mother and Father; Bendaradon, third son of Daracha, the first daughter of the Mother and Father; Tarphajan, Klacuffa, and Naralyne, son and daughters, firstborns of Sesstarra, third daughter of the Mother and Father; and himself—Aceldune, Kingdomborn, last son of the Mother and Father born out of Time by Sanctus' will for such a time as this.* He shook his head slowly. *Nine of us. But ten stones?* His troubled thoughts leaked into the minds of his companions.

"There should have been a tenth." The Dark One brooded paying the entangled and perplexed Colorless no heed. "But she is a tricky one . . ."

Why us? Naralyne asked.

Aceldune breathed into their linked minds. *I am not sure. In reality, our blood is no stronger; we are no less vulnerable to the Dark than any other Colorless—*

But we are the seed of firstborns, all of us have at least one parent in direct line of descent from the Mother and Father; all have a parent or sibling directly linked to the Prophecy, or who protect the spaces between this realm and the Source. Valon whispered catching on.

The Colorless gazed at the Dark One.

He fears us because of the Prophecy. He fears who we might be and what events our testing might precede. Tarphajan said.

He wants us because he thinks it will disrupt the Prophecy. Klacuffa agreed.

And he may just be right. Fembra said. *We are not invincible.*

Xillion snorted. *Let him just try to claim us!*

Xaxell grinned and pounded paws with his twin in mid-air. *We can give him a fight worth having!*

He doesn't mean to fight fair, Xaxell. Bendaradon said nervously.

The Dark One stalked further around the circle. His black breath flew as he fumed. "She hid herself in the *deepest foundation!* Curse her!

But I have trapped her there and soon I will find the way to take her back. I am Sgarrwrath and there will be no hope!"

In the pitch black, Aceldune broke the silence of their connected thoughts. *Who is the tenth and why does he want her so vehemently?* But silence was the only answer.

* * *

In the Heart of the Earth:

Earth may as well have been iron. Sian Seela gazed around her lonely prison: earthen walls yet they stood resolutely against her. Deep furrows disfigured their faces, stained by her blood where talons broke from use as she fought to escape this entombment, and flesh cracked open where the scales of her paws had violently torn away. The earth could not have held her longer than she wished to be held; she could sense how the earth despised the power holding it in place. No, this was the Dark One's doing. He was stronger! Stronger than her breath for she could not yet breathe the Flame, stronger than her unproven blood; stronger than her talons that could crush bones and pierce Guardian scales but could not penetrate this wall of wet dirt! Dank, stale air filled her nostrils again and again with each hard breath. A cloud of heat stifled those breaths before they could fully satisfy her parched lungs. Her little burning heart seared faster in her heaving chest as the dark pressed in around her.

She could hear it clawing through the layers of soil, slowly, laboriously—hungering for her *life*. Earthworms dropped in upon her in disordered clumps to escape this dark power. She whimpered softly as she hobbled forward to touch the earthen wall. Her broken leg dragged awkwardly behind her. Her broken wing lay limply at her side. Her colorless paw pressed hard against the wall. "You will not have me so easily!" She said softly.

With a talon, she carved three crescents into the baked earth: two back to back forming an "X" shape with one curling overhead. *Protection.* They came to life with a silvery glow. The power of the Guardians extended out, spreading around her in all four directions. As long as it held only someone very special or very powerful could pass beyond them. For the moment, she was safe. The Dark One could not have her yet. He could not touch her. Not without the Stone of Existence twisted to his purpose or Guardian power faltered.

She whimpered softly again, lowering herself onto the earth and laying her head between her paws. The only light came from her flaming eyes fixed with sadness upon the ancient Guardian rune. Her sweet voice rose from deep within the heart of the earth to sing the song of her people beneath what was left of the Guardian Moon.

"Ageless Mother, shine down on us. Guide through Darkness till the Light of hope is reclaimed. Great Ones bleed while fires burn. Each crescent bares a tale that must end. Remember the blood from which you came."

LettheLightshineforthandawakenHope.LetMhoragarise.Letthe Promised come.

Chapter Fifty-Two

DESPAIR

Loriath, Kingdom of the Elves of Light

LettheLightshineforthandawakenhope.LetMhoragarise.Letthe Promised come.

Light flashed white and painful behind Cadclucan's eyes. Its whisper filled his ears as the pain filled his head and crept down his spine, radiating through his body. He lifted the Stone of Existence from around his neck with a grimace; without its weight pulling at his shoulders, his pain lessened but did not dissipate entirely. A thorn remained buried in his chest. He didn't feel whole without the stone, yet to bear it was an excruciation beyond comprehension. His fingers were slow to release it; their tips lingered upon the stone's smooth face, extending their departure. Swallowing the lump in his throat, Cadclucan clenched his hand closed, pulling away after a horrible moment of uncertainty, finally letting his hand fall, still in a fist, to his side. The stone lay there, a lifeless symbol of all that was good, right, and could be, and all that was at this moment so far away.

"It hurts you." Maizie's voice shattered the silence.

Cadclucan flinched at the sound of her voice. Memory of the future twined in the back of his mind. Her fateful words had started that vision, and now they too were set in stone. He turned, amazed he had not sensed her approach before now. A held breath escaped his lips. "No," he breathed. "It does not hurt me. At least not in the way you think. The stone longs for its true master, the One beyond Time to come into Time. You cannot know the weight of such a desire." His voice was low and soft as if he spoke of secrets, which Maizie supposed was exactly the case.

She held out her hand toward him. "Baculus?" she hesitated. "What is coming is—"

Cadclucan pulled her close, silencing her with a kiss.

Every thought scattered from her mind except for the one that exalted in his caresses.

His action had been an impulsive one. The longer he touched her, the more hesitant he became till his lips hovered over hers, so close she could feel their warmth, so far she could see the grimace of agony twisting them.

Maizie's heart throbbed in rapture in her chest. She looked up into his eternal eyes and watched as a crimson hue leaked through the Flame.

Abruptly, he stepped away, turning his face from her; his blood answered the *Darkness* whispering in the distance, yet she imagined this offering was given in exchange for her blood. *If the price of freedom was blood . . .*

Then I would surely pay it, the Guardian whispered. His thoughts invaded her own.

Maizie was not surprised to find once again that he knew her thoughts. Dare she hope for more? *If love*, her mind formed the word with timidity, *bled . . .*

Cadclucan turned toward her, his eyes softening in response to the timid and hopeful gaze of her shy eyes. He could not deny her this, whatever their future might be. *It would surely be for the other half of itself.* His words came into her like a caress. Maizie walked forward into his arms. "But Guardian blood is not the cure," he whispered as she wiped the blood from his eyes. "And love cannot hold back this *Darkness*."

"But can love endure it?" Maizie lowered her head. "Baculus, will ours survive the course laid before us now?"

Cadclucan did not answer. He couldn't. Maizie pressed her face to his chest, breathing in the scent of him and the Light within. In his arms, it was easy to have hope, though a fresh wash of blood came from his eyes as he gazed into the black of the future. His arms tightened around her. *Darkness* filled every sight; its black breath clogged every sound, burying every hope in its abyss, but out of that emptiness loomed a vacant throne. Images of the future flew rapidly through his mind; not all came into focus, yet those that did made his blood run cold.

Darknessdrapedtheland.Silentshadowssweptacrosstheworld.All life drew back from them as they passed.

"No!" a young mother screamed. Sweat dripped down her face. In the light of a fire, the shadows stood erect like men.

"Not my baby!" the mother screamed as these shadows yanked a still bloody newborn from her arms.

Cadclucan closed his eyes against the vision, but it did not prevent him from seeing.

Massive bonfires encircled the summit of a great hill. Erect shadows danced between these fires while the infant's screams filled the dark. A jagged knife glowed in the light of the flames, and so too did the perfect mark upon the newborn's face—the Mark of the Promised whole and untainted. The orange flames leaped higher, hungry for the baby's life.

The infant's screams continued; more screams joined with them as Time rushed with its secrets before Cadclucan's eyes, leaving a trail of ash and bone mounting up around the throne in the blackness that buried the Prophecy in horrors untold.

A storm was gathering all around him and at its eye was the cry of innocent blood rising from the heart of the earth. This blood was yet unshed, but the time of its shedding was rapidly approaching. The earth was shaken apart by the black breath, and a fathomless Darkness opened before his eyes. Mountains fell and new rose in their place. These new mountains were black, binding all the universe to the One Whose Name is not Spoken, framed from the carcasses of the dead of every race and all manner of living things. Screaming trees were swallowed in the blackness. Water stopped flowing. The seas dried, and all that lived within lay suffocating beneath the boiling sun.

Father, Cadclucan thought as he gazed upon the sun. It ruptured into a thousand flaming balls before falling into **Darkness.**

Mother, he nearly cried out as the moon turned to blood and poured into nothingness.

"Can we survive it?" Maizie asked again as the Guardian drew in a ragged breath.

"Life passes to life," he said quietly. "Hope rekindles, but the Dark One will never stop." He pulled away from her. What he had seen and the burden he carried remained in his knowledge alone and pulled him further from her side out into the night without a backward glance.

The moon hung low upon the heavens, slowly waning toward darkness and darkness toward a new *darker* dawn.

*   *   *

Red stained the black horizon—the first warning sign of a new day. Lorshin could feel the Sun's approach in every nerve ending. Their uncomfortable twinging would intensify into excruciating pain in the final hour before dawn, and then he would burn. He deserved to burn. No, more than that he *wanted* to burn so great was his shame as he watched the ground rot around him. He had been a fool to think that Sithbhan had ever been his opponent. His lover was a mere pawn in a game started centuries before. He knew now that to battle a beast, he would have to become one, yet that part of him that still longed for Light rebelled. His actions had only sunk him further into the black mire of choice. Isentara was safe for now, but not his people. Nor himself. So, did he gamble the last of his sanity and his soul or did he give himself to the Sun that would purify him with fire?

All around him the trees roiled and moaned. The rustling of leaves and creaking of branches sounded like a storm but the air beneath remained still. He reached out to touch the nearest tree only to recoil from the palpable suffering, which was rising out of the earth. Never had he felt such madness. Not even his own!

A sob rasped from his chest in response to the anguish. He was on his feet and running before he could draw another breath. Come Sun, come *Darkness*, come Hope—an end was all he desired now!

Epilogue

THE SEASONS

Loriath, Kingdom of the Elves of Light

Though the Sun hung low, the Moon lingered in his sight. Cadclucan stood alone on the highest of the golden bridges wrapping between the oldest of the giant redwoods. For once the Elves left him in solitude, sensing his need to be alone. The sounds of their singing and dancing in halls of artificial light reached his ears even at this height, yet he was unmoved by their merriment. His flaming gaze divided between *Darkness* and Light, fixing upon the thin sliver of the Moon's waning crescent. By Night's reemergence tomorrow, the Moon's face would be hidden and soon enough all would come to know the meaning of the two faces of the Guardian Moon. He sang the ancient song, his deep voice resounding through Loriath—ancient and powerful—full of secrets.

"Ageless Mother, shine down on us. Guide through *Darkness* till the Light of hope is reclaimed. Great Ones, bleed while fires burn. Each crescent bears a tale that must end. Remember the blood from which you came." His voice rose with wordless melody.

Loriath fell silent as they listened.

"What is the Great One doing?" their little ones asked.

"Remembering," the elders answered. "The deeds of the past must never be spoken where enemies may hear."

Guardian voices bathed in Light flowed to surround Cadclucan, whispering around the Stone of Existence. He bowed his head and sang, the words and melody coming from deep inside him. "In the still of the night, great warriors arise! Chains must be broken, hope restored— carved into stone, sealed with ancient blood. Never bow beneath the tormentor's claw, 'til stars fall to leave a naked sky. Remember and be free. Dreams gilded with heroes blood. Ancient beacon of starlight calls. Clouded hope forged the past. Fated choice has sealed its ending— crushed beneath another's curse! Blood cries from the earth. Fight! Fight! 'Til our souls rest beyond the Sun, Flame returned unto Flame!"

In the back of his mind, he remembered. He remembered a past, and he remembered a future.

"To every season, there is an added sorrow. Consider the beautiful flowers of spring that wither in the heat of the summer sun, the trees that bring forth bud only to have those garments fall and rot upon the ground, the ground that freezes in winter, locking up its bounty, but to every sorrow, there is a purpose. There is always the promise. There is always Hope." His own words echoed back to him.

His voice continued to rise wordlessly, shattering the long Guardian silence with memory as old as Time—memory etched within the Flame by its Source. *Light flowed to him from the far reaches of the earth. Darkness watched and waited. Between the two gathering storms, a boy with eyes of amber Flame arose. The universe spun rapidly around him, mimicking the swirl of the golden blood shining unnaturally in his flesh. This boy walked into the blackness, shining brighter than the Sun ever had—casting the blackness into burning shadows. Flame crackled all around him, inside him, burning out through his eyes.*

Light built around him, seething out of once sealed portals into a world driven mad by need. Cadclucan sighed, "Mhorag, arise."

The boy with the golden blood looked Cadclucan squarely in the eyes, the world turning beneath his feet, the seasons slowly decaying as Darkness triumphed over Light.

The boy smiled, and Light burst around him as never was seen before.

Cadclucan raised his hand toward the sight while the vision endured; memory seeped through his veins, and a future beckoned. He gazed in silence, with tears in his eyes, at this vision of this glorious being. His heart soared in exaltation at the presence, until a brooding black film stained the horizon. In the next instant, sadness came out from the child to stroke his soul.

The boy sighed and slowly turned away. As he turned, closing his bright eyes, a piece of Sun broke away and fell to the earth. Possibility and reality meeting at last.

Darkness.

Acknowledgments

A special thanks to the One who taught my hands to write. Not every artistic person has the unwavering support of their family when it comes to their craft, so I must begin with four very special people. Mom: Thank you for hugs, unusual names, editing, for encouraging me to keep going when I would have given up, and for just being there. Dad: Thank you for giving me pushes in the right direction even when I resist them. This series is in memory of my brother, Isaac, without whom Sgarrwrath may never have found his voice. To the best nephew a girl could have, Riley, I love you. Thanks for the free promotion, representation and abundant inspiration.

Thank you to my furry writing companions: Smokey "Shakespeare" Kennedy and his assistant Misty Kennedy for: keeping me company, for playing with the letters on the screen without seriously hurting the manuscript, for giving inspiration, and for forcing me to take breaks from my obsession to enjoy the sun! And to the new recruits: Shadow "The Clown" Kennedy and Mittens "Princess Wigglebutt" Kennedy thanks for the entertainment, and for unexpected but much enjoyed "editing".

A special thanks to the Hackman family who provided the computer that made writing this novel possible until a new computer could be purchased. Huge thanks to all of you who unknowingly inspired characters in this novel: firstly to my nephew Riley for being my "Master Summoner" and storyteller; to Kelly Ramey, Katurah Hackman, Bethany Hackman, Abbie Weiskopf, Dad, Mom, all the Cornerstone Baptist Junior Youth kids, and of course my feline friends.

Here is a shout out to Sgarrwrath's Facebook friends and Twitter followers. I won't list you by name, for fear I may forget someone, but I appreciate your interest in an artist struggling to carve out a place in a difficult industry. Also, thanks goes out to all the people who purchased *Sgarrwrath*, helping to make this next installment possible. Thanks to the Harford County Public Library who invited me to the Local Author Gift Extravaganza of October 2013. Owen and Pat Bunce, Jen Antley, Savannah Phelps, Kathy and Tom Mc Donaugh, Charles Arthur, Naomi Klimowicz, Michael and Tiffany Childress, and Lora Reheard thanks for going out of your way to come out and support me that day. It really meant a lot.

Thanks to the Institute of Children's Literature and the Long Ridge Writer's Group for the excellent writing courses that helped me hone my craft. Thanks to my high school English teachers, Miss Danielle Zawodny and Mr. Kline, who saw the talent and nurtured it (you too, Mom).

Thank you to the Xlibris team that worked on this novel. It's awesome! Thanks to Janet Fulcher Photography for taking such a beautiful author's photo. All who are reading this, I invite you to Like Prophecy of Hope Saga on Facebook for the latest news and fun facts.

Lastly, here is a shout-out to all who love Dragons, Fantasy, and Science Ficiton! Let the Saga continue . . .

Sneak peak at

Mhorag, Prophecy of Hope Book 2
*w*here the story continues

Excerpt from

The Coming

The Kingdom

A rawn grew still. It seemed that both *Darkness* and Light were capable of infinite patience. How long had it been? Another day? Another Age? The noise of wars won and lost rose from the universe below. Cries of betrayal, violence, and death were as incessant as the vile beating of that ruined heart down there in the blackness. He could hear what he could no longer see. The Light made him blind to all but itself. Oh, how he wished it would quell his other senses, yet he shuddered at the thought. Oblivion was a trap of the *Darkness* he knew all too well. Truth in all its painful yet beautiful array was the glory of the Light.

Sanctus had called this the agony of Hope. Arawn wondered if the agony would ever fade away. It was unlike anything he had ever experienced before in life . . . more excruciating than the illusions of the *Dark*, yet as pure and intoxicating as the Light that cradled it. He marveled in its strangeness. How was it that Hope was knit together of bitter opposites that daily grew beyond his comprehension? The agony of Hope was a monstrous and disturbing netherworld, maddeningly beautiful and foreboding, held stagnant through Time by Sanctus.

In all his years, Arawn had never known temptation so great. He wanted this perfection with every fiber of his being, and yet he feared its call. All this played out in the silence of his mind. Gradually he succumbed.

Hope. Did he dare to embrace it? Could it really be something more wonderful than he could ever imagine? Or was the *Darkness* still playing tricks on his mind?

Thud. Thud. Thud. Thud.

Arawn's eyes flashed open. *Light.* Everywhere there was only Light. "Sanctus!" he screamed. The brilliance burned his blinded eyes with the sheer white Flames. He groped around desperately. His panic grew as his hands clutched at nothing.

Thud. Thud. Thud. Thud.

"Sanctus!" Arawn shrieked, spinning around wildly as the beat of the ruined heart taunted him.

"Arawn," Sanctus said softly. His voice sounded further away than it should have.

Arawn froze.

"I am here," Sanctus said.

"What is happening to me?" Arawn screamed.

"Nothing is happening to you."

"But my eyes!"

"Look closer," Sanctus said gently. "The change is upon me. It is coming from within the Orb of Power that contains Flame's Source."

"Sanctus?" Arawn whispered, his voice heavy with concern and fear. "What is happening to you?"

Sanctus didn't answer. Arawn sought for him through the blinding intensity of the Light. His shallow breaths echoed through the silence. His hesitant footsteps resounded like thunder as he drew near Sanctus's bowed and blazing form. Sanctus had taken the Orb of Power upon himself, but within the covering, another was rising, burning brighter than the Sun below their feet. This presence emerged like the petals of some exotic flower, awakening to a new day, shedding droplets of dew in the glittering Light. Only these droplets crackled and flared in white fire, burning brighter and brighter as they spread. The brilliant tendrils reached out to touch Arawn. He recoiled. The strange Flames were surprisingly cool and insubstantial like a shining mist; vivid, yet allusive—an oasis in a barren desert—a Light from within Light. Something so beyond comprehension had never appeared before the eyes of living creatures in all the Ages since time began.

Arawn knew this as surely as he knew the sound of that corrupted heart down there in the *Darkness* he had forsaken. He watched openmouthed as it took on a vaguely familiar shape. The furthest reaching points of Light were the tips of wings, the likes of which only the Guardians possessed. A beautiful head, shaped like a horse's and crowned with a single iridescent horn, appeared as the presence rose up with a noble cry. A glittering mane tumbled down its long neck. From the top of the head to the end of the long, thick tail, the massive body was made of Light, divided into a covering of tiny, close-knit, scale like Flames. The outer edges were a royal purple, fading into the familiar cerulean blue of Guardians' Flame and finally into the blinding white that shone brighter than the Sun. Within this Lightshadow of the new

Guardian stood the silhouette of a young boy. Golden blood spiraled freely through his frame. His eyes of amber Flame fixed upon Arawn with startling clarity—piercing straight through him.

"Mhorag," Arawn gasped in recognition.

Even in silhouette, Mhorag had a regal leonine quality. He shook himself, shedding water and Flame as his mane of Light billowed in a wind made of his own breath. The divided Flames continued to flow, some back into Sanctus, some back to Mhorag, and some rippled over Arawn's flesh with unbridled power. The Source laughed melodically at Arawn's startled gasp. Rods of golden amber Flame burst from his shining, playful eyes.

Sanctus smiled. "The Time has come," he said. "The orb can no longer contain you."

Mhorag sprang up and away, still laughing, and shot out of the kingdom like a flying comet. Arawn leaped out of the way, swinging back and around, narrowly missing the flaming plumage that whipped past just inches from his face. A wake of the royal fire crackled as it mysteriously froze before shattering into nothingness with a deafening bang. A shockwave rippled through the Kingdom, knocking Arawn flat on his back at Sanctus's feet.

The Kingdom trembled violently at the departure of the Source. As his presence faded, the Light seemed but a dim reflection of itself, fading into a gray haze, though nothing had really changed. Arawn sprang forward to the brink of the Kingdom as the tail of the Lightshadow broke into space. In rushing descent, Mhorag tore through the labyrinth of spinning planets and stars, a shrinking Flame in the blackness of space, plummeting down, down into Sanctus's creation. Arawn watched until the living Flame was nothing more than a tiny, delicate spark in the heart of the earth. How could something so small and insignificant possess such power? How could it leave such a vacancy in the Kingdom as if a hole had been ripped in the fabric of eternity? What was this longing that had been planted in the empty place his heart had once occupied?

Arawn looked questioningly at Sanctus and back again. "What is happening?" he whispered. "I don't understand."

"Since before the beginning, this Hope has lived here within the Orb of Power," Sanctus answered as he lifted Arawn from his knees. "Mhorag has always been waiting for such a Time as this. To a hurting world groaning for release, his coming is the Cure."

The Light whispered around them, *Let the Light shine forth and awaken hope. Let Mhorag arise. Let the Promised come.*

Arawn stared wide-eyed down at the tiny Flame streaking toward the *Darkness*. "The One Whose Name is not Spoken has grown strong, feeding on the fear and violence of the Races. *Darkness* is too great," he whispered. "It will crush him."

"You know the *Darkness* is capable of much more."

Arawn nodded, unable to frame the words. *Corruption. Death.* He trembled as the *Darkness* stirred.

"Don't be afraid," Sanctus said quietly.

Arawn teetered on the edge of the Kingdom, watching with numb horror. Sanctus held him back with a hand on his shoulder. "Do something," he pleaded in a strangled cry.

Sanctus shook his head. "This must be. Do not be afraid."

The Sun and Moon were eclipsed as Mhorag streaked across the heavens. Day and Night parted before him, their sky cloak thrown overhead. Power poured from him, summoning every soul to the coming of Hope as he vanished from Arawn's sight.

"Do not be afraid," Sanctus whispered.

Darkness.

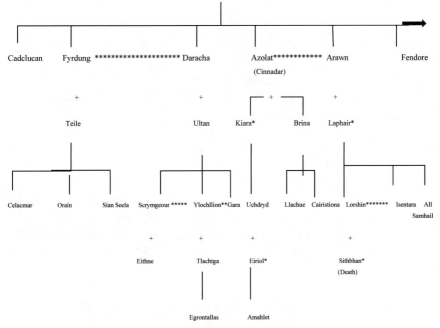

Urgilis + Casara

Father and Mother of all Guardians

Honored by Sanctus and placed in heavens as the Sun and Moon

Cadclucan   Fyrdung ******************** Daracha   Azolat*********** Arawn   Fendore
                                                    (Cinnadar)

          +   +   +
       Teile   Ultan   Kiara*   Brina   Laphair*

Celacmar   Orain   Sian Seela   Scrymgeour ***** Ylochllion**Gara   Uchdryd   Llachue Cairistiona Lorshin******* Isentara All
                                                                                                                                  Samhail

          +   +   +   +
       Eithne   Tlachtga   Eiriol*   Sithbhan*
                                                    (Death)

                  Egrontallas   Amahlet

*By the name means they are not Guardians
*   *   *Means Twins or other multiple birth scenarios

Glossary of Major
Characters Names and Places

Amahlet: (Om ah let) Daughter of Uchdryd and his Astoni wife, Queen Eiriol; she is the Chosen One or the One veiled in weakness spoken of in the Prophecy.

An Taoseach: (an TOO shah ch) The supreme royal title of the true and rightful king of Isear.

Arawn: Fourth son of the Father and Mother. As a Colorless, he fell into Darkness. In order to set him free, his three older brothers cut out his heart and carried him to Sanctus where he continues to live. Sgarrwrath uses an illusionary version of him still. He is the father of the Samhail.

Armahad: (Arm a had) is the An Taoseach of Isear—an all-powerful king over a hidden Race of Men.
Upon his face is the Mark of the Promised. He descends from Nudhug in a direct line, and when the Races see him, he becomes the first emperor of the world.

Azolat: (Az oh lat) is the third son of the Father and Mother of all Guardians; he is the Guardian of the Astoni, and their name for him is Cinnadar (Sin adar).

Bynthroenine: (Been throw neen) is the secret realm of the Guardians.

Cadclucan: (Cad Cloo can) the eldest son of the Father and Mother of all Guardians, he is the Guardian of the Stone of Existence. He is also known as Baculus (Back ool us), the name given to him by the Elves of Light.

Cait: (Kate) She is the sister of Kinjour, an orphan, and eventually an adopted daughter of the An Taoseach

Cartiman: the name of the Council dome where the Guardians ruled and guided the Races during the Golden Age. Sgarrwrath destroys it during the Darkening War.

Celacmar:(Sell ack mar) eldest son of Fyrdung and Teile, he is a Guardian of the Prophecy.

Colorless: These are the young, unproven offspring of the Guardians. They are powerful but that do not know how to control that power. They require guidance and when necessary the control of a Proven Guardian. When the Colorless reach the Time of Testing (aka Coming of Age), they are sent out of the secret realm into the world to be tested and earn their color. This testing can happen in numerous ways, but there are a couple of key rules governing the outcome: i. They must use their power in the service of another; i.e . . . Their actions must not taint the purity of the Light.

Dianara Mountains: is the mountain range that overlooks the Nameless Forest where the Samhail live. It is the sight of incredible Darkness and despair and is destroyed when the Samhail fall.

D'Faihven: (d FAY ven) One of the Summoners. Of the Giant Race.

Document of Unification: This is the signed agreement between Armahad Caladrius, the An Taoseach of Isear, and the leaders of the Resistance races joining them into one kingdom, the Empire of Light.

Dullahan: (Duel a han) He was the first of all the created. The great white hound of the Kingdom.

Egrontallas: (Egg ron tallas) is the son of Ylochllion and his wife Tlachtga; he is born to be the Guardian of the Promised king.

Empyrean: The hidden name of power.

Esarian: (Es ar ian) is a young human child who is a Master Summoner; High Commander of the Resistance

In the days of Aramahad, An Taoseach of Isear. After a vision upon Firinn's Pinnacle, he becomes the Firebrand who will prepare the way for the coming of the Promised.

Fenachdra Willowbark: (Fen ach dra) is an elfin Summoner who fled from the Resistance after the fall of the Samhail. Whereabouts unknown.

Fendore: is the fifth son of the Father and Mother, a Guardian of the Fairies. He gave the Fairy Face the gift of super speed.

Firinn: is the pinnacle of truth, the footstool of Sanctus.

Fyrdung: (Fear dung) is the second son of the Father and Mother of all Guardians; he is a Guardian of Water and the Giver of the Mark (see Isearians). He is also known in Isearian mythology as Caladrius (Cal a dree us), a great white bird.

Gnoll: (Nol) He is a deformed and twisted creature who serves Sgarrwrath and loves Death.

Goldya: (Gold Ya) She is an orphan and eventually an adopted daughter of the An Taoseach.

Guardians of the Prophecy: There are nine of them. Their names are Gara, Scrymgeour (Scr im gar), Llacheu (latch oo), Eithne (eyeth na), Orain (oh Rain), Ylochllion (yule ock, lion), Tlachtga (tl ackt ga), Uchdryd (Youk drid), and Cairistiona (Care is Tiona). Together they are the keepers of the nine trees that grew from the Nine Grains of Power spoken of in the Prophecy. They are joined by the Nine Guardians of the trees who are subordinate to them. The Guardians of the Prophecy are responsible for the protection of: the Chosen One, the Mark, and eventually the reforging of the Summoning Stones.

They are also defenders of the Prophecy and appear to ensure it is upheld.

Gyceal: (Guy KEEL) one of the Enechelbrah who aid the Elves of Light.

Isear: is the hidden kingdom of the hidden line of Men.

Isentara: (I SEN tara) is Lorshin's twin sister. She is the only Samhail to escape enslavement to the Darkness by seeking refuge in the protection of the Guardians in Bynthroenine. Nicknamed: Isen

Jysine: (JY seen) is a human Summoner apprenticed to Fenachdra in the beginning of the Darkening War.
    She is bitten by a Samhail and thus cursed. She falls with the Samhail into Darkness.

Khartang: (Car Tang) one of the Enechelbrah who aid the Elves of Light.

Keliah: (KEL I ah) is the Queen of Isear, the wife of Armahad Caladrius and eventually the first empress of the World.

Kinjour: (KIN jor) is an Isearian orphan who dreams of being a knight. He is taken into Armahad's household, becomes the Champion of the Realm and the adopted son of the An Taoseach and his queen.

Laeginlast Thornecrowne: (Lay JIN last) He is the right hand of the Elf Queen, Knight of the Realm

Liacin: (lie a KIN) is the heir to the Royal House of Caladrius.

Lorshin: He is Prince of the Samhail, eldest son of Arawn and the human Laphair. He is the lover of Death and the bestower of the Forbidden Kiss spoken of in Prophecy.

Maizie: She is queen of the Elves of Light; the star-crossed love of the Guardian Cadclucan.

Manarc: (man arc) A captain in the Mydrian Guard.

Mhorag: (mHor ag) He is the Promised Guardian King; Hope; Cure; residing in the secrecy of the Kingdom within the Orb of

Power. He is the Source; the Living Flame and the object of Sgarrwrath's ancient lust. (see Empyrean)

Mydrian: (mid ree ann) are the elite army of bodyguards whose entire lives are devoted to the protection of the An Taoseach, his family, his crown, and his throne. They are absolutely loyal, secretive, spending their whole lives in either service. You are born Mydrian. To be a royal bodyguard is a birthright but must ultimately be earned secret rights held once a year. (A sort of graduation that either ends with service or death. No one outside their "society" will ever be counted among them. They are almost like a country within a country having their own laws, and hierarchy outside the authority of the An Taoseach yet submissive to Crown, Mark and Throne.

Nithrodine: (nith ROW dean) is the name of the town that is the capital of Isear. Nithrodine Castle is the royal palace.

Nothaniel: (NOTH a Neil) He is one of the Elves of Light. He is a scout and warrior.

Nudhug: (Nud hug) He was the first An Taoseach of Isear. The Mark of the Promised was first placed upon him by the Guardian Fyrdung during the Great Exodus following the Guarding War.

Nulet: (null et) He is one of the Summoners. Of the Poeth Race.

Orlok: (or LOCK) He is one of the Summoners. Of the Dwarf Race.

Resistance: After the Exodus of the Guardians, a large number of the Races join together in a last alliance against the Darkness (see the list of Resistance Races and their leaders).

Rowlyrag: (ROWL y rag). The name means gray rock. It is on the highest peak of the Dianara Mountains and is the sight where Sgarrwrath took Arawn—before his brothers freed him—and where he then gives Sithbhan the power of Death.

Samhail: The Children of Arawn and Laphair, and those turned by them. They call themselves "Likeness." because they possess the speed, strength, and flaming blue eyes of the Guardians, though they cannot take Guardian form. They have been cursed with an unquenchable hunger for the fingerprint of Flame that is hidden away within all living things. Sunlight can kill them.

Scarrow: Shadow People. They are the seven daughters of Poulderon, Lord of Darkness (Night) and Diastrilis, Lady of Light (Day). Day and Night are eternal beings, while their children will one day fade away, as all shadows fade. Six of the Scarrow feel this is unjust and will stop at nothing to prevent it. They steal life to extend their own. The Guardians exiled them, but with the Guardian Exodus, one of the six returns and is tempted by the Darkness.

Sgarrwrath: (SGarr wrath) He is the ancient evil born out of Dullahan's lust. He has long existed in formless Darkness. He possesses access to the Flame through Arawn's withered heart. The Dark One; the One Whose Name is not Spoken

Sian Seela: (See ANN Seal ah) is the eldest daughter of Fyrdung and Teile and is one of the Colorless sent out for her Time of Testing. She is captured by Armahad Caladrius and later is trapped in the deepest foundation of Nithrodine, Isear.

Sithbhan: (Sith ban) is one of the Scarrow returned from exile. She is given the power of Death.

Summoners: They once were able to call Guardians from the secret realm at will. With the Styarfyre (STY ar Fire) orbs, they could draw upon the power of the Guardians. Summoners are chosen at birth from among each race and spend the rest of their lives living in the "Guardian Path"; they are Keepers of History, Law enforcers and Judges. They lead the Resistance in the Darkening War. Few are left among them with a will to fight. A child leads them now. Though the Styarfyre orbs have been broken, the shards still give them access to a small measure of power, and in the absence of the Guardians it is to them that the Races come for counsel.

Teile: (Teel) is the wife of Fyrdung. She is a Guardian of Animals.

Trin Thibodeaux: (trin thib ODOO) A scout for the Resistance of the Fairy Race.

Yelizaveta: (Yell iza veta) is one of the daughters of Armahad Caladrius and his wife. She is inflicted with an aging disease. Her life proves to be Armahad's weakness.

Zrene: (ZR een) She is the last of the Calianith, slain in the Guardian War, revived by Death and Sgarrwrath's dark powers. She has her own plans and agenda but is ultimately destroyed at the hands of Lorshin.

Resistance Races

Astoni: They are the offspring of the only Scarrow content with her life and a human male. They are both flesh and shadow. On average, they live longer than humans by nearly 500 years. In the Days of the Darkening War, they are ruled by King Zoan. They live in the Kingdom of Evanthra (ee VAN thra) by the Pool of Azolat.

Centaur: They are half human, half horse and have a very gentle nature. To look at them, they have a very woodsy, tied-to-nature appearance. Despite their gentle natures, they are handy in war and are skilled fighters. Their swords are of the best craftsmanship; the metals for their creation harvested from the fertile soils of their homeland. Their ancestral home is the Kingdom of Amhorazia (am HOR azia) which is a land known for vast orchards and deep blue lakes. In the Days of the Darkening War, the Centaur are ruled by Queen Hempress, who is supported by her untitled, hulking consort, Cyrock.

Dwarf: They are cold like the land of their nativity. They are manufacturers of weapons of mass destruction
In the Days of the Darkening War, they are ruled by General Ickluck Lorndop. Their ancestral homeland is buried in the great Ice Cap of the Far North.

Echoes of Guardian Sorrow: (see Faedran) These are the little dragons that live inside the Dark Elves.

Elves of Light: a Race that separates themselves from the Resistance in the early days of the Darkening to align themselves with Cadclucan, the last Guardian remaining in the world who takes refuge among them. Though not officially part of the Resistance, they oppose Sgarrwrath. They are ruled by the young Queen Maizie. Their homeland is the vast coastal forest affectionately known as Red Wood. The forest sweeps down from the North, following the course of three mighty rivers that intersect into one on the outskirts of Isear, a Kingdom of Men. Most Elves live centrally in a huge amber and gold city called Loriath (Lori ath). Loriath is protected by magical barriers that make the city invisible.

Enechelbrah: A Race of armoured red horses. Much bigger than average horses. Despise strangers and Darkness. Cannot be tamed or bridled but serve at will. They make their home on the other side of a dimensional portal contained within the Elves' city of Loriath. They have no ruler.

Faedran: (FAY dran) Sometimes referred to as Dark Elves, the Faedran are really their own separate Race.

They enjoy a symbiotic union with little dragons (made from the Guardians shedding breath, blood, and sorrow). They live in the Light ways of Solais (soul ace) that are the foundation of the whole world. They are ruled by Hakan (hay can), Kateirah (Ka tear ah), and Ethany (e THany). The little dragons cannot live long outside their bodies nor they outside the little dragons' power. Neither can survive long outside the Light ways.

Fairies: They are medium-sized beings, insectile with antennae, and wings like those of a cricket but eye-catching like a peacock's plumage. They were given the gift of super speed and "FLY" by running really fast, leaving a trail of silver dust in their wake. During the Darkening War, the Fairies served as scouts for the Resistance. They are ruled by Caesar Umber III, but it is his ambassadors that come to sign the Document of Unification as he can never leave their kingdom or it will die. Their kingdom is also behind a magical barrier known to outsiders as the Vale of Tears as it is visible, glowing from within because of the residue of silver dust caused by the Fairies themselves. Their kingdom known to them as Faedom is divided into five provinces: Summerton, Winterton,

Springington, and Fallton and in the middle is Ougashade where Caesar lives in the great tree.

Faun: Half human, half deer, they are very shy and so gentle they are seldom seen. They are ruled by their Seneschal, Tuernok in the days of the Darkening War. They live in the wild roaming and grazing in fields and fertile valleys and mountain ranges where Humans seldom go.

Giants: They are good friends of the Centaur and the Faedran. Because of their size, they are good in a fight, but by nature, they are prone to cowardice. They can disguise themselves as boulders. They are skilled farmers and love good earth. For Ages, the best vegetables have come from their ancestral land and been sold or traded among all the Races as part of the alliances formed under the Guardians at Cartiman. Their homeland has been stolen leaving Giants in poverty. In the Days of the Darkening, they are ruled by King Dubber.

Gnome: The Gnomes live in bogs made of their own waste, which they manufacture to make power.
Rather disgusting beings but useful, they are under the leadership of the Gnome Commander, Fugwort.

GWE: Gnome War Effort: The industrialized effort to fashion Gnome Waste into bricks. Each brick will provide a day's worth of illumination when burned.

Humans: They are mostly a nomadic Race by the Days of the Darkening War. All their kingdoms have fallen. They have no rulers and feuding among different factions is common. (The Humans of the Kingdom of Isear are a separate and unknown branch but when the An Taoseach is made known to them all Humans join into one kingdom.)

Kot: Half cat, half dolphin, they spend some time on land but mostly in the sea. They hunt in the reefs, and their favorite prey is shark. They live in prides ruled by Suzerainty. The leaders of one such pride are Eek-ash and Uleya (OOL ay ah). In general, they have a special dislike for humans who have hunted them.

Merar: They are a water-dwelling race. They prefer fresh water and are only able to breath outside the water with special devices they have made. They are not as fierce as the Kot. They live in schools of no more than a hundred led by a matriarch but as a whole they are ruled by King Akule (ACK ool).

Poeth: They are tiny. They live in volcanoes. They have fire for hair and teeth like a shark's. They are very, very bad-tempered. They are ruled by King Wirtbam (wert bam).

Shee: They are winged humanoid females with two thighs that fuse into a single leg. At the end of their lives, they build a cocoon, their foot breaks off, and from it a new Shee is born. They live in caves deep in forests. In the days of the Darkening War, they are ruled by their elderly Mother Superior, Subara (Sue bar ah).

Sylph: They are creatures of the air. They are ruled by their Queen Astraya (A STRAY ah).

Trolls: They live underground and eat the bad stuff to keep the earth pure and fertile. In the days of the Darkening War, they are ruled by their king, Porig.

Edwards Brothers Malloy
Thorofare, NJ USA
February 13, 2014